S0-BAJ-547

TEMPTRESS

*Also by Lisa Jackson
in Large Print:*

Dark Sapphire
Deep Freeze
Impostress
Mystery Man
Mystic
The Night Before
Obsession
See How She Dies
The Shadow of Time
Tears of Pride
Unspoken
Whispers

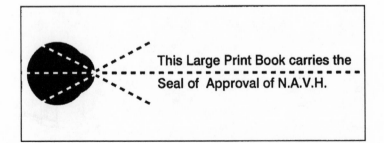

This Large Print Book carries the
Seal of Approval of N.A.V.H.

62342116

TEMPTRESS

LISA JACKSON

Thorndike Press • Waterville, Maine

Copyright © Susan Lisa Jackson, 2005

All rights reserved.

This is a work of fiction. Names, characters, places, and incidents either are the product of the author's imagination or are used fictitiously, and any resemblance to actual persons, living or dead, business establishments, events, or locales is entirely coincidental.

The publisher does not have any control over and does not assume any responsibility for author or third-party Web sites or their content.

Published in 2006 by arrangement with NAL Signet, a division of Penguin Group (USA) Inc.

Thorndike Press® Large Print Romance.

The tree indicium is a trademark of Thorndike Press.

The text of this Large Print edition is unabridged.
Other aspects of the book may vary from the original edition.

Set in 16 pt. Plantin.

Printed in the United States on permanent paper.

Library of Congress Cataloging-in-Publication Data

Jackson, Lisa.
    Temptress / by Lisa Jackson.
        p. cm. — (Thorndike Press large print romance)
    ISBN 0-7862-8393-9 (lg. print : hc : alk. paper)
    1. Middle ages — Fiction.   2. Large type books.
  I. Title. II. Thorndike Press large print romance series.
PS3560.A223T46 2005
  813'.54—dc22   2005033978

ACKNOWLEDGMENTS

I would like to thank everyone who helped in the creation of this novel. First and foremost, my sister, Nancy Bush, also an author, who helped me with the editing and proofing of the pages, all the while plying me with Hot Tamales (yes, the candy) and diet Pepsi and assuring me that "we can do it." Second, Claire Zion, my editor, for her patience with this project, and third, my agent, Robin Rue, for being a calm voice of reason.

There were tons of others who gave me time and support and provided laughter when I needed it. To all my friends and family, thanks!

As the Founder/CEO of NAVH, the only national health agency solely devoted to those who, although not totally blind, have an eye disease which could lead to serious visual impairment, I am pleased to recognize Thorndike Press* as one of the leading publishers in the large print field.

Founded in 1954 in San Francisco to prepare large print textbooks for partially seeing children, NAVH became the pioneer and standard setting agency in the preparation of large type.

Today, those publishers who meet our standards carry the prestigious "Seal of Approval" indicating high quality large print. We are delighted that Thorndike Press is one of the publishers whose titles meet these standards. We are also pleased to recognize the significant contribution Thorndike Press is making in this important and growing field.

Lorraine H. Marchi, L.H.D.
Founder/CEO
NAVH

* Thorndike Press encompasses the following imprints: Thorndike, Wheeler, Walker and Large Print Press.

PROLOGUE

Wybren Castle, North Wales
December 24, 1287

'Tis time.

The voice was soft but insistent, like a flaxseed lodged in his collar, a tiny irritation relentlessly pricking the back of the neck, ever nagging. Reverberating through his head, it urged him onward as he slipped through the gloom of the keep.

You know you cannot wait any longer. Redemption is at hand. For you. For them.

He flicked an anxious tongue to his lips, tasted the salt of his sweat though it was freezing within the castle walls, his own breath fogging and mixing with the smoke from the smoldering rushlights. His muscles ached with tension and fear; his ears strained to hear the quietest footfall lest he be discovered. Still he hesitated.

You must do it. Now. All is in place. The guards are asleep from all the revelry, their minds sluggish from too much ale. The guests, too, with their full bellies and

7

wine-sotted minds, sleep as if dead. And the lord's family, all of them, are near dead already, their cups having been washed with the potion. Their rutting has ceased. Hear them snore through the doors to their chambers.

From the depths of his cowl, he looked over his shoulder, checking the hallway one last time and then, knowing God was speaking to him, lifted his unlit torch to the embers of the hallway sconces. With a crackle and hiss, the oil-soaked tip caught fire, casting the dark corridor in flickering, deadly shadows. Swiftly he bent down and touched his torch to the bit of braided oil-doused cloth that he'd tucked under the doors moments earlier and then watched in fascination as the quick little flames sped beneath the door to the dried rushes spread thickly upon the chamber floor.

First the baron, he thought, and then the rest.

He worked with speed, praying softly, lighting each wick in succession along the corridor. His heart hammered wildly, sweat and fear sliding down his spine. Should he be caught, he would be imprisoned, quickly judged a traitor, and then hung until he was twitching, near death. Before he took his last breath, he would be

8

removed from the gallows, his body drawn and quartered, his entrails spilling out while he was yet alive, and then, upon his death, his head would be skewered upon a pike and placed on display high above the wide wall walk, an example to all who might consider this kind of treason.

Do not fear. Your cause is just. You are the Redeemer.

Smoke began to fill the hallway, seeping stealthily beneath the doors.

He calmed his fears. 'Twas done. The rest was in God's hands, or those of the devil. He knew not which, nor did he care. For the voice that urged him on came from within, the nagging insistence arising from a deep part of his own desire, the words only amplifying what he wanted so desperately. And yet he heard them as surely as if someone had whispered them against his ear. He told himself they came because God wanted vengeance. He was but the servant . . . unless it wasn't God who spoke so intimately to him.

Unless it was a demon or even Satan himself.

He glanced around the arched ceiling of the hallway, breathing shallowly as if expecting an angel of darkness to swoop down before him as the smoke rose in thin, evil wisps.

Yet no apparition appeared.

Whether the voice he heard was from heaven or hell, the deed was done. Redemption and, aye, vengeance were at hand. At last.

At the end of the corridor, he tossed his torch onto the floor and then swept rapidly down the stairs, his footsteps making no sound as he eased out of the keep and into the black, moonless night.

Soon someone would rouse.

Soon an alarm would sound.

Soon it would be over.

And justice, at long last, would be served.

CHAPTER ONE

Castle Calon
January 12, 1289

Morwenna moved upon the bed.
Her bed?
Or another's?
Lifting her head, she saw the glowing embers of the fire, red coals casting golden shadows upon the castle walls. But what castle? Where was she? There were no windows, and high above the walls, past creaking crossbeams, she spied the night sky, dozens of stars winking far in the distance.
Where was she?
In a prison? Held captive in an old, forsaken keep whose roof had blown away?
"Morwenna."
Her name echoed against the thick walls, reverberating and turning her blood to ice.
She twisted on the bed and stared into the shadows. "Who goes there?" she whispered, her heart thudding.

" 'Tis I." A deep male voice, one she should recognize, whispered from the dark corners of this seemingly endless chamber. Her skin crawled. With one hand she clamped the bedding to her breast and realized that she was naked. With the other hand she searched the bed, fingers scrabbling for her dagger, but it, like her clothes, was missing.

"Wh-who?" she demanded.

"Don't you know?"

Was he teasing her?

"Nay. Who are you?"

A deep chuckle from the gloom.

Oh, God!

"Carrick?" she whispered as he appeared, stepping into the light, a tall warrior with broad shoulders, deep-set eyes, and a chiseled chin. She couldn't trust him. Not again. And yet a thrill pulsed through her veins and erotic images stole through her mind.

He stepped closer to the bed and her heart pounded, her mouth suddenly desert dry. She couldn't help but remember the feel of his sinewy muscles beneath her fingertips, the salty taste of his skin, the male smell of him that had always stirred her.

"What are you doing here? How did you

get in?" she asked but realized she didn't know where she was.

"I came for you," he said, and she trembled inside.

"I don't believe you."

"You never did." He was close to the bed now and leaned even nearer. Her heart thudded as he slowly pulled his tunic over his head, and the fire glow caught his sinewy muscles as they moved. "Remember?"

Oh, yes . . . yes, she remembered.

And cursed herself for it.

"You should go," she told him.

"Where?"

"Anywhere but here." She forced the words out.

His smile flashed white. Knowing. Oh, he was a devil. Isa was right. Morwenna should never have allowed him close to her, let him into this room without a ceiling.

But you didn't. You don't even know where you are. Perhaps you're his captive and this is your prison cell. Could it not be that he is keeping you here as his slave, to minister to him, to lie with him, to do his bidding?

"If you won't leave, then I will," she said, her gaze sliding away from his face to search the floor and the pegs near the door for her clothes.

"Will you?" he taunted, settling onto the bed next to her and running a finger down the side of her jaw. Her skin prickled in delight. Her blood rippled with lust. "I think not."

"Bastard."

He laughed at her, ran his finger ever lower, pushing aside the bedclothes, baring her breast, watching the nipple pucker under his perusal. Though Morwenna knew she was making a devastating mistake, she turned her face up to his, felt the warmth of his breath against her skin, knew that she would never be able to resist him. A deep warmth invaded that most intimate of regions and she sighed as he worked his way lower, callused fingers trickling down her willing flesh.

Lowering his head, he placed a kiss upon her bare abdomen.

She moaned, heat pulsing through her body. Then she sensed they were not alone, that unseen eyes were watching their every move. Someone or something with evil intent.

From where? The open ceiling where she saw stars shooting across the

*heavens . . . or closer? In the room with
them?*

*"Morwenna!" Someone was calling her,
but she could not be disturbed, not when
this man she had loved with all of her
heart had returned. "Morwenna!"*

"Morwenna!"

Her eyes flew open.

The dream evaporated like a ghost
chased by morning's light.

The dog at her feet gave out a disgruntled snort.

"God's teeth!" She sat straight up in
bed, pushed her hair out of her eyes. It had
been a dream. All just a cursed dream.
Again. When would she ever learn?

There was no one in her chamber, no
mysterious warrior about to seduce her, no
old lover returning. She was alone. And yet
. . . something felt amiss, like a breath of
wind in a sealed tomb. Her skin prickled as
she drew the bed linens close.

"What a ninny," she muttered, forcing
herself to breathe normally.

She was in *her* bedchamber at Castle
Calon, in *her* room, in *her* keep, the one
her brother Kelan had entrusted to her.
She glanced about the large chamber with
its vibrant tapestries and whitewashed
walls. The ceiling, rising high above the

15

crossbeams, was very much intact, the fire in the grate burning embers, shutters on the windows allowing only a few gray wisps of the coming dawn inside. Nothing was disturbed. Even the dog, a cur she'd inherited when her brother had assigned her to Calon, had been sleeping soundly, his snoring ruffling the fur of the rabbit coverlet tossed carelessly over the foot of the bed. She was letting the old rumors about the keep being haunted bother her; that was it.

"Lady Morwenna!" Isa's frantic voice echoed through the hallways.

Morwenna started. Her dog, suddenly wide awake, sprang from the bed to bark wildly as if the old deaf thing was sounding an alert.

"Hush, Mort!" Morwenna commanded.

The beast lowered his speckled head and growled in low disobedience.

A thunderous knock erupted on the door. "M'lady?"

"Coming!" Morwenna yelled, irritated at the urgency in Isa's voice. The old woman was forever concerned about the future, her ancient eyes imagining danger and darkness in every corner. Morwenna threw on her tunic and raced across the fresh rushes to the door just as the pounding re-

16

sumed upon the thick oaken panels.

"What is it?" she demanded, unlatching the door and pulling it open to find Isa's face colorless, her lips tight. Beside her in the darkened hallway stood one of the huntsmen. Jason, a tall, gangly man with bad skin and teeth to match, was worrying his hat in his hands. "What's wrong?"

"A man was found outside the castle gates," Isa said, breathless. Strands of once-red hair were visible beneath her cowl and her ice blue eyes blinked nervously. "Near dead, he is, and beaten to within an inch of his very life." Her eyebrows knitted together and her thin lips tightened. "The attack was so savage that no one . . ." She took in a deep breath. "Not even his own father would recognize him." Isa shook her head and her cowl slid to her shoulders. "I doubt he will live another day. Tell her, Jason."

" 'Tis true," the huntsman admitted. "I found him while chasin' down a stag just before dawn. Stepped over a rotten log and there he was, covered with leaves and dirt, barely a breath left in him."

"So where is he now?"

"In the gatehouse. Sir Alexander thinks he could be a spy."

"A near-dead spy," Morwenna clarified.

Isa nodded, and she looked as if she wanted to say more but held her tongue.

"Has the physician seen him?"

"Nay, m'lady, not yet," Isa said.

"Why not?" Morwenna demanded. "Nygyll needs to examine the man immediately."

Isa didn't reply. Her feelings against the physician were strong.

Morwenna ignored them. "Have the wounded man brought into the keep, where it's warm. Mayhap he can be saved."

" 'Tis unlikely."

"But we shall try." Morwenna's gaze swept the corridor to land on the door of a room now unoccupied. "Take him to Tadd's chamber."

"Nay, m'lady," Isa said swiftly. " 'Tis unsafe . . . only a few doors down from you."

"Did you not say he is near death?"

"Aye, but you cannot trust him."

"You, too, think he's a spy?"

Isa nodded, her wrinkled face becoming more so as she thought. She glanced at Morwenna, worried the hem of her sleeve with gnarled fingers, and then looked quickly away.

The hairs on the back of Morwenna's neck rose. "There is something you're not telling me," she said and remembered the feeling in her dream, that she was being watched from unseen eyes. "What is it, Isa?"

"There is trouble brewing, something I sense but cannot yet envision." The old woman suddenly gripped Morwenna's forearm and her eyes were instantly dark as midnight, her pupils dilated as if she had, indeed, just experienced one of her premonitions. "Please, Lady," she whispered, " 'tis your safety I fear for. You must not take a chance."

Morwenna wanted to argue but couldn't. Too many times in the past Isa's premonitions, her visions of the future, had proved true. Had she not declared that the potter's wife would have triplets, all boys, and die with the birthing of the third one? Hadn't Isa predicted the lightning strike in the bailey at Penbrooke, and within a fortnight, the tree in the bailey's center had been cleaved and charred from a bolt that narrowly missed Morwenna's brother Tadd? Then there had been the mysterious death of a merchant's wife. Isa had sworn the woman had been poisoned, and when all was said and done, it was proved that her husband had, indeed, forced the poor woman to drink hemlock because he'd discovered that she'd been bedding the miller.

For most of her sixty-seven years Isa had been able to see things others could not.

"Fine," Morwenna said. "See that the man is brought into the great hall, where it's warm, and have someone . . . Gladdys, open the hermit's cell in the north tower. 'Tis large enough for a pallet and has a grate for a small fire. Get the fire started and sweep out the vermin. Then make certain that the man's wounds are cleaned and that the physician examines him before he's moved into the tower."

Morwenna pretended not to notice the shadow of distrust that passed through Isa's clear eyes at the mention of Nygyll, the castle's physician. Isa and Nygyll had never gotten along and barely tolerated each other. Nygyll considered himself a man of reason, a practical if God-fearing man, while Isa believed in spirits and the Great Mother. Nygyll had been with Castle Calon for years, while Isa had moved here with Morwenna less than a year ago.

"It may be too late to save the injured man," Isa reminded Morwenna.

"Then send someone for the priest."

There was another nearly imperceptible tightening of the corners of Isa's mouth. "The priest will not be able to help —"

"Did you not say the wounded man was near death?" Morwenna reminded her. "He may be a man of faith. Should he not have a priest's blessing and prayers if he's about to die?" Morwenna didn't wait for an answer. "Send someone to find Father Daniel. Have the priest meet us in the great hall."

"If you wish."

"I do!" Morwenna snapped.

The hunter took off at a fast clip and Isa, too, hurried away, presumably to carry out Morwenna's orders. Her long cape billowed behind her as she hastened to the stairway, where, before she disappeared, she glanced over her shoulder at Morwenna, her old face knotted in worry. She appeared to want to argue further, but she reluctantly descended.

"By the saints," Morwenna whispered once she was alone again.

Sometimes Isa seemed more trouble than she was worth. Considered odd by most who met her, she had helped raise Morwenna and her siblings. A faithful servant to Morwenna's mother, Lenore, during her lifetime, Isa was now steadfastly at Morwenna's side.

"Fie and feathers," Morwenna muttered as she walked deeper into her room, tossed a mantle over her head, and stepped into her shoes. She'd just made her way out of her chamber, Mort at her heels, when a door creaked open and Bryanna poked her head into the hallway. Sleep lingered in her blue eyes and her curls were a tousled dark red mass around her head. "What's happening?" her sister asked around a yawn. Though sixteen and nearly four years younger than Morwenna, the girl often seemed a child.

"A wounded man was found near the keep. 'Tis nothing," Morwenna said, hoping to stop the tide of Bryanna's ever-rampant curiosity. "Go back to bed."

Bryanna wasn't to be easily deterred. "Then why all the noise?"

"Because of Isa. She is certain the man is a spy or enemy or something." Morwenna rolled her eyes. "You know how she is."

"Aye." Bryanna stretched one arm over her head, but she seemed no longer to have slumber on her mind. "So what is to be done with him?"

"What do you think?"

"Questioned and fed. Mayhap cleaned a bit."

Morwenna nodded and kept the news to herself that the man was about to expire.

What purpose would it serve to tell Bryanna about his condition? Until Morwenna had seen the man herself, she decided she would seal her lips. As it was, gossip about the wounded warrior would travel lightning fast through the keep and Bryanna wasn't known for her ability to keep a secret.

"What kind of man is he? Another huntsman? A soldier? A merchant attacked by thugs?" Bryanna's imagination was beginning to run away with her. "Perhaps Isa's right. Mayhap he's a spy, or worse. A henchman for —"

"Stop!" Morwenna held up a hand and cut off her sister. "I know not who or what he is yet, but I will as soon as I speak with him."

"I'll come with you."

Morwenna sent her a look guaranteed to intimidate even the boldest of men. "Later."

"But —"

"Bryanna, let the captain of the guard question the man, determine if he is friend or foe, allow him to be seen by the physician and get some rest, and *then* if he awakens and I think it's appropriate, you may see him."

"You think it's not safe?" her younger

sister challenged as her eyes sparkled with excitement.

"I don't know," Morwenna said, realizing belatedly that she'd used the wrong tack, that she was only whetting Bryanna's appetite for adventure. Exasperation tainted her words as she said tersely, "We'll wait. That's all."

"But —"

"I said, that's all!"

"You cannot tell me what to do!"

Morwenna lifted one black eyebrow, silently challenging her sister. "I have no time for this." She turned quickly and made speedy tracks along the hallway, leaving her younger sibling pouting as she leaned against the doorframe of her room. Morwenna felt Bryanna's rebellion seething behind her but ignored it. Let the inquisitive girl stew in her own juices. So what if she was angry? Bryanna was always getting into trouble.

Just like you, her conscience reminded her.

"Bother and broomsticks!"

She heard voices floating up the staircase and scurried down the two flights of steps. Smoke from recently lit rushlights touched her nostrils, and the aromas of sizzling meat and baking bread wafted from the

24

kitchen and through the labyrinthine hallways of the keep. Servants were scuttling from one chamber to the other, carrying laundry, cleaning grates, sweeping stairways. Candles were being replaced and lit, and they offered a bit of warm light on this chill winter day.

As Morwenna reached the first floor and stepped into the great hall, the main door was thrown open. Several soldiers hauled a stretcher upon which a man, or what was left of him, lay unmoving.

Morwenna's breath stopped at the sight of him. Though she'd warned herself that he would be difficult to gaze upon, she hadn't realized how fiercely he'd been attacked. His face had been pulverized and was now swollen and bruised, blood crusting over the wild gashes upon his cheek and forehead. Dirt and leaves clung to hair as black as obsidian, and his eyes were mere slits cut into puffy lids that were varying shades of purple and green.

His clothes were matted with soil and blood, his tunic slashed to reveal his bare chest and recent bloody gashes that were still raw.

Morwenna's stomach turned over.

"By the gods!" a horrified voice behind her whispered. "Is he alive?"

Morwenna's heart sank. Turning, she spied her sister standing on the stairs between the first and second floors. Bryanna had tossed a rust-colored tunic over her chemise but hadn't bothered with shoes. Standing in her bare feet, she shivered and gaped at the scene in the large room below. One hand was raised to her mouth; her eyes were round, her skin as white as alabaster.

"Of course he's alive!" Morwenna said.

"Barely," one soldier muttered. "Poor bastard."

Bryanna's face twisted. "He looks horrid. Dead."

Morwenna snapped, "Didn't I tell you to go back to bed? Leave us!"

Having seen enough of the gruesome display to satisfy her morbid curiosity, Bryanna rapidly made the sign of the cross over her chest and then raced barefoot up the stairs as if the devil himself were chasing her.

Good! Morwenna was in no mood to deal with Bryanna's histrionics while attempting to calm everyone.

The great hall, so recently asleep, was teeming with activity. The castle dogs, too, were unsettled, the old bitch pacing and growling while Mort, sensing a chance to best the beast, stole her spot near the fire.

26

Servants hurried in with fresh towels and steaming pots of water. Others lit candles and cast worried looks at the wounded man. Sheeting was laid upon a table near the fire where two boys were busily adding wood and pumping the bellows.

The man on the stretcher moaned though his eyelids didn't so much as flutter as he was transferred onto the table. Who was he? Why had he been attacked so violently? He whispered something, a word, and yet it was indistinguishable.

"What's going on here?" Alfrydd, the steward, strode into the room. He was a scarecrow of a man, his tunic always hanging oddly from his scrawny shoulders. His voice had a nasal goose-squawk quality to it and he was a worrier who sometimes put Isa to shame, but he was loyal and true, a brave heart trapped inside a skeletal body. "Oh, m'lady," he added quickly as his gaze fell upon Morwenna. "Excuse me, but I heard that a prisoner had been brought up here rather than to the dungeon and I was uncertain that this was a wise decision."

" 'Twas mine," Morwenna said, motioning to the wounded man, "and he's not a prisoner." Again the man tried to whisper something, but it was unintelligible.

Alfrydd nodded as if in agreement, but he couldn't hide his shock when his eyes landed on the bloodied, beaten piece of humanity laid upon the table. "Has the priest been called?"

"Aye, and the physician," she said and then added impatiently, "Where the devil is Nygyll?"

As if he'd been waiting to hear his name, the physician burst through the outer door, bringing with him the scent of fresh rain and a gust of wind heavy with the promise of snow. A tall man with an easy gait and an air of arrogance, he walked purposefully toward the table where the wounded man lay. Isa was on his heels, taking two steps to his one. "Isa claimed there was an emergency," he said. "Ah . . . I see. Who is he?"

Morwenna shook her head. "We know not."

"Friend or foe?" Nygyll was already cutting away the rest of the man's tunic and leaning near, listening to his rasping breath.

"Again, 'tis not known."

"His clothes are those of a poor man."

Yet he was suspected of being a spy. How odd . . .

"Where's the hot water?" the physician demanded, and a serving girl set a pot on a nearby table while another placed a stack of towels near the steaming water. "I'll need a mash of yarrow." His eyes narrowed on the first serving girl. "Send someone to the apothecary."

"I'll go," she said and hurried away, her skirts billowing.

Carefully Nygyll began to clean the wounds, first tackling those that seemed the most life threatening.

Again the main door opened, and this time two men talking low entered in a rush of biting winter wind. Alexander, captain of the guard, a muscular man with curling brown hair, a square jaw, and eyes as brown as sable, was leaning down and talking to Father Daniel, the keep's priest, who appeared as weak as the soldier seemed strong. No matter what the season, the priest forever remained pale, his skin nearly translucent, his eyes an icy blue, his red hair thick and wiry, his expression dour. He was a man of the cloth who seemed to take the burden of being God's messenger as a heavy, sometimes unbearable load. His eyes met Morwenna's for but an instant, and then he quickly looked away.

Before the door could close, Dwynn, the half-wit, slipped through. A man of twenty-odd years, he'd been cursed from birth with the mind of a child. He caught Morwenna's eye and sidestepped around the priest, slipping out of her direct line of vision. She'd never understood his fear of her, for she'd tried to be kind to him, but he seemed to want to always avoid her, which, this morn, considering her foul mood, was just as well.

Isa, watching the physician tending to the man's wounds, sidled up to Morwenna. "We cannot move him" — she jutted her bony chin toward the beaten man — "at least not to the hermit's cell in the north tower as the floor has rotted through. Also, the cell in the south tower is occupied by Brother Thomas, so that leaves us with the dungeon or the pit or —"

"The drawbridge pit? The dungeon?" Morwenna said, shaking her head vigorously. "Isa, no. We will not treat this man as our enemy. We will put him up in Tadd's chamber with a guard at the door if you feel unsafe. There is no reason to assume this . . . man, near death as he is, will do us any harm." She studied the older woman's worried eyes and noticed Dwynn, ever nearby, fiddling with the ragged hem of his sleeve. How much of the conversation did he really understand? Though everyone claimed him to be an idiot or a half brain,

Morwenna often wondered if his dull-wittedness was a ruse. "Come, let us give Nygyll some room to work." She pulled Isa into an antechamber beneath the stairs. "Why does Sir Alexander think the man to be a spy?"

"I know not," Isa whispered.

"But you believe it."

"'Tis not just that, m'lady," Isa said, lowering her voice, her eyes not meeting Morwenna's.

"Then what . . . Oh, by the gods, don't tell me it's one of your visions again."

Isa's thin lips tightened and her eyes narrowed. "Do not mock me, child," she said, reverting from the affable servant to the nursemaid who had raised Morwenna. "The things I've seen have proved true and you know it as well."

"Sometimes."

"Most times. Did you not notice his ring?" The old woman's eyes had grown dark.

"What ring?" Morwenna asked, a growing sense of dread invading her.

"The gold ring the wounded man is wearing. 'Tis a ring with a crest. The crest of Wybren."

Morwenna's heart seemed to stop. The castle walls closed in on her. "What are you saying, Isa?"

The old woman's eyes were sharp, the wrinkles around her lips more pronounced. "That the man who lay near death in the great hall may well be Carrick of Wybren, and the ring he wears is cursed."

"Cursed? Carrick? By the gods, Isa, have you gone mad?" Morwenna demanded.

As if he'd heard the name, the man cried out in pain, and then deliriously he whispered, "Alena." Morwenna froze. No . . . it couldn't be. But the raspy voice again murmured in desperation, "Alena . . ."

Morwenna's heart dropped as she heard the name of the woman who had become Carrick's lover, his own brother's wife. Alena of Heath, younger sister to Ryden of Heath, the man to whom Morwenna was now betrothed. Oh, God. She felt sick inside and felt as if the eyes of everyone attending the wounded man had turned to her.

"I knew it," Isa whispered, but there was no hint of triumph in her voice. Her lips tightened as she looked from the beaten man to Morwenna. "I believe this man is indeed Carrick of Wybren," she said softly, her old fingers worrying the stone that was suspended from the cord she wore around her neck, "and if he is the cursed traitor, the murderer, may the Great Mother save us all."

CHAPTER TWO

"This cannot be," Morwenna said, feeling faint and chiding herself inwardly for her weakness as the wounded man's desperate cry for Alena echoed through her brain. "Carrick . . . Carrick is dead, along with the others." Suddenly chilled, she rubbed her arms and repeated what she'd believed to be true. "He and his family all perished in the fire." *As did his lover, Alena.*

Isa shook her head, and her face was lined with worry. "There was talk that he escaped. A stableboy claimed he'd seen Carrick ride off on his favorite steed a short time before the fire was discovered."

"Idle gossip," Morwenna insisted, though her confidence was waning.

"Charred remains. Only identified by the pieces of clothing and jewelry that weren't destroyed. All that was left of the family members were blackened corpses that were little more than bones."

"You were not there." Morwenna's stomach turned at the picture Isa painted. Her head was pounding, her pulse thundering in her ears. *Could it be true? Could Carrick truly have survived and was he now lying half-dead in her keep?* Nay, she would not believe this nonsense. 'Twas only an old woman's deepest fears.

Isa let out her breath slowly, as if sensing Morwenna's disbelief. "See for yourself, m'lady."

Morwenna did just that. Without waiting for Isa, she made haste to the great hall, where the crowd was yet gathered around the beaten man. The servant had returned with a mash of yarrow and Nygyll was carefully applying the healing herb to his patient's wounds. The priest moved his hands and muttered prayers over the stranger's beaten body, which was all the more visible as he'd been stripped of his filthy, blood-soaked clothes. His chest was bare, black hair swirling over flat, thick muscles to arrow downward and disappear beneath a sheet draped over the lower half of his body. Dark impressions, bruises, and ugly bloody gashes covered the taut skin stretched over his torso, shoulders, and arms.

"Will he live?" Morwenna asked and glanced down at one hand where the knuckles were cut and had bled, two fingernails nearly missing.

" 'Tis too early to tell," Nygyll said with a deep frown. He ran experienced hands along the stranger's limbs. "I think none of his bones have been broken aside from ribs, which may have cracked." The physician's thick eyebrows knotted, his eyes narrowing. " 'Tis hard to believe, with the extent of his wounds, but again, too early to tell. If he rouses, we'll see if he can use his arms or legs."

Nygyll lifted one of the man's hands. As Isa had stated, a ring encircled a dirty finger. It winked in the candlelight, and Morwenna's mouth went dry at the sight of the crest etched into the gold. Her heart jolted . . . and a memory, as clear as ice, cut through her brain. . . .

It had been over three years past. Summer. They'd been riding and had stopped near a mountain stream. Carrick, nineteen and already a blackheart, had plucked a wild rose and handed it to her. One irreverent eyebrow had risen and a smile had toyed at the corners of his mouth as, with a flourish, he'd given her the bloom. She'd felt it then, that if she took the flower, she would pay a price, yet she'd gladly accepted the red-petaled gift and cut her finger on a thorn hidden be-

35

neath a smooth green leaf.

"Ouch!"

"Ah, m'lady," Carrick had mocked, "one must always be careful. That which appears most innocent ofttimes proves to be the most deadly."

"What is that supposed to mean?" she'd asked as he'd lifted her finger to his lips and sucked the drop of blood that had appeared upon her skin. She'd caught sight of the ring then, not for the first time, as it glinted in the hot summer sun. "Do you now want to speak in silly riddles?" His mouth was warm, the tip of his tongue gentle and wet as it touched her tiny wound. She felt a tingle that ran up her arm and down her body to settle deep in that moist, most intimate part of her.

" 'Tis not silly. 'Tis true." Again the knowing lift of a dark eyebrow even as his teeth had brushed against her fingertip.

Something warm and hot unwound within her, and fearful lest she fall into a deeper state of wanting, she yanked her finger away only to see the flash of his deadly smile and the sparkle of amusement in his clear blue eyes.

"Afraid?" he'd taunted.

"Of you?" she'd thrown back at him, baiting him as she stepped closer. "Nay, Carrick, just careful."

His laugh had been rich and full, echoing off the canyons and ricocheting through Morwenna's heart. She'd fallen in love with the blasphemous beast soon thereafter.

"M'lady?"

Morwenna blinked, suddenly conscious that Alexander had addressed her. Father Daniel's whispered prayers had ceased and everyone attending the weakened man seemed to be staring in her direction.

"Excuse me," she said, clearing her throat and feeling heat steal up her cheeks, as if everyone within the keep could read her thoughts. "What is it?"

The captain of the guard said softly, "If I may, I would like a word with you."

"Yes. Of course. Come. To the solar," she said and quickly motioned him up the stairs. "Do not move this man," she ordered the physician, "until I return or send word otherwise."

"As you wish." Nygyll barely looked up as he cleaned a particularly nasty wound above one of his patient's swollen eyes.

She hastened up the stairs with Alexander at her heels and was grateful to get away from the wounded stranger with his horribly battered body, tattered clothes, and disturbing ring.

The solar was a large room that could be

reached from the hallway or her private bedchamber, and as she entered, one of the serving girls who had cleaned out the ashes and relit the fire bustled out.

"M'lady," she said, bowing her head as Morwenna passed. "Is there anything else I can do for ye?"

"Aye, Fyrnne, if you could bring the captain and me some warm wine, 'twould take off the chill."

The serving girl offered a gap-toothed smile. Springy red hair surrounded a face splashed with freckles. "I'll bring it up right away," she said and scurried off down the hall, her skirts rustling the fresh rushes she'd strewn upon the floor.

"You wanted to speak to me," Morwenna prodded as the captain of the guard hung near the door. "Please, take a seat." She motioned to the two chairs near the fire and settled into one of them. "Tell me what's troubling you."

" 'Tis the prisoner," he said and reluctantly, it appeared, took a seat as the fire crackled and spit, offering golden light that played upon his rough-hewn features. A big man with a crooked nose and dark, anxious eyes, he'd been a part of Calon, one of the servants and soldiers she'd inherited with the keep.

"What about him? And remember, Sir

Alexander, until I'm certain that he's our enemy, I shall consider him a guest."

"That could be a mistake, m'lady." His thick fingers rubbed the hilt of his sword nervously, tracing the intricate carving on the weapon's handle.

"Why?"

"Mayhap we should consider him an enemy until he proves otherwise."

"You think he's dangerous?"

"Aye."

"But he's near death." She tapped a finger on the worn arm of the chair and tried not to think that the man could be Carrick. Nay, that was impossible. "I doubt he'll harm anyone."

" 'Tis never a sin to be careful," he said, and Carrick's own warning, issued on the summer breeze so long ago, again teased her mind. *"One must always be careful. That which appears most innocent ofttimes proves to be the most deadly."*

Alexander's dark gaze touched hers, and not for the first time did she notice something in those brown eyes, something he quickly disguised as he glanced away.

A sharp rap on the door broke the uncomfortable silence. " 'Tis Fyrnne, m'lady," a soft voice called.

"Come in, please."

"The cook, he thought ye might like a little nibble as well." Carrying a wide tray, the servant bustled in. She set the tray upon the small table between Morwenna and the captain of the guard.

"Ah, thank you," Morwenna said as Fyrnne left a basket of warm bread and small dishes of jellied eggs, salted eel, and baked apples. Morwenna's stomach grumbled as she offered Alexander a cup. "That will be all, Fyrnne."

"As ye wish."

Once Fyrnne slipped outside the door, Morwenna turned her gaze onto the captain of the guard. "Now, tell me, Alexander. You think the man downstairs is dangerous. Why?"

"He was found not far from the castle, hidden in a copse of trees that overlook the road to the rear gate."

"And beaten within an inch of his life. Did he have any weapons upon him?"

"Aye, a dagger strapped to one leg, within his boot. And a sword."

"Sheathed?"

"Aye."

"Was there any blood upon it?"

Alexander shook his head and took a swallow from his cup. "Nay."

"So he did not even defend himself from this attack?"

"Not with a weapon that we can determine. The sheriff and some of his men are searching the area near the spot where the man was found."

"For others?"

"To try to learn what happened."

"Was he robbed?"

"Not of his weapons, nor of his ring, but he had no horse nor cart nor purse upon him, so, aye, he could have been."

She plopped a jellied egg into her mouth and ignored the pounding of her pulse as she chewed. *The man downstairs may be Carrick.* Were there not rumors that he had escaped the blaze that had taken the lives of his family? Was there not gossip that a stableboy had seen him ride off? Had it not been conjectured that Carrick himself had started the fatal blaze? Why? What reason would cause him to kill his entire family? It was certainly not to inherit the keep, as he had let everyone think himself dead. No one had seen him in over a year, since the rumor spread by the stableboy.

Until now.

"It seems to me we should fear those who besieged this man rather than the man himself."

Alexander studied the contents of his mazer before looking directly at her. "He

41

wears the ring of Wybren."

Her heart nearly froze. "So I saw, but Wybren is not our enemy."

"There is much amiss at Wybren."

So there was. Everyone who noticed the ring would remember the blaze that ravaged Wybren Keep a year ago last Christmas Eve and the accusations that Baron Graydynn, now lord of the castle, had done little to squelch. "You are speaking of the fire?"

"It killed at least seven people. Nearly every member of the baron Dafydd's family, including his wife, five children, and his daughter-in-law. The only one who escaped was his son Carrick. And there is talk that it was murder."

She fingered her mazer of wine. "You think Carrick set the fire, murdered his family, rode away, disappeared for over a year, and now, somehow, lies battered upon a table downstairs in the great hall?"

" 'Tis possible." Alexander had been reaching for a piece of eel but stopped, his hand hovering over the platter.

"But not probable. Why would he do it? Why kill his family and disappear?"

"I know not. Mayhap he had a grudge."

"Against his *entire* family? There were seven bodies accounted for. *Seven*," she reminded him as well as herself. "Sir Carrick somehow escaped the blaze — or . . . or so it seems. But there is no evidence he is the one who set the fire. The man downstairs either stole the ring on his finger or someone placed it there." She finished her wine and wiped her lips with a linen napkin. Her fingers were shaking. "Why don't you take me to the place where he was found? In the meantime, have him transferred to Tadd's room across the hallway." Tadd was her brother but rarely visited, for which Morwenna was usually grateful, but today she would have sought solace in his counsel, disrespectful though it may be. "You may post a guard at the man's door, but we will treat him as a guest until we find reason to think he is a foe."

"But, m'lady —"

She gazed at him sharply and felt her chin hike upward, the way it involuntarily did each time anyone dared defy her or insinuated that because she was a female she was any less a leader than a man would be.

Alexander caught the gesture. "As you wish."

"I'll get my mantle and meet you at the stables. Tell the stable master to ready my horse."

He looked about to protest but set down his cup and nodded before quickly exiting the room.

Morwenna let out her breath. She brushed her fingers clean of crumbs and slipped into the next chamber. Closing the door, she tried to dismiss thoughts that the wounded stranger downstairs might be Carrick. 'Twas a foolish notion, as she'd so recently told Sir Alexander. She glanced at her bed and remembered her vivid dream, the heat and lust, the wanting and desire, and then waking to the feeling that she'd been observed as she'd writhed on the bedclothes. Another silly thought. Aye, Castle Calon was an intricate keep, one with many sets of stairs and hallways, some of which she had yet to explore, but no one was lurking in the shadows, watching her from gloomy corners. 'Twas only her too-fertile imagination running away with her again.

She slid on a warm mantle, pulled her gloves on with her teeth, then dashed down the curved staircase to the great hall, where soldiers were lifting the wounded man onto a stretcher.

He let out a moan as his body was shifted and for a second she thought his swollen eyelids might flutter open, but he only groaned and didn't waken as soldiers raised the stretcher from the table.

"Will he survive?" she asked the physician. Nygyll shook his head and wiped his bloody, wet hands upon a towel. " 'Tis doubtful. He is in a sorry state. Too many wounds. He appears strong, but it will take much fortitude for him to prevail. He will have to want to survive."

" 'Tis in God's hands now," the priest added, making the sign of the cross over his own chest and shaking his head, as if in judgment of the poor soul lying before him.

"Then I guess I have little to fear if he's inside the keep," Morwenna said. The priest turned to leave, but Morwenna placed her hand upon his arm. "Father, a minute, please," she said, and the priest's icy gaze met hers. Quickly she dropped her hand. "The man wears a ring with the crest of Wybren." She noticed a barely perceptible tightening of the priest's lips. "The crest of your brother Graydynn's keep. The crest of the keep where your uncle Dafydd's family died."

The priest said nothing.

"There is . . . Some are concerned that the wounded man is Carrick. Your cousin."

"The traitor."

"So it's said."

45

Father Daniel's gaze followed the soldiers hauling the stranger upstairs. "Oh, it's more than said. It's the truth."

"Did you recognize him?"

"No more than did you," the priest said, and she could only catch her breath. "You knew him, did you not?"

"Aye, but —"

"It is impossible to tell who he is."

"Until he heals."

One of Father Daniel's eyebrows lifted. "*If* he heals. As I said, 'tis in God's hands now." He made the sign of the cross over his chest and then added, "But, of course, it would be prudent to notify my brother that his enemy, our cousin, may have been captured."

"When I'm certain that the man is truly Carrick," she said, watching as the soldiers rounded the corner of the stairs. "Rumors may reach him at Wybren before morn but until we are certain *who* he is, they will just be that — rumors."

Who would beat the man so badly and then leave him for dead? Why? she wondered. Had it been robbery — the work of cruel thieves? Then why were some of his valuables not taken? Had the robbery been thwarted; had the would-be killers been scared off before they'd stolen all they wanted and killed their victim? Or had the harsh beating been for revenge? For what misdeed? What sin had this man committed to warrant such a brutal attack?

And why is he wearing the ring with the crest of Wybren?

Morwenna had no answers to any of her questions and was pacing when Alexander returned, Bryanna following him like an orphaned pup. "That man is *staying* in the keep?" she whispered, her eyes bright as she looked over her shoulder as if expecting the wounded man to appear like a specter behind her.

"Aye."

"Is it not dangerous?" Bryanna asked with what seemed to be great anticipation.

"I think not, as he's unconscious and barely breathing." Ignoring her younger sister, Morwenna turned to Sir Alexander. "Let us be off to the place where the huntsman found our guest. Mayhap we will be able to determine what happened."

Alexander snorted. "Guest," he said under his breath.

"I'll come, too," Bryanna said, and she flew toward the stairs, nearly bumping into the priest in her haste. "Excuse me, Father," she managed and then called back to Morwenna, "Just give me a minute to get my things."

Father Daniel's eyes met Morwenna's, and she saw there the unspoken recriminations and something more, something murky and dark — even forbidden — lingering in their blue depths only to rapidly disappear. As if he, too, was aware of what passed between them, the priest glanced quickly away and hurried toward the eastern corridor and the chapel beyond.

"I don't know what good this will do," Alexander grumbled as Morwenna gazed after the priest.

What were Father Daniel's secrets? For that matter, what were everyone within this keep's most private thoughts? A chill settled deep in her bones. Not for the first time she felt estranged from everyone else in the keep, a shepherd who knew not her flock. She'd been here less than one year. She was the outsider.

"M'lady," Alexander said, clearing his throat.

"What? Oh!" She remembered his statement. "I, too, know not of what we'll find in the forest, Sir Alexander, but let's take a look, shall we?"

Morwenna nodded to the guard and waited as he pushed open the heavy door to the outside. Mort, who had been snoozing before the fire, stood and stretched. As she stepped into the inner bailey, a rush of winter wind screamed bitterly over the winter grass to burrow deep through Morwenna's mantle and slap at her face. Ignoring the icy blast, she bent her head and made her way along the well-worn path to the stables with Mort tagging at her heels. The grass was yellow and trodden, crisp with frost, puddles along the pathway showing bits of ice.

Two boys, noses red, wool caps pulled low over their ears, hauled firewood toward the great hall while another carried pails of water. A girl, not quite in her teens, was throwing seed and oyster shell for the chickens, which clucked and pecked at one another. Feathers scattered as the hens hurried out of the way. The smell of smoke, fermenting beer, animal dung, and rendering fat tinged the cold air. In the pens, pigs grunted noisily and goats bleated as they were milked.

The castle was at work, everyone at a task; the momentary disturbance of the wounded man was seemingly forgotten. She glanced up at the wall walk and saw sentries posted, as always. Merchants and farmers were flogging their beasts as huge carts were pulled through the crusted ruts of the main road leading into the keep.

Morwenna ducked along a path leading

49

past the alewives' hut, where the women were talking loudly, discussing the discovery of the wounded man.

". . . beaten so badly his own mother would not recognize him," one woman — Anne, a true gossip — whispered.

"A robber, no doubt, who deserved his fate," another responded.

"Or else some husband caught him raising the skirts of his wife," Anne confided.

Chuckles erupted and Alexander let out a disgusted breath. "Women," he muttered as Morwenna lengthened her stride and maneuvered away from the nattering crones.

She walked swiftly alongside the armorer's hut. The steady ping of a hammer molding chain mail could be heard over the nasty hiss of a goose as it chased a small, interloping rooster out of Morwenna's path.

As she passed through a final gate, Morwenna glanced at the heavens. The clouds were ominously gray and thick with the promise of more rain.

"I know not what you expect to find today," Alexander said gruffly as they reached the stables and Mort found a favorite post, where he lifted his leg.

"Nor do I, but mayhap my curiosity will be satisfied."

He tossed her a doubtful look as she walked inside. The smells of hay, horses, leather, and dung assailed her and the wind no longer pulled at her hair. Morwenna walked unerringly to a stall where her favorite little jennet was already saddled and waiting.

Dark eyes bright, Alabaster snorted loudly and tossed her white head, jangling her bridle.

"Ready to run, she is," John, the stable master, said. He reached down and patted Mort's head. "There's somethin' in the air that's got all the horses ill at ease this morn." Straightening, he frowned and rubbed the back of his neck. "Somethin' they don't like."

"Like what?"

He glanced at her as he reached for the reins to Alabaster's bridle and shook his head. "Don't know, but I feel it, too." He stroked Alabaster's neck.

A frisson of fear slid down Morwenna's spine. John seemed a solid man, a sensible, staid soul, nothing like the cackling ale-wives or the disturbingly quiet priest.

"'Tis only the cold and the winter, John," she said lightly, though she sensed he didn't believe her and, in truth, she, too, was unnerved.

Ever since the damned dream about Carrick.

Dream?

Or omen?

She pushed her wayward thoughts aside and followed as John led her horse outside. Ever eager, Alabaster, nose to the wind, tail plumed, stepped into the crisp morning and began to pull at the reins. "Calm down, there," the big man said, smoothing the horse's neck. As white as a ghost, with gray stockings and muzzle, the jennet had been Morwenna's horse for the past four years. "Be careful, m'lady," John advised. " 'Tis slippery this morn, the ground frozen. You take care."

"I will, John," she said and, at the skeptical rise of his bushy blond eyebrows, added, "Promise."

"Oh, I'm not doubtin' ye," he said quickly, though his face flushed and his bulbous nose turned even redder as she swung onto the mare's back. Footsteps flapped along the path, and Bryanna, her face chapped from the wind, her dark curls flying behind her, rushed around the corner. "Wait for me," she said breathlessly. "I'm coming with you. John, I need a horse."

Morwenna inwardly groaned and the

stable master looked up at her. She nodded to him and he motioned to a boy who was mucking out the stalls.

"Kyrth, saddle Mercury for the lady. Did ye hear me, lad?"

The boy tossed down his shovel and, brushing his palm across the seat of his breeches, gave a quick nod. "Aye. 'Twill be but a minute." He ducked under the low-hanging roof and disappeared into the stable while Alexander mounted his own steed, a bloodred stallion who pranced near enough to Alabaster that she turned her white head and tried to take a nip out of the larger horse's flank.

"Steady, girl," Morwenna cautioned. "You don't want to pick on someone so much stronger, now." But as she spoke to the horse, an image flashed through her mind, a picture of herself with a sword, going toe to toe with Carrick. He was far stronger than she, over six feet tall and muscular. Though she was quick on her feet and deadly with a sword, he had easily disarmed her, leaving her breathless as he pointed his weapon at her heart. They had been in a castle courtyard, alone, the sweet scents of honeysuckle and roses wafting through the evening air, and her back was pressed hard against the stones of one wall.

"You lost, m'lady," Carrick had told her, his eyes glinting in the coming dusk.

"This time." She'd tossed her hair out of her face and met his gaze as the sword didn't move. She was breathing hard, sweating from exertion, her heart pumping. Carrick, too, was flushed, a sheen of perspiration covering his brow.

"Every time."

"You flatter yourself."

His smile had been slow and sensual. "Mayhap I must, for no one else will."

"And now you're begging for a compliment."

His grin had nearly been evil. "But you won't give me one, will you?"

She'd tossed back her head and laughed. "That's where you're wrong. I believe with all my heart that you, Carrick of Wybren, are the most handsome and arrogant and prideful snake I've ever met."

"Snake?" He feigned shock. "I'm wounded!"

"Asp?"

" 'Tis the same."

"Both speak with a split tongue, do they not?" she'd teased, and as a spark had flared in his eyes, he'd dropped his sword, letting it clatter to the stones, and swiftly pinned her against the wall with his body.

His lean muscles had strained over hers, calf to calf, thigh to thigh, chest to breast. She'd barely been able to take in air, he was so tight against her.

"You're a vexation, Morwenna," he'd said, his breath whispering against her ear, his hands holding hers over her head, then moving slowly downward, stroking her muscles. Her heart had been a wild thing, pounding and pumping. He'd kissed her then, his face pulsing hot, his lips hard and insistent and that tongue she'd so recently decried working its magic upon her. With an unwilling moan, Morwenna had melted against the courtyard walls. . . .

"Let's be off!" Bryanna's voice sliced through Morwenna's daydream as if it were a cleaver. She let out her breath, noticed Alexander staring at her, and flushed hot in the cold air. Clearing her throat and giving her head a sharp little shake, she pushed the memory aside as Alabaster trotted from the stable, Mercury in tow.

With the stableboy's help Bryanna mounted and took the reins in her gloved fingers. "Let's be off," she said again breathily, excitement flaring in her eyes.

"Aye." Alexander nodded.

Losing no time, they rode through an open gate to the outer bailey, where sheep, cattle, and more horses were penned. In the orchard, skeletal trees stood, shivering in the wind. Only a few hardy winter apples and a scolding black crow were visible in the naked branches.

As they passed under the raised portcullis of the back gate, Alexander mumbled something under his breath about a "fool's mission." He lifted a gloved hand to the guard and then spurred his mount down the frozen road leading toward the river.

Outside the protection of the thick castle walls, the wind raced fiercely, once again slapping at Morwenna's face and tugging at her hair. Ignoring the cold, she urged her mount to keep up with the swifter horse and felt Alabaster stretch out, her legs extending into an easy gallop as they veered off the road, raced across a fallow field, and headed toward the woods on the north side of the keep. Whooping happily, Bryanna clung like a burr to Mercury's neck and followed gamely. To her younger sister, this morning was a lark, a welcome breath of excitement. To Morwenna the situation was far more grave and troublesome, yet she, too, felt exhilarated with the rush of the wind and the clods of dirt flying up from beneath her horse's hooves.

It felt good to escape the castle walls. Her spirit seemed to soar, to be unburdened, for as much as she loved Calon, there was something within the keep, something dark and sinister that she didn't understand, a gloom she was all too glad to shed this morning.

You've listened to Isa too long.

You've had one too many disturbing dreams.

Alexander slowed at the edge of the forest, and as the horses breathed loudly, hot breath streaming from their nostrils, he found a deer trail that had been recently trampled by many horses' hooves.

"This way," he said, and Morwenna's short spurt of elation faded with the darkness of the surrounding woods. Following behind Alexander upon his mount, Morwenna heard the sound of voices drifting through the forest. As they passed beneath a tattered canopy of leafless trees and through a patch of scrub brush, the voices became louder. In a small clearing they found the sheriff, two of his men, and Jason, the huntsman. All the men had dismounted and were studiously surveying the ground beside a near-frozen creek. They looked up at the sound of the horses, and hats were quickly swiped from their heads as they lowered their eyes.

"M'lady," the sheriff said as she climbed off her jennet.

"This is where the man was found?" Alexander asked. He hopped to the ground and Bryanna, as well, slid off her horse.

"Aye, behind that log, near the big rock." Jason pointed to a large boulder with flat surfaces, sharp edges, and several dark splotches that ran in reddish rivulets to pool in small puddles upon the ground.

Blood.

Inwardly Morwenna shivered.

Alexander asked, "Have you discovered anything?"

Payne, the sheriff, shook his graying head. He had wild silver eyebrows, a high forehead, and lids that drooped over the corners of his eyes. Even so, Morwenna thought he saw more than most people. "There is not much to see. The remains of a campfire over there" — he pointed to a small pit where charred wood was visible and then moved his hand toward a stand of yew — "horse dung over there, and of course the blood on the rock along with some dark hairs. Probably a head — his head — smashed against it."

Bryanna let out a sound of protest, but the sheriff continued. "There are hoofprints, of course, and boot prints all around." He motioned to the ground. "Many of the impressions are unclear, but . . ." He squatted as he stared at the ground. "It seems that there are at least two different sizes of feet involved, and I would guess from the trodden underbrush that there was a struggle near this rock." He scowled as he glanced about the copse of trees lining the small clearing. "Some of the smaller branches of a few trees are broken, but we can't be certain they were snapped in a struggle, though that would be my assumption." He rubbed his beard thoughtfully and his eyes narrowed upon the area, as if he was imagining the events that had occurred. "I'd say that the man Jason found here was ambushed at this spot, fought off his attacker or attackers, lost the battle, and was left for dead."

"Or whoever was attacked prevailed and the man we have in the keep is the criminal. With what we know, we cannot determine who began the struggle here." Alexander walked over to the rock and eyed it. "The man Jason found may well have been the assailant and his intended victim escaped."

"Or his body is yet to be found in the woods," Payne said as if to himself, and Morwenna shuddered. "But the beaten man's weapon had no blood upon it — his dagger was sheathed when he was found." Payne stood, a knee popping as he straightened. " 'Tis a mystery. The best answers will come from the prisoner once we talk to him."

"He's not a prisoner," Morwenna said.

"A guest then?" Payne snorted as if he thought the idea absurd. "Something happened here, Lady Morwenna, something violent and criminal." As he said the words, a gust of wind rattled the branches of an old oak tree, almost as if it were the whisper of fate. Payne's gaze focused hard on Morwenna. "As I hear it, the wounded man is wearing a ring with the crest of Wybren, and one has to wonder how he got it."

Morwenna nodded stiffly, her mind wandering again to the identity of the wounded stranger.

"Was the ring stolen?" Payne continued. "A gift? Is he somehow connected to Wybren? There's been much trouble at that keep ever since the baron Dafydd's family was killed and his nephew Graydynn became lord." Payne scowled, his face grim, his nostrils flaring, as if he'd smelled something rotten. "I suggest you keep the stranger under lock and key, at least until we can determine his identity."

"A guard will be posted at his door."

The sheriff glanced at the bloodied rock. "Let's hope that's enough."

"He's near death. I doubt we have much to fear from him."

"But what of his attacker? What if he returns?" the sheriff asked thoughtfully.

Alexander said, "If he was attacked."

"There are many questions here and few answers." Payne clucked his tongue as the wind swept through the forest with a keening sigh. "Far too few answers."

CHAPTER THREE

Every bone in his body ached as if the pain would never stop. Muscles he hadn't known existed throbbed and his face felt afire, as if someone had taken a dull knife and peeled away his skin. He heard sounds . . . . disembodied voices talking over and around him, as if he were truly dead, the words whispering across his burning skin like the wings of moths. Still he was unable to move. Couldn't so much as flinch.

He tried to speak, but no sound escaped his lips.

Where was he?

His mind was blurry and dark, as if he were lying in a fog-shrouded forest.

How long had he been here?

He tried to open an eye, but pain sliced through his brain, and he could do little but let out a moan and try to fight the blackness that pulled at the corners of his consciousness and threatened to drag him down in that blissful abyss where there was no pain, no memories. His mouth tasted foul, his tongue thick. He attempted to move a hand.

Agony ripped through his body.

He made another stab at speech, but his lips would not move and his voice failed him except to murmur a groan. As if from a distance, bits of conversation pierced through his pain from voices who had no faces.

"He stirs," one old woman said.

"Nay, 'tis only the moan of a dying man. I heard he whispered Alena of Heath's name when he was brought in."

Alena . . . Deep inside he felt something stir. *Alena.*

"But he weren't awake then, nor is 'e now."

"But —"

"I'm tellin' ye, he's not awake. Watch." He felt a hard hand upon his shoulder and all the fires of hell swept through him in a painful blast. Yet he could not move. "See . . . he's as close to death as any man should be, and 'twould be a blessing if he passed." The heavy hand was lifted.

"Do ye think he's a highwayman?" one worried female voice asked nervously. "An outlaw, then?"

"Mayhap" was the response from a surer, steadier voice. That of the older woman. "I believe 'e were a 'andsome one. I wouldna be afeard of 'im searchin' me skirts."

"Oh, ye're awful, ye are," the voice said. "How can ye tell, what with all his bruises and swelling? 'E looks more like a hog's carcass after Cook has hacked off the meat fer sausage."

Both women cackled before he blissfully drifted off again.

Later . . . how much time had passed he knew not, but his pain had lessened considerably and in his half-oblivious state, he heard prayers, intoned without inflection, from a man he presumed to be a priest, a man it seemed who thought his soul was about to leave his body, and it sounded, from the tenor of the priest's words, that that very soul was about to plunge straight to the depths of hell. So days had to have passed . . . several days, he thought.

He tried to lift an arm to let the priest know that he could hear, but his bones were too heavy and he was able to only listen as the priest, without much conviction, asked that his sins be forgiven.

His sins.

Had there been many? Or few?

And what had they been? Against man? Woman? God?

As he lay aching in the darkness, he didn't know, couldn't recall, didn't care. He only wanted the remaining pain to go

away, and as the priest left, he wondered if it would be better to embrace death rather than endure.

His periods of consciousness were thankfully brief and this one was no exception. As he began to slip away again, he heard a door creak open and then quiet footsteps.

"How is he?" This voice was that of a woman. Whispered, so as not to disturb him, he presumed, but clear and filled with an underlying authority. A voice that touched a far corner of his memory, a voice he knew instinctively he should recognize.

"About the same, m'lady" was the response from a gruff male voice.

M'lady? The lord's wife? Or daughter? He had to fight to keep from slipping back into the murk of unconsciousness.

She sighed loudly and the delicate scent of lilacs reached his nostrils. "I wonder who he is and why he was found as near to the castle as he was to death." What was it about her voice that was familiar? Had he known her?

Think, damn it! Remember!

"We all do," the man said.

More footsteps. Short. Hurried. Nearly frantic. "Has he awakened?" Another

woman, older, he thought, with anxious threads running through her words.

"Nay. Not yet." The priest again.

"By the Great Mother, I trust him not."

"Aye, Isa, we all know," the man said.

The older woman is Isa. He tried to commit her name to his memory and remind himself that she believed in the old spirits as he battled the blackness picking at the edges of his brain.

"As you've said." The younger woman again.

"Lady Morwenna, he is healing. Mayhap we can now transfer him to the prison," the older woman suggested.

Morwenna?

Why did that name strike a chord in him?

Try to remember the younger woman, the one who seems to have some power here, is Morwenna.

"Look at him, Isa. Does he look like he could harm anyone?" Morwenna demanded.

"Sometimes things are not as they appear."

"I know, but for now, we will not treat this man as a prisoner."

A prisoner? What had he done for anyone to think that he should be locked away?

More footsteps. Louder. Heavier.

He struggled to stay awake, to learn of his plight.

"M'lady," a man said gruffly, and with him came the smell of rainwater and horses, a hint of smoke, and a rising of the hairs on his arms, as if this unknown man with the deep voice was an enemy.

"Sir Alexander." The younger woman's voice. *Morwenna's* voice. By the gods, why was it so familiar? Why did her name resound in his mind? Why the hell couldn't he remember?

"How is he?" the man Alexander inquired, though there was no hint of interest in his voice. *He is the enemy. Beware!*

"About the same. He's not yet awakened, though the physician says he's healing and you can see that his wounds have scabbed over, the swelling lessened. Nygyll says no bones were broken, that most of the wounds were of his flesh and, as he's not gotten worse, no organ was damaged significantly."

Such good news, he thought wryly as he decided Nygyll was the physician. Another name to be committed to memory.

"Should we not send a messenger to Wybren and notify Lord Graydynn?"

Wybren? He knew in an instant that

they were speaking of a castle. *Lord* Graydynn? That didn't sound right. Or did it? Graydynn? Aye . . . surely he'd known a Graydynn . . . or had he? His stomach knotted more painfully and he sensed something was wrong, so very wrong. *Graydynn!* He tried to conjure up the man's face but once again failed and was left with a sour taste in the back of his mouth worse than before.

"Send a messenger to Wybren and tell the baron what?" Morwenna asked in a tone of disbelief. "That we have a near-dead man we found in the woods and that the only identification we have is a ring with the crest of Wybren upon it?"

"Yes," Sir Alexander said. "Mayhap the baron or one of his men could identify this one and we could then determine if he's friend or foe."

" 'Tis a good idea," the older woman said hurriedly, almost as if she and Sir Alexander had planned this conversation in advance. "Then we would know once and for all if the man is Sir Carrick."

Carrick? His heart nearly stopped before racing wildly. He was *Carrick? Carrick of Wybren?* The name pounded through his brain in a way none other had. He tried to concentrate, to think past the pain, to remember. Was he Carrick?

"Not yet," the younger woman said. "I agree, eventually we will have to contact Lord Graydynn, but let's wait until we find out more about the stranger."

"And how will we do that?" Isa demanded.

"We'll talk to him, once he awakens."

"*If* he awakens," the older woman said with a disgusted snort. "It has been over a week since we found him and yet he doesn't respond."

Over a week? That long?

Isa added, "He may never awaken."

The crone's words were like a prophesy, for struggle as he might, he was losing the fight and soon he slipped back into the oblivion of darkness.

" 'Tis not idle gossip," the fat merchant insisted. Wedged into the chair before the fire in the great hall at Heath, he licked his fingers and then plucked another jellied egg from the platter laden with wedges of cheese, slices of salted eel, and dates. "I was at Calon but two days ago. The guards who knew me well, they stopped me and questioned me and searched my cart. They would not say why, but later in town I was playing dice and having a few cups when I spied Wilt, the apothecary. Though he had to be urged into speaking, he finally admitted that Carrick of Wybren had been located and brought to the castle."

Lord Ryden, sipping from his mazer, listened while the obese man told the story of a savagely beaten, near-death stranger found close to the castle gates. Ryden's blood heated and he tried to tamp down his anger, or at the very least, disguise it. The thought of Carrick of Wybren infiltrating the fortress that was Calon infuriated him. It mattered not that Carrick was near death; the fact that he was close to his fiancée, Morwenna, caused Ryden to clasp his mazer in a death grip.

The merchant was caught up in his tale. He gestured wildly in between bites and, no doubt, exaggerated the captive's wounds and the ensuing mayhem at the keep, playing up his own part in risking his life to bring Ryden the information.

But the tale had merit. This was not the first person to have brought him news of Carrick's capture, which was all the more distressing.

Ryden wasn't a man who deluded himself. He knew that Morwenna of Calon had agreed to become his bride only after she'd been jilted by Carrick. Ryden had no illusions that she loved him; nor did he love her. But Calon was her dowry, so the marriage would be a strong union, solidifying two baronies that abutted each other into one stronger, with vaster lands over which he would rule. He itched to see it happen and wouldn't let anything or anyone stop him.

Especially not Carrick of Wybren, the lying spawn of Satan who had bedded and then mercilessly killed Ryden's sister, Alena, in that unforgivable fire. Ryden felt his rage return as he thought of the sibling who was young enough to be his own daughter. She'd had so much life within her. With straight flaxen hair, a melodious, near-naughty laugh, she'd also been blessed with a twinkle of devilment in her gold eyes. She'd been beautiful, had known it, and at the age of seventeen had pronounced she was madly in love with Theron of Wybren and had married him scarcely six months later.

Ryden hadn't been fooled. Alena was too much of a flirt to settle down with one man, and not long after the nuptials there had been trouble, rumors abounding that she had taken up with Theron's brother Carrick. Ryden had even sent a spy to watch his sister, and the spy, curse his soul, had never returned. Just taken his hefty fee and disappeared.

Now, as the merchant rambled on, losing pieces of fish in his heavy beard so hasty was he in stuffing the food into his thick throat, Ryden silently considered his options. He'd known of Carrick's fate long before this smug trader had driven his cart through the gates of Heath.

Managing to appear only slightly interested, Ryden sipped from his cup, plotted his revenge, and heard the man out. Carrick would have to be dealt with; he'd known this from the moment he'd heard that the wounded man brought into Calon was suspected of being the missing son of the dead baron Dafydd.

Eventually the merchant's story petered out, which, it just so happened, was when the trencher was empty, and Lord Ryden rose, signifying that the audience was over. He thanked the man profusely, then passed him off to the steward with instructions to buy more of the merchant's wares than the castle actually needed.

The fat man left happy and thinking Ryden was his ally.

But then it was obvious the seller of goods was a fool who liked to think he was more cunning than he was.

So many were like him and they were so obvious, their motives clear to anyone with a brain. But Ryden outwardly treated the slob with respect. Though Ryden had a small army of his own trustworthy spies and was perfectly capable of looking after his own affairs, it never hurt to have another set of eyes watching out for his interests. So he managed a thin smile just to show that he appreciated the fat man's efforts and then let it fall from his face as the tradesman waddled off with the steward.

Once he was alone, Ryden simmered, rage burning like cinders in his blood. He walked to the fire and stared into the flames, conjuring up the conflagration at Wybren and the horror that had ensued.

Carrick.

Morwenna's lover.

"Hell," he muttered and spat into the flames. They exploded and sizzled, shooting sparks. He told himself to bide his time with Morwenna. Somehow he would have to be as patient with her as he had been with his other wives, perhaps even more so. Both Lylla and Margaret had been headstrong women, rulers of their own keeps, but Ryden had remained ever patient with each of them, intent upon his ultimate purpose, and in so doing had increased his lands threefold.

When he finally married Morwenna, his wealth would again grow, his holdings widen. To add to her allure she was young enough to provide him with an heir. A son. At last! Lylla had borne him a daughter, a frail thing like her mother, and they'd both died of a fever within three months' time. He'd married again, and Margaret, nearly as old as he, had been a cold widow when he'd taken her as his bride and she'd turned out to be barren as a stone. He could have been mounting a statue for all the good it did to try to impregnate her. She'd died within five years, wasting away until she was barely skin and bones, the physician at a loss as to what was happening. All the urine examinations, blood-lettings, leeches, herbal pastes, and potions had been for naught and, he supposed, for the best. Margaret's only merit had been that she'd been wealthy.

Ryden had shed no tears for her for she'd been a fussy, demanding, self-serving woman who had blamed everyone but herself for her own misery.

But Morwenna was young and spirited. Surely fertile. He smiled at the thought of bedding her and imagined losing himself in her. Getting her with child would be a pleasure. She was sensuous without knowing it, tall and finely muscled, her buttocks round, her breasts large enough without being ponderous, and he imagined she would enjoy the lovemaking as much as he. Oh, to feel her strong legs surround his torso as he plunged into her again and again, pushing hard against her, making her cry out in pleasure and pain. For what was sex without the pure, animal rutting of it? The domination of male over female . . . Ah, yes, he felt himself grow hard with the thought of it.

Dominion — that was what he craved more than anything else on heaven and earth.

He couldn't wait to claim Morwenna as his bride.

Aye, 'twas a fine, fine union, the best he'd ever planned and one he would have pursued were Morwenna an old, fat, hook-nosed, addled crone. The fact that she was young and supple with firm breasts and a trim waist was but a little sugar on an already tempting pie.

He licked his lips in anticipation.

Ryden of Heath wasn't about to let any man, least of all Carrick of damned Wybren, change his destiny. He would become husband to Morwenna of Calon no matter what.

CHAPTER FOUR

Morwenna escaped the chapel and felt anything but holy. Her thoughts throughout the dreary service had been with the stranger, and though she'd made the sign of the cross, listened to Father Daniel's prayers, fingered her rosary, and whispered her own words to God, she'd done so without any thought or consideration. Her prayers had been merely a matter of habit, and all the while she'd considered the wounded man. Friend or foe?

Carrick?

Could he possibly be?

Her heart leapt at the thought as she walked through the frosty afternoon, and she experienced a warm sense of something close to vengeance run through her blood. Was it possible? Could destiny have served up the blackheart that she'd loved so fiercely, giving her the power over his fate? She felt a pang of guilt at that turn of thought, probably because he was in such a bad way. Had he been healthy, she would have readily thrown him to the wolves of

Wybren. To Graydynn. To the hangman, if he was a murdering traitor. But he'd been near death when they'd found him, and her hard heart had cracked a bit as she'd stared into that battered face.

Somehow the wounded man had survived. Though the physician had warned her that the man would probably die within twenty-four hours, he had prevailed.

It had been more than a week since he'd been discovered near death. Surely he would survive, a man whose will to live was this strong.

So, Morwenna, what will you do with him? You, as lady of the keep, hold his fortune in your hands. What if he is Carrick? Or . . . what if he isn't?

"Bother and broomsticks," she muttered, as confused now as she had been when he'd been carried into the keep upon a stretcher. Wrapping a scarf more tightly around her neck, she barely noticed the servants and freemen working in the inner bailey. The farrier was pounding out horseshoes while girls collected eggs or singed the hair and pinfeathers off dead chickens, and the laundress frowned at the dark sky. Morwenna was hardly conscious of the efforts of those around her. Her body, however, responded, her stomach rumbling as she passed by the baker's hut and the scents of fresh-baked bread, apples, cinnamon, and cloves assailed her.

"Morwenna, wait!" Bryanna cried as she hurried out of the chapel. Morwenna glanced over her shoulder to find her sister picking her way through near-frozen puddles to catch up with her in the garden where last year's flowers had withered and a bench placed near a fountain was slick with ice.

As if reading her older sister's thoughts, Bryanna demanded, "What if the man in Tadd's chamber is Carrick?"

" 'Tis not possible. Carrick likely died in the fire with the rest of his family." Morwenna kept walking, holding her cloak tight to her body. They passed by a trellis where a few rose hips still clung to a dark, leafless vine. She didn't want to speak with her sister about Carrick or whoever the devil that man was. She and Bryanna had exhausted this conversation a dozen times since they'd seen the damned ring of Wybren on the wounded man's hand. "He's . . . dead." She glanced at her sister. "And so is this discussion."

"You were in love with him once," her sister charged, and Morwenna nearly stumbled over a rock in the path. "And now you're promised to Lord Ryden of Heath."

Morwenna's jaw ached. She couldn't think of Ryden. Not now. "I was *never* in love with Carrick," she said, as much to convince herself as her sister. "Aye, 'tis true that I *thought* I loved him, but it was all just foolish youth." After all, had not he also bedded Alena before and after his flirtations with Morwenna?

"He broke your heart."

Inwardly Morwenna cringed, felt the lie of denial leap to her tongue. Instead she stopped short near the carter's hut and wished to the heavens above that she didn't have to have this conversation.

"It was a long time ago. Three years have passed."

"I know, but if this man does prove to be Carrick, what will you do? Either he set the fire at Wybren and is a criminal, or he escaped the fire and whoever set it may be after him . . . and either way Lord Ryden will not be pleased to think that you are harboring an old love who might also be a criminal, a murderer."

"Or a victim," she said and spied the challenge in her sister's eyes.

"I knew him not, but I doubt Carrick of Wybren was a victim," Bryanna said. "A rogue, aye. A blackheart, yes, but never a victim." She didn't wait for an answer but hurried off, leaving Morwenna alone with her cold, troubled thoughts.

The fire could have been accidental, Morwenna told herself and wouldn't believe that Carrick had intentionally killed all of his family. To what end? True, if his father, Dafydd, and older brother, Theron, had died in the blaze, he would become lord. But only if he could get away with their deaths. And he would have to come forward and challenge his cousin Graydynn for the barony. Graydynn, Lord Dafydd's nephew, had inherited the keep after the inferno, and if Carrick did happen to be alive, he had not surfaced to challenge that claim to the inheritance.

Because he was a traitor. A murderer!

"Oh, for the love of Saint Peter," she mumbled under her breath, and the carter, leaning over a wheel with broken spokes, lifted his head.

"M'lady?" He straightened, his nose red from the cold, straw-colored hair sticking at odd angles from beneath a woolen cap. "Is there something I could do fer ye?" He wiped his nose with the ragged sleeve covering his arm.

"Nay, Barnum, 'tis nothing." Forcing a smile, Morwenna walked back to the garden and sat on the solitary bench. She looked up at the sky, where dark clouds glowered, promising an early dusk. The day was as gloomy as her spirits. Glancing upward, toward the small window of the room where the wounded man lay, she imagined a castle overcome by fire, the panic that would ensue, the long lines of people with buckets of water being passed from hand to hand from the well and ponds as the flames burned and crackled. Commoners, servants, soldiers, and the lord's family would try to beat out the fire with wet rags or buckets of sand and prevent the spread of flames. Thatched roofs would be frantically doused, young children and livestock herded away. Pigs would squeal, people scream, dogs bark, horses shriek as the flames leapt ever closer, destroying all in their paths as black smoke roiled to the unforgiving heavens. Pandemonium would ensue, and if the wind were to shift in the wrong direction . . .

She shivered and wrapped her arms around herself. Could someone have intentionally started the fire at Wybren?

But why?

Personal gain?

Revenge?

Abject hatred?

She bit her lip and stared up at the small window. Was she harboring a murderer? And if so, was he the one man who had touched her heart, only to break it? Steeling herself, she stood and headed out of the garden again. If the man in Tadd's room truly was Carrick, then she should deal with him as she would anyone suspected of a crime. She would hand him over to Lord Graydynn. Perhaps there was a price upon his head, a reward.

That thought should have given her a sense of anticipation. Or a little thrill of satisfied revenge. Instead it only dampened her spirits all the more.

"You're pathetic," she growled at herself. *And the man in the chamber is* not *Carrick of Wybren.*

"We've found out nothing more than we knew a few days ago," the sheriff admitted later that day. He was warming his legs before the fire of the great hall and holding his cap in his hand as he shook his head. "My men searched the surrounding villages, listened to the local gossip, and asked questions of innkeepers, farmers, merchants, anyone who might have been a witness to or heard about the beating. Not one person had anything to offer."

"The only people who know what happened are the man upstairs and whoever did this to him," Morwenna said.

"But it looks as if there was quite a struggle. I'd hoped we would find someone with bruises and scars he couldn't explain, but we haven't. There was a farmer who'd been nearly trampled by his horse, a huntsman who'd fallen from a ridge while chasing a wounded stag, two boys who'd gotten into a fistfight, and that was it. Whoever did this to the man we found either has hidden his injuries well, had received none, or has disappeared. We also looked for someone who had ended up with an extra horse, assuming that our *guest* was riding. But you know that finding a stolen steed is a difficult thing to trace, animals being traded and sold all the time."

"Mayhap we're making too much of this," Morwenna said. She was seated near the fire and staring past the sheriff's legs to the flames. "A man was found beaten and left for dead. 'Tis a crime, yes, but one we can't solve without the victim's word. We've acted as if our own keep was threatened, but could this not have been a simple highway robbery?"

"Then why not take the ring? 'Tis valuable gold for melting down."

"Maybe someone or something scared the attacker off before he could snatch it."

"Or if this man we've got here was the attacker, his victim was somehow able to escape with his horse and leave him behind." The sheriff clucked his tongue and rubbed the bridge of his nose. "What does the physician say?"

"He now expects him to live."

"Good." Payne adjusted his hat upon his head and his eyes glittered with a hardness that Morwenna had never before witnessed. "Then when he awakens, we'll see what he has to say."

"If it be the truth."

Payne's mouth twisted cruelly. "What are the chances of that?"

Twilight had descended upon the keep, and the Redeemer slipped silently through the corridors. Moving stealthily, he hastened down the staircase to what had once been the archive chamber. Thirty years past, after a particularly nasty bout of thievery, the room had been changed into a storage chamber, where seldom used items had been left to collect dust and become vermin-riddled and forgotten. Few even remembered that the room existed.

Listening for footsteps and hearing none, he slid a rusted key into the lock. With a low, resonant creak the door swung open. Stale air greeted him as he held his torch aloft and then quickly closed and locked the door behind him. Quietly he walked unerringly to the small grate on the floor, reached between the rusted bars, and found a latch that he unhinged. Straightening, he walked to the back of the chamber and pushed against a notched stone. Immediately the back wall moved on noiseless hinges, opening to a yawning dark staircase and a web of narrow corridors that had been built into the old keep during its construction.

His shoulders brushed against the walls on both sides as he slid into the corridor, where the air was dry and lifeless. He heard the scratch of tiny claws as rats and other unseen vermin scrambled out of his path. Yet he smiled. No one knew of these ancient, hidden hallways, and those who did believed them to be a myth. Only he knew how to access them and use them to his advantage.

He came to a V in the narrow passage and turned unerringly to the right, climbing ever upward, the soft leather soles of his shoes making no sound over the accelerated rate of his own breathing, the pumping of his heart. For in a few minutes he would be in his viewing chamber near he ceiling of the keep, where hidden he would be able to look down on her.

Morwenna.

Lady of the keep.

Sensually innocent.

His groin tightened at the thought of her, of watching her, and a dryness settled in the back of his throat. Unseen, in weeks and months past, he'd viewed her slipping out of her tunic and chemise. He had spied upon her as she'd settled into a scented tub, the round, rosy nipples of her breasts visible beneath the dark water. He imagined suckling there, tasting her, touching her, the sweet ecstasy of dominating her. As he'd watched, his agony had been exquisite. Gingerly he'd slid his fingers into his breeches and slowly caressed himself, restraining his eagerness, extending the torture of not having her. He'd been careful not to speak, determined not to let out so much as a soft groan to give away his presence. Nor had he relieved himself of the discomfort. Nay, no matter how long he was hard, no matter how much sweat and desire ran down his skin, no matter how much his muscles strained and his cock ached for release, he'd forced himself to wait.

For her.

All of her.

In his mind's eye, he imagined his lips behind her ear, his teeth at her throat. . . . He shook at the image, and beneath the folds of his tunic, his member responded. Gritting his teeth, he climbed ever upward in the slim, forgotten staircase.

On the third level aboveground, the corridor split into two pathways. He veered toward her chamber and again up a narrow set of flat stones.

Almost there!

He left his torch in an empty iron holder and then continued upward, his fingertips running along the rough, familiar walls as he mentally counted each step. As quietly as a cat, he slunk to his hiding spot, where, through the slits between the stones, he peered downward. Though his view was partially blocked, he saw most of the chamber. Licking his lips, praying that the fire was stoked bright enough so he could see her upon her bed, he pressed his face to the crack between the stones, his nose flattening with his effort. His heartbeat was pounding a wild tattoo in his eardrums, his fingers damp with anticipation, his cock ever thickening as he scanned the dark chamber.

It was impossible to see her, but he strained and he listened hard, holding his breath, hoping to hear her gentle breathing, the rustle of bedclothes, the soft rush of a sigh as she dreamed.

Nothing.

He strained. Yet he couldn't see her, didn't hear a sound over the hiss of the fire.

Anxiously he moved his gaze over the chamber so far beneath him, past the bed and the stool holding a basin, along the rushes of the floor to the alcove where her clothes were hung, past the chairs positioned at the grate . . . Damn!

A rising sense of panic flooded him. His hands began to shake.

Look again! Do not be fooled by the shadows!

Was she not in the bed?

He squinted hard.

Were the bed sheets rumpled but empty?

Nay! The miserable dog was there, curled into a useless ball. But the beast was alone, breathing shallowly, guarding no one! Wretched, useless cur.

Disappointment welled deep within and rage seared the corners of the Redeemer's brain.

Where the devil was she?

Where? The question echoed and ricocheted through his brain, and his erection began to wither and die. All his plans for this night, ruined! He leaned his forehead against the rough stones and slowed his breathing. As he did, an ugly realization began to dawn upon him.

Suddenly he knew with a deadly certainty where he'd find her. Cold sweat slid along his neck and shoulders, and his nostrils flared as if he'd encountered a rank smell.

Carrick! The Redeemer's lips curled in silent fury. A hatred as dark as the very heart of Satan curdled through his bloodstream.

She's with her lover. With Carrick of Wybren. She is forever drawn to him!

The Redeemer's hands became impotent fists.

Patience, he silently warned himself, *patience. 'Tis not only a virtue, but a necessity.*

He turned so quickly he nearly stumbled, but caught himself, scraping his fingers upon the wall.

Mentally chastising himself, he raced along the hallway, snagging his torch and then slowing to creep past the juncture leading downward. He sucked the spittle from his lips and moved as swiftly as possible.

Along the less-familiar corridor, he had to fumble for the bracket and then left his torch in the waiting holder. Fury pounding at his temples, he edged upward to another viewing post, a spot that would allow him to look down upon the prisoner, who lay motionless upon his bed.

Alone.

Yes!

Relief slipped through the Redeemer. Mayhap the fascination he sensed Morwenna had for the prisoner was only his own fear getting the better of him.

Then where is she?

A good question, he thought. A very good question.

One that bothered him.

He could search the castle, but he didn't have the time. There was a chance that he would be missed.

It was a chance he dared not take.

CHAPTER FIVE

"Who are you?" Morwenna whispered as she slipped into the room and stared down at the beaten man. Biting her lip, she ran a fingertip along his bruised cheek as she gazed upon him. The room was dark, only the glow from the firelight allowing her to view his distorted features. Swollen eyes, discolored skin, and a beard covering his jaw. Was he really Carrick?

Her throat constricted at the thought.

Don't believe it. This man could be anyone. A thief who stole the ring with its crest of Wybren. A man with hair as dark as Carrick's. An imposter who happens to be of the same height.

But why would he pretend to be Carrick of Wybren, a man who was thought to be either dead or a traitor to his family, even a murderer?

Murderer. She shrank from the thought. Surely not Carrick. Aye, he was a blackheart. True, he took her virtue along with her heart, but a killer? Nay. She couldn't believe it. Wouldn't. Looking intently at the stranger, she attempted to see Carrick's face beneath the bruised features, imagine the man she'd loved so recklessly lying upon this bed, his eyes shut, his chest barely rising and falling with his shallow breaths.

Over the past ten days, he'd begun to heal, yet the scabbing and swelling destroyed the natural contours of his face. *Think, Morwenna, think. You saw him naked. Were there not old scars or marks upon his skin that would confirm that he is Carrick?* She closed her eyes for a second, envisioned the rogue she remembered.

Tall, with a chiseled jaw and a nose that wasn't quite straight, teeth that flashed in sarcastic humor, eyes that seemed to see to the far reaches of her soul. His hair had been black, with a bit of a wave, his muscles taut and close to the skin, not an ounce of fat upon his frame. Scars? Had there been evidence of an old wound upon his body? A birthmark or mole upon his skin?

For the past three years she'd tried to forget him, to force her mind away from the vibrant images of a man who had so heartlessly left her, a man who everyone had warned her was a callous rogue, a man to whom she'd so recklessly offered her heart.

Now, looking down at him, studying the battered lines of his face, she knew not who he was.

So her efforts had been wasted.

Unable to sleep, she had risked leaving her chamber and made her way to the latrine and then waited until the guard himself had gone to relieve himself before slipping inside the prisoner's chamber. She would be found out, of course, but at least she wouldn't have to have the discussion or argument at the door. And, truth be known, the guard, Isa, Alexander, even the sheriff himself could complain mightily about her conduct, but there was little anyone could do about it. She was the lady of the castle. Her word was law.

Again she glanced down at the man, studying him intently. Could it be? She cleared her throat and then whispered, "Carrick?"

No response. Not even the slightest movement of an eyeball beneath his discolored eyelids. She bit her lip. Carrick had blue eyes. She wondered as she stared down at the wounded man just what color his were.

There was one certain way to find out. Carefully, her finger trembling, she touched his eyelid. Some of the swelling had decreased over the past week, and she was able to force his eyelid upward. The bloody orb beneath made her cringe. The white part was bright red but the iris was as blue as a morning sky.

Like Carrick's.

Her heart jolted as the pupil shrank and seemed to focus on her.

Because of the light?

Or because the bloody bastard was awake?

"Can you see me — hear me?" she demanded and then let the eyelid close and felt a fool in this chamber where the embers of the fire glowed a deep scarlet. She braced herself and tried again. This time she touched his bare shoulder and whispered into his ear. "Carrick!"

Was it her imagination or did the muscles beneath her fingertips tighten a bit?

Her heart jolted.

You conjured up his response.

Ignoring her doubts, she cleared her throat. Felt her pulse leaping.

"It's Morwenna. Remember me?" *I'm the woman you lied to. The woman you promised to love. The woman you turned your back on.* "Carrick?"

Again that tiny tension beneath her fingers.

94

Could he hear her?

Footsteps sounded outside the door. "What the devil?" a gruff voice muttered. "Bloody hell!" The door flew open to bang against the wall.

Was it her imagination or did she again feel a reaction where her fingers touched the wounded man's skin?

"M'lady?" Sir Vernon the guard demanded. A big brute of a man, he'd already unsheathed his sword and was surveying the interior of the chamber as if he expected to be ambushed at any second. "What're you doin' here?"

"I couldn't sleep," she admitted.

"You shouldna come into this room alone, especially when I'm not at my post." At his own admission some of the bristle seeped out of him. "I mean, I was just down the corridor, in the latrine takin' a . . . Oh, m'lady, forgive me. I shouldna have left my station."

" 'Tis all right," she assured him, stepping away from the wounded man's bed. "I let myself in and nothing is amiss." She offered the guard her best smile. "Worry not, Sir Vernon." Sliding one last glance at the man on the bed, she added, "I don't think he will do anyone any harm for a long while."

"But if he's Carrick of Wybren, he's a murderin' bastard and he canna be trusted." Vernon pointed at the unmoving man with his sword and then, realizing the inanity of his actions, rammed his weapon into a sheath strapped to his thick waist.

"I don't think I have any concerns from him."

Vernon glowered, bushy eyebrows slamming over furious, dark eyes. "Even sleeping, Lucifer is dangerous."

"I suppose you're right, Sir Vernon," she said, though she wasn't convinced the man was evil. Nor could she say for certain if he was Carrick. Only he, and perhaps his assailants, knew his true identity.

So what if he is Carrick? What will you do then?

"Good night, Sir Vernon," she said.

"And you, m'lady." As if determined to prove his valor, Vernon stood with his feet apart, spine stiff as steel.

Morwenna walked the few feet to her chamber, kicked the door closed, and flung herself onto her bed. What had she been thinking? What had she expected to learn by slipping into the man's chamber? By touching him?

Mort let out a soft woof, his tail pounding the covers for a second, and then

he sighed loudly and slipped back into slumber.

Absently Morwenna petted the dog's thick ruff, but her thoughts were jumbled and far away. She owed Carrick nothing: no allegiance, no concern, and least of all love. Her lips compressed as she remembered the day he'd ridden away. Cowardly. Before dawn. Leaving her alone in the bed.

She'd felt a breath of wind stir and had awoke to find him gone, the sheets where he'd lain still warm and rumpled, the small room where they'd taken shelter still smelling of the dying fire and the musk of the morning's sex. She'd heard a cock crow as she'd walked to the window and imagined she'd seen him and his horse on the horizon, the fog shrouding his image, the pain in her heart so suddenly intense her knees buckled and she'd had to bite down on her lip not to cry out.

She'd known then he wasn't returning. Would never. And yet she'd gone after him, intent on confronting him, on telling him what she suspected, nay, knew to be the truth. . . . Oh, she'd thought she'd come away from the meeting with a shred of dignity, a bit of pride. And she'd been mistaken.

That's what you get for trusting a rogue,

for giving your heart away so recklessly.

Now, lying upon her bed, her jaw tightening and tears threatening her eyes, she forced her mind back. She'd cried her last drop for that coward.

And what about you? Why had you not told him the truth when you had the chance? Were you not just as cowardly as he? Why did you give him the chance to flee?

She gnashed her teeth at the unanswered questions that had chased after her for what seemed a lifetime. Had she secretly known that he would abandon her and had she tested him, unwilling to force him to her, keeping her lips sealed and *waiting* for him to leave her? So that she could chase after him, find a horse, hop on the beast's broad back and . . . and . . .

She squeezed her eyes shut. A hot blush of embarrassment flooded her face. What good was it now to think of what had happened or what could have been? Blinking rapidly, she banished the wayward images, refused to conjure up any forlorn, self-pitying feelings for herself. She'd survived his betrayal. Had become stronger for it.

As it turned out, the beast had done her a favor!

What if the near-dead man is proved to

be Carrick? What will you do?

'Twould serve the blackheart right if she was to return his lying hide to Lord Graydynn. Wybren was less than one day's journey on horseback, even shorter if one took the old road and forded the river near Raven's Crossing. Graydynn might pay well to have the traitor returned.

Elsewise, she could, as Sir Alexander suggested, jail him in the dungeon. Let him suffer a while. 'Twould serve the scoundrel right!

Nay.

She sighed at her silly fantasies.

She knew better than to try to get back at a man who had wronged her. 'Twas petty. And foolish. Besides, the beaten man was most likely not Carrick but a simple thief who had been attacked on the road.

And yet . . . there was something about the stranger that jogged her memory and caused her pulse to quicken.

"Idiot," she chastised herself as she pulled the bedclothes up to her neck, causing the dog to reposition himself. Before she closed her eyes, she glanced around this chamber that had been her own for less than a year. Sometimes . . . 'twas silly, she knew, but . . . sometimes she felt as if she was being watched, as if the room itself had eyes.

By the gods, what was she thinking? 'Twas only her tired mind playing tricks upon her. Besides, 'twas something she could not voice, for if she did, her brother would surely take away her privilege of running this keep. She'd had to beg Kelan, who ruled over several baronies, including Penbrooke, to give her the chance to become the lady of Calon. Now, if Kelan knew she was thinking the castle was haunted, or someone was glowering at her from the shadows, or that there was a chance Carrick of Wybren was sleeping in a bed across the hallway, Kelan would surely interfere and, mayhap, think again about letting a woman be in charge of this castle. Mayhap Kelan would order Tadd, who was off fighting for the king, back to rule. Perhaps he would want Bryanna, sent to Calon as Morwenna's companion on the hope the girl would grow up, to return to Penbrooke to be with him and his wife, Kiera. Kelan was still the ultimate ruler.

The man lying across the corridor is not Carrick. Do not be fooled!

Muttering angrily at herself, she dared not face the demeaning truth that in her heart of hearts, she hoped the beaten man was Carrick of Wybren, that he would recover and realize how far she had come from that silly little girl who had loved him so wildly and that she was now a woman who was his equal, who would no longer leap at the chance to be with him, who would now never willingly abandon all others for the sake of her love . . .

"Stop it!" Her voice hissed and bounced off the thick walls. What had gotten into her? Was she finally believing Isa's dire warnings, the old lady's ever-constant muttering of death and doom?

The wounded man is not Carrick! Get that through your thick skull!

The moon was a dull orb shrouded by an ever-thickening fog. Weak light filtered through the bare trees as Isa knelt on the muddy banks of a swift creek and the barest of breezes snatched at her cloak. "Great Mother be with us," she whispered, her heart heavy. Using a stick to draw her rune, a symbol that looked much like a rooster's claw, in the damp earth, she prayed for safety. The wind kicked up a bit, bringing with it a chill of something she couldn't see but something she felt, the very soul of evil.

"Stay back!" she cried as if whatever was out there would heed her. A shiver of pure fear slid down her spine. Reaching into her pouch, she tossed a combination of mistletoe, rosemary, and ash slivers into the air, hoping the particles would catch in the wind and provide protection for Lady Morwenna and all who resided in the keep.

What the devil had her brother the baron Kelan been thinking when he'd given in to his sister's determination and allowed Morwenna, alone, to become Lady of Calon? 'Twas not a job for a woman. Though Morwenna was smart as any man, she was still a female. Many a woman had run a keep, to be sure, but usually their will was imposed through a man, a baron who knew not that his wife was maneuvering him. But this, to allow a woman alone to oversee so large a barony, was unnatural.

True, Morwenna had promised to marry within the year. Though the wedding banns had not yet been posted, Lord Ryden of Heath Castle had asked for her hand and Kelan had agreed.

Isa frowned and a cold worry settled in her heart. This coming marriage was not a good match.

The baron was good-looking, aye, and athletic, despite his years. The man was nearly Isa's age, for the love of the Mother

Goddess, too old, though he appeared a decade younger. Lord Ryden was used to doing things his way, which did not bode well.

Morwenna was headstrong and opinionated, willing to speak her mind. As had been his other, now-dead wives.

But Morwenna had agreed to the union, an inner voice reminded her. *Despite your advice, admonitions, and premonitions.*

"Bah." Isa tossed down her stick and dusted her hands on her old tunic. Morwenna had agreed to marry Ryden only as it was expected that she take a husband. After her disastrous love affair with Carrick of Wybren, she'd turned to an older, steady man, one who had courted her with the intent of a wolf upon prey.

Nay, 'twas not good. And it would not have happened if Morwenna had not given her heart to the rogue of Wybren.

Carrick.

It all came down to that cowardly beast.

Isa hated the man. It wouldn't surprise her if he was behind the murderous fire at Wybren. Carrick had no loyalty, no integrity. A bad seed, he was, a rogue who took after his father, Baron Dafydd, who, despite the love of a fine, beautiful woman, had been known to lift the skirts of servant girls, widows, and even the wives of his friends. Dafydd had been a ruler without conscience when it came to women, and all the while his wife, Lady Myrnna, had suffered in pinch-lipped silence and ignored the rumors of infidelity and bastards being born as she had tended to her own brood of five children. Rumor had it that Dafydd, outside the bounds of his marriage bed, had fathered daughters, sons, even a set of twins. . . . Isa wanted to dismiss the stories, or at the very least accept them as exaggerations borne on idle, bored tongues. But the rumors of Dafydd of Wybren's excursions into the beds other than his own were legendary and, no doubt, had some nugget of truth within them.

The wind slithered through the bare trees, tugging at Isa's cowl and the hem of her tunic. She felt the cold of winter settle into her bones.

Isa scowled into the darkness, her eyes searching the gloom for any sign of life, of the presence she felt. But nothing moved.

She turned toward the castle.

Snap!

The crack of a brittle twig breaking echoed through the darkness. Isa spun quickly. She stared in the direction of the sound. Searching the foggy shadows, she saw nothing in the skeletal trees, no movement, no dark figure crouching near the creek. Her old heart clamored, though she reminded herself there were creatures within the forest that meant her no harm, animals who moved in the night and were more frightened of her than she was of them.

Yet something here had shifted. She felt it again, that subtle and dangerous change in the air. Her skin crawled. "Who goes there?" she demanded hoarsely, her fingers slipping into her pocket for the little dagger she always kept with her. "Show yourself!"

No answer.

Just the murmur of the wind through rattling branches, the soft hoot of an owl high above, and the sluice of icy water rushing downhill.

Isa's ears strained. She licked her cracked lips and told herself she'd been mistaken. No hidden eyes were watching her every move. No one had seen her pagan rite. Fingers clenching around the hilt of her knife, she slowly backed toward the keep. Careful not to trip on the exposed rocks and tree roots, she eased along the path and away from the menace she felt was glowering in the woods.

'Tis only your imagination running wild, Isa, she told herself, *nothing more. The breathing you hear is from your old frightened lungs gasping for air. The snap of the twig was probably the weight of a passing boar or stag upon the trail.* But she hadn't heard the grunt of a creature rooting, nor caught the stink of an animal nearby.

Nay, whatever she'd sensed lurking in the darkness had been silently and malevolently watching her, for what purpose she knew not.

Glancing over her shoulder, she saw Calon looming upon the hill, the wall walks thick and sinister looking, the dark towers spiring high into the night. She had been opposed to Morwenna being sent here and longed for the safer days at her lady's childhood home of Penbrooke. But Isa's voice had not been heard. Morwenna had bargained hard and long for her own keep and Kelan had eventually granted her the barony — one that, Isa feared, came with its own history, bloodshed, and peril.

Had she not seen the signs?

Had her dreams of bloodshed not been vivid?

Did she not know that danger lurked within and without the walls of the castle?

"By the saints," she whispered and, once near the gate, turned and hurried up the muddied road to the gatehouse, half expecting some nightmarish beast to leap out and tackle her.

None appeared.

No dark dragon or messenger from hell assailed her.

As she hastened beneath the raised portcullis without incident, she released hold of her little knife, sent up a thankful prayer to the Great Mother, and tried to calm herself. What she imagined was just her own fear congealing in her mind.

Nothing malevolent lingered in the forest.

Nothing evil skulked through the barren trees.

Nothing unholy was watching over Calon.

Or was it?

CHAPTER SIX

"I swear to ye, I left my post but a minute, and the lady, she slipped into the room." Vernon's face was red, his jaw set with conviction as he stood nervously in front of Alexander's desk, his big fingertips rubbing against each other.

Alexander had called Sir Vernon to his chamber in the gatehouse. The door was ajar and the sounds of men's voices, the clink of chain mail, and the scrape of boots filtered through the crack.

"I was in the latrine takin' a piss," Vernon explained, then caught himself, for the excuse was feeble. "Lady Morwenna *is* the lady of the keep. She can go where she pleases."

And a stubborn one she is, Alexander thought, though he didn't say as much. He remained quiet, his eyes steadfast on Vernon's flushed features; he'd learn more from silence and patience than if he led an inquisition.

The big guard shook his head. "I know I shouldna have left me post and . . . and had I been there I could have tried to dissuade her or accompany her in to see the prisoner —"

Alexander had but to raise one eyebrow for Vernon to quickly correct himself.

"— I mean, to see her guest, but . . . ah, hell's bells, Sir Alexander, I was wrong. There! I admit it. Take me to the dungeon if ye must, or banish me from Calon, or cut off me right nut, but, Christ Jesus, even a saint needs to take a piss now and again."

Alexander's other eyebrow lifted of its own accord and he leaned back in his chair. Vernon was a good man. Simple but true of heart. He would walk through fire if asked but could be distracted all too easily.

As captain of the guard, Alexander had no choice but to punish any disobedience. Leaning forward, resting his elbows on the scarred table, he eyed the soldier who had been so true of heart. "You're relieved of your duty, Sir Vernon."

The big man's shoulders slumped a fraction and he seemed about to protest but wisely held his tongue.

"You can spend the next two weeks on the wall walk," Alexander said, his gaze holding Vernon's. "Mind that you don't leave your post for any reason. If you need to relieve yourself, you can bloody well do it through the crenels."

Vernon's heavy jaw worked beneath his beard, but he didn't argue.

"After a fortnight, I'll reconsider."

"Thank you, sir," Vernon muttered, and as he opened the door he nearly stumbled over Dwynn, the half-wit. "Out of me way," Vernon said and skirted the smaller man, who watched him pass. Dwynn entered the chamber. There was a slyness beneath his dull expression, a bit of cruelty in his blue eyes. Alexander didn't trust him. Then again, he didn't trust anyone.

"Something I can do for you?" he asked Dwynn as Vernon's bootheels rang down the stairs.

"The lady, she told me to . . ." He paused, scratching his chin, rolling his eyes upward as if to search his brain. "To . . ."

"To what?" Alexander asked, his patience stretched thin as Cook's gravy.

"To visit her."

"Visit her?"

"Yeah. She wants to talk to you." Dwynn seemed pleased with himself; his eyes were suddenly bright, his thin lips curving into a self-congratulatory smile.

"In the great hall?"

"Aye. The great hall. Yes." Dwynn's

head was bobbing up and down rapidly as he turned and half ran down the stairs.

Alexander pulled his mantle from a hook and swung it over his shoulders. His heart was beating a little faster at the thought of seeing Morwenna, though he told himself he was being foolish.

Again.

Being near to her was as much a curse as it was a blessing, he thought unkindly as he headed down the stairs of the gatehouse.

From the first moment he'd seen her, he'd been smitten.

He remembered that day all too vividly.

There had been rumors running rampant that a woman was to become the ruler at Calon, and Alexander had received a missive from Sir Kelan of Penbrooke that his sister would be sent to oversee and run the keep. Alexander had thought the idea ludicrous. A *woman?* A woman with no man to guide her? 'Twas foolishness. Laughable. Nearly sacrilegious. To Alexander's way of thinking, a woman running the keep was sure to be Castle Calon's ruin. He'd even gone so far as to silently call her Lord Morwenna, for surely she was a woman who had something to prove, a female who thought herself a man. Probably an old hag of a woman who wore breeches, swilled ale, and was ugly as a sow.

And then he'd seen her.

Riding like blazes on that white jennet through the gatehouse and into the bailey. Black hair streamed behind her, crimson skirts billowed as she leaned over the horse's neck, and she moved as easily as if she were one with her mare. "Run, you miserable beast," she'd cried, and the little horse had raced faster, gray legs stretching over the grass in the bailey, chickens and geese scattering and squawking, peasants and serfs abandoning their jobs to watch in awe as she pulled back on the reins near the great hall and the horse, panting and wild-eyed, slid to a stop.

With her tangled hair, flushed face, and incredible eyes, the woman had hopped lithely to the ground, her boots sinking into the mud. Even so, she was taller than most women and had a regal bearing she wore as easily as her mantle. She'd seemed oblivious to the fact that the hem of her dress was becoming dirty, or that rain was beginning to drizzle from the sky. A smile unlike any he had ever witnessed had toyed with her full lips, exposing perfect teeth.

"Who's in charge here?" she'd demanded of the small crowd gathered at the spectacle. She had eyed the people, her chin naturally lifted, her eyebrows arching.

Carpenters, laundresses, the priest, and a dozen others had stood near the keep's stone steps. But none had uttered a word. All had seemed dumbstruck.

Alexander had hurried down the stairs of the gatehouse and was striding across the trampled expanse of grass. "M'lady?" he'd asked. "Lady Morwenna?"

She'd turned swiftly and he'd seen her full in the face. Intelligent midnight blue eyes narrowed imperiously as she studied him. "And you are?"

"Sir Alexander. Captain of the guard. At your service." He'd knelt in the mud and she'd laughed, a deep, throaty, yet merry sound that had touched his soul.

"Oh, please, do not . . ." Glancing around the bailey, she saw that others had bowed their heads. "Oh, well . . . We'll have none of that. Not today. I'm tired, hungry, and in dire need of a bath. My horse needs —"

Alexander nodded toward a page gawking from beside a hayrick. "George, take the lady's horse and see that the mare is fed and groomed." His gaze returned to the lady's face. "Come inside. I'll introduce you to the servants, and I assure you, your every need will be attended to." He motioned to the small crowd that had gathered. "Everyone, back to work!"

Before anyone could move, more horses thundered into the keep. A party of seven, two women and five men dressed as guards, passed under the portcullis and into the inner bailey.

To another page, Alexander said, "You there, Edward, alert the stable master that we have more horses to stable. They'll need to be cooled, brushed, watered, and fed. Have John send his son Kyrth and one of the other grooms to tend to them."

Edward nodded, his hair darkening in the rain as he dashed off toward the stable.

"Lady Morwenna!" an old woman bouncing uncomfortably in the saddle of a swaybacked horse yelled as she frantically tried to stay astride.

The lady's eyes crinkled at the corners. "That's Isa," she whispered to Alexander. "My old nursemaid. She's never quite gotten over the fact that she brought me into the world. Sometimes it's best to pretend that she's the ruler. . . . It makes things go more smoothly. As for my sister" — Lady Morwenna hitched her sharp chin in the direction of the younger woman, who was easily riding a bay gelding and now drawing up on the reins — "definitely do not ever allow *her* to think she rules."

As the small party approached, it was evident that the guards who had accompanied Lady Morwenna were unhappy with their headstrong charge. All five of the soldiers wore stiff, uncompromising expressions as they reined in their horses and dismounted.

"They warned me to stay with them," Morwenna admitted quietly, and then she cleared her throat. "I believe I'm in trouble."

No, Alexander had thought at that moment, *I'm* in trouble. For in the few moments that he'd known her, he was falling hopelessly in love with her. Which was ridiculous, something that never happened to him. Oh, he'd been smitten upon occasion, but usually after a few pints of ale and always with a fetching lass whom he would forget the next day. But never, in all his thirty years, had he felt this unlikely, unwanted, and desperately ill-advised pull on his heart. 'Twas foolish, and Alexander prided himself for clear thinking. He'd reached his position at Calon through bravery, intelligence, and, aye, a bit of scheming. He'd hoped that after that fateful day, his wits would return to him and his first impression of the lady would fade into laughable nothingness.

Of course it hadn't. His life had shifted from the moment he'd laid eyes upon her. And now his lot was cast.

Though it was impossible, though he was not, nor ever would be, of her station, he loved Morwenna more than any man should love a woman.

And it was all for naught, he knew now as he pushed open the gatehouse door and was slapped with a blast of winter wind.

Lady Morwenna was promised to another man. A baron. A man as wellborn as she.

And a man who was a cur. Bile rose in the back of Alexander's throat. Lord Ryden of Heath. A wealthy baron who was nearly twice her age and had already buried two wives. Alexander's nostrils flared and one fist clenched as he strode up the slight hill toward the keep.

There was naught he could do. He'd been born the only son of a laundress, with no father nor mention of one. That he had risen to his position here, at Calon, had been because of cunning, grit, and ambition. His bravery in battle was for one purpose and one purpose only — to gain power.

But with all he'd done, he could never become a nobleman.

And as such, he would never be able to win a place in the lady's heart.

CHAPTER SEVEN

"Do not punish Sir Vernon," Morwenna ordered as she and the captain of the guard sat before the fire in the great hall. It was obvious Alexander was irritated, angry with his sentry, and, she supposed, himself. "It was my fault. I plotted to fool him," she admitted. "I was awake and waited until he'd gone to the latrine before slipping into the room."

Alexander looked at her, then glanced away. " 'Tis my duty to see that you are safe, m'lady," he reminded her. "How can I do this if you trick the guards I've assigned to you?"

" 'Tis not your fault."

"Then whose?"

"My own."

He frowned then, his expression as dark as midnight. "There is another issue here. If you can fool my guards so easily, then others may as well. Others who mean you or this keep harm."

"Punishing Sir Vernon will not change that."

He raised an eyebrow in dispute. "You don't believe in making an example of him?"

"Not when I was the one who duped him."

"Ah . . . 'duped him.' My point exactly. One should not be able to 'dupe' a guard in my service. I'm sorely disappointed in Sir Vernon."

"And in me?" she asked, watching denial form beneath his beard. "Do not lie to me, Sir Alexander."

"I would hope that if you wanted to do anything that is the slightest bit unsafe, you would confide in me so that I see that you are protected," he said, his gaze locking with hers again.

"You worry too much, Sir Alexander."

"You pay me to worry."

"I pay you to protect the castle."

"And yourself," he said, taking a long draft of wine, his eyes for a second betraying him and conveying emotions he quickly disguised.

"I appreciate your concern."

Clearing his throat, he set down his cup. "Sir Vernon's penance, if you will, is to spend the next fortnight on the east wall. Afterwards . . . we'll see."

"Would you send me to the wall walk as well?"

He grinned, a slash of white teeth

showing in his beard. "Nay, m'lady, I fear I would have to lock you in the highest tower and keep the key on a chain around my neck."

"At least 'tis not the dungeon."

His dark eyes sparked and she thought he was about to tease her further and say he'd love to cage her behind the iron bars of the cells within that lowest level of the keep, but he only shook his head, his smile fading, the joke between them dissipating in the air as the physician slipped down the stairs and hurried into the chamber.

"If I may have a word, m'lady?" he asked.

"Of course."

Sir Alexander was on his feet quickly, his backbone snapping into a stiff, authoritative stance. Half a head taller than the physician, he stared down at the man but seemed slightly embarrassed at being caught smiling and drinking wine with the lady of the keep. "I'll take care of the situation, m'lady," he said with a quick bow of his head.

"I think, Captain, you should hear this as well," Nygyll said.

"You have news of the man?" she asked, waving both Nygyll and Alexander onto the stools near the fire. A boy added wood to the logs already burning in the grate and a silent girl poured another mazer of wine after meeting Morwenna's gaze and receiving a nod.

"The patient is improving."

"Is he?" She couldn't help but feel a bit of elation. "So soon."

"He's a strong man."

"Aye." She'd seen his muscular arms and torso for herself, sensed that he was a warrior of sorts despite his tattered clothes. Alexander's expression was grim and he fidgeted as if he was in a hurry to be off.

"We've all heard the rumors," Nygyll continued, studying his hands, "that the patient might be Carrick of Wybren."

" 'Tis just that, gossip and supposition, because of the ring he wears."

"The ring is missing," Nygyll said softly.

"What?" Morwenna froze.

"I said, the ring is not on the man's finger."

"But it was there last night. . . ."

"Last night?"

"Yes. Late. I saw it with my own eyes." Or had she? When she'd looked over his bruised body, she'd searched for moles or scars or . . . Surely the ring had been on his finger. If it had been missing, she would have noticed. Wouldn't she?

Nygyll must have read the doubts in her eyes.

"You must be mistaken," Sir Alexander cut in. "The prisoner, er, patient has been under guard from the moment he was brought to Calon."

"You're certain the ring is gone?" Morwenna asked the physician.

"You can see for yourself."

Shooting to her feet, Morwenna was across the great hall within seconds. Sir Alexander was but a step behind her with Nygyll on his heels.

Morwenna flew up the staircase, ignored the guard, threw open the door to Tadd's chamber, and found the black-and-blue man where she'd left him last night. The patient, as hideous as ever, hadn't moved. He lay upon the bed, his near-black hair curling over his bruised forehead, the crusts of blood dark against his battered flesh.

Quickly she walked to the far side of the bed, where his right hand was hidden beneath the covers. Without a thought, she tossed back the blankets and saw his fingers, the knuckles swollen and cracked, the fingernails broken.

As Nygyll had said, the man's hand was bare, the third finger of his right hand lacking the ring.

Her stomach turned over. "How could anyone remove it?" she demanded. "His fingers are swollen, his joints . . . Dear God." She saw it then, flesh ripped from his finger, his knuckle red with fresh blood.

"The finger is broken; the joint as well," Nygyll said as he walked into the room behind Sir Alexander.

In her mind's eye Morwenna witnessed the gold band being ripped from the unconscious man. "Holy Mother," she whispered.

Alexander viewed the still man's damaged hand. " 'Tis not possible," he said, though without any conviction as he stared at the bloodied evidence.

The physician shook his head. "The sentry failed." Before the captain of the guard could defend his men, Nygyll added, "Whoever wanted the ring was desperate and had to work fast." His gaze landed on the beaten man's discolored face. "He is lucky."

"Lucky?" Morwenna repeated, her stomach roiling.

"That the finger wasn't severed." Nygyll's mouth tightened as he picked up the man's bloodied hand. "Whoever wanted the damned thing could easily have sawed off the finger beneath his joint."

"For the mercy of God, who would do such a thing?" she whispered, feeling herself blanch.

"I know not." Nygyll's gaze traveled to the larger man standing next to him.

Alexander's jaw slid to one side and his eyes thinned as he looked around the room. "On my word, m'lady," he vowed, his eyes grave and burning with a quiet fury, "we will find the bastard who did this."

"Mayhap you should question the guard," Nygyll suggested.

Alexander skewered the physician with an uncompromising glare. "Mayhap you should do your job, physician, and let me handle mine."

"Mayhap you should see that yours is done properly!" Nygyll answered hotly and then turned to Morwenna. "Obviously someone got past the sentry, entered the room, and then ripped the damned ring from the patient's finger and crept back into the night. No one, not even the guard, saw the culprit, and the ring is missing. We are fortunate that nothing else happened, for just as easily whoever it was could have slit this man's throat." He motioned to the patient and then turned his back upon Alexander, as if the soldier wasn't worth consulting.

Noticing a serving girl poking her head into the room, Nygyll lifted an arm and snapped his fingers. "You there, Mylla, stop your gawking and be useful." His pursed lips were white around the edges, his nostrils flared in agitation. "I'll need hot water, fresh linens, and yarrow for the wound . . . oh, and some comfrey. Send someone to the apothecary — that's right, comfrey and yarrow. Do you understand?" As the girl nodded and hastened off, Nygyll turned his gaze toward Morwenna again. "Now, m'lady, if you'll excuse me," he said, his voice losing its hard, imperious edge. "I do need to tend to my patient."

"Of course." She cast one last glance at the wounded man, and the knots in her stomach tightened. Who would do such a thing? Why? Was the gold crest of Wybren the reason for the stranger being attacked? Who would want it? Its value would only matter to members of Castle Wybren unless the ring was melted down. Or could it be that the ring was a trophy, a little prize to remind the attacker of how he had somehow duped the owner? Had the assailant returned and finished his act of thievery?

Then why not, as Nygyll suggested, just lop off the finger and be quick about it?

Muttering under his breath, Sir Alexander was but a step behind her as she marched toward the stairs.

"Who would do this?" she demanded.

"I know not. But I will find out." Alexander's voice was stern as steel. "Whoever did this is making a point, showing us all that he can move through the keep at will. He wants us to know about him; he's flaunting his power. Elsewise, why not just kill the patient and be done with it?"

Something inside her curdled and bumps of fear crawled across the backs of her arms. "He's trying to prove that the man is vulnerable."

"Not just the patient, but everyone in the keep," Alexander said soberly.

"How could anyone have gotten past the guard . . ." she began, then remembered how easily she had duped Sir Vernon.

" 'Tis exactly what I intend to find out."

Voices calling out orders, tinkling laughter, and the scrape of table legs sliding over the floor rose to greet them.

"Morwenna!" Bryanna came rushing in through the open door near the bottom of the stairs. Catching sight of her sister, she hurried up the few steps separating them. "Is it true? Did someone really steal Sir Carrick's ring?"

"We don't know that the patient is Carrick of Wybren," Alexander cut in.

"But the ring?" she demanded. "It's missing? Someone got past the guard?"

"So it seems," Morwenna said, irritated, as she continued to the bottom of the stairs and walked through the great hall, where boys were adjusting the tables and benches and Alfrydd, the steward, was surveying their work with a practiced, if doubting eye.

Near the grate, Dwynn was tending the fire, tossing in chunks of mossy oak that caused the flames to crackle and spit. His gaze followed the tiny sparks as they climbed toward the high ceiling.

Mort, resting in the corner, gave out a soft yip as he rose to his feet and, wagging his tail, approached. Noticing the dog, Dwynn cast a glance at Morwenna and scrambled up. Nervously he rubbed the sawdust and slivers from the knees of his breeches as he turned back to the flames. "M'lady," he said, his head hanging a bit, as if he'd been caught stealing from Cook's larder. "I was jest . . . I mean . . . the fire . . . it needed —"

"It's fine, Dwynn," she assured him, and a smile stretched from one side of his mouth to the other.

"You like it?"

"Yes, thank you," she said, though her mind was elsewhere. Dwynn, satisfied, grabbed an empty basket and headed outside. Morwenna paid him little attention, as Bryanna was still demanding more information.

Though she lowered her voice, Bryanna was flush with excitement, her eyes glowing with exhilaration. "Tell me," she insisted. "Carrick, er, the patient, he's unharmed?" As if realizing her words bordered on the ridiculous, she added swiftly, "I mean, no one hurt him any further."

"Not that we know. Nygyll is with him now."

"I'll alert the sheriff, m'lady," Alexander said, "and report back to you."

"Good."

With a tip of his head, he strode out the main door, pausing only to say something to the guard. The man listened, nodded curtly, and straightened his spine as Alexander disappeared, the door banging shut behind him.

"What does it all mean?" Bryanna asked, tugging at Morwenna's sleeve. "First the man is found beaten, near death, perhaps ambushed. And then while he's unconscious, under guard in this very castle, he's robbed!"

"I know not," Morwenna admitted.

"Do you think the person or people who beat him live *here?*" She gestured with one hand, indicating the entire castle.

"I don't even know if the ring was truly his. He could have stolen it."

"Why didn't whoever attacked him and left him for dead take it then? During the fight?"

"Mayhap he was scared off." Looking over her sister's shoulder, Morwenna noticed that Dwynn had returned to the fire. He now squatted near the iron dogs supporting the back log, poking at the embers and, she suspected, straining to hear every word of the conversation. From the corner of her eye Morwenna watched as he jabbed the iron poker hard at a stubborn piece of wood, his face reflecting the gold light from the flames. He seemed so childish and innocent that Morwenna doubted her assumptions about him. Why consider him calculating?

As if he felt her eyes upon him, he slid a glance in her direction. For a heartbeat, she thought she noticed a shadow passing behind his eyes before he turned away again, his childlike demeanor restored as he stared once more at the greedy flames.

"Maybe someone else stole the ring,"

Bryanna was saying, lowering her voice to a whisper.

"Someone else?" Morwenna repeated, steering her sister out of the great hall, away from hidden ears and prying eyes.

"The thief!" Bryanna said in exasperation. "He could be among us even now. Any one of the servants or the merchants or even the guards could be a traitor." As if to add conviction to her words, she lifted an eyebrow, then watched as a maid with an overflowing basket of laundry headed for the stairs.

"You're making more of it than there is," Morwenna said discouragingly, all the while shepherding her sister to the stairs leading to the solar.

But Bryanna's eyes were bright with the mystery and excitement of the theft. That was the trouble with the girl; Bryanna rarely understood how dire a situation might be. "I think mayhap you're not making enough of it."

Oh, how wrong you are, Morwenna thought but said only, "Time will tell. Sir Alexander will locate the thief." Morwenna hoped her words were filled with more conviction than she felt. What did she really know of the inhabitants of this keep? Bryanna was right. Most of the servants and peasants who resided here understood far more about Calon than did she. She'd heard the rumors that the castle was haunted, that ghosts could be heard creeping through the walls, but she didn't believe them, even when she herself had felt the weight of unseen eyes upon her. 'Twas her mind playing tricks upon her, nothing more.

Or so she tried to convince herself.

CHAPTER EIGHT

From his hiding spot behind the beehives, Runt, the spy, eyed the main door of the keep. Two guards flanked the great oaken portal and they were both wide awake, their gazes sweeping the darkened inner bailey. Fortunately for Runt, the night was heavy, fog clinging to the crenels, hiding the towers and wisping around the smaller buildings within Calon's thick walls.

Surely there was some way to gain entrance to the great hall, he thought, wondering how to slip inside without being seen. He was an ordinary-looking man and enough people knew him as a local peasant that no one paid him much notice during the day. But at night he would stand out, and the guards, ever vigilant, had been even more so since finding the man who'd been attacked in the forest nearby.

Runt itched to see the wounded stranger with his own eyes, but so far he'd been thwarted. If the rumors proved true and the wounded man was indeed Carrick —

A gloved hand flattened over his mouth,

cutting off his scream.

Another held a blade to his throat. "Shhh!" his attacker hissed into his ear. "If you value your pathetic life, don't make a move."

Runt's knees turned to water and he nearly pissed himself.

The blade pressed into his neck, and he squeezed his eyes shut, certain he was drawing his last breath.

"I know why you're here," the voice, raspy and faint, as if disguised, said. "And I'll tell you what you want to know. Aye, the man who was found is Carrick of Wybren. Aye, he is near death. And, aye, it is imperative that you tell the man who sent you of him."

Runt wanted to argue, to lie that he was just an innocent, but the razor-sharp edge of the knife kept him from saying a word. "Tell your master that you found this out from the servants. Make no mention of our meeting, for if you do, I will know of it, and I will slice your throat so quickly, you will not know what happened until you see your own blood pouring from your neck."

Runt's Adam's apple bobbed and sweat rolled down his forehead.

"Understand?" the voice demanded, and before Runt could answer he felt warm breath against his ear. "Understand?" A prick of the knife, just enough to pierce his skin.

Runt nodded quickly.

"Good. Since you found your way in here, I trust you'll find your way out past the guards. Do not fail me," his attacker warned, "or I swear I will hunt you down and slaughter you."

The blade and hand were quickly removed as his attacker hurried away through the rising mist. Runt slumped against the dormant hives and slowly let out his breath.

So he'd been discovered.

Was known to be a spy.

And yet was left to live.

For now.

He swallowed back his fear and straightened. Who was it who had caught him, who had stolen upon him so quietly that he'd not heard so much as a step? Had it been a man or a woman? Runt knew not, nor did he care. It mattered not. What did matter was that he make his way out of Calon before whoever it was who had just left him returned.

Pain screamed through his body.

He was on fire.

Burning up from the inside out.

He felt the sweat, the salt seeping into his wounds, and was barely aware of anything other than the intense agony that ripped through his body.

I'm alone, he thought, for he heard no voices, no scrape of the soles of boots upon the stone floor, no breath rasping in and out of lungs as someone hovered over him.

Gritting his teeth, he pushed aside the pain, tried to think beyond the agony.

Think! he told himself. *Where are you? Who are you? Why are you here?*

But, Christ Jesus, the pain . . .

No . . . think not of it! Concentrate, damn it. Figure out what is happening. Look about you! Now!

With all his willpower, he attempted to open an eye and failed. His lid didn't so much as twitch.

I'm blind, he thought miserably. *I can't see.*

No! You can't lift your eyelid . . . yet. Try again! Time is slipping through your fingers.

His fingers . . . oh, God, how they ached.

God in heaven, how long had he lain here?

Where was he? Some castle, though he couldn't remember hearing its name.

There had been talk of placing him in the dungeon but *she* — Morwenna — had been against it, and it seemed that she was the lady of the keep. *Morwenna*. By the saints, why was that name so familiar? It echoed through his mind . . . *Morwenna, Morwenna, Morwenna* . . . teasing at him, conjuring up memories that came so close to the surface only to submerge again.

How do I know you?

What did it matter? He was dying. No one could survive this kind of pain and live. His eyes burned, his head felt as if it were twice its normal size, his body ached, and his hand . . . Christ Jesus, his right hand felt as if it was splitting apart. 'Twas as if Satan himself had severed the finger . . . or all his fingers. Clenching his muscles, concentrating so hard his head pounded, he tried again to raise his hand, to open his eyes . . . but could not. . . . His body trembled . . . his empty stomach wrenched and suddenly the blackness beckoned him again, slowly and seductively pulling him under.

Sweet, sweet oblivion was calling to him, promising him relief, and, curse his cowardice, he let himself fall willingly into her waiting, comforting arms. . . .

'Twas dark.

The castle was fast asleep.

The Redeemer crept through the secret corridors and stepped carefully, his ears straining to hear any noise that seemed out of place. Though he believed no one else knew there were hidden hallways and tunnels within this keep, or those who had once heard the rumors of secret passageways didn't believe them, he was still cautious. Wary. So he strained to listen.

But he heard nothing other than the sound of his own heart pumping madly. Excitement sizzled through his bloodstream as he made his way through the tomblike corridors. He felt a sensation of power that was nearly godlike and it pleased him. He had much to do tonight.

First, a stop with the prisoner.

Noiselessly he moved through a narrow passage and up the stairs to an alcove where a body could barely squeeze through. Then, in this nearly airless cubicle, his fingers touched the wall in front of him and inched across the rough stones until he found a tiny crevice wherein the mortar was missing and a latch was hidden. Deftly he fingered the lock, and pushing with his feet, he moved a small section of the wall inward.

Agilely he slid into the room where the wounded man lay.

His blood was pumping, racing through his veins. His body tingled in anticipation. It would be easy to kill the bastard now, when the castle was asleep and the guard was snoozing at his post. So easy. Perhaps too easy.

There would be risk with his sudden death here at Calon. Questions. An inquisition.

But if the man were to die at Wybren, all the questions and theories about the fire would die with him. A morbid justice would be served if Carrick returned to Wybren to pay for sins not his own, a traitor hanged for all to see. . . . Aye, that would be so much better, and yet the Redeemer found the wait agonizing. As long as the man lived, there was a chance that all the Redeemer's plans were for naught. 'Twould be so easy to place a hand over the man's nose and mouth and hold him down as the hellion struggled for air that would never reach his lungs. Or it would be simple enough to bring a vial of poison to this locked room, break the seal, and pour the deadly liquid over the man's cracked lips.

'Twas tempting.

So seductively enticing.

He itched to put an end to the man's pathetic life.

137

In the near darkness, the Redeemer eyed his adversary. Still clinging to life. Still a threat. And yet still useful. Somehow this beaten pulp of an individual had to be blamed for the carnage at Wybren. Had to.

The Redeemer would see to it.

It had been a blessing in disguise that the man had been found and dragged to this keep, he reminded himself. A blessing. Others wanted him dead. Others had tried to silence him . . . and failed.

The Redeemer would not.

But the deed had to be done in the right manner.

And so, for this night, the wretched cur would live.

Only to die at the hangman's hand.

Smiling to himself, the Redeemer slid through the shadows, crawled carefully into the passageway, and slipped into the tight corridor. He found a small handle cut into one of the stones and strained to pull the facade closed behind him and then, with a bit of difficulty, hooked the old latch. It was a wonder no one in the keep knew of the series of secret tunnels and false walls that had been built, most likely, as escape routes in case of a siege.

He sometimes worried that the prisoner might find this means of escape, but the traitor was in no shape to try to find a way out of his guarded chamber. Nor was he treated as a prisoner, which, should he awaken, might lull him into a sense of complacency.

Satisfied, the Redeemer made his way in the darkness. He had other matters to deal with.

Licking his lips in anticipation, he made his way along the narrow stone corridor. In his mind's eye, he was already gazing down upon Morwenna from his private viewing alcove. He would be able to watch her sleeping form unseen.

And undisturbed.

Ah, yes . . . the thought of her lying there was enough to create a stirring deep in his loins, and his member began to twitch eagerly.

He nearly stumbled in his urgency and had to force himself to temper his lusty anticipation. *Patience,* he told himself, but already fire sizzled through his blood.

Rounding a final corner, he slipped quietly to his viewing stage and peered through the narrow opening between the rocks.

Tonight he was rewarded.

Faint light from a dying fire gave off just enough illumination for him to view her.

She lay upon the bed, the covers rumpled as if she slept fitfully, her hair a tousled dark mass upon her pillow.

His throat turned to dust. His heart pounded mercilessly at his temples. His shaft, already aroused, became stiff as steel.

She moaned softly and turned away from him, and he spied the curve of her spine, the outline of her rump beneath the covers. He imagined himself crawling into the bedclothes, molding his body to hers, feeling the hill of her buttocks rubbing eagerly against his crotch.

Sweat broke out upon his skin and he swallowed against the craving so visceral, so raw, so primal that his entire body shook. He imagined her mouth, the sweet taste of her as his fingers twined in that thick mass of curls and he guided her lower, the scrape of her tongue upon his flesh an exquisite torment.

Morwenna, he silently cried, pressing his face to the shallow slit in the mortar. *I am here. Soon we will be together.*

But he would have to wait.

He had much to do before he could claim her.

Much to prove to her. To himself.

To them.

Again she turned, restless in her sleep, rolling over so that she was facing the wall behind which he stood, his cock throbbing. He sucked in his breath as the coverlet fell away and exposed one breast, the top of a nipple. . . . Glorious, glorious woman. So beautiful. So full of life. So unaware.

But their time would come.

And soon.

It had to be very soon.

CHAPTER NINE

"The beast threw a shoe. Fix it!" Graydynn ordered, sweat running into his eyes, his hair flattened by the rain. He was tired and on edge, his early morning hunt having proved fruitless . . . just as his night had been. He slapped the reins of his steed's bridle into the palm of a surprised and cowering stableboy.

"Aye, m'lord," the boy muttered through crooked teeth that crowded his mouth.

"And make it soon."

"As you wish." The boy bowed his head and swiftly led the stallion away under the overhang of the stable. Graydynn smelled the scents of horse dung and urine mingling with dust. He strode toward the keep, leaving his guards to do what they would with their sorry beasts.

His mood was as dark as the clouds rolling toward the mountains, and the headache building behind his eyes pounded with every clang of the farrier's hammer against his anvil. Chickens squawked, ducks quacked, the damned pigs squealed, and even the castle dogs, on long leads, were barking their fool heads off.

All the noises of the castle grated on his nerves, and he wished for someone, anyone, on which to take out his frustration. Christ Jesus, this was not what he'd anticipated upon becoming Lord of Wybren.

He'd imagined sitting in a padded chair, ordering servants about, collecting taxes, and spending each and every night with a beautiful serving wench willing to do every erotic act his fertile imagination conjured.

He saw himself as Lord of Wybren, his dominion and reputation ever-spreading, the luxuries and fruits of wealth bringing him satisfaction and fame. Oh, he'd thought of rebuilding the keep and filling it with the spoils of other baronies that he planned to conquer. He saw himself as master of not only Wybren but also every land touching his . . . and in his deepest fantasies he thought of himself as a conqueror who could, should the fates be kind, exist on a par with Alexander the Great or even Hannibal. Graydynn would be a legendary ruler who would rival Llywelyn ap Gruffudd, the leader who united all of Wales, in reverence.

And yet since he'd taken control of Wybren, none of his dreams had come true. The cost of rebuilding the fire-gutted great hall had surpassed the revenue from taxes. The gloom and grief of the servants and freemen who worked for him had not improved much since the burial of Lord Dafydd and his family a little more than a year ago.

Graydynn snorted at this irony. Dafydd, the old baron and Graydynn's uncle, had been a liar and a cheat, the man who had lifted more hems than the local seamstress and had fathered more than his share of bastard children. What Graydynn did know as true was that Dafydd had robbed Graydynn's father of his rightful inheritance, and it was only because of the fire that Graydynn had succeeded him.

He felt a smile twist the corners of his mouth at the thought of the blaze that had elevated him to baron. Satisfaction burned through him.

At least some justice had been served.

He'd almost forgotten his bad mood as he passed by the armorer's hut and Runt approached. A wiry man with a pointed nose, buckteeth, and dark eyes that missed little, he'd been named Roger at birth but had been called Runt from the time he'd been a lad able to scurry about. There was something about him that gave Graydynn pause, a nervous twitch that could stretch a man's already dwindling patience to the breaking point.

"My lord," the smaller man whispered, ducking his head in what was supposed to be a bow. "I have news." Dark eyes blinked with excitement.

Graydynn pulled off his gloves. "Of what?" he asked without interest. Runt was known for his theatrics.

The little man lowered his voice. "Carrick."

"Again?" Nodding to the guards, Graydynn entered the great hall and had but to look at a page to send the lad hastening off in search of wine.

"Yes, yes. But this time, I swear, all that I know is true."

Disgusted, Graydynn whirled on the spy. How many times since the fire had Runt come to him with the same story? Ten times? Twenty? "And how am I to believe you?"

Runt's lips slid into a small, supercilious smile and his large nostrils flared even farther. "I heard it from Gladdys, a maid who serves the lady Morwenna."

Graydynn's groin tightened at the mention of the ruler of Calon. Morwenna. Sister to Baron Kelan of Penbrooke. So beautiful. So proud. And so damned arrogant. He envisioned the curve of her jaw and the arch of her eyebrow in response to a subordinate who proved foolish enough to challenge her.

The page delivered his wine and Graydynn shoved thoughts of Morwenna aside. He took a long swallow from his cup before settling into his chair near the fire. "And what says this serving maid?"

"That a man, beaten to a pulp, only inches from death, was found not far from Calon's gates." Runt glanced around quickly and then leaned in close enough so that Graydynn could smell the sour stench of old beer upon his breath. "The maid, she attended the wounded man, and she swears he was wearing a ring with the crest of Wybren upon it."

Graydynn's eyes met those of the spy and he couldn't disguise his interest. "Carrick?"

"As I said." Runt was pleased with himself and didn't bother hiding it. Yet Graydynn sensed there was another emotion beneath his satisfaction, something that didn't quite fit.

"And how do you know that this serving

wench —" He snapped his fingers impatiently. "What is her name?"

"Gladdys."

"Yes, Gladdys. How do you know she is not lying or . . . mayhap teasing you?"

Runt's eyes shined, as if he had been anticipating just this question. His expression was nearly a sneer. "Because Gladdys dare not lie. I know something about her, something she would not want anyone to hear."

"So you're blackmailing her?"

Runt chuckled low in his throat, but his fingers worked nervously as if he was overly anxious to relay his news. "Just insuring that what she tells me is true, so that I can pass on to you only the best information. I thought you would be pleased."

"I am," Graydynn said. Knowing the spy's information would cost him, he added, "And you'll be paid for your services, as always. Just as soon as I verify for myself what you've told me."

"Do so, m'lord, and you'll see that I speak the truth. Carrick is lying in a guest room at Castle Calon and he's hovering near death."

"Not expected to live?"

Runt swung his head side to side. "That's the beauty of it, Lord Graydynn.

Gladdys overheard the physician, Nygyll, speaking with Lady Morwenna. It seems Carrick's only chance of survival is a miracle. 'Twould be easy enough to kill him. A little poison, a hand over his nose and mouth . . . no one would know." His eyebrows lifted while his lips drew downward in an expression of dull innocence.

Yet, Graydynn sensed, something wasn't quite right. He'd never trusted Runt, though he'd employed him often enough. Spies' allegiances could be purchased too easily.

He would have to tread slowly and carefully. He had other spies at Calon and then there was his younger brother, poor, tormented, ever-atoning Daniel, who somehow thought himself a martyr, envisioned himself a saint, when, in reality, Daniel was just another sinner who thought he could repent his way into heaven.

Ridiculous!

"There are many at Calon who are . . . unhappy that a woman is now their ruler," the spy said, cleaning the fingernails of one hand with the thumb of the other, as if he'd just thought of something insignificant. "And now there is Carrick within the keep."

"What are you suggesting?"

Runt flipped a bit of filth from his nail onto the rushes. "Only that it would be an . . . opportunity to set old wrongs right . . . if someone were to see that the lady is . . . incapacitated and Carrick is blamed for it."

"You're speaking of killing Morwenna of Calon?" Graydynn said, his eyes narrowing.

"There are mercenaries who will do anything for a price."

"If Morwenna were to die, her brother Lord Kelan of Penbrooke would avenge her death."

"As would Lord Ryden, her intended, I realize." The spy's smile faded and a deadly gleam shone in his dark eyes. "I'm just saying that if some ill fate happened to the lady while Carrick was in her care, he would be blamed."

"Is he not under lock and key?"

"Sentries, like soldiers and serving maids, can be bribed. Even the captain of the guard has a price."

"Does he?" Graydynn said, trying to tamp down his excitement, for he didn't trust Runt. His suggestion may well be a trap; he could have been sent to Wybren by someone who had paid him.

"Of course he does," the little rat of a spy said. "We all do, m'lord. Even you."

"You think I should send word that Sir Carrick has been located?" the sheriff of Calon asked as he and Sir Alexander walked between the tightly packed huts. Their boots crunched along a muddy path where the dirt was near frozen and the puddles sparkling bits of ice. Hammers pounded and saws chewed through wood as the beekeeper's hut's roof was being repaired. Carpenters and thatchers moved quickly to replace the sagging overhang in the chill morning air.

It had been nearly a fortnight since the wounded man had been found, and castle life seemed to be returning to normal. The excitement and concern about the stranger had eased as everyone had returned to their ordinary tasks of running the castle. Merchants, farmers, and peddlers had been allowed again to freely pass through the gates, the wheels of their heavy carts creaking, horses and oxen straining at their harnesses.

The morning was brisk and clear, the ground hard with frost, and the air sharp with the bite of winter. The scent of brewing ale mingled with smoke from the farrier's forge, dung from the animals, and the acrid odor of rendering fat.

Huntsmen who had been out at dawn were returning with a gutted stag, several squirrels, and two rabbits hung on poles. Jason, the man who had discovered the beaten stranger, was among the group. He glanced up and found Payne staring at him. He looked quickly away, almost as if he were guilty of some unknown crime. The sheriff made a mental note to question the man again as Alexander finally answered him about notifying Wybren that Carrick had been located.

"Rumors travel quickly and it is only a day's ride to Wybren. No doubt Lord Graydynn has already heard of Carrick's capture."

"And his ambush." Payne scratched at his beard. There was something here he didn't trust.

"Aye. The assault."

They stepped to one side of the path as the kennel master, with six shaggy dogs straining upon their leashes, passed.

"Slow down, ye miserable curs," the kennel master growled before nodding to the sheriff. "Anxious they are, this morn."

Once the man and dogs were out of earshot, Payne asked Alexander, "Have you spoken to Lady Morwenna about contacting Lord Graydynn?"

"Not recently."

"So you want me in agreement with you first, is that it?"

"I thought it would be best if we both approached her."

Payne understood that the two of them would be more persuasive together. Pursing his lips thoughtfully, he headed past laundresses kneeling near huge wooden tubs. The women were up to their elbows in steaming sudsy water and filthy clothes swirling together. "A two-pronged attack, then."

"Not an attack," Sir Alexander said quickly, his face hardening. "A suggestion."

"From the both of us."

The bigger man nodded, squinting as a gaggle of geese, honking noisily, flew in formation overhead beneath the high, filmy clouds. The sheriff slid Alexander a look. "Do not tell me you are afraid of the lady?"

"Afraid?" Sir Alexander snorted in disgust and then spat, as if the idea were absurd. Nonetheless his cheeks darkened to crimson and the lines in his face seemed to crease a little deeper. "Of course I do not fear her. I'm here to protect her and all who reside within this keep. That is what I have in mind. If Lord Graydynn hears that Lady Morwenna is harboring a criminal, that, indeed, we have detained Sir Carrick here, Graydynn will be furious."

"Aye."

"And he'll be angry that he wasn't informed. Sir Carrick is a wanted man. There is no telling what Graydynn will do."

"You are assuming that the wounded man is indeed Carrick of Wybren."

"Aye."

"And you also assume that he massacred his family, then fled Wybren."

"Aye." Alexander nodded sharply, without so much as a second's hesitation. "So many people are dead because of Carrick. The murdering bastard killed not only his parents, but his sister, brothers, and sister-in-law as they slept. 'Tis a wonder no servants or peasants were killed as well."

"And why do you think that is?"

They had reached the great hall, and Alexander took in a long breath and then squared his shoulders as they climbed the steps and passed by the guard at the door.

"Because the assault was planned. Whoever did it wanted only the lord's family killed."

"You said 'whoever,' yet you're certain the culprit was Carrick."

"He was seen fleeing the castle."

"By one stableboy," Payne reminded him, feeling the warmth of the interior of the keep reach his skin as he yanked off his gloves. Boys were stoking the fire and replacing the candles and rushlights in the sconces on the walls while girls washed down the long oaken tables, all the while chatting and giggling as they worked. By the fire one of the castle dogs stood and stretched, its black lips pulling back in a yawn as it eyed the newcomers and then settled into its spot near the grate.

"The man we've got locked upstairs was wearing the ring of Wybren," Alexander said as he reached the base of the stone steps and then paused to skewer the sheriff with his intense gaze.

"Agreed," Payne said slowly, still thinking.

"So what you're saying, Payne, is that you don't believe our captive is Carrick? Or you don't believe that Carrick is the criminal?"

"I know not who he is or what he's done . . . but I think we should tread carefully."

" 'Tis best if the news of what has happened here reaches Graydynn through our own messenger and not idle gossip. That way we are assured that he learns the truth."

Payne couldn't disagree with this line of reasoning and yet he felt as if alerting Graydynn could be the same as waking a sleeping dragon. The current Lord of Wybren wasn't known for his patience.

Alexander started up the stairs and his steps quickened. "Let us speak to the lady. 'Tis her decision."

That it is, Payne silently agreed. Payne was not one to suffer fools, but in this case he pitied Alexander, for it was obvious he was in love with the lady and that love was futile. Stupid. A ridiculous notion. Not only was Lady Morwenna promised to Lord Ryden of Heath, the pompous ass, but even if she were not, she was of a station far above that of the captain of the guard.

He shook his head and followed. He only hoped Alexander's unrequited love for Morwenna had not clouded the captain of the guard's judgment. If that was the case, then everyone in the keep was in jeopardy.

CHAPTER TEN

"But, m'lady," Alfrydd said, "you need to attend to matters beside the prisoner, er, guest. Aside from the band of thieves that has been bothering the farmers and merchants as they travel —"

"The sheriff and captain of the guard are dealing with them," Morwenna cut in, angry that the steward suggested she was ignoring her duties.

"Aye, 'tis true. But there are other issues," he persisted. "The taxes must not be ignored. They have to be collected in order that we run this keep. Jack Farmer is only one of the men who owes two years of bodel silver. His house, as well as those of others — and I have a list of their names — is on your land and therefore taxed by bodel silver —"

"I understand," she cut in.

But the steward wasn't finished. "Then there's the agistment tax. We haven't collected as much as we should have because some of the farmers have let their animals graze in the woods but have as yet refused to pay you."

Alfrydd was standing in front of Morwenna at her desk in the solar. With a long, skeletal finger, he pointed to the ledgers where a scribe had entered the records of all the taxes, tithes, and fees collected for the past three years. Families who were in arrears were listed on another sheet of parchment. "There are also several people, including Gregory the tinsmith, who owe chiminage as they've carted their goods through the woods and not paid! And . . . and . . . see here." He tapped the ledger page. "No heriot collected from five families this past year. That's five horses we don't have in the castle's stable."

Morwenna scowled. Heriot was one of the taxes she didn't like. One, she thought, designed by men for men. "I find it hard to take the best animals from a family who is grieving for the loss of their husband and father, especially when those horses could provide the wife some income."

"I know, m'lady. But you must make the collection and pass on the king's share to him." Alfrydd smiled kindly. "I don't mean to sound callous, but it is expensive to run this keep, and everyone you collect from receives the benefit of your protection. 'Tis a privilege to pay these paltry fees."

"Tell that to Mavis, the wheelwright's wife, and her five children. Explain to them why I must take their strongest mule as they have no horse. That mule is probably used to till the land on their small plot. And tell them that not only will I take the mule, but I'll be expecting fodder corn as well."

"Everyone must help feed the horses for our army."

"And that of the king, I know, I know!" She tossed up her hands in disgust and stood abruptly. "But Mavis Wheelwright has six mouths to feed including her own and no husband to provide for her. What's she to do? Look to another man to help sustain her and her children?"

"The oldest boy can help —"

"Aye, a lad barely eight years old." She let out a long sigh.

"And a strong boy who could help the woodcutter or the mason or —"

"We'll *not* take Mavis Wheelwright's mule," she argued, feeling her cheeks warm with color and knowing her eyes were blazing. "Nor will she have to pay fodder corn this year or next. After that, we'll see."

If Alfrydd intended to argue any further,

he thought better of it and held his tongue. "As you wish," he muttered dourly and scooped up the ledgers.

"Yes. As *I* wish," Morwenna bit out and then, seeing his lips fold in upon themselves, felt immediate remorse. The man was only doing his job and he was doing it thoughtfully. She suddenly felt as if a huge weight had settled heavy upon her shoulders. In all the years of clamoring to be treated as an equal to her brothers, in her prayers for a keep of her own, never had she considered some of the tasks and responsibilities thrust upon her, nor thought of the hard decisions she would be forced to make.

"Thank you, Alfrydd. I do know that you are only looking out for the good of Calon," she said more softly. He nodded at her as he left the room. As she settled into her chair, the captain of the guard and the sheriff were announced. A bare moment later the two men were striding into the solar.

"M'lady," Alexander said, "if we might have a word."

"Certainly." She braced herself.

The two men's expressions were hard and set, their demeanors stiff, as if they were about to impart bad news. *Carrick,*

159

she thought and her stupid heart clutched.

"It's about the patient," Alexander stated.

Of course. Her fingers curled over the arms of her chair. "What about him?"

"I think, mayhap, it's time to tell Lord Graydynn of him."

Dear God, not yet. Not until I know for certain! "Do you?" she asked, forcing herself to remain calm. "Why?"

After only a second's hesitation, Alexander spoke first, explaining his reasoning, specifically his concerns about Baron Graydynn's reaction should the Lord of Wybren be told by others that she was harboring a traitor and criminal.

Morwenna wanted to argue, and a rising sense of panic started deep inside at the thought of sending Carrick to his uncle. Tamping down her fears, she listened, quietly biding her time, attempting to remain neutral and unbiased until she'd heard the two men out, trying silently to quell an anxiety she couldn't name should she have to give up the patient.

Were the two men standing before her in agreement? She couldn't tell. As Alexander stated his case, the sheriff remained quiet, almost studious, while the captain of the guard listed off his reasons for sending a messenger to Wybren.

Once Alexander paused, Morwenna trained her eyes upon the sheriff. "Am I to assume you are in agreement — that a messenger must be sent to Wybren?"

Payne hedged. "I'm not sure. 'Tis possible the man is not Carrick, and there seems to be no reason to inform Baron Graydynn unless we are sure of the patient's identity. However, Sir Alexander makes a good point that it would be much better if you were to send word of the situation rather than have gossip, rumor, and who knows what kind of lies seep through the gates of Wybren."

So that was it. She would have to make a decision regarding Carrick's fate. "I was hoping we could wait until we were certain of who the man is."

"Aye, that would be best." Payne rubbed the back of his neck.

"But, after this much time, impossible," Alexander said, his big face earnest. "Perhaps a note to Graydynn, carefully worded so as not to anger him or let him leap to any assumptions, would do for now." A muscle worked beneath his beard. "I fear the gossip has already reached him as it is."

Morwenna leaned back in her chair and rested her chin on her clasped hands. Alexander was right. She knew it. The sher

knew it. Yet she was reluctant to send the missive.

"What if Lord Graydynn sends his army, or even comes himself, to retrieve Carrick and take him to be hanged for treason? What if the man isn't Carrick?"

"Then who is he? A common thief who stole the ring from a dead man?"

"He could be anyone," Morwenna said, though in her heart she felt the man lying in Tadd's chamber was indeed Carrick of Wybren. "He could have stolen the ring, yes, or found it. Or perhaps won it in a game of dice. It may even have been given to him."

Alexander snorted his disbelief, but the sheriff was slowly nodding. "There are many reasons the man across the hallway might have had the ring, but until he awakens and tells his story, we won't know what they are."

"Even then, he might lie," Alexander stated.

Payne's eyebrows rose and he nodded his head. "Possibly."

" 'Tis not a chance we should take. M'lady, I think it best to let Graydynn of Wybren know that you've taken in a stranger, a wounded man, possibly a soldier, and that he was found wearing a ring

bearing the crest of Wybren. You could tell him that you are waiting until the man regains consciousness to decide who he is and what you will do with him, if anything. Doing so, you'll avoid risking Graydynn's ire and, possibly, his retribution."

She turned her gaze to the sheriff. "You agree?"

The sheriff nodded slowly. "For the most part."

"But you have reservations."

He smiled. "Of course, m'lady. I always have reservations."

She trusted these two. Alexander was always concerned about Calon's safety and Payne was interested in justice. Though she'd known each man less than a year, she felt that they were true hearts.

Or so you think. What do you really know of them? Only what they want you to see; only what you've heard from the servants and peasants within the castle, people who are more loyal to them than they are to you. What had Isa said?

"Trust no one, Morwenna. No one."

Both men were staring at her, waiting, and she couldn't help but wonder if they had conspired to confront her, each acting out his predesigned role.

"M'lady?" Sir Alexander nudged.

Morwenna bit her lip and weighed each alternative. She didn't want to risk alienating Wybren, nor did she want to act in haste.

"I'll think on this tonight, and if I decide to inform Lord Graydynn, I'll send a messenger tomorrow."

"By then it may be too late," Alexander pointed out. "Graydynn may hear the rumors."

"He may have already," Morwenna said. "Wybren is but a day's ride."

"Or less." Payne was frowning thoughtfully and scratching at his chin.

"Then a few more hours won't change things," she said, dismissing them. "On the morrow I'll make my decision."

She only hoped it would be the right one.

"Why is it you hate Carrick so much?" Bryanna asked as she pretended to embroider. She tugged impatiently upon the thread. It was evening, the fires burning bright, and Isa felt it then, the evil that lurked within this castle.

'Twas as if the walls themselves had eyes.

"He broke your sister's heart." They were seated in Bryanna's room. Isa warmed her old back against the blaze of the logs in the grate. It seemed that with each winter the aches in her joints worsened. She rubbed her hands together and noticed how her knuckles had grown over the past few years.

Bryanna lifted a shoulder and, frowning at her work, pulled at the knotted thread, then muttered something unkind under her breath. "It happens often, does it not, a heart being broken?"

"Aye, but not with Morwenna." Isa knew of Morwenna's unborn babe, of course, though Isa had never revealed it to anyone, including Morwenna. For the loss of that little one, Isa would never forgive Carrick. Nor would she ever reveal that he'd left Morwenna for Alena of Heath, the woman who had married his brother Theron; Alena, the sister to Lord Ryden, to whom Morwenna was now promised. Oh, 'twas an impossible knot. As bad as Bryanna's pathetic attempts at embroidery. On top of all this mess, there were the ever-present rumors that Carrick had murdered his family as they'd slept.

"You know more than you're willing to say."

"About a lot of things," Isa admitted. "We all have our secrets."

"You speak in riddles."

"You ask too many questions."

Bryanna snorted but didn't disagree. "There's talk of sending him back to Wybren."

Isa nodded; she'd heard the same rumor. In Isa's opinion, returning Carrick to Wybren was too good for the beast. "Your sister told you this?"

"Nay, it was Fyrnne. Oh!" Bryanna looked up sharply, her round eyes pleading. "Please do not rebuke her. I overheard her speaking with Gladdys as they carried the laundry downstairs, and they said Sir Alexander wants Morwenna to send a messenger to Graydynn of Wybren about Carrick," Bryanna explained, her words coming out in a rush, tumbling over each other. "Of course Lord Graydynn will demand that the traitor be returned."

"Of course," Isa agreed. She'd already thought the same. Good. The sooner that Carrick was out of the keep, the better for everyone. Especially Morwenna. "Still, the serving girls shouldn't gossip."

Bryanna nodded but grinned, one dark eyebrow arching sagely. "No one should, Isa. But we all do; that's the fun of it. 'Tis a woman's nature and, I suppose, a man's as well." She glanced down at her embroidery hoop and sighed at her limited progress.

"This is hopeless." Angrily she clipped the thread with her teeth, then tossed the hoop onto her bed, where she ignored it. Leaning forward, her eyes reflecting the firelight, she asked, "How did Carrick kill his family?"

"I'm not sure. 'Tis only conjecture that he set the blaze, remember."

Bryanna stared at Isa. "But you believe it."

Isa picked her words carefully. "I believe that he is capable of many things, even murdering his family, though I don't understand why. It makes no sense." She rubbed the thick bumps of her knuckles. "But it's said that while the baron and his family were all sleeping, Carrick sneaked through the hallway and set the fires. Some people, perhaps the constable, think that he even poured on the floor oil or something that would ignite the rushes even more quickly and cause smoke to seep and spread under the doors into each of the chambers. The lord and lady, Baron Dafydd and Lady Myrnna, were in one room; their children Alyce, Byron, and Owen as well as Theron and his wife, Alena, were asleep in their chambers." She frowned. 'Twas a tragedy.

"Where were the guards?"

"I know not, but some say they were

asleep at their posts."

"Did no one awaken?"

Isa sighed and bit her lip. "There was a suggestion that all of the people who died may have sipped from the same jug of wine, that it may have been tainted."

"With poison?"

"Or something to make the family members sleep through the smoke and flames." Isa stood. She'd said enough. Too much perhaps. She shivered as a cool breath of air touched the back of her neck, and she glanced upward to the walls that rose so high to the ceiling, to the dark spots where light never seemed to reach.

"What do you think Morwenna will do?" Bryanna asked.

"I know not," Isa said, walking to the bed, where she picked up the embroidery hoop. Deftly she removed several of the ungainly stitches, then handed the hoop to Bryanna. "I'm sure your sister will make the right decision."

It was a lie.

Deep in her heart, Isa knew, as she left the room, there was no right choice. She'd seen the face of death in her dreams, sensed his breath upon her skin, knew he lingered close, waiting for just the right moment, ready to pounce.

It was only a matter of time.

'Twas dark.

The night lay mired in a dense fog that blocked the moon.

The Redeemer stood near the crenels of a high tower and felt moisture ooze through his heavy cloak and dark cowl. A dampness pressed against his face, cool and soothing, and yet there was a disturbance in the night. Though he could not see through the veil of mist, he knew that she was down there, by the creek, whispering her spells and drawing her runes in the dirt.

The old one.

Isa.

She was dangerous.

And evil.

Had she not seen visions that had, time and again, proved true?

'Twas a miracle that she had not yet unmasked him and destroyed all that he had worked for.

Though he outwardly disdained anyone who believed in the tripe that was peddled by the old ones — the pagan ways — he could not deny that some of their magic seemed to exist.

In the windless night, he thought he

heard her raspy voice whispering through the bare trees, calling to the spirit of Morrigu, the Great Mother, pleading for safety from an unseen menace, asking for guidance and protection.

Deep in his cowl, a smile tugged at the corners of his mouth.

'Tis too late, Isa, you old witch . . . much too late. Silently he fingered the knife strapped to his waist.

All your prayers to the Great Mother are for naught.

CHAPTER ELEVEN

"I said, 'twill be all right, Sir James. Let me pass."

Her muffled voice floated to him as if in a dream, and mayhap he was dreaming for he kept drifting in and out of consciousness, mindful that time was passing, listening, as if through a tunnel, to voices of people as they attended him. But the tenor of her voice, Morwenna's, was different than the others. It touched a chord deep inside and brought him closer to the surface.

He tried to move his arm and to his surprise it shifted. Just a bit. His heart beat faster and sweat beaded his brow as he concentrated. With renewed determination, he attempted to slide his right leg to one side and it, too, moved only slightly, but his calf definitely slid an inch beneath the bedclothes.

Christ Jesus, he wasn't a cripple!

He tried his fingers and they responded. As did his toes.

His heart jolted, pounding wildly with the effort and the sudden exhilaration of knowing that he wouldn't have to lie unmoving on this bed forever.

"Sir Alexander will not like this." A muted male voice, the one she called Sir James, argued. "I'll be losing my post, just like Vernon did."

"I'll take full responsibility," she insisted. "In fact, I'll tell Sir Alexander myself in the morning."

The patient panicked. Soon she would slip into the room and he would have to make a choice. Try to speak and reason with her, show her that he was healing, or to remain unmoving and pretend to yet be comatose.

If he was to prove that he was mending, mayhap the guards would become more vigilant, or, worse yet, he might be sent to a prison cell to insure that he did not escape. . . .

Sir James said, "But, m'lady, 'tis my duty to protect you and —"

"The patient hasn't moved since he was brought in here nearly two weeks ago. I'm certain I will be safe enough with him."

"Nay —"

"Stand aside, Sir James, and keep to your post here at the door. I'll call you if I need you," she said firmly, and the patient heard the door creak open only to shut softly a few seconds later.

"Wait. Lady Morwenna!" the man's voice was muffled before the door squeaked as it was shoved open again. "The door should not be closed. Please, m'lady, let it remain ajar." The guard must've poked his head into the room as his voice fairly boomed, jarring loudly through the patient's brain.

"Fine," she said with a sigh of disgust.

"As you wish."

"Thank you, Sir James," she said and then after a few seconds admonished herself under her breath, "Fie and feathers, Morwenna, who is the ruler here? Why do you let them bully you? Would Kelan let a soldier tell him what to do? Nay. Sir Alexander and Sir Payne and all the rest try to tell you what to do because you are a woman, despite the fact that you have all the power of the lord of the castle."

Her voice grew closer. Louder, even though she was whispering in ire. "Damn it all. Even the men beneath them and the serving girls do the same. Treat you as if you are a child rather than the lady of the manor. 'Tis an insult." Her footsteps, which the patient had heard approaching his bed, abruptly stopped. "God's eyes, do not let them get away with it!" The sound of her footsteps receded angrily as she marched away from him. "I've changed my mind, Sir James," she shouted so loudly the patient nearly jumped out of his skin. "The door will remain shut."

"Nay, m'lady —"

"Do not argue with me!" The door banged closed. "I should lock it," she muttered under her breath again and then, footsteps stronger, advanced to his bed.

His every nerve ending was taut, and for the first time as he tried to open his eyes, he felt his eyelids rise just slightly, barely slitting but allowing in a gloomy light and a bit of motion. Pain burned through his pupils as his vision adjusted to the soft light of a fire that crackled in the grate.

"So, Carrick." Morwenna's voice held no warmth. " 'Tis time for me to send a messenger to Wybren."

Carrick, if that was his name, felt himself tense, every muscle painfully tightening. Wybren was familiar, the castle name reverberating through his brain. Faint, horrifying memories of smoke-filled corridors, burning tapestries, and crackling flames consuming everything in their path seared through his mind. Holy God, was he responsible for the blaze? Was he truly the beast who had brutally murdered his own family as they'd slept?

A dark malevolence burrowed deep into his soul. He envisioned someone lifting a burning torch from its sconce and sweeping it over the tinder-dry rushes and dusty tapestries of the keep. Could it have been he? Could he really have plotted the deaths of each of his family, have planned the horrific fire? Sickening visions of burning hair, eyes rounding in horror, blackened, searing flesh appeared before him.

No! No! No!

He could not have masterminded the unthinkable!

Despair took hold of him. Wrenched his guts.

What kind of man was he?

Or was it all a lie?

Some dire scheme concocted to make him appear a villain for someone else's crimes?

"Who did this to you?" she asked, leaning closer.

In his mind's eye he saw muddy boots aimed at his abdomen. Heard voices yelling angrily, horses' shrieks of terror ringing through the woods. Smelled smoke from a campfire. Felt the sharp, painful crack as the toe of a well-aimed boot smashed against his ribs. Men cursed, clubs thudded against his body as he writhed on the ground. Who had done this to him? *Who?*

Had whoever it was left him for dead? Or had the son of a dog who had beaten him to within an inch of his life intentionally left him to be found and brought here, to this castle?

But why would someone do this to him?

And why had he been defenseless? Though he couldn't remember much about himself, he sensed that he'd been a strong man, a warrior, one who would not submit to a beating.

By the gods, he felt as if he were going mad as he listened to her voice, felt her presence so near.

"Can you hear me?" she asked, her voice whispering across his skin. "Carrick?"

Again the too-familiar name. He didn't move.

"I need to talk to you."

He remained still as stone even when he felt her finger poke gently at his shoulder. "Can you not hear me? Sir Carrick of Wybren, please, awaken."

It was all he could do to breathe naturally.

Another prod. Harder this time. Her voice sounded more desperate as she said,

"Carrick, by all that is holy, please, please, talk to me."

He resisted. Nothing good would come of letting her know that he could hear her. Not yet. He set his jaw and endured yet another jab before she gave up and let out a disgusted puff of breath.

"So this will be my decision alone. You won't help me."

If her remark was meant to goad him into speaking, if it was one more test, he ignored it and didn't so much as lift an eyebrow. Yet she continued to speak. If not to him, then to herself.

"Well, I suppose I should not have expected more! However, you may as well know that Sir Alexander is insisting that I send word to Wybren of your . . . condition and, er, situation. And I must tell you that everyone here at Calon, including Isa and the physician and the priest and the sheriff, agrees that Lord Graydynn must be notified that you have been . . . well, 'captured' isn't the word I would like to use, and 'apprehended' isn't quite right, either, but that you are here, as my guest, recovering from your wounds." She was moving around the bed, the sound of her voice shifting as she circled him, and past the veil of his lashes, he saw bits of color as

177

she passed, her form seeming to float about him.

His eyes caught a glimpse of her — long black hair that curled wildly around a small face. Her features were blurry as she passed, but he saw an image of a white dress that caught the firelight and eyes — incredible blue eyes — that stared at him as if he was more than a curiosity, as if he was a deep enigma. His throat nearly closed at the sight of her and the images faded and danced in his head. He felt he remembered her, so beautiful, but that was just a fleeting thought and he didn't know how much of his memory was real nor how much his mind had created.

His head pounded. He wanted to scream. Instead he clenched his jaw and hoped she didn't notice.

Her voice came to him again over the gentle hiss of the fire. "Some people claim you were in alliance with Graydynn, that you killed all the members of the family in an attempt to gain the lordship and that Graydynn then turned on you, named you as a murdering traitor. Is that possible?" She was suddenly closer to him, her warm breath fanning his face. "I wonder."

He stared up at her through the slits that were his eyes, and in the shadowy light she didn't seem to notice that he could see her. For a second, he thought perhaps he might be able to speak, to squeak out some words, but thought it better to hold his tongue, to listen and then plan his next move, if, indeed, he was able to.

She touched the side of his face with cool fingers and he fought the urge to flinch. Somehow he managed to feign unconsciousness. "Oh, Carrick," she whispered, despair lacing her words. "How you vex me." Her finger slid along the side of his jaw, along beard stubble and yet creating a sensitive path upon his bruised skin. "But then, you always have."

He felt her tremble slightly. "What am I to do with you? Send you to Wybren and Graydynn's justice? Keep you here as . . . a patient or a prisoner?" Her finger slid down his neck to rest at the crook of his shoulder, and despite his wretched pain, his concentration centered on that one spot where his bare skin met hers. Heat seemed to radiate from that one fragile point of union.

"I loved you, you miserable bastard," she admitted, and a part of him wished she wouldn't bare her soul. "I wanted to marry you, to have your children. . . ." Her voice caught and for a second he thought she was finished. Yet more words, angry now, boiled up from her, and the touch of her finger was stronger, as if she wished to poke him hard. "But you left me, didn't you? For Alena, I'm told."

Alena. The name sparked a memory in him, yet he could not recall her image. She, too, had been his lover?

" 'Tis a low cur who would steal his brother's wife."

His insides twisted. What was she saying? He bedded his brother's wife?

"So, you see, Carrick, 'tis a difficult decision I have. How much do I owe you?" She paused, as if thinking. "Nothing!" she finally spat. "Less than nothing. You left me and our child for Alena."

Our *child?* He had sired a babe? With her?

No . . . something was wrong here. Very wrong. Aye, he remembered Morwenna's name and Alena's as well, but . . . but he knew nothing of a child. He was certain of it. Mayhap he was imagining all this. His mind had been wandering and perhaps his weary brain was creating visions — dreams from the potion the physician had administered with the hot water and broth that had been spooned down his throat.

That was it. Perhaps he'd only imagined

he'd been examined by the physician, listened to the drone of the priest's dour prayers, felt all sorts of eyes upon him while he pretended sleep. Mayhap he'd been alone and they had all been apparitions. Imaginings. Just the other night he had been certain that a malevolent being had appeared, slipped through the solid wall, and stared down at him with evil intent. . . . This, too, could be a dream. That was it. The lady was not in his chamber.

But the pressure on his skin spoke otherwise and he closed his eyes completely.

Morwenna's finger dragged along his shoulder toward his chest. His heart pounded. His blood heated. "By the gods, Carrick," she hissed angrily, "I should have let you die!"

Despite her ire, he felt a swelling between his legs as the tip of her finger pressed to his neck, where, he was certain, if she looked she would see his pulse pounding erratically.

"Ah, Carrick." She let the finger trail downward along his rib cage, causing the coverlet to bunch and his chest to be exposed to the cool air. Slowly she traced his breastbone, causing the pain in his ribs to turn into excruciating, seductive torture. "I lost you," she admitted sadly. "I lost the

babe. And mayhap it was all for the best."
Her voice broke a bit, and he felt a rending
deep into his soul. What was it about this
woman that touched him so? Why did her
words scrape into his heart?

'Twas the medication the physician had
given him, the foul-tasting stuff that had
been forced across his tongue. Or the pain
— that was it! He was creating enticing,
erotic images because of the agony he'd
endured. . . . This woman wasn't really in
the room with him. Or so he mutely
prayed, for he felt his groin tightening and
his cock respond to the erotic movements
of her hand. Sweat dampened his brow
and he bit down hard so as not to cry out
as the coverlet slid ever lower, exposing
more of his flesh to the cool air of the
chamber. He let one eye open a slit as he
watched her, neck bent, hair falling forward before she tossed it over her
shoulder.

"If I remember, you had a birthmark on
your thigh, near the juncture of your legs."

What! He nearly cried out.

In one swift motion, she tossed the coverlet aside, and he felt the brush of air
upon his stiff shaft.

She gasped. "Holy Mother," she said in
a swift breath as she stared at his naked

form with its rock-hard appendage pointed upward. "Carrick . . . oh, by the gods . . ." The coverlet was flung over him quickly, his member beneath the bedclothes shriveling. A flush of color bloomed up his neck even though a part of him wanted to laugh out loud.

Served her right.

"Oh, dear, oh, dear, oh . . . damn!" She blew out a long breath and glanced up at his face. "Can you hear me, you cur? Did you . . . no . . . oh, God, Carrick, you rotten, sick piece of dung, if you heard one word of what I said, I swear I'll . . . I'll cut out your miserable heart and *then* send you to Wybren and pay the hangman myself to dangle your body from the crenels!"

She hurried out of the chamber, her footsteps quick and frantic. He heard her start to stumble, swear, and then catch herself as she threw open the door.

"M'lady?" the guard asked. "Are you all right?"

"Fine, Sir James."

"But you look like you've just seen a ghost."

"I said I'm fine," she repeated breathlessly, and then the door slammed shut and he was alone. Again.

CHAPTER TWELVE

So she was still in love with the cur!

From his hiding spot, the Redeemer watched in silent, white-hot fury. A bad taste climbed up his throat and he was shaking in the tight, musty passageway. He had heard only bits of her whispered conversation, not enough to piece together what she was saying, but he witnessed the pained look upon her face, noticed how her finger lingered and trailed over the wounded man's flesh, and then how she'd tossed off the coverlet in a burst of anger, gasped, then thrown it over him quickly again. As if the sight of his manhood had stunned her.

From his position, with her body blocking his view of the patient, the Redeemer hadn't caught a glimpse of the naked man, but from her reaction, he assumed she saw something that shocked her . . . something out of place.

Was the man so powerfully endowed — like a rutting stallion? Or just the opposite, his member tiny and flaccid?

Or missing?

Whatever the case, Morwenna had been repulsed and enraged.

Though it appeared as if the man on the bed hadn't moved a muscle, instantly Morwenna had sputtered and spat invectives as she'd backed away from the patient she'd heretofore been so insistent upon protecting.

Perhaps things were changing for the better.

The Redeemer waited for a few minutes and then slipped quietly down the familiar passageways to his favorite spot where he could view her chamber. Nose pressed to the smooth stones, he silently watched as she stripped off her long white tunic, flung herself onto her bed, and pounded her fist upon the bedclothes, startling her sleeping dog and sending him barking crossly.

"Hush, Mort!" she commanded irritably.

Ah, she was a wild one. The Redeemer watched her release her fury and he considered what it would be like to mount her, to place his teeth on the back of her neck, to enter her and ride her hard, pushing against her, listening to her pant, twining his hands into the thick rope of her black hair or reaching around her and grasping her breasts in his hands, gripping them so hard she would cry out with a blissful agony.

It was difficult waiting for it.

Envisioning the future.

Planning for that inevitable night and remaining patient.

He ran the tip of his tongue around his suddenly dry lips and stared down at her, her temper now reined in, her legs drawn up and one arm flung around her knees, her other hand rubbing the scruff of the old dog's neck as he quieted. Black hair fell in unruly waves down her arms and back. She was without a doubt the most seductively beautiful woman the Redeemer had ever set eyes upon.

He lowered his hand to the uncomfortable bulge pressing against the laces of his breeches. Slowly he undid the leather strings and let his fingers reach inside.

He stiffened.

Anticipating.

His fingers surrounded his cock and he thought about the future and the delights it would hold.

Would it not be sweet, sweet justice to savagely claim her as his own?

In the small alcove that was her room, Isa used her dagger and carved a rune for protection into the single white candle. Then she tied a black string around the candle's base before positioning it in a ring of seven smooth stones she'd anointed with oil and placed in a large platter.

Ignoring the feeling that unseen eyes were watching her, she carefully scattered herbs over the stones. Her heart was beating wildly, her nerves strung tight. If Father Daniel discovered that she was practicing her magic within the keep, he would be furious, banish her, thrust her old bones into the deadly winter alone, but she had to risk his wrath.

Too much was at stake to worry for her own safety.

She felt the malevolence within the cold walls of Calon, sensed a dark, living evil that seemed to ooze throughout the castle.

How many nights had Isa woken from a vivid dream of such dark foreboding that she'd barely been able to breathe? Each time she'd witnessed a faceless phantom, his features hidden in a dark cowl, his identity murky as he brought death and destruction to those she loved.

Nay, she could not trust Father Daniel to protect this keep from the curse that was Carrick of Wybren. Daniel was a weak man whose piety seemed a sham, a facade behind which he hid. As for Carrick of Wybren, he was cut from the same fabric as his father: a man who could not leave a maiden untouched. Had there not been rumors abounding about Dafydd of Wybren's wenching ways for years? A few had lived, others had been born dead, others had been rumored to have been born defective, only to linger and die early on, the result of a curse Lady Myrnna had asked an old sorceress to invoke.

Isa cringed at the memory. Lady Myrnna had come in the night, pleading with her to do something, *any*thing to stop her husband's whoring. Though she'd pretended Dafydd's rutting with others hadn't bothered her, she'd been shamed to her soul and had threatened to take her own life. Isa's sister, Enid, had refused to help Myrnna, and so Myrnna had traveled to Penbrooke and begged Isa for the favor.

Now it seemed that age-old curse had come back to haunt her in the form of Carrick of Wybren, for Isa was certain the near-dead man was he.

From the moment the wounded man had been carried through the gates of Calon, Isa had sensed the evil within the keep increase. Pulse with life. Grow restless. And the ever-changing, sinister malevolence had become more bold and dangerous. She felt its hot breath against her back.

But she had to be strong.

To fight.

As she was this night.

Using a piece of straw she'd taken from a broomstick, she touched the dry blade to a rushlight and watched as the thin little strip ignited. Carefully she lit the candle. A single bright flame flickered in the small room, casting eerie shadows upon the wall and reflecting in the bowl of water sitting near the taper.

"Great Mother, be with us," Isa whispered, her old heart beating frantically. "Bless this keep and hold it safe."

The wick sizzled. Beeswax began to melt down the sides of the single candle in thin streams. As she prayed, the warm wax reached the taper's base, streaming over the black thread, heating the crushed herbs, and scenting the still, cloying air with laurel, Saint-John's-wort, and rue.

Isa closed her eyes and softly chanted. "Morrigu, Great Mother, hear my plea. Keep us safe. Banish the evil from within these walls. Morrigu, Great Mother, hear my plea. . . ." Over and over she whispered the words, reaching upward to touch the worn stone with a hole upon it dangling from her braided leather necklace. Ever faster she chanted, as the minutes passed by. She rocked slightly to the rhythm of her own words, felt the spirits within the castle moving. She concentrated solely on ridding the castle of all evil. "Morrigu, Great Mother, hear my plea. Keep us safe. Banish —"

She felt it then.

The shift.

A repositioning of the stars and moon.

Her old heart clutched as she opened her eyes, her words failing her as she saw the candle, burned half down. Beyond the melted taper was the bowl of water, where the still surface and her own reflection began to swirl with shadowy images that moved faster and faster, as if a whirlpool were within the shallow basin. The reflection of her face became distorted and twisted, her mouth opening wide as if in a silent, horrible scream.

Isa's fingers rubbed furiously at the stone dangling from her neck, but the horrifying vision didn't disappear. Nor did it congeal into something she could understand. Her face splintered and she saw only pieces of the changing images, shards of pictures that drove fear straight to her soul:

A small dagger slicing downward.

The wicked blade flashing silver in the moonless night.

Blood. Oozing over the sides of the bowl.

And the crest of Wybren floating in the thick, red water beneath her own startled expression.

And then the god of death looking over her shoulder, his hard face so close that she turned quickly, knocking over the candle, causing the water within the bowl to slop.

Her heart knocked so loudly she was certain Arawn of the underworld was in the room with her.

But there was nothing.

Just darkness.

And the promise of death.

CHAPTER THIRTEEN

"Forgive me, Heavenly Father, for I have sinned." Father Daniel bowed low, his head nearly touching the stone floor of the apse, the rushes brushing his face. Closing his eyes, he tried to concentrate, but the fire in his blood ran hot even now. Though he'd tried to fight temptation and had prayed for relief, wanton images flickered through his mind, robbing him of sleep, making his words catch in his throat as he tried to speak. Even his prayers were interrupted by sinful thoughts.

Of women.

Morwenna and Bryanna. The tall older sister with her dark hair, regal stance, and imperious stare was as seductive as the younger one with her bright eyes, riot of reddish curls, and low, sensual laugh.

He imagined himself bedding them, singly and together, and the erotic images that seared his brain wouldn't leave him alone. 'Twas as if he were in a hell of his own making. Aye, that was it; Satan had somehow slipped into his mind. He closed his eyes and his body shook with a need so violent it frightened him.

God will punish you, Daniel. He knows your thoughts, and if you do not atone, if you are unable to force these unholy images from your mind, God will destroy you and all that you hold dear. The plans and dreams you have for your life will be decimated. Know that the Holy Father will punish you.

Mayhap He already has, Daniel thought desperately, his hands curling into fists, clenching over the straw and herbs of the rushes.

"Please, Father, forgive me and help me. I have had lust in my heart," he admitted, his head bowed before the crucifix. But even now his restless mind wandered to the women, such beautiful, tempting creatures. "And . . . and my body betrays me. My thoughts are impure. I see the lady and her sister and I . . . I . . . fall victim to being mortal. I fight the urges, but, Father, please help me." Tears burned at the back of his eyes, for he knew that prayer alone would not atone for his sins.

He needed to be punished.

"Help me banish all lust from my mind and my body," he prayed, his voice catching, tears drizzling from the corners

193

of his eyes. Oh, he was weak. Pathetically so.

In despair, he made the sign of the cross. He had started to rise when he heard something, the scrape of a boot, nearby. As if someone had been in the chapel with him.

His heart clutched as he thought of his desperate prayers. They were for God's ears only.

Awash with embarrassment, he glanced over his shoulder and found the door to the outside ajar, perhaps pushed open by the wind — the latch was forever broken. Mayhap it was nothing. But the hairs on the backs of his arms lifted and he thought he heard, over the rush of wind, the sound of retreating footsteps. He pulled himself to his feet. Had someone been listening at the doorway? Had whoever it was heard his guilt-riddled confession?

Without wasting a second, he made his way to the door and stepped outside. The night was raw and bitter, the wind fierce enough to cut through his cloak, the slanting rain so cold it was nearly ice.

Tossing up his hood, he bent against the wind and followed the main path leading through the garden. No one was visible, but the gate was open, banging in the wind as if someone had been in too much of a hurry to secure the latch. Who? Had someone been spying upon him?

He flew over the flagstones and into the inner bailey, where, because of the weather, few men were gathered, only a few guards at their posts and Dwynn, who, hat pulled down nearly over his eyes, was carrying a basket filled with firewood toward the great hall.

"You there," Father Daniel called, his boots sliding on the mud as he caught up with the younger man. Dwynn halted, rainwater dripping from his hat's brim. "Did you see anyone enter the chapel a few minutes ago?"

"Nay, Father." The half-wit shook his head quickly but hitched his heavy basket with surprising ease and started for the great hall again.

"No one?"

"Just the guards."

"Here, let me help you," the priest offered, more to have a chance at conversation with the man than to ease his burden. Rain was peppering the ground, splashing in puddles, blowing sideways. "You're certain no one hurried outside — from the garden there?" Daniel pointed toward the open gate.

"Who was it?" Dywnn asked.

"What? Oh, I don't know, but I believe someone was in the chapel and ran outside. This way." Daniel peered through the driving rain and thought he saw a shadow, a figure, disappear along the path leading to the stable, but as he blinked the rain from his eyes, the image vanished.

"Then he left if he's not still there," Dwynn reasoned.

"What?"

"Whoever was in the chapel. Didn't you say there was someone there?" Dwynn asked, his eyebrows slamming together as if he was trying to concentrate. The poor half-wit was absolutely maddening. "Alfrydd, he wants the wood," Dwynn continued.

" 'Tis a sin to lie, Dwynn. You know that." The priest was firm.

"Aye, Father." Dwynn's steps didn't so much as falter.

"And God, He hears everything. Not just prayers."

No response.

'Twas impossible. Either the man didn't understand or wouldn't reply. They were near the back entrance of the great hall now. "God would not like it if you lied, Dwynn. He would punish you."

Dwynn shouldered open the kitchen door and nodded as he passed through. "He punishes all, Father. Every one of us."

That He does, Daniel thought morosely as he glanced upward to the windows on the third floor where Lady Morwenna and Lady Bryanna had their private chambers. Sleeting rain fell upon his upturned face and yet it did nothing to dampen the rage burning in his soul.

Sir Vernon wrapped his mantle more tightly around his torso. 'Twas a night not fit for man nor beast, and yet he stood outside, huddled against the sleet that had started to spit from the dark sky. Slowly, head bent, he walked from one corner of the curtain wall to the next tower. He stamped his feet loudly as they seemed frozen within his boots. Though he'd told himself he would never sip from his small jug again while on duty, tonight he ignored his promise to himself. It was just too damned buggery cold not to have a nip of mead to warm his belly.

"Hell's bells," he growled as he took a long tug and felt the warmth burn its way down his throat. He let out a belch and, satisfied for a while, slipped the jug back into its hiding spot deep in a cranny he'd found in one of the walls of the east tower.

From his vantage point, Vernon looked down upon the inner bailey, where only a few fires glowed in the huts huddled along the base of the walls. All was quiet. Serene, had it not been for the blasted sleet. His gaze swept past the inner gate to the outer bailey, a much larger piece of land still surrounded by these thick walls. All there seemed as it should, no dark shadows stealing across the yellowed winter grass. No gang of thugs collected near the well nor in the orchard. Listening, he heard only a few grunts from the pigs pushing each other aside as they settled in for the night and the creak and swish of the windmill as its sails turned in the same breeze that rattled the bare branches of the trees in the orchard.

All was well on this moonless winter night. He thought about another sip from his jug, but then decided to wait. It was hours yet until morn and he should save his precious mead. He blew on his gloved hands and turned toward the south tower.

Something moved in the watch turret.

"Blimey." What the devil was that? Another guard? Who was posted there this evening? Geoffrey? Or Hywell? Or . . . Vernon squinted and started walking quickly along the east wall. Sleet peppered his face, and a bit of apprehension crawled up his back, but his eyes were trained on the dark figure that seemed to have appeared out of nowhere.

Whoever it was had his back to Vernon and was staring through the crenels. "You there," Vernon yelled, reaching for the hilt of his sword as he closed the distance between them. "What're ye doin' up here?"

The dark figure turned, still hidden in the shadowy battlements, his face concealed deep in his cowl. "Brother Thomas?" he guessed, for the man was wearing the guise of a monk. Vernon hurried forward, glad for the company, any company, though it was believed the hermit of the keep, Thomas, was mad. "Ye're a far piece from yer room," Vernon admonished gently as he neared the other man. "Needin' some fresh air, are ye?" He didn't blame the solitary monk. Who could stay in a single room, praying and lying prostate, seeing no one save the serving boys who brought up porridge and water and took away the buckets of excrement? God in heaven, what a life.

Vernon let go of his weapon. The old man was no threat and probably only looking for a little respite from his cramped quarters. "Er, Thomas," he called, still several feet away, "I don't know what yer vows are, but if ye'd like a nip or two, I've got me a jug in the tower back there. . . ." He hooked a thumb toward the east tower. "It could warm yer belly if not yer soul on a cold night like this one."

Still the man did not speak and for a second Vernon thought he might have had his tongue cut from him long before. Perhaps as some kind of idiotic sacrifice. Vernon shivered at the thought and kept walking, and as the distance between them lessened, he dismissed his idea of self-mutilation. More likely Thomas had taken a vow of silence and would not break it. Not even for a drop of ale. Aye, that was it! Vernon was near the tower now and said, "Brother, I hope ye didna take offense at my offer. It's just so bloody cold tonight."

The man stepped forward, offering his hand.

Vernon smiled, glad for whatever company the monk could provide. "Aye, it's a night not fit fer Lucifer himself," he said, bridging the small distance between them.

A bit of a grin flashed white in the darkness.

The monk raised his arm quickly.

In the dim light Vernon recognized the weapon.

Small.

Curved.

Deadly.

"What the bloody hell!" Vernon scrabbled for his sword.

With surprising agility, the monk spun Vernon around.

The larger man twisted, but his boots slid on the icy wall walk.

In an instant, his attacker was upon him.

Fingers surrounding the hilt of his weapon, Vernon tried to unsheath his weapon and whirl around. But it was too late. He felt his head pulled back by the hair.

The dagger plunged downward.

Vernon's scream died in his throat as the wicked little blade sawed into his thick throat in a jerky, uneven movement.

With a thud, Vernon fell, his head cracking against the merlon. Then, lightheaded, he gazed at his murderer helplessly, recognized him but was unable to scream as his lifeblood seeped onto the cold, flat stones of the wall walk.

CHAPTER FOURTEEN

"Lady Morwenna! Please open the door. 'Tis I, Isa!"

Morwenna groaned and opened her eyes. The dog beside her gave up a soft growl.

"Coming!" Morwenna called, reaching for her tunic as the dog roused and barked. A headache pounded in her skull and her eyes felt as if they had sand in them. "Don't start," she admonished him as she padded to the door, then flung it open. "Why are you forever beating against my door in the middle of the night?" she demanded, still cranky as she'd slept little since her visit to Carrick's room.

At the thought of her visit, she felt color rise up her neck, for as she'd lifted the coverlet, she'd seen . . .

"Something is horribly amiss," Isa insisted, and her old eyes were round with worry, her face as pale as a ghost, her lips bloodless.

"What? What is wrong?" Morwenna was instantly awake though her head still throbbed from lack of sleep.

Isa slipped into the room and shut the door as the dog growled low before settling onto the bed again. The room was cold, the fire having died in the few hours since Morwenna had flung herself onto the bed in anger and despair.

Isa's voice, as she spoke, was a low whisper, as if she was afraid that the very walls had ears. "There is death, m'lady. Death here." She jabbed a finger at the floor. "Within the walls of Calon."

Morwenna's skin crawled. "Death? Nay, Isa."

"Yes!" Isa hissed. "Tonight."

"Whose?"

"I know not."

"What do you mean?" Morwenna's eyes thinned suspiciously. And yet she could not shake the sense of dread that Isa's words had brought. *Carrick! Someone has killed him.* "Tell me," she demanded.

"I was . . . I was asking for protection from the Great Mother —"

"Casting a spell?"

"Nay! Only praying."

"Not practicing any of your magic? You know how Father Daniel feels about —"

Isa's fingers surrounded Morwenna's wrist in a clawlike grip. "Hear me out, child," she ordered, as if she were again the nursemaid and Morwenna her young charge. "*I saw death tonight.* Here. In this keep. By someone's hand. Mark my words, Morwenna, there has been a murder in this castle."

"Yet you cannot say who was killed or why or even who did the deed," Morwenna pointed out, not wanting to believe her. "Am I right?"

"Trust me," Isa begged, the desperation in her voice so real it chased away any of Morwenna's remaining doubts. Dread seeped deep into her soul.

"I do." How many times had Isa proved herself in the past? Too many to count. She tossed her hair out of her eyes. "Is it Carrick?" she demanded.

"Nay . . . I think not," she said, and Morwenna felt a second's relief before panic assailed her.

"Bryanna? Oh, God . . ."

"Your sister yet sleeps," Isa said. "What I saw happened in the towers. . . . I saw the moon above a turret and then the face of death as clearly as if Arawn stood in front of me."

Arawn, Morwenna knew from years of Isa's teaching, was the god of revenge and death and the overseer of Annwn, the underworld.

But Isa wasn't finished. "As his image

disappeared, I saw the White Lady upon the battlements. . . . Oh, Morwenna, there is death sure in this keep tonight."

"Then let us find it," Morwenna said. She fished a long mantle from a peg and tossed the cloak over her head. Before the mantle had settled over her body she yanked on her boots and followed Isa into the dimly lit hallway, where a breath of cool wind caused the candles in the sconces to flicker eerily. From the edge of her eye she thought she saw a shadow move swiftly around the corner, as if someone had been lingering near her door and now was creeping swiftly and stealthily away. Her skin crawled for a moment, and then she told herself she was imagining things, but her dog froze in his footsteps. Nose to the air, hackles standing stiff and threatening, Mort glared at the darkened corner and growled deep in his throat.

"Just a minute," she ordered the older woman. Fear thrumming through her, Morwenna took off after the shadow with Mort fast on her heels, barking loudly, black lips pulled back as he snarled. She rounded the corner and found the corridor empty, not a soul in sight. And yet the rushlights quivered, as if someone had recently passed. Or was it from the breath of wind she felt chasing down the corridors?

Mort slid to a stop beside her and gave off a quick, nervous bark.

"Lady Morwenna," Isa called. "This way."

Morwenna stared down the shadowy hallway, and as she had so often in the past few days, she felt unseen eyes watching her, someone hiding and eavesdropping and watching. Goose bumps rose on her flesh. "Is anyone there?" she demanded.

But there was no sound.

"Fie and fiddlesticks," she muttered under her breath.

"Hurry!" Isa called.

Morwenna glanced at Mort. The speckled dog whined, his nose twitching, ears flat, head down, but he didn't run down the hallway.

"A fine guard dog you are," she admonished, turning and hurrying to catch up with Isa.

"What were you doing?"

"I thought I saw someone in the hallway."

Isa's eyes rounded further, and then she flicked a hand as if swatting away a bothersome insect. "There was no one in the corridor when I came."

"You think I'm imagining things?"

"I know not," Isa admitted as she hastened down the curved staircase.

Neither do I. Morwenna didn't like the admission, even to herself. She'd always had a mind of her own, been often called stubborn or mule headed as a child, and now she was torn, not believing what her own senses suggested, for 'twas nonsense. Folly. No one could be watching her. At least no earthly being. As she stole one last look over her shoulder, she felt a coldness invade her soul.

After checking with Sir James and seeing Carrick lying upon his bed, and then tapping softly on Bryanna's door before cracking it open and spying her sister sleeping, Morwenna followed Isa down the stairs to the great hall.

The vast room was empty and dark, the sconces dead, the embers from the banked fire glowing a soft, bloodlike red. The castle dogs, once asleep, lifted their heads to let out disgusted woofs before yawning and returning to their curled positions near the grate.

At the door, Isa whispered, "Please, m'lady, hurry!" and then ordered the guard to stand aside.

"But —" the skinny man started to object.

" 'Tis all right, Sir Cowan," Morwenna assured him. "Isa needs to show me something."

" 'Tis the dead of night," he protested.

"Aye. Worry not. I go to see the captain of the guard."

"Mayhap I should go with ye."

"No. Stay here. Allow no one, save ourselves, inside!" Morwenna ordered.

Isa pushed her way outside to the inner bailey and the icy moonless night. Sleet slanted from the dark heavens and there was a chill in the air, a chill more frigid than the icy drops slashing from the starless sky.

"We'll find Sir Alexander," Isa said, still pale as death, her legs sweeping quickly over the frozen earth toward the gates of the inner bailey.

Hurrying past the well where a bucket suspended from a thick rope creaked and swayed, they half ran down an icy path that skirted the peasants' darkened huts and led to the gatehouse where most of the garrison was housed.

A sentry high in the watchtower saw the movement and shouted down at the intrusion. "Who goes there?"

Morwenna turned her face toward the voice, and icy drops rained upon her cheeks. " 'Tis I, Lady Morwenna. I'm with Isa, Sir Forrest. Awaken Sir Alexander and let us into the gatehouse."

"Lady Morwenna?" the man repeated, obviously unsure that he'd heard correctly.

"Aye! Now hasten, Forrest! 'Tis freezing out here!" she commanded, wiping her face with her sleeve before wrapping her mantle around her and eyeing the east, hoping to spy the first few glimmers of dawn in the winter sky. But the night was dark as obsidian, seemingly impervious to any shards of morning light.

"Right away, m'lady!" Sir Forrest called down to her.

"Finally," she muttered under her breath as his footsteps clattered down the stairs in the gatehouse and other muffled voices could be heard through the thick stone walls. Within seconds the door to the gatehouse was shoved open and Sir Forrest, a gangly man whose head always seemed a bit too large for his body, appeared. He escorted them inside. "I've alerted Sir Alexander. He should be —"

"I'm awake though 'tis the middle of the night," a gruff male voice announced as the captain of the guard, tightening a belt over his tunic, made his way down the stone steps. His hair stuck out in unruly clumps and his surly gaze landed on Morwenna. "What's wrong, m'lady?" he asked, his eyebrows beetling into one thick line over his nose. "It must be something serious."

"Aye," Morwenna said as she stood in the main hall, where a fire burned bright. Several men were warming their backs at the grate, three others were playing dice at a scarred table, and from the nearby chambers that angled off the main hall came the cacophony of men snoring. Soldiers, jailors, guards, and the constable's servants, all wrapped in their cloaks, were sleeping on the rushes strewn across the floor.

Never before had Morwenna been in the gatehouse at night, and though she was lady of the manor, the ruler over these men, she felt uneasy and nervous, as if she'd trespassed into a forbidden area, a place few women ever entered.

To add to her discomfort, Alexander was watching her with his dark, penetrating eyes. Waiting. For an explanation. She rubbed her arms to ward off a chill and wondered if perhaps she'd been rash to believe Isa's fears. "There has been a murder within the keep," she finally stated.

"*What?* A murder?" He stared sharply at her, all traces of sleep dissipating from his eyes. Deep in his beard, his lips became blade thin. "Who was killed? Where?

When?" Alexander reached for his sword and scabbard mounted on the wall near the fire. "Why was I not told?"

"We haven't found the victim yet."

"What? You haven't found . . ." He left his weapon on the wall and held up his big hands as if in surrender. "M'lady," he said, again pinning her with his steady gaze, "I don't understand. How would you know if someone has been killed if there is no body? Did someone confess? Nay?" he guessed, seeing the gentle shake of her head. "Then did someone witness this murder? Who?"

Morwenna cleared her throat and felt increasingly silly. "Isa has had a vision."

"Pardon?" he said.

"Of death," Isa interjected, her ice blue eyes sober and determined. "I've seen a brutal killing in my mind's eye."

"A vision?" Alexander repeated, one thick eyebrow elevating. He glanced at Sir Forrest, and silent communication passed between the two men. They thought this a joke. "In your mind's eye."

"Do not mock me," the old woman warned, her visage as savage as that of an eagle. "It happened on the wall walk." She pointed toward the east. "I sense your disbelief, Sir Alexander, and I know that I've amused you. But trust me, this is no joke. Someone was murdered tonight in this very keep."

"But you know not who?"

"Not yet. Let us go there now . . . to the east tower," Isa insisted.

"The east tower."

"Must you repeat everything I say? Yes, the east tower!" she spat, exasperation evident in her voice at the thickheadedness of the captain of the guard. "Please, come along. We must hurry!"

Alexander's gaze traveled toward Morwenna. "Is this what you wish, m'lady?"

"Aye, Sir Alexander." She swallowed back her doubts. "I trust Isa."

"Then so shall I." In an instant he pulled down his weapon and strapped the scabbard to the belt at his waist, and then he motioned to Sir Forrest. Without another word, he led the way up the stairs to a doorway leading to the wall walk, the wide alleyway high above the bailey that encircled the keep. Here the wind blew fiercely, screaming through the crenels and swirling around the towers. Somewhere in the distance an owl hooted over the sound of boots scraping against stone, whispered conversation, and the dread thudding in Morwenna's heart.

What if Isa was wrong?

Then she would be relieved, for there would be no death in the keep. So she would be embarrassed for believing the old nursemaid. So what? 'Twas not a sin, nor even a sign of being addled. And yet she knew that if Isa's vision proved to be untrue, Morwenna, for believing in the old nursemaid's dream, would be the subject of wagging tongues and doubting minds, the butt of more than one joke. Serving girls would cover their smiles as she passed, pages would lower their voices but laugh behind her back, and the older men and women would share knowing glances that said they'd always believed a woman was not fit to run a castle such as Calon.

And yet if the opposite proved true and Isa was correct, then one of the people within Calon was now dead. Killed by a murderer's hand.

While Morwenna had promised to protect all those who served her.

'Twould be far worse.

Embarrassment she could suffer.

An innocent being killed she could not.

They walked swiftly along the wall walk, and Alexander asked, "Where's Sir Vernon?"

Morwenna's heart nearly stopped.

"He was assigned to the east wall." Sir Forrest was squinting into the night, across the battlements. "I saw him earlier and he was at his post."

"Oh, Great Mother, please, no . . ." Isa said and began to chant. Morwenna, cold from the inside out, felt a new sense of dread as she conjured up Sir Vernon's fleshy face and glittering eyes beneath bushy eyebrows. Surely there was some mistake.

"He's known to take a nip or two," Sir Forrest was saying as they worked their way eastward. "Mayhap he fell asleep while . . . What's that?" The guard's voice had grown strangely worried.

"What?" Alexander stared straight ahead, his gaze seeming to sharpen on the east tower. "God's teeth!" Swearing under his breath, Alexander began running, his boots ringing against the stones.

Morwenna's heart froze as she saw the dark, crumpled shape of a man lying on the wall walk. "No!" she cried, racing forward fast on Alexander's heels. Not Sir Vernon. Not the heavy man with the deep laugh whom she'd tricked. Not the knight whose punishment was this very duty. Throat dry, she ran faster, her heart echoing with dread.

But she recognized Sir Vernon's face, now pale with death, a thick pool of dark blood congealing beneath his cheek pressed hard against the stones. His eyes stared sightlessly ahead and his sword lay impotently by his side.

"What in God's name is this?" Alexander said as he bent beside the big man, felt for a pulse.

"Is he — ?"

Alexander shook his head and slowly closed the slain soldier's eyes as Sir Forrest and Isa reached them. Isa was panting, praying, her skin as bloodless as Vernon's. She fingered a stone hanging from a leather strap at her throat and leaned heavily against the battlements. "As I saw," she said without an ounce of satisfaction.

Alexander straightened. "If you saw this, then who did it?" he demanded, his voice shaking with rage.

"I know not."

"And yet you envisioned the death?" His dark eyes flashed in the night.

"I saw him fall, I saw the face of Arawn and later the White Lady."

"Images of death," Morwenna explained.

Alexander turned his fury on Forrest. "Sound the alarm! Wake all the sentries! Have all the gates checked so that no one escapes and place double guards at every entrance to the keep. Have the garrison check every nook and cranny of this castle for a murderer."

"And how will we recognize him?" Forrest asked. "Who is the cur?"

"Yes, how will we know him?" Alexander advanced upon Isa, who, trembling, was propped against a merlon. Isa's pale eyes were glassy, her fingers rubbing the stone frantically, as if the mere act of kneading the smooth rock would remove the vision and turn back time.

Morwenna said, "She knows not; she said as much earlier."

"But she could try to conjure up the vision again, could she not?"

"I don't know." Morwenna shook her head. "Sir Forrest, send someone for the physician . . . and the priest." She stared down at the corpse of Sir Vernon and blinked rapidly against tears. "He was not married?"

"Nay," Alexander said.

"Good. At least he has not left behind a widow or child," she said, but it was little comfort on this night that was as black and cold as Satan's shroud.

CHAPTER FIFTEEN

"I told you, Carrick of Wybren is cursed," Isa whispered as they stood in a chamber of the gatehouse. She was rubbing her hands over her upper arms and her gaze darted about the room, searching every dark corner for a murderer.

As the sconces flickered, Father Daniel, grim as ever, was administering last rites over Sir Vernon's body.

Outside, the castle began to stir to life. Roosters crowed, men shouted, sheep bleated. Cowbells clanged but the wind, so fierce in the night, had died. Dawn was stretching over the eastern hills and shafts of pale light sifted through the small windows. Most of the soldiers had been sent to search the keep; the few that remained stood in stony silence. Sleep, dice, women as well as food and drink had been forgotten at the sight of Sir Vernon's unmoving, blood-smeared corpse.

Father Daniel whispered prayers over the slain man while the physician stood to one side, patiently waiting for the religious rite to be over with so that he could examine the corpse. Both men's expressions were grim as they faced death from opposite sides, one from the spiritual, the other concerned with the physical body.

Sheriff Payne and Sir Alexander were positioned nearby, while Forrest was posted at the door.

"Listen, m'lady," Isa insisted, her eyes wide with fear, her old lips flat against her teeth. "As long as Carrick of Wybren is within this keep, we are all doomed!"

The priest lifted his bowed head and his hard eyes found Isa's. "If anyone is doomed," he said slowly, his lips thin and without color, his eyes flaring with a nearly manic fire, "it is those who pray to pagan gods and goddesses."

Isa's gaze never faltered. She took a step toward the priest. "Since Sir Carrick has been brought into this keep, there has been naught but turmoil and death, Father."

"Perhaps if we all had greater faith, God would bless this castle." The priest's smile was fixed. Practiced. He slid a cool glance toward Morwenna. "My lady, 'twould be best if all spells and runes and prayers to the unholy cease."

"You think Sir Vernon was killed because of Isa's prayers?"

"The Holy Father would not be pleased."

"And you, Isa, you think Sir Vernon was killed because of a curse upon Carrick of Wybren?"

"All of Wybren is cursed," the old nurse-maid said boldly, and the priest snorted his disgust.

Sir Alexander stepped closer to the table upon which Sir Vernon lay. "No matter. The fact is Vernon is dead. A murderer somehow invaded this keep."

"Or resides here," the sheriff said as he tugged at his beard. "Physician, can you tell us what kind of blade was used to slice the man's throat?"

Nygyll was already examining the body. He tilted up Sir Vernon's chin, exposing the ugly gash beneath his beard. "Let's see. . . . You there, Sir Forrest, go and see what's taking so long. I've already asked the steward to have someone bring me hot water and fresh cloths from the great hall."

Morwenna's stomach turned. She'd seen dead men before and had helped those who were wounded, but Sir Vernon's death was different. Personal. Not only was she indirectly responsible for sending him to his post upon the wall walk, but it was her duty to care for and protect all those within the keep. And she'd failed. Aye,

Vernon had been a soldier and a sentry, a man who had sworn his allegiance to her and to Calon, a man who had vowed to protect her and who knew the dangers of his position, yet Morwenna experienced a gnawing guilt that somehow she'd brought this death and destruction with her when she'd come to Calon. Had it not been for her, would not Sir Vernon be alive this day?

She looked up and caught Dwynn staring at her. The addled man had somehow wakened and found his way here. Which was no surprise. It seemed he was always about, no matter what time of day or night, especially if trouble was brewing.

The door to the gatehouse opened and Gladdys, carrying a basket of towels, hurried into the room. She was followed by George, the page, lugging a heavy cauldron of steaming water.

"Put the basket there," Nygyll ordered, pointing to a bench, "and set the pot on the hearth so it stays warm," he said with an edge of impatience to his voice. "You there, Dwynn, help the lad!"

Dwynn reached for the cauldron's handle and some of the hot water slopped onto the floor, a stream running into the fireplace to hiss against the hot coals.

"God's teeth, what's the matter with you?" Nygyll muttered, glowering at the half-wit as he reached for a towel and dipped it into the steaming water.

Dwynn, silent as usual, pointed an accusing finger at the page, but Nygyll had turned away and was cleaning the crusted dark blood from the wound at Vernon's neck.

" 'Tis not a straight cut," the sheriff said, bending closer.

"Humph," Nygyll grunted.

"What the devil is that all about?" Alexander asked as the wound became more apparent.

"Shave him," Payne suggested.

Morwenna watched as Nygyll found a sharp blade and carefully scraped away the dark beard that grew down the dead sentry's neck. Slowly the ugly gash was revealed, and as Payne had said, the wound was far from a neat, clean slash. The hideous cut sliced downward from Vernon's left ear, then up slightly near the point of his chin, down again on the other side of his jaw to finally slash upward and end near his right ear.

"Jesus," Alexander whispered.

The sheriff stared gravely.

" 'Tis a W," Isa said, and some of the

soldiers in the room glanced at her for many could not read. "For Wybren."

"Or witch," Father Daniel said quickly, his lips flattening over his teeth as his eyes narrowed on Isa.

"By the gods, it's something," Payne finally whispered, and Morwenna felt a shiver race down her spine as she, too, stared at the uneven gash.

"A warning?" she asked.

"Or someone trying to place the blame on Carrick of Wybren." Alexander looked at Morwenna, unasked questions in his eyes.

"Carrick has not awakened," Nygyll said as he dried his hands on a clean towel. "I have attended to him, and he's had no response." He glanced up, his eyes focusing on Morwenna for an instant before looking at Sir Alexander. "Even if the patient had managed to wake up and have full use of his limbs, which I doubt, he could not have gotten past the guard. He's trapped in his chamber. He could not have done this," he said, motioning to Sir Vernon. "Take this," he ordered Gladdys, the doe-eyed serving maid, as he slapped the dirty towel into her open hands. She flinched, then obediently placed the blood-soaked cloth into a pile with the other soiled rags.

"He obviously died from his throat being slit," the sheriff said.

The physician turned back to the corpse and folded Vernon's bloodstained hands over his chest. Nygyll's gaze settled on the sheriff and he nodded. "I found no other marks upon the corpse aside from a bruise where he cracked his head against the battlements or the floor of the wall walk, so, yes, his throat was slit and he bled to death." He glanced at the dead man. "Aside from what killed him, I would note that he's fat and, I suspect, infested with lice or fleas or worse. Not exactly a prime example of Calon's army."

Hurried footsteps sounded in the hallway outside. "What's going on here? Where's my sister?" Bryanna's voice floated into the chamber half a step in front of her. "Oh!" she cried as Morwenna turned toward the doorway. "What happened?"

"Sir Vernon was killed a few hours ago," Morwenna said.

"Killed? How?" Bryanna gasped, her wide eyes rounding as they discovered the bloody corpse. "Oh, God!" One hand flew to her throat. "No!"

"Get her out of here before she gets sick," Nygyll said.

Morwenna had seen enough. "Come,"

she said to Bryanna and shepherded her into the hallway, then outside to the crisp morning where the tanner was scraping a deer hide and the armorer was cleaning chain mail in casks of sand. Morwenna barely noticed the activity, her thoughts centered on the slain guard. Who had done this to him? Why? Vernon, though a soldier, seemed a gentle soul at heart.

"Wha-what happened?" Bryanna asked as she and Isa hurried to catch up with Morwenna. "Who . . . who . . . would harm, I mean kill, Sir Vernon?"

"We know not. Yet." As they made their way past the dyer who was boiling fabric in a vat filled with green liquid, Morwenna explained about Isa's vision and the ensuing events.

They reached the great hall just as she finished.

"You are saying there is a killer in our midst," Bryanna whispered as they slipped into the warmth of the keep.

"So it appears."

"What are you going to do?" Bryanna asked.

"The guards are searching the castle. The sheriff and some of the soldiers are questioning people in the town and surrounding villages."

"But he may have escaped," Bryanna said as they climbed the stairs to the solar. "Should you not send a messenger to Penbrooke?"

"No." Despite the murder, she wasn't about to ask for help from her brother Kelan. At least not yet. " 'Tis not Kelan's problem."

"He'd want to know about it."

Morwenna nodded, thinking of her brother as she removed her gloves and mantle. Tall, proud, determined, Kelan would not only want to know what was happening here but would no doubt send an army led by himself or their brother, Tadd.

Morwenna tossed her mantle over a stool and frowned when she considered the younger of the two. Tadd was as handsome as Kelan, but as irresponsible as Kelan was reliable. She wanted neither one of her domineering brothers telling her how to handle the situation. "And if you were lady of the keep, Bryanna," she asked, folding her arms under her breasts, "would you so quickly run to either of our brothers?"

Bryanna snorted as she plopped onto a bench near the fire and sat studying its flames. "Nay," she admitted, shaking her head, her long curls showing red in the firelight.

"Kelan might help," Isa advised.

"I think not." Morwenna walked to the window. From the elevated position, she could look down upon the inner bailey, where the morning was starting just as if it were another day and there had not been a brutal murder within the keep.

The farrier was already pounding out horseshoes at his fire, a boy working a bellows to keep the embers hot while the big-muscled man was straining to curve and then flatten the red-hot iron as it was molded into horseshoes.

Not far off, a freckled girl of about five was busily gathering eggs, while her gangly redheaded sister was flinging seeds into the air, strewing them for a flock of cackling chickens that flapped and pecked angrily at one another around her feet. Near the center of the bailey two straw-haired boys, the miller's sons, were hauling pails of water from one of the wells, slopping far more water than Cook would have liked, while three huntsmen on horses were being detained by guards beneath the portcullis leading to the outer bailey.

And all the while Sir Vernon lay dead. Killed by an assassin's hand. Morwenna rubbed her shoulders, and as if reading her thoughts, Bryanna sighed loudly.

A quiet knock sounded on the door.

"Who is it?" Morwenna called over her shoulder.

"Alexander, m'lady."

"Come in."

He entered and his expression was as grim as it had been in the gatehouse. "If I may have a word," he said, glancing at the two other women.

"Certainly," Morwenna agreed, eager for any news. She could not just sit about. "I'll be right back," she said to her sister and Isa. Quickly Morwenna followed Alexander into the hallway, where rushlights burned and flickered. She closed the door behind her. "What is it?"

"A messenger arrived at the gatehouse just minutes ago. We detained him, of course, but he swears he's from Heath Castle and it appears he is. All was in order. He brought this." Alexander handed her a letter, rolled tightly.

Her heart nose-dived as she recognized the unbroken seal from the house of Heath. Lord Ryden's seal. She contemplated not opening the damned letter. The last thing she needed right now was to deal with the man to whom she was betrothed. But Sir Alexander was waiting, and deciding she could not put off the inevitable, she broke through the wax and unrolled the letter. It was short and to the point. Lord Ryden had heard from a traveling merchant that there was trouble at Calon, that Carrick of Wybren had been found half-dead at her castle gates.

Dear God. Did this mean that the news could have traveled to Wybren as well?

Of course it has. . . . You are foolish to think otherwise!

Her shoulders slumped. What had she been doing? Trying to protect Carrick?

Or keeping him held nearly a prisoner until he woke up so you could demand answers, not only of his attack but of why he left you for his brother's wife?

She closed her mind to that line of thought. She had to face what was happening now, whether she wanted to or not. She would have to contact Graydynn immediately. As for her intended . . . what was she to do with him?

Lord Ryden not only offered her his help with returning the traitor to justice at Wybren, but also promised to visit her as soon as was possible. If all went as he planned, he'd arrive at Calon in three days' time.

Morwenna stared at the letter and then crushed it in her hand. She felt no joy at the prospect of seeing him again. If anything, she felt anger with herself for accepting his proposal and a silent fury that she still harbored feelings for Carrick though she was loath to admit it to anyone . . . even herself. What was wrong with her? Why did she still care about the man who had betrayed her, and what on earth had possessed her to promise herself to Ryden of Heath? She must have been mad!

And it had been a grave mistake.

She'd known it nearly as soon as the words of "I will" had passed her lips.

And Ryden has another reason for coming, does he not? Did he not vow to avenge his sister's death?

Panic nearly strangled her. Surely Ryden wouldn't take matters into his own hands, not here in Calon, where she was ruler. Or would he?

So lost in her thoughts was she that she'd nearly forgotten that Sir Alexander was still standing only inches away from her, his dark eyes filled with unspoken questions. Questions she had to answer.

"Lord Ryden will be visiting," she announced, forcing a lilt she didn't feel into her voice and tamping down her rising sense of dread. "In three days' time."

A muscle worked beneath the thick

beard of Alexander's jaw.

"I'll tell Alfrydd, so that he can prepare."

"Thank you," she said, though her heart was even heavier than before. What would she say to the man? She didn't love him, never had and never would, but now, because of her rash decision, they had an agreement and love had never been a part of it. Often, marriage was not about love.

And if he wanted to inflict his own swift justice on Carrick, she would forbid it. Here, her word was law.

She notched her chin up a bit. Forced a smile. "It will be good to see Lord Ryden again."

Alexander silently accused her of the lie.

"Was there something else?" she asked and felt her cheeks warm under his steady gaze.

The captain of the guard cleared his throat. Finally he looked away. "Yes, m'lady. You said that you would decide today if you were going to send a messenger to Lord Graydynn," he reminded her. "To tell him about the capture . . . er, the discovery of Carrick."

Morwenna nodded. Despite the horrid events of the early morning hours, she'd not forgotten about Graydynn, a man she'd met more than once, a cold, hard-edged ruler whose expression was always of irritation or boredom. "Aye. I've given it much thought," she admitted, clasping her hands behind her back as they reached the great hall, where trestle tables were being arranged for the morning meal. "I'll see the scribe this afternoon and compose a letter, though I'm not certain yet when or if I'll send it."

"But, m'lady, what good will it do here, at Calon? You could send the letter by messenger. Sir Geoffrey would be a good choice to carry it. He was a page at Wybren and knows Lord Graydynn. Or perhaps Father Daniel, as he is Lord Graydynn's brother."

Morwenna was vexed. "If the baron does not know that Carrick was found outside my castle gates, I'm not ready to reveal that Carrick is here."

"Why?" he asked, and the damning question seemed to ricochet around the corridor, bouncing off the whitewashed walls and repeating itself over and over in Morwenna's brain. *Why? Why? Why?*

She had no answer. " 'Tis my decision," she said tightly. "I'll do what *I* think best."

"Against the advice of those sworn to protect you?"

"Yes, Sir Alexander, if I deem it necessary. I'll consider all you've said, but in the end, 'twill be my determination and mine alone."

"M'lady —"

"That is all, Sir Alexander." She lifted her chin a bit and glared up at him. He hesitated slightly, gave a stiff nod, and turned on his heel.

As he left, she let out her breath and saw that the letter in her hand had been crumpled until it was no longer legible. Which was just as well.

Until she learned the truth, she wasn't ready to turn the patient over to Graydynn of Wybren. Not yet. Not until she was certain the wounded, silent man was Carrick.

She only hoped she had enough time before the word of his attack crossed the entire realm.

CHAPTER SIXTEEN

The patient lay still. He was weak, his stomach crying out for food, his lips dry and cracked from lack of water. Though he remembered having broth forced down his throat and water poured over his lips, he felt parched.

He'd woken this morning and opened his eyes to find that he could see much more clearly. He could move without as much mind-searing pain. He could move his hand to touch his face, and he'd felt the swelling, but the agony that had been a part of his body had diminished.

Earlier, he'd nearly let on that he was conscious when he'd heard the guards talking, catching muted bits of conversation that he'd pieced together. The guards talked of a murder that had taken place in the keep and that the Lady Morwenna was sending a messenger to Lord Graydynn of Wybren to announce that she was holding Graydynn's cousin Carrick as hostage or prisoner.

He tried to remember Graydynn. . . .

Surely he should have some feelings about the lord — his cousin? But he could conjure up no image of the man and was left with only a disquieting fear that if Graydynn found out about him, it would be his death sentence. What little he could remember of the Baron of Wybren was that he had been a surly, jealous man . . . or had that been Graydynn's father . . . what was his name? He concentrated but ended up with only a headache for his trouble.

The images in his head were hard to catch, just fleeting thoughts that ran away the second he tried to capture them.

He remembered Wybren Castle. Or some parts of it. Could still smell the fire . . . witnessed the flames climbing up the walls. Or were those thoughts just imaginings, dreams he'd concocted from all the conversation he'd heard while lying here unable to move?

He'd been forced to listen to gossip about a great fire at Wybren, a fire started by Carrick, the man everyone assumed him to be. Carrick the traitor. Carrick the murderer of seven innocent souls. Carrick the hideous. Was it possible? Had he really so callously killed his family?

If so — why?

His feelings for what he remembered of

his family were hard to sort, his memories broken and jumbled. . . . He did think he had brothers and sisters . . . aye, and he hadn't been fond of all of them. But their faces were a blur to him — murky images that evoked sensations of restlessness, pain and, aye, jealousy and hatred.

Was it true?

Was he the monster everyone believed?

He set his jaw and forced the damning questions from his brain. He didn't have the time now to concentrate. Soon the guard would check on him. He had to act quickly.

As he had throughout the day when alone, he forced one leg to move. Again. It swung off the bed without too much pain.

He tried the other and felt the sluggish muscles protest as he shifted so that both feet landed on the floor.

Now the real test.

Slowly, thinking he might fall into a heap, he pushed himself to a standing position. To his surprise his legs were able to bear his weight. For the first time.

Taking a deep breath, he took one step.

Pain burned up his leg.

His knee held. He took a deep breath.

Another step.

He nearly fell, then caught himself.

235

Sweat covered his body. Every little movement was an effort. But his knees didn't buckle.

Again he tried to walk. He felt some pain, but with each step it lessened a bit, his stiffened muscles loosening. To his surprise most of the agony he'd experienced when he'd first awakened in this chamber days before seemed to have eased.

He had no real plan, just an understanding that if he didn't escape, he would surely be sent to Wybren to face Graydynn's justice, whatever that might be. He couldn't remember his cousin but instinctively distrusted the man, who would doubtlessly hang him and then draw and quarter him for treason and seven deaths.

Unless you are not Carrick.

Surely Graydynn would see that you're not the traitor.

Or are you?

He had to bear at least some resemblance to Carrick, as everyone's reaction to him was the same: he was the killer. Even if he remembered his true identity and protested his innocence, it would be to no avail. Even if there was doubt as to his identity, because of the damned ring being found with him, he would be considered at

236

the very least a thief.

There was more, as well.

The person who had benefitted from the fire had been Graydynn. So did it not stand to reason that Graydynn or one of his soldiers may have been behind the tragedy at Wybren? Mayhap the stableboy who had witnessed "Carrick" ride away had been paid to make the claim.

Only he could uncover the truth, and there was no time to waste. Every so often a guard, or a servant, or even the lady herself would visit his room, and if he was discovered awake, he would have no chance of escape, no opportunity to redeem himself, no way to uncover the truth.

If he were not to ferret out what really happened at Wybren, then who?

No one! You, alone, must do it.

He would start tonight. Slowly, ears straining to hear anything from the hallway on the other side of the large oaken door, he walked the perimeter of the large chamber, and as he did, his gaze swept the walls and floor. He studied the corners and where the individual stones butted against each other. Somewhere, he knew, there was another entrance to this room, a hidden doorway. Unless he'd dreamed of the man standing over him, of the quiet sound of stone scraping against stone as a secret portal opened. He'd not been able to move his head or cast his gaze about when his nocturnal visitor had arrived, but he'd been awake enough to know that whoever had hovered over him that night had made his way through a secret entrance in the corner opposing the doorway to the hall.

Carefully he lifted a rushlight from a wall sconce and held it aloft. Was he wrong? His nightmares from the pain so vivid that he believed them? Gaze inching over each stone, he scrutinized the wall and floor, touched the smooth stones and rough mortar, and found nothing.

'Twas just a dream, he decided, but the rushes on the floor caught his attention. They had been strewn randomly, straw and dried flowers scattered over the stones, but in one spot, close to the far corner of the room, they'd been pushed into a small pile, as if swept together.

Heart thudding, he knelt closer, ignoring the jab of pain that ran up his leg. He ran his fingers over the flat stones of the floor and noticed the tiniest scratch upon the surface of one large stone. *Here,* he thought, *here is where the bastard entered.* Narrowing his eyes, he focused hard on the wall above the scratch. Nothing seemed amiss.

"Damn," he muttered but refused to give up.

Surely, if there was an entrance, it would have to be cut squarely, so that the door would move easily. And it would have to be raised ever so slightly from the floor.

In pain, he lay upon the floor directly in front of where he suspected the door to be. He closed his eyes and concentrated, and yes, he felt the slightest hint of a draft that moved beneath the area where the door should be. So where was it? How did it move?

"M'lady!" The sentry's voice from the other side of the door.

Damn.

"I'd like to see the patient."

"Again?" the sentry demanded.

He jumped to his feet. His knees protested and he bit down hard to keep from crying out.

There was a heart-stopping moment of silence.

He crept back to the bed.

"Now, Sir James," Morwenna said. "And I'll hear no argument about it."

Then came the sound of a lock opening, and he dived into the bed, his body screaming with the effort. He managed to slip beneath the covers and close his eyes just as he sensed the door swing open.

"I'd like to be alone with him," Morwenna ordered.

His heart was knocking so loudly, so quickly. Surely she would be able to hear it.

"Sir Alexander won't like it."

He forced a calm over his muscles, breathed deep through his nose.

"I'll handle Sir Alexander, and I see no reason to have this conversation again."

He slowly let out his breath.

There was a tense moment in which the patient could feel the guard's indecision before he said reluctantly, "As you wish, m'lady."

She waited a few minutes, as if giving herself time to compose herself or to make certain they were alone, and then he heard the sound of quick footsteps as she approached his bed. His every nerve ending was taut, aware of her movements as she slowly walked around his resting spot. At first she didn't speak and it was all he could do to feign unconsciousness.

"Well, Sir Carrick," she finally said, as if she expected him to hear her. " 'Tis done." A few seconds passed and he still pretended to sleep, not daring to move a muscle. She plunged onward. "As I promised, I've composed a letter to Lord Graydynn, though it's still in my keeping. If I decide to send the letter and Baron Graydynn isn't away but is actually residing at Wybren, he could know within a day's time that you are here at Calon." She waited as if she expected him to say something.

He concentrated on his breathing.

Sensed her stepping closer.

Her voice lowered to the barest of whispers as she inched her mouth so close to his ear that he felt the warmth of her breath slipping across his skin. "Listen, Carrick, and I pray to God that you can hear me: I know not what you did at Wybren, and even though you are a scoundrel — nay, much worse, a piece of pig dung — I find it impossible to believe that you killed your family, that you're a murdering traitor. That is even lower than I would expect of you."

Again the hesitation, and it was all he could do to keep his eyes shut, his body relaxed as if in slumber.

"But what happens to you next is not my decision. No matter what I believe. It is my duty to my ally to report that we've found you. So if you can hear me, let me know. Move your eyelids or your fingers or . . . Oh, fie and fiddlesticks!" She blew out an exasperated breath. "I don't even know what I'm doing here. 'Tis a mistake." She straightened, and he no longer felt the heat pulsing off her skin but imagined her pushing her hair away from her face in frustration. "So . . . Oh, by the gods, this is mistake. . . ."

He thought she might leave, sensed that she'd turned toward the door again, and then she abruptly wheeled and faced him. "So, damn you, if you awaken, it would be best for you if you called for me. . . ." Her voice broke and she took in a long, shuddering breath. "I should hate you and I've sworn that I do . . . but . . . 'tis a lie. I do not. I . . . I wish there was another choice. I wish that . . . Oh, we both know that wishes are for ninnies! Just . . . just please believe that I do what I do with a heavy heart."

It was all he could do to lie motionless. Yet he did. And when she approached again and her lips brushed against his temple, he thought he might groan in the sweet agony of it or, worse yet, be unable to keep his arms pinned to his sides rather than pulling her down upon him.

With all his strength, he managed to remain unmoving and was able to breathe as if he were asleep. He didn't so much as flutter an eyelid and waited, seconds ticking by, his entire body seeming to center on that tiny spot near his hairline where her warm, pliant lips touched his skin.

His pulse pounded wildly, his blood ran hot, his heart thundered in his chest. Could she not hear the pounding, nor see the jump of his vein in his throat, nor notice the beads of sweat erupting upon his skin?

He strained to appear deep in slumber, his breath coming through his lips in soft little puffs, his muscles slack, his eyes closed.

"Carrick! Can you not hear me? Please, please, awaken!" she whispered desperately against the shell of his ear.

Do not listen to her. Don't let her see that you can hear her.

"I need to talk to you. . . . By all that is holy, Carrick, wake up," she ordered.

When he didn't respond, she let out an angry sigh. "I hope you rot in hell!" she vowed.

He thought she would leave then, prayed she would end this sweet torment, but instead she lingered, moving closer again, her breath racing across his skin as, once again, she leaned over him. His guts twisted. He nearly groaned. She placed her

243

lips upon him and then slid a kiss across his bearded cheek to his mouth.

Oh, God, no!

He tensed.

Felt her breath mingle with his.

No!

Her smooth, supple mouth touched his.

How could he ignore this? The warmth that invaded his blood, the tingles that ran through his entire body, the raw pulse of need that rushed through his veins? Desperately he fought the urge to surround her in his arms, to crush his mouth against hers, to taste the salt upon her skin. . . . His groin tightened and he became so stiff he ached. Heat radiated from the innermost part of him. He refused to let his mouth respond.

As if to test him, she rimmed his still swollen lips with the tip of her tongue, and he nearly moaned aloud before she straightened, leaving his mouth tingling, his body desperate for release.

"By the saints, Carrick," she said on a disgusted sigh, "I fear you're doomed. If you will not waken, there is nothing I can do to save you."

He knew his manhood was rock hard and he half expected her to throw back the covers as she had before. She didn't. Instead her voice turned harsh as she whispered, "I swear on my mother, Lenore of Penbrooke's, grave, if you can hear me, you son of a wild dog . . . if . . . if this is all an act . . . then you're a worse bastard than even I imagined, and I'll send you to Graydynn and gladly accept whatever punishment he metes out for you. If you're pretending about this . . . this state you seem to be in and I find out, trust me, Carrick, you'll rue the day you crossed me!" Her anger seemed to pulse through the room. "I will never forgive you!"

He reacted then. Instinctively he opened his eyes and his hands captured her wrists, holding her fast.

She gasped, startled. Her heart pounded a thousand beats a minute and she tried to pull away.

He held her as if his life depended upon it. "Help me!" he rasped, forcing the words out through vocal cords that strained. "Help me!"

"Oh, my God, you can hear me!" she cried. "Carrick, oh, God . . ."

The world spun, darkness threatened. Still he grasped her wrists.

"I cannot believe you're awake," she said, as if through a long tunnel. As if the effort of holding her were too much, he dropped her arms and fell back against the bed. Groaning, he tried to stay alert, to tell her . . .

"Carrick!" she cried, but he couldn't respond. Fingers grabbed his shoulders, pulling at him. "Please, talk to me . . . oh, no . . . don't do this. Don't you dare do this!" she ordered.

He heard the desperation in her voice, felt her shake his shoulders roughly, but he was already drifting away, his energy spent from his earlier efforts to stand and walk, as well as the effort to deceive her. Now he was being sucked under by the blackness again, and though he fought the sensation, it had its talons dug deep into his brain.

"You bastard, do not leave me again. . . ." But he was quickly fading and she knew it. "You . . . you miserable blackheart, you deserve whatever fate decides for you!"

He felt a rush of air as she turned quickly and her footsteps pounded to the door. He heard her say something unintelligible to the guard and then shout, "God's teeth, Dwynn, you nearly scared the liver out of me! Why are you forever lurking about?"

He caught a glimpse of a man hurrying away. Then the door slammed shut with an echoing thud. As if Morwenna were closing him out of her life forever. He felt a second's pang of regret, and then, blissfully, he faded into unconsciousness.

CHAPTER SEVENTEEN

His horse was panting in the moonlit night, lather appearing upon his dark hide, his wet sides heaving as the Redeemer slid from the saddle to the near-frozen ground. His boots sank deep into the mud near the stream that ran through the forest of Calon. He cast a glance at his steed. The ride had been long and arduous and the stallion's breath spewed out of his nostrils in twin shots of steam. The beast deserved to be walked, groomed, fed, and watered and yet there was no time.

Holding the bridle in his gloved hands, he allowed the animal a few long swallows of water from the icy brook where the water splashed over stones and cut beneath overhanging roots. Seconds later, fearful that the horse might become ill, he pulled his mount away from the rush of the water, swung up into the saddle again, and rode to a small clearing where he stared up at the battlements rising on the hillside.

This keep was not his home. Nor would it ever be. A strong fortress it was, but it was smaller than Wybren by half, the square towers not the perfectly rounded turrets that were mounted high on the walls of Wybren, the battlements of Calon not as steep. The only assets this castle had that Wybren did not were the labyrinthine secret passageways and the woman. Oh, yes, the woman. His pulse quickened at the thought of her. Morwenna. Proud. Tall and striking. A woman with intelligent blue eyes that seemed to see past his facade to the man within.

The chill of the night seeped through his hood and mantle, reaching to his bones. He thought of a warm fire, a cup of wine, and a hot, supple woman to chase the coldness from his soul, but he would have to wait. There was much to do.

Since Sir Vernon had been found, it was much more difficult to ride through the gates of Calon. He had to be careful, making sure his excuses for leaving, should they be checked, would be verified. No one in the castle doubted his need to leave, nay, it was a necessity, and yet everyone was being more closely observed since Vernon, the fat old fart, had been killed.

The Redeemer smiled as he remembered the act, the surprise on Sir Vernon's face, the gasp of horror as he realized he was about to die, the satisfaction that came to the Redeemer as Vernon sputtered a bloody last breath.

Though killing Vernon had not been in his plan, he'd been unable to stop himself, had been pressed to find a way to service his bloodlust. When he'd seen the single sentry rooting around in the cranny cut into the wall walk, he'd known the man would have to die. Though he hadn't realized it, Vernon had come too close to discovering a latch for a hidden door, one the Redeemer used to make good his escapes. If the simpleminded soldier had been left up on that walk, searching for places to hide his jug, there was a chance he would stumble upon the Redeemer's private labyrinth, and if that had been allowed to occur, all his plans would have been threatened, perhaps exposed. No other sentry had paid the slightest mind to the small little cuts in the towers and curtain wall, and the Redeemer had felt safe. Until Vernon had started poking around.

It had been necessary to stop him.

That part had been easy.

And enjoyable.

As the Redeemer remembered the exact second Vernon's eyes had met his, the instant of fear and confusion, he felt satisfaction. The guard had recognized him and then, quick as a bolt of lightning sizzling to the ground, the Redeemer had struck with all his fury, flinging his body upon the bigger man's back, drawing his blade and plunging it deep into his prey's thick neck, reveling in the guard's pathetic struggles, his flailing arms, reeling body, and finally the moment the life seeped out of him as he'd tumbled to the hard stones of the wall walk. . . .

The Redeemer had been forced to work fast, and luckily the downpour had leached the blood out of his dark cape.

In the end he'd duped them all.

Tonight, astride his mount, the Redeemer smiled to himself and felt a tingle of excitement, a thrill hasten up his spine in anticipation of his next kill.

This one would be more difficult but even more satisfying.

The wind sighed through the trees, causing dry leaves to swirl and dance and the fronds of ferns to sway. Somewhere he heard the sound of a woman's voice intoning indecipherable words without a bit of inflection.

A chant.

His lip curled in disgust.

The old hag was at it again.

Whispering her blasphemies to unholy gods and goddesses.

He tied his horse to a tree and, following the path of the stream, stepped stealthily through the underbrush and leafless trees, moving silently and ever closer to the sound that murmured through the shadows.

Finally he saw her.

In a small clearing near the stream, she was huddled upon the cold, bare ground, her cape spread out behind her in a pool of black cloth as she busily dug in the soft soil near the creek. As she worked, she never gave up her litany, sending up prayer after prayer of worthless pleas for protection.

Stupid sow.

Worthy only of death.

From the shadows of the forest, he let out a long breath and allowed himself the fantasy of killing her. In his mind's eye, he saw his gloved hands circle her pathetic, scrawny neck. He imagined lifting her from the forest floor, holding her so that her legs would kick uselessly, her spindly arms flail in the air as he slowly and surely squeezed the breath from her.

His hands itched to do the deed.

His blood pumped in anticipation.

Why wait?

She stood suddenly.

Whirling, she stared into the forest, her pale eyes searching the darkness. As if she sensed he was there.

He froze.

Held his breath.

"You, Arawn," she yelled, spitting out the name of the pagan god of the underworld. "Begone!" Her voice was loud and crackled through the still night. The fear he had hoped to see in her ancient visage was missing. In its place was steely determination.

She took a step forward, her chin thrust out, her gray hair falling free around her wrinkled face. "I fear you not," she swore and tossed a handful of dirt or herbs or dry leaves into the air. The tiny dark pieces seemed caught in a whirlwind that swirled and danced in the moonlight. "Go back to the darkness where you were spawned and leave us be!" Her lips pulled into a hideous snarl.

The Redeemer swallowed hard, wondering for a heart-stopping instant if she could, with those ice blue eyes, see through the dense blackness of the forest to the spot where he stood.

"Die!" she called out. "Go back to the demon who sired you!"

Fear grasped his heart for the merest of seconds, but soon it was chased away. She was bluffing. She had no power.

Nonetheless, he knew that he had to kill her.

Soon.

Before she exposed him.

When her back was turned.

He found the latch.

Etched deep in one of the stones near the corner, a tiny piece of metal protruded. He glanced back at the bed where Morwenna had bent over him and kissed his lips. Where he'd fallen into a deep deathlike slumber only to awaken refreshed. He knew not how long she'd been gone but feared he had precious little time before someone discovered him missing. There was a chance that once he opened this door and stepped through whatever portal opened, he would never see her again. He didn't know what lay beyond the doorway, should it open, but whatever was behind this wall would lead to another room, or a hallway, or a chamber that would not, he believed, be guarded. It was his chance for escape. His only chance. And he had to take it. Before she sent him to face Graydynn.

He worked the tiny piece of metal, shoving it with his fingertips, pulling at it, trying to make it budge, but nothing happened.

This had to be it.

Or was it locked?

Did whoever had visited him have a key?

Try again!

Sweat beaded his brow and he pushed harder, placing his finger atop the damned piece of metal and pressing down with all his strength.

He heard a soft, nearly indistinct click.

Without a second's hesitation he pushed on one of the stones near the floor and it along with several others moved, sliding silently outward. He smiled as he realized that this small door was invisible because it was uneven, the stones not cut squarely as a normal doorway would be but the opening created around the shape of the stones, the mortar that should have held them together cut.

Knowing he had little time, he grabbed a torch from its iron cradle and slid carefully into the small opening. He found himself in a tight, musty passageway that was barely wide enough for his shoulders. It ran along the back wall of this room, and, he presumed, behind the next chamber if there was one. There were sconces upon the wall, places to mount lights, and the floor, as he examined it, showed many footprints in dust that had accumulated for what he guessed was decades.

So who had used this corridor? Who was the person who had sneaked into his room, the dark presence that he'd felt staring down upon him?

And where did this path lead?

He considered that Morwenna herself might know of this dark passageway and then discarded the idea. Why not use it to visit him; why do battle with the guards? No, he guessed, she did not know it existed. Nor had he heard anyone speak of it, though, of course, he'd been conscious very little. Yet from the smell of the airless hallway, he suspected it was seldom used.

But someone knows about it and that someone has visited you.

Setting his jaw, he knew there was only one way to find out who. He decided he had some time to explore this hallway, for if he was discovered missing, the alarm would sound, alerting him to the fact that soldiers would be searching for him.

Perhaps he could find a means of escape.

And then what? his mind taunted.

But he had the answer. He would seek out the truth, whatever that might be. Was he, indeed, Carrick of Wybren? If so, had he truly mercilessly slaughtered his entire family as they'd slept? A bad taste crawled up the back of his throat at the thought. Nay, that couldn't be. And yet he had vague memories of Wybren, of life at the vast castle with its tall spires and thick battlements.

He located the latch from the passageway side of the wall and he pulled the stones into their original position, sealing the doorway. If anyone was to look in on him now, they would find him gone and know not how he escaped.

He thought of Morwenna and her harsh words about sending him to Wybren and Graydynn's justice. 'Twould serve her right to discover him missing. A smile curved across his lips until he remembered her kiss and his foolish response.

He could not want this woman.

At least not until he found out who he was.

After marking the closed door with black char from an old rushlight, he started down the narrow hallway. His torch offered a flickering, uneven light that reflected against the ancient, dusty stones and caused a skittering of rodents' claws as rats or mice or whatever else scuttled out of his path.

He swiped at cobwebs, and his thoughts

turned toward the questions that had haunted him from the moment he'd awoken. If he wasn't Carrick, then who was he? Why was he left beaten, near death, close to these castle walls? Had he been on his way to Calon and been ambushed? Or had he been dragged to the place after he'd been attacked and then left? Had whoever was behind the assault been scared off before he was able to finish his job, and who the devil was he? Or she? Did the attack upon him have anything to do with the mysterious visitor who had come to him using this passageway or was his ambush somehow connected to Morwenna?

If only he could remember!

He felt that if he learned just a little more, found one more piece to the puzzle that was his life, everything else would fall into place and his memory would return.

Is that what you want? his voice nagged. *What if, indeed, you are Carrick? What will you do then? Give yourself up? Face Morwenna? Return to Wybren?*

"God's teeth," he whispered, his lips cracked, his voice creaking. 'Twas of no use to wonder. He'd find out soon enough.

Bare feet sliding over the cold stones, he moved silently along the hallway until he came to a fork in the tight corridor. Making another black mark on the wall to indicate which way he'd come, he veered toward a set of steps and began climbing until he reached another hall. Perhaps this hidden corridor opened to a tower, and he imagined flinging open a door and feeling cold air, fresh with the scent of rain, upon his skin. It seemed decades since he'd been outside, smelled the forest, felt the dampness of fog upon his cheeks. He stepped carefully and soon came to a wider spot in the passageway. He stopped, felt a slight rush of air, and put his hand to the space between the stones. The slits were for ventilation, he decided, but placed his face to the opening and looked beyond to a wide chamber with vivid tapestries upon the walls, a crackling fire burning brightly in the grate, a large bed in the center of the room, and a woman . . .

His heart stopped.

He drew in a swift breath as he recognized her.

Morwenna of Calon.

The lady of the keep.

Lying half-naked in the bedclothes.

Sleeping and unaware . . .

The back of his throat went dry as she sighed and turned over, the coverlet slipping low enough that he caught a glimpse of the dark circle of her nipple before she drew the sheeting to her chin.

Carrick's heart thundered. He bit down on his lip and studied the bed.

The bedclothes were rumpled as if she'd been restless and had not been able to fall easily asleep. A speckled dog was curled into a ball upon the bed with her and didn't so much as glance upward as Carrick watched.

He looked again at her. God, she was beautiful. He felt a stirring deep in his blood and silently cursed himself for the desire that burned through him. What was it about this woman he found so intriguing, so maddening, so downright irresistible? And why now, when his very life depended upon her whim, did he fantasize about stealing into her chamber, sliding under the covers, and pressing his body against hers? He imagined the feel of her softer muscles yielding to the gentle pressure of his own. He could almost hear her moan of surrender, feel the trace of her fingers along his skin as she scaled his ribs . . .

Stop it! Stop it right now! You have no time for this, no time!

His gaze lingered for a second before he forced himself to step backward. He took a deep breath, clearing his mind of the forbidden images, cooling the fire that was crackling through his veins.

Think, man, think! You need to concentrate and gather information. It's imperative you form a plan. You cannot be distracted. Not by Morwenna. Not by any woman.

Mentally chiding himself, he surveyed the small area where he now stood. Wider than the rest of the corridors, it had obviously been constructed so as to view the chamber below.

Why?

And for whom?

Sentries? A jealous husband? Spies within the keep?

Frowning, he noticed the disturbance in the dust on the floor. Recent footprints. So he was not the first to have stared down at the lady's chamber. An eerie sensation brushed the back of his neck. He had little doubt that whoever had visited him the other night had also stood in this very spot and watched Morwenna as she'd slept, or dressed, or bathed. Whoever it was had heard her most intimate conversations, seen her when she thought she was entirely alone. Whoever it was, he sensed, was the enemy. Any lingering thoughts that she

260

might know of these secret corridors were banished and he realized that not only he, but she as well, had enemies within the stone walls of Castle Calon.

There was treachery afoot and somehow it involved him.

Both he and she were being watched by someone, perhaps manipulated by that same dark enemy.

Morwenna let out a long, soft sigh, and he couldn't help himself but leaned close again to catch another glimpse of her as she slept so peacefully. Her dark hair tumbled around her face and down her back, her breathing was soft and steady, her eyes were closed, the sweep of her eyelashes resting upon her cheeks. Her mouth was slightly open and he remembered her kiss and her confession that she didn't believe him to be a murderer.

But someone is.

Probably someone she trusts.

He thought of all the voices he'd heard, the glimpses of men who had observed him. The steward, guards, priest, and physician had all been in attendance. And what of the old woman who seemed to hate him so?

He had no answers.

Yet.

But he would find out who was behind this . . . set a trap for the bastard — that was it.

His mind was rushing ahead. Somehow he had to flush the enemy out. The first step was to know his lair, and this was it.

Using his torchlight for illumination, he leaned down and stared at the footprints. . . . Most were smudged and there was nothing distinctive about them; they were the size of an average man, one whose feet were close in size to Carrick's own. And though the slits in the wall were not level and several were set at a lower height, it seemed that most of the prints were at the same one that was comfortable for a person of his own height. He saw nothing else that would help him unmask the voyeur, no bit of fabric from a robe, no careless dropping of a personal effect, no hairs caught on the sharp edges of the sconce . . . though this sconce was probably not used often for fear the light would shine through the slits in the wall, allowing whoever was below to know someone was watching.

So who had been watching her?

Without an answer, he walked along the narrow passageway. There were other wide spots between the stones, and he was able to view another woman, one with dark reddish hair splayed upon her pillow as she slept — the sister, he guessed. He moved farther on to what appeared to be the solar, which was now empty, and then to the empty room with the rumpled, empty bed, the chamber where he'd been held as a captive guest. He guessed this viewing area was directly above the hidden doorway that he'd used to enter the passageway. Were there portals from all the rooms — one from Morwenna's?

He searched for other hidden doors or latches along the flight of narrow stairs and at the floor level of the lady's chambers, the same level on which his own room and secret doorway were located, but discovered none. He also checked the dust on the floor of the passageway for signs of disturbance. Though there were footprints leading everywhere, it seemed that most were concentrated in the viewing area over Morwenna's room. Whoever used these secret hallways knew them well and used them to secretly observe the lady of the keep.

Carrick felt a quiet rage steal through his blood, not unlike the emotions he experienced whenever he thought of Morwenna marrying Lord Ryden, a fact he'd learned from gossiping servants.

Jealousy?

His jaw tightened. He had no right to any kind of possessive feeling toward her. According to her, he'd thrown away her love, left her when she was with child.

He slapped at a cobweb and frowned. What kind of a man had he been? One who would ruthlessly kill his family? One who would turn his back on his woman and child for a dalliance with his brother's wife?

No wonder someone had decided to beat the snot out of him.

Moving stealthily, he came upon a small room no larger than a cupboard. As his torchlight illuminated the tiny chamber, he discovered how the person who walked these hallways was able to get in and out of the castle undetected. He was disguised in the clothing that he left here: a monk's robe, a dark cowl and cloak, a soldier's uniform, a farmer's humble tunic and cap . . . disguises. And weapons. He found two knives, a sword, an ax, and several carpentry tools. Whoever used these hallways had plotted carefully.

As would he. He slipped on the soldier's tunic and tucked the breeches, belt, pouch, and boots that were a part of the uniform beneath his arm. Then, hardly believing his good fortune, he stole the smaller knife and slipped it into his sleeve.

Afterward he explored for as long as he could and discovered several tunnels, one leading to the chapel, another to a dungeon's cell that was empty, the rusted gate unlocked. He saw several other offshoots from the passageways, but he didn't have time to search them. Time was passing and though he wanted to examine every inch of this hidden maze, his strength failed him and he was suddenly weary, his muscles aching after so much sudden use.

Fearing that he might be discovered missing, and in the search that ensued the passageway that he might need to use as a means of escape be found, he inched backward.

Retracing his way to his chamber, he was careful to disturb little and his ears strained to hear even the slightest sound that was out of the ordinary, lest he, with only a small weapon, run into the person who walked these passageways with ease and knowledge.

At each branch from this hallway, he cleaned off the charcoal markings so that whoever had been using the hidden corridors wouldn't notice a change and instead scratched the stones near the floor. Making mental notes about the passageways that branched from what he sensed was a main arterial, he headed toward the room where he'd spent so many days and nights. He would explore again, if he had the opportunity. Surely there were more rooms one could slip in and out of, perhaps more tunnels leading to other buildings within the heart of the castle.

There was much he could do.

But first, he needed rest. Fatigue was setting in, his muscles protesting. He stripped near the door to his room and tucked his newfound clothes into a dark, musty passageway that appeared, with its lack of footprints and profusion of cobwebs, to be seldom used. Keeping the small knife that he would hide beneath his body, he headed toward his own chamber again.

He would have to escape, he thought as he unlatched his door and stepped naked into the chamber where he'd lain for two weeks.

And he would have to leave soon.

Before Morwenna made good her threat to send him to Wybren.

CHAPTER EIGHTEEN

"Help me!"

The words echoed through her mind, just as they had since last evening when she'd visited Carrick.

She couldn't shake the memory, nor ignore the desperation she'd heard when he'd finally spoken. His plea chased her even now as she hurried along the wet flagstones that cut through the garden and led to the chapel.

Carrick had grabbed her arms, looked directly into her eyes, and begged her to help him only to fall back against his pillows. Had he known her or had it been part of his delirium? His words had been with her all night and into the day, and though she'd checked on him twice since, he hadn't roused again. She'd mentioned that he'd appeared to awaken to the physician, but Nygyll had examined Carrick and only shaken his head.

No one had seen him stir.

Except you, her mind nagged.

"Bother and broomsticks," she muttered,

her breath coming out in a cloud as she reached the chapel door.

Carrick's cry for help had been too long coming. Too many people knew that he was within her keep to have his whereabouts hidden or to help him in any manner other than to bring him to justice.

Quietly she stepped inside the chapel and slipped off her hood. She was tired from lack of sleep and drained by the thought of what she must do.

You don't have *to do anything. You are the ruler of this keep, Morwenna. Do not forget. Do not feel duty bound.*

Her gaze swept the interior of the chapel, its coved ceilings, whitewashed walls, and long tapers burning in iron sconces surrounding the carved altar.

The chapel was empty. Morwenna stepped through the intimate room and felt, instead of being closer to God, as if she were somehow trespassing through a forbidden chamber, treading in an area where she should not set foot.

Which was silly.

This was God's house, in the keep where Morwenna was the lady, the ruler, the law. What was wrong with her? Her skin crawled and she mentally chided herself. It seemed that all Isa's talk of omens, curses, and demons was getting to her.

Listening hard, she walked toward the communion table and thought of calling out to Father Daniel. But she held her tongue, something in the vacant room forcing her silence. She genuflected near the altar, stared up at the figure of Christ upon the cross, and thought fleetingly of all her sins. In her life she'd collected many, and so many surrounded Carrick of Wybren, an old lover who now seemed her bane. Oh, how she'd lain with him, so trustingly giving her virtue, so joyously lying in his arms, so happily realizing she was with child — his child.

And all the while he was bedding his brother Theron's wife. The old pain twisted inside her like a knife to her womb, and she couldn't help wondering if there would ever be another babe.

Yes, she'd sinned more often than not and, she was certain, she wasn't through. There would be more. Her fingers touched the hem of her pocket and she frowned. Her decision, though already made, weighed heavily upon her.

Yesterday she'd met with the scribe, had told him what she'd wanted to say as he'd scratched out her words. Then she'd sealed the letter that was Carrick's fate. It now rested in her large pocket and she, ridiculously, felt like a traitor as she set her plan in motion. Finally she would officially admit to Lord Graydynn that she was harboring his cousin, the traitor to Wybren.

She was planning to seal Carrick's fate forever.

'Tis your duty, her mind told her, and yet she felt tricked, trapped into a corner, forced into making a decision that still felt wrong, kept her thoughts in constant turmoil. Ever since the stranger had been carried through the gates of Calon nearly a fortnight earlier, she'd had little sleep and no peace whatsoever.

Nonetheless sending Carrick to Wybren would only make things worse. Well, 'twould be done. She fell to her knees, made the sign of the cross, and prayed for guidance. Through the windows she heard muted sounds of men talking, axes striking, the mill wheel grinding, but above those noises of the castle at work there was another sound, soft and low, a droning . . . nay, more like a chant. Ever steady, it whispered through the chapel, bounding off the walls.

Instinctively she climbed to her feet and stepped to one side of the apse, where she peeked through the slits of a curtained doorway to the private chamber of the priest. She nearly gasped as she peered through the small opening and spied Father Daniel lying facedown in front of a small communion table, a cruder version of the chapel's intricately carved altar.

Her stomach twisted in revulsion.

The priest lay naked, his white skin nearly translucent, red welts visible upon his back as he prostrated himself. In one hand he clasped a small prayer book, in the other he gripped a leather whip so tightly his knuckles bulged from his fingers. Obviously he'd been flailing himself, using the weapon to . . . what? Expunge demons from his soul?

"Forgive me, Father," he said, and his voice was a wet rasp. He sobbed and sniffed. "For I have sinned. Oh, I have sinned. I am not worthy of Your love."

Blood began to rise to the surface of the red streaks upon his back, and Morwenna noticed other wounds, scars from earlier floggings. She nearly retched. What would drive a man to whip himself until his flesh was raw?

Rather than risk being discovered spying upon him, she slowly backed away from the curtain. Intending to sneak out the way she'd come, she inched toward the door.

Crack!

The heel of her shoe hit the doorframe, and the noise seemed to reverberate through the chapel.

The chanting stopped abruptly.

Damn.

She heard the rustling of clothing and feet as Father Daniel quickly dressed and knew she would be found out. There was no way to hide that she was in the chapel. Rather than try to run away, she flung the main door open as wide as it would go. It slammed back against the wall.

"Father Daniel!" she said in a loud whisper, as if she'd just entered but didn't dare yell inside the chapel. "Father Daniel, are you here?" she called again. Treading loudly, she walked to the altar and slipped to her knees.

She was just making the sign of the cross over her chest when the priest, fully robed, swept into the room. He was still carrying his prayer book in his one hand, but the other was empty, no whip in sight.

"Oh!" she said, as if surprised to see him. "I — I was looking for you."

"I was in my quarters. Praying," he said a bit breathlessly, and his face was flushed as he cleared his throat. He stood over her, looking down. She was still on her knees and close enough to smell the blood upon his skin. He managed a thin, patient smile that curved his lips but didn't add any warmth to his eyes. Those eyes regarded her with an intensity that made her want to squirm. She saw his feet shift beneath his cassock, and in this position, her knees pressed to the cold floor, she felt submissive and vulnerable. Her skin crawled as he asked in a quiet, silky voice, "Is there something I can help you with, my child?"

She cringed inside, and when he touched her on the shoulder, she wanted to flinch. "Aye, Father," she said, nodding. "Please." She finished a quick prayer and then climbed hastily to her feet. "I — I need your counsel." This was better. A tall woman, she nearly looked him in the eye.

"Of course." He seemed to relax a bit as they walked out of the chapel and into the garden, where water from last night's storm dripped from the eaves and puddled in footprints in the earth. As nothing was in bloom, the garden looked as desolate as Morwenna felt.

"What's troubling you?" the priest asked.

"There are several things, including Sir Vernon's death."

"A tragedy."

She agreed. "I also must deal with the

stranger who was brought to us, the wounded man."

"Ah." Father Daniel nodded as they walked through the garden gate, and dark clouds moved across the sky. Two boys ran by, laughing, their noses running, as they chased after a squealing piglet. A dog bounded behind them and nearly knocked over a boy toting two pails from the well. Water sloshed over the sides of the buckets and the boy cursed roundly before spying the priest. He quickly hurried toward the kitchens.

Father Daniel stared after the lad as Morwenna said, "It's been suggested that I tell Lord Graydynn, your brother, that we have possibly apprehended Carrick."

"He may already know." Father Daniel returned his attention to Morwenna. "Wybren is not far away."

"All the more reason to give him official notice." She met his eyes and withdrew the sealed letter from her pocket. "I was hoping that you would take this to Wybren. Since Baron Graydynn's your brother, I thought 'twould be best if the news came from you."

She handed him the letter.

"And what would you have me tell him? Aside from what you've written?" he asked as they made their way past the candlemaker's hut toward the great hall.

"Just that we're not certain that the man is Carrick, of course, because he was so badly beaten as to be unrecognizable. And even though he's healing, it's difficult to see his features, to be sure that he is Carrick."

"You doubt that he is?"

Morwenna swallowed hard. Did she? Rather than answer, she said, "When you meet with Graydynn, please mention that the man who was attacked came to us wearing a ring emblazoned with the crest of Wybren, but that the ring has since been stolen."

"And would you have me tell him that another man was murdered, possibly at Carrick's hand?"

"Nay!" she said quickly, surprised at the question. She had to make herself clear. "As I said, we're not certain of the stranger's identity, and it's unlikely that he slew Sir Vernon, for our guest was under guard at the time of the attack."

Father Daniel studied her face intently. "So you still defend him?"

"We know not what happened to Sir Vernon."

Father Daniel shook his head as if she

were a naive child, and then he touched her shoulder again, and even through her tunic she felt the coldness of his fingers upon her skin. "Oh, we know he was savagely murdered; we only do not know who did the heinous deed." He winced a bit, as if his cassock had shifted to rub against the new wounds upon his back. He dropped his hand. "Whoever took Sir Vernon's life will have to answer to the Father."

"And to me."

"Oh, Lady, please, place your trust in God. Have faith. Only He can right this wrong." The words were said with conviction, but there was something else in the priest's expression, something more troubling. "Remember the passage from Romans, Morwenna: 'Vengeance is mine; I will repay, saith the Lord.' "

Morwenna pulled her arm away but held the priest's intense gaze with her own. "But in my keep, Father Daniel," she pointed out as a breeze tugged at her hair, "please remember that justice is mine."

She left him standing near the candlemaker's hut and marched up the stairs into the great hall, where two guards stood. Geoffrey held the door open for her and she felt the warmth of the room seep into her bones.

She was letting the events of the past two weeks get to her, starting to believe all of Isa's silly notions of curses and omens and bad luck. She'd become rattled enough that now she was doubting the priest, a man who had dedicated his life to God.

And a man who flogged himself performing some kind of painful, self-inflicted penance.

What was it that tore so at Father Daniel's soul?

What sin had he committed that he felt the need to flail at his own flesh?

Yanking off her gloves as she climbed the stairs to her chamber, she passed by Fyrnne and Gladdys. She felt their eyes upon her and told herself she was imagining things. Ridiculously she was beginning to believe that no one in this keep was who they first appeared to be.

"You're as bad as Isa," she said once inside her room, where the fire was burning bright, a tub and a bucket of warm water waiting for her. Mort was snuggled upon the bed. He gave up a bark as she entered. "Miss me?" she teased as the dog wiggled, tail slicing the air frantically until she walked over to him and scratched his ears. He rolled over, offering up his belly to be rubbed. "I guess so."

She kicked off her shoes, petted the dog, and told herself that for just a few minutes, she would quit worrying. There was a bucket of hot water resting on the coals, and she considered having a handmaiden help her with the bath and then thought better of it. She wanted a few minutes alone.

She wound her hair onto her head, stripped out of her clothes, poured the water into the towel-lined tub, and then sank into the warm depths.

"Aaah," she whispered to herself and using lavender scented soap washed her body before unwinding her hair and lowering herself even farther into the warm water. She scrubbed her hair and skin and felt the tension ease from her muscles. It was heaven. All of her aches, all of her worries, all of Isa's dire warnings of curses and omens and death seeped away.

But as she lazed in the tub, her mind wandered and she did think of Carrick. He was healing, and as she'd stared at him in these last days she'd become convinced that, yes, it was he lying across the hall, he who had awoken suddenly and begged her to help him, he whom she had loved so impetuously, so madly, so rashly.

Too easily she remembered what it had

been like to be with him. She'd spent her days fantasizing about the weight of his body upon her, the feel of his flesh against hers, the erotic touch of his lips to hers. Each night had been spent in hours of lovemaking, of skin touching skin, of straining muscles working together, of hot, gasping breaths and mind-splintering, furious joinings of bodies and souls.

Her heart contracted and she felt that same dark void that had been with her since the morning she'd lost the babe, as if part of her life had ended.

Dipping a cloth in water, she squeezed it over her face, letting the drips run down her cheeks.

She wondered if she would ever feel as she had three years earlier or if those emotions were forever lost to her, killed by Carrick's betrayal. For a fleeting moment she considered Lord Ryden and knew that she would never feel the same breathless, dizzying, soul-rending glory with him that she had had with Carrick. And she also knew that not only did she not love him, she could not marry him.

'Twould be a sham of a marriage. A disastrous mistake that she would forever regret. 'Twas too late to write to him as he was on his way to Calon, so she would wait until he arrived and tell him face-to-face, no matter what her brother thought. She knew she would be able to convince Kelan that the marriage could not happen.

Leaning back in the tub, she glanced up at the ceiling and that shadowy part of the wall that loomed above the crossbeams. Was it her imagination or did she see something . . . a reflection of light in the mortar between the stones? 'Twas impossible.

And yet . . .

She covered her breasts with a wet cloth and gazed upward, but whatever she'd seen was no longer visible. Probably just her imagination again.

Nothing was amiss.

Not right now.

Not for the moment.

There was no evil within the castle walls.

Listening to the crackle of the fire, hearing the muted sounds of voices echoing from the chambers below, she closed her eyes and ignored the feeling that hidden eyes were watching her every move.

CHAPTER NINETEEN

The sheriff didn't like the turn of his thoughts. Seated in his wooden chair, he stared into the fire and felt the same restlessness he always did when he was close to finding a culprit but hadn't yet been able to figure out who the criminal was.

His boots were warming by the grate and he stretched his legs so that his stocking feet felt the heat of the glowing embers. The scents of Sarah's mutton pie still lingered, and both his belly and the cup at his side were full.

He and Sarah lived within the castle walls in a substantial structure of stone with three full rooms and a private entrance, only a short walk to the great hall. He used the first room to conduct business; citizens of the town would find him there and could lodge their complaints. Lately it seemed that everyone had one. Neighbors squabbling, the insistence by Tom Farmer that one of the carpenter's sons had stolen his goat, several merchants and farmers complaining about a band of thieves near

Raven's Crossing, a charge that one man's boar had run amok, breaking through a fence and destroying two bags of seed for spring planting, and on and on.

Payne's head throbbed, for on top of all the normal complaints were the business with Carrick of Wybren, or whoever the man was, and Sir Vernon's vicious murder.

He rubbed his chin as he stared into the hungry flames and all the while he considered what had happened to Sir Vernon. The guard's slaying had been for a reason. Vernon's unusual wound, the slash in the shape of a W upon his throat, was a hint to the killer's mind. And mayhap something the bastard wanted everyone to see and know, a macabre taunt.

Certainly the wound had been intentional.

A clue to the killer's identity?

Or an attempt to turn Payne's head from the true culprit, more a diversion than an actual indication of who the killer was?

Why would someone kill Sir Vernon?

Plowing his nose into his mazer, Payne considered the big man's demise and took a long swallow of ale.

Somehow, Payne was certain, Vernon's death was linked to Carrick of Wybren. But there was no way Carrick could have crept from his sickbed, passed the guard, climbed up the guard towers, slit Vernon's throat, and then returned undetected. No, Sir James, the guard at Carrick's door, hadn't moved all night.

Unfortunately there had been no witnesses. None. No one interviewed since the slaying, including all the sentries stationed around the keep, had seen or heard anything unusual during the storm. Nor had they spotted any person unknown to them.

The people who had been sighted out in the storm had generally had good reason: Father Daniel had been returning from visiting the millwright's ill daughter, as had the physician, Nygyll; Alfrydd had been double-checking the locks on the stores of spices. Isa, the old sorceress who claimed to have "seen" the death, had been alone in her chambers. The tanner had been awake, but he'd seen nothing out of the ordinary. The apothecary, Samuel, had upon his return from the town spied Dwynn hauling firewood into the kitchen, though it had been the dark of night. The kennel master and stable master claimed they were sleeping near their charges. Alexander, captain of the guard, had also returned and been asleep, as had all of his men who hadn't been actively guarding the keep.

Everyone had been talked to officially, and afterward there had been the buzz of gossip swirling through the keep, words whispered in the corridors, towers, and pathways. Speculation in the fields and huts. Guesses and jokes over games of dice or cups of ale.

Payne had listened to all the rumors. He'd hoped that someone might inadvertently slip and give out new information, but he'd been disappointed. 'Twas as if the killer had appeared, killed Vernon, leaving the savage, bloody W on the big guard's throat, and then disappeared again. He imagined that the criminal was strong, clever, and trustworthy, for Vernon had been a big man, a trained soldier who would not give up his life easily.

'Twas a mystery. Payne drummed his fingers on the arm of his chair. Mayhap he'd been going at this all wrong. Mayhap it wasn't Vernon's death on which he should concentrate. The killer wanted him to consider Wybren. Why else had Carrick's ring been stolen and Vernon's throat slashed so significantly? Certainly the two crimes could be linked and were most probably connected to Carrick's brutal attack.

Was the killer trying to force Payne into examining the murders of the family of Dafydd of Wybren more closely? Seven people had been killed that night. *Seven!* And now the man thought to have set that fire was here, not even under lock and key.

Why had this stranger not been killed? Why left for dead only to survive? A mistake made by whomever had assaulted him? In the beaten man's state it would have been easy enough to slip a blade between his ribs and nick his heart. He would have easily bled to death. But no . . . either the attacker had been frightened off, or he had intended for Carrick to survive, to live.

Why?

Just so he would suffer? Mayhap the killer planned to return and finish the job.

Why had a ring been stolen? And again the robbery victim not killed? Was the attacker's purpose *not* to take his life? To have him sent to Wybren and face judgment? Why then not just bind him, throw him over the back of a mule, and haul his near-dead body to the gates of Wybren?

Payne frowned, took a swallow from his mazer, and decided that the stranger's attack had something to do with Calon, with Lady Morwenna. Most of the trouble within the keep, including this latest spate of horrors, had occurred since she'd been handed the barony by her brother less than a year ago.

Why then kill Vernon?

"Bah," he muttered into the bottom of his cup. Mayhap his theory was all wrong. Mayhap he should concentrate on those who would benefit from Carrick of Wybren's death. Was it possible that Sir Vernon had stumbled onto something that the killer wanted to remain hidden? Overheard a conversation that might implicate someone?

He shoved the fingers of one hand through his hair, making it stand on end.

"Come to me, husband," his wife, Sarah, called from the bedroom. A big woman with pillowy breasts, silver blond hair, and cheeks like apples, she was the one person he trusted in the world. A truer heart no one would ever find. "You'll not solve the puzzle of Sir Vernon's death drinking ale and staring at the embers."

"Many a crime has been solved right here," he countered, and she laughed that deep, throaty laugh that he'd loved for nearly twenty years.

"And many have been solved here, in the bed."

He smiled and took another swallow of ale, feeling its tangy warmth slide down his throat. He never tired of her. Never. She'd been with child when they'd wed and he was certain, all those years ago, that she was not a woman he would want to spend the rest of his life with. But he'd been wrong.

She had known.

As she knew so many things.

She patted the bed. "A good night's sleep will help you," she said, and he turned, looking over his shoulder, raising an eyebrow to stare through the open doorway. He saw her half lying on her side of the mattress, the covers hiding little of her enticing breasts, her come-hither smile always tempting.

"So you're thinking I need sleep." He drained his cup, slammed it onto the floor, and then stood and stretched. Mayhap she was right.

"Sleep? Aye, well . . . eventually."

"You're a wench, Sarah." In his stocking feet he walked into the bedroom only to stand over her when he reached the edge of their bed. The room was near dark, but he saw her. She'd aged so much in the years since their wedding. Her skin was no longer tight, lines fanning from the corners of her eyes and etching around her mouth. Her hair no longer shone with the luster of youth, yet she was still beautiful to him.

Never had he strayed. Never had he been tempted. "A wench, I say."

"Only for you, my love." She chuckled then, that deep, throaty sound that touched his heart and made him smile. "Every other man in this keep thinks I've got ice in my veins. Only you know better."

"Fools. All of them." He pulled off his tunic and unlaced his breeches as she watched.

"Let me," she offered, and the covers slipped away as she reached forward, her fingertips lithely loosening the leather laces.

A tiny smile played at her lips as she met his gaze. She reached into his breeches with warm, knowing fingers. "I think we might not get much sleep tonight, Sheriff," she teased, moving her fingers up his chest to tangle in the gray hairs that sprouted there.

Weary as he was, he didn't care.

He had to leave.

Now that Morwenna knew he was awake, that she suspected he'd heard her desperate confession and angry rantings, now that she was determined to contact Lord Graydynn, Carrick had to find a way to escape.

He was about to search the passageways again when he heard the laundresses arrive. He recognized their voices as they flirted and teased Sir James in the hallway before stepping into Carrick's chamber.

"So no one knows who killed Sir Vernon," one woman was saying as she changed the bedclothes on which he slept.

Killed Sir Vernon? The sentry who had been at his doorway? The deep-voiced man who had argued with Morwenna and had subsequently been relieved of his duty? Vernon was the man who had been slain?

He'd heard some of the guards talking but hadn't been able to make out their conversation, and though he'd sensed a change in the atmosphere, he hadn't understood what had happened.

He waited impatiently, silently hoping the gossiping hens would give him more information.

"Nor does the sheriff have any idea who took the ring," the other woman with a high-pitched, wheedling voice agreed.

Deft hands moved him with practiced ease. He risked lifting an eyelid and saw a woman wearing a scarf wound tightly over her large head. Her face was fleshy, her lips curved in upon themselves, her movements brusque and practiced. The other woman was a birdlike thing with frizzy brown hair, fair skin, and dark eyes. She tossed the dirty bedclothes into a basket and snapped the fresh linens out of their folds.

"If ye ask me, there's been nothing but trouble in this keep since this one" — the larger woman tapped the side of the bed — "was dragged in here. I'm beginnin' to believe what Isa says, that he's cursed."

Cursed?

"I just don't know why the lady keeps him here, him being a murderer and all," she continued.

"So ye believe that he truly is Carrick of Wybren."

"Who else? Look at him. Now that he's healing, it's more obvious than ever. The lady, she knows it, too. She is finally sending word to Lord Graydynn." She clucked her tongue. "Such a waste. A handsome man, son of a baron. What would make him do such a thing?"

"Money or a woman," the birdlike maid said. "Unless he's just plain mad, there is no other reason. And I've never heard it said that Carrick of Wybren was out of his mind. Treacherous, aye. A blackheart who had an eye for the ladies. Mayhap even mercenary, but mad? Never."

"And yet seven people were killed — eight, if ye throw in Sir Vernon. This man here — Carrick of bloody Wybren — is a murderin' bastard, and the sooner the lady sends him to Lord Graydynn, the better. Maybe then we can all rest easy again; maybe then this curse will be lifted."

Quickly, as if spurred by their own words, they finished their job and left him alone in the clean bed.

Until this moment he had accepted the fact that he was Carrick. The name was familiar, and mention of Wybren brought back memories. Surely he'd been there. Lived there. Was he the vile bastard? In his mind's eye he saw a huge keep with round towers and turrets, a wide inner bailey, sweeping fields, and a moat that ran from the river and surrounded most of the castle. His head pounded as he remembered pages shouting near the quintain, an old farrier bending horseshoes, the huntsmen returning with stag and boar and pheasant through a portcullis that yawned wide . . . or had it all been a dream?

Nay . . . his family had lived there. . . . He saw faces, a large, swaggering father

291

and a milder, hard-lipped woman who was his wife . . . his own mother? His jaw tightened as he tried to draw up the images, but they were unfocused and skittered in and out of his mind, just as did his name.

What about Morwenna? Did you know her?

His throat went dry at the thought of her. How could he forget her with her heart-shaped face, smooth skin, and curling ebony hair? In the few moments he'd seen her, he'd noticed her eyes, a deep, dark blue and quick with intelligence, surrounded by a sweep of black lashes and eyebrows that arched in interest or doubt. In those fleeting instances she'd spent in his room, she'd displayed violent changes in temperament. She'd been wildly passionate, filled with despair, blazing with hot fury, or coldly determined. She'd sworn at him, accused him of all kinds of vile acts, and yet she had kissed him with tenderness and longing, an ache and heat he'd felt himself.

And in their few, brief meetings he understood one truth: Morwenna of Calon was still in love with Carrick.

Christ Jesus, if he could only talk to her, plead his case, ask her forgiveness.

For what?

What sins have you committed?

Do you think you truly are this horren-dous monster who is capable of de-stroying his entire family?

No! he silently raged. *Impossible!*

His fists curled impotently and he heard her voice, soft and low, instructing the guard to let her inside.

His heart sank.

He would never be able to keep up this pretense. She knew that he could hear, could speak.

A key turned in the lock and he braced himself, every muscle straining.

He recognized her scent: Morwenna.

Whoring wench!

The Redeemer had watched as Morwenna slipped out of her room. She'd bathed and washed her hair, then nearly fallen asleep in the tub, her breasts rimmed by the soapy water, her dark nipples puckering as the temperature in the room chilled.

Oh, to suckle from her. To touch her. To rim his tongue over each little bud and to bite down . . . He'd let out a low moan at the thought, and her damned dog had looked up, barked, and growled.

Morwenna had suddenly roused,

wrapped a towel around herself, and, following the dog's lead, looked upward to
the very place he stood. Her eyebrows had
knotted, her lips flattening in anger. She'd
stared hard, as if she could actually see the
narrow, nearly invisible slits, and then said,
"What did you hear?" to the stupid, mangy
mutt. She then quickly donned a scarlet
tunic and cinched it with a silvery belt.

Still eyeing the wall suspiciously, she'd
started combing out her hair near the fire
when a sharp knock registered on the door.
Morwenna had visibly started as the dog
charged to the door to bark and snarl crazily, all the while wagging its fool tail.
What a useless creature.

Gladdys, that little goose of a maid, had
announced herself before entering. Then,
sending the mutt a glance suggesting she'd
like nothing better than to kick him over
the castle wall, she had helped Morwenna
finish drying her tangled loose curls.

Disgruntled, the speckled beast had
growled but settled into a ball on the bed
again.

Nearly two hours later, after dismissing
the serving maid, trying and failing at
sleep, Morwenna had climbed out of bed,
thrown on a long black robe, cinched it
around her slim waist, and made her way

to the prisoner's chamber. And make no mistake, the man in the bedroom across the hall was a captive. Lady Morwenna could lie to herself and call him what she would, a guest, a visitor, or a patient, but the man was a hostage, held in a room, awaiting judgment.

Which was only fitting, the Redeemer thought, smiling to himself. Silently he had followed Morwenna's movements, knowing with instinctive, gut-burning clarity where she would turn. Deftly, he had padded through the narrow passageways and waited, only to see her appear in the patient's chamber.

The Redeemer's back teeth clenched as he studied her.

Innocently seductive.

Intelligently alluring.

Her gaze centered on the unmoving man on the bed.

With naked fascination, he observed her every move, heard the low whisper of her voice, and felt the hate pulsing through his veins.

He should have killed the man when he had the chance, should have heeded his baser instincts rather than enjoying the wait, drawing out the pain, seeking satisfaction in a judgment yet to be passed.

He licked his lips and reached for the dagger strapped at his waist. A few seconds alone with the man and he would send him straight to hell.

Patience! his mind screamed. *You've worked too hard, spent too much time planning what will come.*

He'd lingered much too long already. And he couldn't take a chance that he would be missed.

You must leave. Now!

If you are discovered missing, all will be lost.

Every muscle in his body tensed. Blood thrummed in his ears. Silently and furiously he lifted his fist, clenching the knife until his knuckles showed white as he wordlessly railed against the gods while he stared unblinkingly through the gap in the stones. He watched her step farther into the beaten man's chamber, walking without so much as a second's hesitation to the cur's bed.

What torment to witness her in another man's chamber, observe the interest in her eyes as she approached his bed.

Curse your soul, Carrick of Wybren. May you rot in the fires of hell for all eternity.

There was a noise from the hallway outside the chamber — no doubt the changing of the guard. He'd tarried much too long as it was, and though he was fascinated with the scene unfolding in the chamber below, he had to force himself away from his viewing area.

There was a chance he'd waited too long.

Mayhap he should just kill the cur and be done with it.

His pulse jumped in anticipation of the deed. His fingers itched to plunge a dagger into the bastard's heart.

No one would know. He could steal into the chamber and quickly do the deed. . . . No one would find his hidden door.

Or would they?

Control, take control of yourself. You have chosen a path — now follow it!

But how much longer could he stand this agony? This wretched, soul-jarring knowledge that she lusted after another man, a traitor no less?

In time, she will see the truth. Realize that it is you she loves, that you and she are destined to be together. Do not *stray. Keep to your plan and now, before 'tis too late, leave!*

Teeth gnashing, he released his stranglehold on the blade and jabbed it into his pocket. He took one last glance through the slits in the wall and then silently crept from his hiding spot.

But he would return.

This night.

After he had made certain no one had missed him.

And if she gave herself to the bastard, he would watch every excruciating moment.

CHAPTER TWENTY

"So, Carrick," Morwenna said, staring at the wounded man and trying to imagine what he looked like without his bruises. His swelling had receded and beneath his beard she noticed the shape of sharp cheekbones and an angled jaw. His forehead was only slightly discolored now, dark hair falling to his eyes. "The deed is done. At dawn, Father Daniel, Graydynn's brother, will ride to Wybren with the news of your discovery."

She watched for any sign that he heard her and found no indication that he was awake. She believed that he fell in and out of consciousness, that at times he knew exactly what was going on while at other times he was unaware of anything. He rarely reacted when touched by the physician or maids in his attendance, and yet she'd seen his eyes open, viewed his erect manhood, heard him whisper another woman's name. He'd shrunken since arriving, what little gruel and broth had been forced over his lips unable to sustain him, and yet he hung on, if not thriving, then at least sustaining.

"I know you can hear me," she said with conviction, though she was lying through her teeth. "And I can prove it." She glanced to the fire, where the embers glowed a soft red. "A coal upon your chest should do the trick. Or the touch of the poker after it's sat for a time in the flames." She was walking around his bed, eyeing him, wondering what it would take to wake him. "You asked for my help once; now 'tis your last chance."

She touched him on the shoulder and then gasped as his eyes opened suddenly and he stared at her from the bed. Her hand flew to her mouth. "You can hear, you miserable slime!" Her pulse was pounding in her brain, her nerves stretched to the breaking point.

"Sometimes," he admitted, his voice a rasp.

"And so you let me rail on and on last night!" she said, embarrassed at her admissions. "Have you no shred of decency?"

"Apparently not."

"What?"

"It seems every person in this keep, including you, is convinced that I'm a traitor, a murderer, a thief, and God knows what else."

She took a step forward, and the question that had been keeping her awake at night sprang from her lips. "Are you Carrick of Wybren?"

"I don't know."

"Answer me," she demanded.

"I wish I could," he said, and there was something in his tone that made her want to believe him.

"What are you saying?"

"That I don't remember."

"Oh, fie and fiddlesticks! You expect me to believe that you can lie there on the bed, talk to me, and make sense, and then believe that you know not who you are?"

"Yes."

"Sorry," she said, shaking her head resolutely. " 'Tis too convenient."

His eyes narrowed and she gasped as he pushed himself into a sitting position. "What do you think?" he asked, that intense gaze not leaving her for a second.

She swallowed hard. "I — I think . . . you are . . . yes, you have to be Carrick."

"Why?"

"Because you look like him, to begin with. Oh, yes, you're still bruised and a bit swollen and it's been years since I've seen you, but . . . still . . . And you were wearing the ring of Wybren." A sudden thought occurred to her and she pointed at his hand. "Did you hide it?"

"What?" He snorted. "Of course not."

"Then you saw who stole it from you?"

"No."

"But you were awake," she said. "You told me you could hear."

"Not always. At first I was awake very little. Only these last few days have I been aware of what has been going on."

She rolled her eyes. "Convenient again, Carrick."

" 'Tis true," he insisted and then grimaced. "But you wouldn't believe me no matter what I said. You don't trust me at all."

"Because you're untrustworthy." She threw up her hands. "Being a liar is the least of your faults."

His jaw tightened. "I did not kill my family."

"Then who did, Carrick?"

"I don't know, but probably the same person who attacked me and —"

"Who was that?" she demanded, and when he didn't respond she folded her arms over her chest. "Don't tell me. You don't remember."

" 'Twas dark. I only remember riding and someone suddenly upon me, as if he'd leapt from a cliff or rock or tree." His face twisted as if he was trying to recall events that were difficult to retrieve.

"And why were you riding to Calon?"

He slowly shook his head. "I don't think . . . I don't remember that Calon was my destination."

"Where were you going?"

"I don't know," he said, and he appeared genuinely confused. And yet had not Carrick been a consummate actor, skilled at the art of half-truths and lies? This man looked like Carrick, but she didn't recognize his voice, rough as it was.

Do not be fooled by him again.

Do not trust him.

And for the sake of all that is holy, do not fall in love with him!

At that thought her knees nearly gave way. *Love him?* How had she come up with that? Though she wouldn't deny, even to herself, that she'd loved Carrick of Wybren with all of her young, naive heart, that was long ago, and she was a woman now. She could not, *would* not fall for his seductive charms again. And yet her fingers went of their own accord to her mouth and she remembered with heart-stopping clarity the warm meeting of their lips, the rush of blood through her veins, the light-headedness and sense of elation that had claimed her.

Foolish, foolish woman.

Squaring her shoulders, she approached him again. "Prove to me that you are not Carrick," she said, and when she saw the questions in his eyes, she pointed to the bedsheet. "Carrick of Wybren had a birthmark high on the inside of his thigh. I, uh, I tried to see it the other night, but . . . 'twas dark, and I felt awkward lifting your coverlet, but now, as it's evident you are able, throw back the bedclothes and let's both look for ourselves."

One side of his mouth lifted beneath his beard. "If you want to see my cock, m'lady," he said, white teeth flashing, eyes glinting a hard steely blue, "all you have to do is ask."

She blushed a dozen different hues of red but managed to keep her voice steady. "I have no interest in . . . your manhood, I assure you," she said, her throat so tight she found it difficult to force words through it. "But the birthmark, yes, I would like to see it."

"As you wish, m'lady," he mocked, lifting a shoulder. Then, wincing with the effort, he levered upon one elbow and tossed off the coverlet.

She was faced with his sheer, unabashed nakedness. His discolored skin stretched over sinewy thighs and strong calves, and the dark hair that covered his legs was thick at his groin, where, to her dismay, his manhood lay flaccid. 'Twas something she'd never seen before, that limp . . . thing . . . in its dark nest. As many times as she and Carrick had made love, she'd never viewed him unaroused. Now she couldn't help but grimace.

Carrick laughed, amused by her discomfiture. "I fear I do not please you."

"You . . . you . . . have never pleased me, Carrick."

His eyes glimmered devilishly. "Never?" He raised a dark, mocking brow. "Then perhaps I should try again."

The glare she sent him had withered many an unwanted suitor, but not this man. If anything Carrick seemed to enjoy her seething anger.

"Look quickly, Lady," he suggested, nodding toward his naked maleness, "for I don't know how long . . . oh, damn."

In front of her eyes his member began to grow and stiffen.

"Sweet Morrigu," she whispered, trying to ignore his ever-enlarging cock by forcing her gaze along the inside of his thighs, searching for the birthmark. Where the devil was it? Her eyes narrowed, but the light in the chamber was weak and his skin still slightly bruised in the spot where she thought the birthmark should be. Or had it been on his other leg, where there was now a scar? Could it be beneath the old scar? She dared not look any closer because his manhood was growing right before her eyes.

"Can't you stop that?" she asked.

"Aye, but first you have to quit gazing at it."

"I'm not gazing at . . . at . . . Oh, for the love of God!"

"Happens at the most unfortunate of times."

She skewered him with another icy glance.

"Really. As if it has a mind of its own."

"Really?" she taunted, refusing to be intimidated. She stepped closer, heard him chuckle deep in his throat, and felt her blood run a little more heatedly through her veins. Which was damned foolish. Suddenly she realized how silly her quest was. "Oh! Cover up!" she ordered.

He had the nerve, the sheer audacity, to laugh out loud. But then he'd always been a rogue. "Satisfied?" he asked.

"No, but . . . What?" Her head jerked up and she glared at him full in the face. She saw the fire in his blue eyes, the irreverent grin slashing across his chin. The bastard was teasing her and enjoying it immensely.

"I asked if you were —"

"Yes, yes, I heard you!" She stepped farther from him, felt the beads of sweat around her neck cool a bit. "Now, please, cover yourself."

"Whatever you want." With a turn of his wrist, he flipped the covers across his body once more, and she let out the breath she hadn't realized she'd been holding. "I'm just here to please you."

"Bloody hell, Carrick," she growled angrily. "Don't mock me."

"You don't like it?"

"No!"

His smile was pure seduction. She felt a tug on her heart. Remembered how it had been with him. The magic of his touch, the warmth of his hands, the erotic pressure of his lips against hers. She felt a blush creep steadily up her neck to stain her cheeks. Stiffening her spine, she forced her thoughts away from the past that was a lie and folded her arms over her chest. "I don't know how you can jest at a time like this. Your fate is in my hands."

"Is it?"

"Yes! God's teeth, Carrick, do you not

understand that tomorrow, upon my command, Father Daniel will ride to Wybren to tell Graydynn of your . . . your . . ."

"Capture."

She looked away. "Had you not been brought into Calon, you would have died. I kept you here as my guest."

"Then I'm free to leave?"

She hesitated. "I have a duty to Graydynn."

He snorted derisively. "How is that? You owe Graydynn nothing." He pushed himself into a sitting position with a strength she didn't realize he'd regained. The muscles in his arms gleamed in the fire's glow and she noticed something smoky and dark in his eyes, something dangerous and yet enticing. "Somehow you believe that I'm a murderer, that I betrayed you as well as everyone at Wybren."

" 'Tis not for me to judge."

He glared at her with disdain. "Oh, Lady," he said, "you already have. What do you think Graydynn will do when I arrive at Wybren?"

"I know not."

"Welcome me with arms wide? Offer me food and wine, perhaps a woman?" he demanded, anger radiating from him. "Or, m'lady, do you think there is a chance he will send me straight to the gallows and the hangman?"

She crumbled inside and shook her head.

"No?" he shot back. "Then let me explain it to you. Graydynn is looking for someone to blame, a goat he can name for all the miseries caused at Wybren. And that goat, should I pass through his gates, will be me."

"How do you know this?"

" 'Tis only natural. I would do the same."

"As easily as you killed your own family? As quickly as you turned your back on me?" she asked, and he was on his feet in an instant, crossing the rush-strewn floor, grabbing her forearms with his strong fingers and standing naked and raw in front of her.

"I did none of those things."

"Then you're not Carrick?" she asked, her voice a whisper, her throat dry as dust as she tried to step away.

"No."

"No?"

He shook his head and beneath the rage, under that layer of hard, masculine anger, she saw a trace of confusion. "No longer."

"Oh . . . so you want to pretend that the past doesn't exist; you want to step forward today as innocent as a newborn babe!" She yanked one arm free. "That's not the way it works, Carrick. We cannot wish away the mistakes of our past. Were that true, I swear, I would wipe away any memory I have of you. You would be dead to me, would never have existed."

"I remember you."

She froze. "What?"

"In bits and pieces," he admitted, his jaw working. "I remember seeing you. Your laugh. That you always rode your horse as if Satan himself was chasing you."

Her heart seized. A dozen memories of being with him on those hot, long-ago days cut through her conviction. Oh, how she had loved him! "How . . . how handy it is for you to remember me now, when I'm about to send you away. And yet you claim you have no recollection of the people who trusted you, the ones who lost their lives because of you."

"Nay." His voice broke and he blinked. "I swear to you, Morwenna, I did not kill any member of my family. I know not if I've ever taken a man's life; the scars upon my body suggest I've spent much time in battle, and there are pieces of memory, tiny little shards of soldiers, and weapons, and a rage that flows through my blood, but I swear on all that is holy, I did not slay my family. Nor . . ." He reached up and wound a thick lock of her hair around his finger. "Nor do I believe I would ever have left you. With or without a child."

Tears burned the back of her eyes. Oh, how she wanted to believe him — his words were a balm to all the pain that had split her heart — but she was not foolish enough to trust him.

"You did, Carrick. That much I know." Closing her eyes, she stemmed the siege of tears and reminded herself that he was a lying piece of pond scum, that he would say anything to save himself. "I was there. You left me."

"Then I was a bigger fool than I can believe," he whispered, and before she could react, he drew her closer so that she was tight against his hard, unclothed body. His mouth descended and claimed hers with a raw urgency that ignited her blood.

No! her mind screamed. *Morwenna, stop this madness now!*

But even as her brain was commanding her otherwise, she gave herself up to the kiss, feeling the sweet, hard pressure of his lips upon hers, opening her mouth at the insistence of his tongue, sensing his fingertips splay across her back as he drew her closer still.

No, no, no!

But she didn't stop. Couldn't. She let her body rule her mind, and as he groaned, her resistence shattered completely. He pushed her tunic off her shoulder and kissed the soft, sensitive spot where her neck met her shoulder.

Warmth uncurled deep inside, need began to throb in the most intimate part of her as he shoved the tunic farther aside, exposing the top of her breast, trailing his warm lips across her skin, causing the breath to be stopped somewhere in her lungs. She knew she was lost. The smell of him, raw and male, mingled with smoke from the fire and ignited her senses. Memories of passion, so long denied, flooded her mind: Carrick lying naked on a field of grass, smiling and curling his finger at her to join him; Carrick slipping into her chamber and pulling off her clothes only to touch her in the most secret of places; Carrick rolling her over in the bed, taking her from behind, slipping his shaft into her moist, hot womanhood as his hands cradled her breasts and she panted and gasped, her nerve endings afire.

Oh, making love to him was sleeping with the devil! She knew she should push him away, put an end to the insanity of staying with him, of kissing him, of making love to him, but she couldn't. Three years she had longed for just this moment, nearly a thousand nights she'd dreamed of him and just as many days she'd cursed his soul to hell.

But tonight . . . just this one night . . . she would forget that he had betrayed her. As embers from the fire glowed a soft red and the rest of the castle slept, she knew she would not deny him but kissed him with a fever born of despair.

When he lifted her from her feet and carried her to the bed, she didn't protest. When his weight forced her onto the mattress, she wound her arms around his neck and looked up at him in eager expectation. When he unlaced her tunic, she waited in breathless anticipation. And finally, when he removed the unwanted garment and she was lying only in a thin, lacy chemise, and she felt as if she could not breathe, as if the air in her lungs was caught somewhere between heaven and hell, she leaned upward and kissed him with all the soul-wrenching passion she'd kept under lock and key for three long years.

"By the gods, you are beautiful, Morwenna," he said, and her soul took flight.

Do not believe him; do not trust this lying bastard.

"So are you."

"Even with these bruises?"

To answer, she let her lips caress a discolored spot over his ribs. He moaned and she moved her mouth, tasting the salt of sweat upon his skin, hearing the sound of his breath being sucked in through his teeth.

"You're a sorceress," he said. He straddled her hips then, his muscular thighs supporting him, his erection stiff and hard against her abdomen. "But I knew you would be." Leaning forward upon one elbow, his face close enough to hers that his breath caressed her face, he tangled his fingers in her hair and then spread hungry, eager kisses upon her cheeks, forehead, and chin.

Her heart beat a wild, erratic cadence, thundering in her ears so loudly she was certain he could hear it. She stared up at his eyes, dark as a midnight sky, and saw not the rogue she had once loved but a new man, one she did not know, or no longer knew, a stranger who was, if she let him, about to become her lover.

Black hair fell over his eyes, bronzed, sweat-dampened skin gleamed in the dim light, sinuous male muscles rippled with each of his movements, and he looked so damned much like the Carrick she remembered, her silly heart squeezed.

For an idiotic second she imagined she was in love with him still, but she quickly chased that thought away. *This has nothing to do with love,* she told herself, *and everything to do with desire and redemption.*

Or was it temptation?

She swallowed hard and reached up to him. It had been a long, long time since she'd been with a man, since she'd lain with Carrick of Wybren only to be shamed. Yet, tonight, she was willing to risk the same heartache, the same pain. Though she was a woman and therefore expected not to give in to wanton sexual need, she refused to deny herself this one night of pleasure in his arms.

She had loved him once with all of her heart.

And so she would allow herself *this*.

She captured the nape of his neck with her fingers, dragged his head to hers, and breathed into his open mouth. He let out a groan and she kissed him fervently. Passionately she reveled in the feel of his lips pressing urgently to hers, the gentle pressure of his tongue as it slipped between her teeth to touch, tingle and taste.

Caught in the moment, she closed her eyes.

With his free hand, he found her breast. Through the silken fabric, he sensuously traced the outline of her nipple with his thumb, and her breast swelled, aching for more.

"Ooh," she whispered, thrumming inside.

She squirmed beneath him, her nipples responding, the yearning between her legs hot and anxious. "Carrick," she cried in a soft whisper that seemed to echo through the chamber. "Oh, please . . ."

He pulled back to stare down at her and grin, that devilish slash of a smile that increased the need pulsing through her. "Pig dung?" he asked, kissing her again. "Is that what I heard you call me?"

"Worse! You . . . you are lower than pig dung."

He chuckled against her skin. "Is that possible?" His tongue rimmed her lips, not quite kissing her.

"Y-yes."

He rubbed his manhood against her. Slowly. Erotically. The stiff shaft hot and hard as it wrinkled the thin layer of cloth separating her from him.

Deep inside she ached. Wanted. Needed.

"What is lower than pig dung?"

"You," she murmured, though her thoughts were far from the conversation and centered on that most private part inside her. God, how she ached for him.

As if understanding her need, he slipped downward, his body sliding against hers. The chemise pulled taut and his lips, moving ever lower, found her breast, still covered by the flimsy cloth. Eagerly he licked her nipple, wetting the fabric, causing her to writhe with the want of him.

He pressed a knee between her legs and she gasped, her fingers digging into his hair. Inside she was palpitating, her most feminine part anxious to be touched. The knee pressed harder and she moaned, hot flesh wanting. Pulsing. Throbbing.

Within the grate the fire glowed red hot, a reflection of Morwenna's own desire. Her fingers dug into his arms, and when his teeth scraped her nipple, she arched upward, forcing her body closer to his, making him take more of her into his mouth. He suckled hungrily and her mind spun.

When he lifted his head, she cried out.

"Patience, m'lady," he whispered, his voice a rasp as he jerked the chemise over her head and she was exposed, her skin visible in the fire glow.

Rough hands caressed her, scaling her ribs to knead her breasts. His tongue and lips were everywhere. Her arms around his torso, she slid one finger down his spine and he jerked, as if a bolt of lightning had run along his nerves.

With a growl, he moved, his knees sweeping her legs apart, his breath hot on her abdomen. "Do not play with me, Lady," he whispered. His breath warmed a trail down her abdomen and to her thighs. He touched her then, his fingers gentle as he opened her, his lips finding that delicate part of her, his fingers and tongue caressing her in such sweet torture that her own fingers clutched at the mattress and perspiration dampened the bedclothes.

He blew into her, hot, wet breath curling inside, and she convulsed, her entire body jerking, her mind splintering into a thousand fragments. She cried out in ecstacy as he slid his body upward. His erection touched her where once his lips had played.

"Now, m'lady," he said, looking down at her and thrusting deep, delving farther than mere breath could reach. She gasped, the back of her neck turning hot. Slowly he withdrew, and she reached forward, fingers digging into his arms. She arched up to meet him as he entered her again, her legs wrapping around his torso, her heart hammering crazily, desire propelling her. All thoughts of the past and future had fled. All that mattered was this one night, and as Morwenna moved with him, heard his breathing become as short and swift as her own, she clung to him, meeting each thrust with her own desperate need. Faster and faster they pushed together, fiercely feeding each other's desire, breaths stuttering in counterpoint to their frenzied lovemaking.

Inside, she was hot, melting, the fires burning brighter and brighter until they seemed to explode and her entire body quivered. In rapture she cried out, clinging to him, holding him, calling his name.

His head jerked backward and every muscle stiffened as he released, spilling his seed into her. "Morwenna," he said, his voice the barest of whispers. "Sweet, sweet lady." Fingers entwined in her hair, he collapsed upon her.

She welcomed his weight. They clung together, soaked and spent, until their ragged breathing was once again steady. Finally, smiling in the near-dark room, he pushed himself upon one elbow and gazed down at her. "You are a vixen," he said, brushing a damp curl from her cheek.

"And a sorceress?" She raised an eyebrow saucily and felt her lips curve into a smile.

"Aye."

"Sorceress!" Shaking her head, she grinned up at him.

"It's better than the names you've bestowed upon me. Let's see, I think I was 'bastard,' and 'son of a wild dog.' Then there was 'pig dung,' and 'rogue' —"

"Shh." She pressed a finger to his lips. "Enough."

"But 'miserable piece of pig dung' was probably your most memorable," he added before kissing her finger and then gently sucking it into his mouth.

"What? Oh!" she whispered as, between her legs, she felt something change, his manhood growing within her again.

He grinned around her finger and one eyebrow arched wickedly. "Oh, m'lady, you did not think that we were yet finished, did you?"

Before she could answer, he withdrew her finger, and the glint in his eye foretold of pleasures yet to come.

"We have much to make up for," he said, toying with her nipples again, his erection suddenly hard and full within her. "So much." Then he made good his promise, pressing against her once more, moving rhythmically while kneading her breasts and crushing hot, anxious lips to hers.

She closed her eyes in the wonderment of it all and refused to think of the consequences.

Damn the morn. Tonight she would give herself to him again and again, and the devil take the morrow.

CHAPTER TWENTY-ONE

No!

The Redeemer watched through the slits in the wall and bit the inside of his cheek to keep from swearing out loud. His nostrils flared in disgust as he stared, witnessing an act so vile it made his insides turn to water.

There, on the other side of the wall, nearly fifteen feet below, the bastard bedded Morwenna. Despite his injuries, Carrick's cock appeared hard and thick, his still-discolored muscles straining in the firelight. His skin was stretched taut over firm buttocks that hesitated only a second before pushing forward, driving the beast's manhood deep into her.

Curse him!

Curse her!

Curse both of their lustful, fornicating souls straight to the fires of hell!

In seething silence he glared, fists and teeth clenching as they rutted like animals, moaning and clawing and sweating.

Revolting!

Immoral!

Nauseating!

And yet he couldn't drag his gaze away, so he observed them in sickened fascination. To add insult to injury, his own nerves reacted to the sexual union, his traitorous mind playing out erotic scenes in which he was involved, his cock as hard as stone and aching for release.

He saw her lips, full in her flushed face as she kissed every inch of her lover's skin.

Oh, that her mouth would touch him so!

That her hands would fondle and stroke him.

That her lips would caress every naked place on his body.

He swallowed hard. Tasted his own blood.

'Twas all he could do not to touch himself, to let loose the demons inside and give in to the pleasure he so craved. How he dreamed of release, to lie atop her and force himself deep into her wet, willing warmth. Over and over he would take her, making her kneel before him, insisting she caress him with her lips and tongue, telling her to stand naked before him and hold her breasts in her own hands as he nipped and tasted of her.

Dreaming of what he would do, he ground his teeth together and nearly cried out from the pain. She was tainted now. Another man's seed inside her, perhaps even now taking root, a child conceived.

His stomach lurched and fury surged through him. He forced himself from his viewing area and silently swore his vengeance. She would not go unpunished, he decided; he would see to it. Familiar as he was with these passageways, he made his way quickly through the dark corridor. Only when he was away from the tiny holes in the wall and around a corner did he breathe again. As he passed, he snagged his rushlight from its iron bracket. He would not lose sight of his plan. No matter how angry he was. How sickened. How painfully his pulse throbbed behind his eyes. He would not be deterred!

Holding his torch aloft, he hurried to the small chamber he used as his storage area. He would need a disguise tonight if he was to go unrecognized in the gray light of dawn.

He thought of Carrick of Wybren. Soon to die a torturous and much deserved death. If not by swinging from a hangman's noose, then at the Redeemer's own hand.

He thought of the killing, and anticipation thrummed through his blood. He imagined slicing his knife across the prisoner's neck. To think that he hadn't killed him before now, when it would have been so easy! He'd had so many opportunities but he'd told himself to be content, to be patient, so that he could savor the kind of justice the bastard deserved.

How better a way to save himself than to have the prisoner killed and blamed for all that he, the Redeemer, had done at Wybren? Had he not planned for Carrick's demise?

What if the man lying now with Morwenna is not Carrick?

What if he's an imposter?

That thought burrowed deep in his brain, but he tossed it quickly aside. Who else would the man be? And his looks, aye, he had the look of Wybren upon him. The Redeemer's lip curled at that nasty thought.

Reaching the tiny room, he peered inside at the clothes neatly piled within. This morn he would wear the clothes of a farmer with dirty, patched breeches, a faded tunic, a cap and . . . He stopped short. Swung his light over the area again, his eyes searching. The monk's garb was in its place, as was the farmer's attire, but the soldier's uniform was gone. . . . *It couldn't be!* He'd left it beside the peasant farmer's disguise.

Blood rushed to his head.

Fear needled into his brain.

Someone had found these tunnels! He searched through the piles, certain he was mistaken. But no. Not only was the soldier's uniform missing but also a small knife, a dagger with a particularly wicked blade.

Panic nearly suffocated him, and he had to take deep breaths of the air in this musty, tomblike room. *Think,* he mutely ordered himself. *Think!*

Had he used the uniform and left it in his own chamber? Discarded it as it was of no use to him? Stashed it somewhere for fear that he was going to be found out?

Nay, nay, and nay! It had been right here. In this secret spot.

Then someone's found it!

Someone knows what you're doing!

Someone is secretly watching you, waiting for just the right moment to come forward and destroy all that you've worked for.

His insides turned to jelly and he held his breath, listening, straining to hear any sound within the maze of hidden hallways that he'd claimed as his own. Something moved in the corner and he nearly pissed himself until he spied a rat frantically disappearing through a hole in the mortar of one wall.

"Stop it!" he hissed, furious with himself. He was alone. Whoever had retrieved the uniform had not made himself known, so the thief, too, had a secret mission, a private reason to be stalking these hallways.

He let out his breath and started changing his clothes, stripping out of a garment many had seen and would recognize.

What about the prisoner? Mayhap he found the hidden doorway to his room.

Until tonight the Redeemer had believed that the man had been unconscious or, even if he had been slightly awake, had been suffering from some kind of delirium, knew not where or who he was. Even if he had awoken, he was beaten and weak. . . .

Not too weak to fiercely bed Morwenna.

Again rage burned through his soul.

Mayhap the man found the doorway and the secret corridors but has not yet discovered how to escape. There is a chance he is only biding his time. While bedding the lady.

"Enough!" the Redeemer spat, tired of the nagging within his own mind. Angrily he pulled the tunic over his head, tearing it in his rage. He began to shake, his fingers fumbling over the leather strings as he attempted to lace the coarse, foul-smelling breeches.

Tucking one knife into his boot and strapping the other onto a worn belt, he tried to push back all thoughts of Morwenna upon the prisoner's bed. But images of her slipped into his mind — dark thoughts of her full breasts with their wet nipples, hard dark buds that the captive had tasted and teased, kissing and sucking all the while plunging into her again and again and again. And, oh, how the wench had loved it! She'd pleaded with him, begged for more, wound her legs around his and pulled him ever closer.

Harlot!

Blood thundered through his veins. Pulsed and sang in his ears as he wended his way through the corridors, his feet guided as if by instinct.

When at last he found the doorway he sought, a tiny portal leading to the kitchen herb garden, he unlatched it and felt a rush of cold, predawn air spray against his face.

His eyes searched the stone steps and the boxes where firewood could be stored; he saw nothing. He studied the patches of dirt where dying plants were visible, their yellowed leaves catching in the dim moonlight. A shadow passed before him on the path leading to the buttery. His heart nearly stopped before he realized it was only a cat leaping onto a cart. He forced his pulse to calm as he slowly surveyed this part of the inner bailey. All appeared as it should be.

For the moment, it seemed, he was safe. Slipping through the doorway, he pressed his body to the exterior wall, careful to stay in the darkest shadows and out of sight of the sentries upon the towers.

He was about to step toward the chapel when he sensed something out of the ordinary. He froze. The hairs on the back of his arms lifted. Surely no one was about, and his feeling of trepidation was the result of the wanton display he'd witnessed in the captive's chamber — that and the discovery that one of his disguises was missing.

But he couldn't take any risks.

Still as stone, listening hard, he peered cautiously into the darkness. The night was cold, only a bit of moon showing through thin, high clouds. An owl hooted and flapped overhead. A few dry leaves rustled in the breeze. But there was *something else*. Something that caused the spit to dry in his mouth.

Slowly, every muscle taut, the hilt of his

knife in his hand, he inched forward, trying to determine what it was that caused his skin to prickle. What was that foreign sound? The one he could barely hear above the gentle swish of the windmill sails in the wintry breeze?

He closed his eyes for a moment, turning his mind to the sound, centering on the noise.

A woman's voice whispered on the wind.

The sorceress.

At it again!

But this would be the last night. Never again would she pray to a pagan god or goddess. Tonight the Redeemer's bloodlust would be satisfied.

He knew that she would return to her room before dawn. All he had to do was wait.

Morwenna shifted on the bed beside him, and he tightened his arm around her for one last second. Then he slid from the bed. The scent of her, feel of her, and sound of her gentle breathing were almost enough to change his mind. Almost. But as heated as their lovemaking had been, he knew that it had been but one night of passion. With the coming light of dawn, they would each see what they'd shared with new, scrutinizing eyes.

She had already threatened to send him to Wybren, and he had little doubt she would go through with her intentions. Despite what they had shared together tonight, he sensed a part of her would be relieved not to have to deal with him any longer.

He watched her for an instant, saw the way her lips parted with her deep, soft breathing, noticed the way her eyelashes swept across the top of her cheek. Something deep inside him knotted, and when she sighed and rolled over, nestling deeper into the covers, he nearly changed his mind and slipped between the linens to lie with her again.

He could not.

He had to escape.

To find out the truth about his past on his own.

His features hardened in the dim light. He planned to go to Wybren, aye, but not under guard, not with his hands bound while the horse he was astride was led through the yawning gates of the castle for all to see, not to be assured of facing the gallows or a dungeon. He would go his own way.

Without a sound he walked to the hidden door, found the latch and, as the portal opened, snagged one of the rushlights, and then crept through the opening. He closed it securely behind him and, using the scratches he'd etched into the stones near the floor as his guide, found his way to the mound of clothes he'd stolen. Quickly he donned the uniform, and though it was a bit too tight across the shoulders, he felt he could, if darkness prevailed a little longer, be able to escape.

As long as Morwenna slept.

Still thinking of her, he carried the boots so as to make no sound and maneuvered through the maze toward the doorway near the chapel. From there he would, when the guards were changing, hurry to the stable and hide until he found a moment when he could steal a horse. He would probably have to attack the stable master or convince a dull-witted stableboy that he was a mercenary recently hired by Sir Alexander, but he was confident that one way or another, he would be able to procure a steed.

Once he did, he would ride like a demon to Wybren.

To face Lord Graydynn as a free man.

And to finally know the truth.

Tonight would be the night, Isa knew, as she chanted prayers to the mother goddess and scratched a rune upon the mud near the eel pond. Faint moonlight cast the night in an eerie silver glow and she sensed that, somewhere within the keep, evil was moving, prowling about in the darkness.

"Keep them safe, Mother," she chanted as she dug her stick deep into the thick soil and scattered her herbs and bark — ash, Saint-John's-wort and rowan — upon her drawing. "For protection, Morrigu," she prayed. "Keep them safe. If I am to be taken, please, please be with the lady. Protect her and her family." She had intoned the same request over and over, and now, with the coming dawn, Isa realized these prayers would be her last.

Slowly she stood, her old knees creaking, fear squeezing her heart. She'd hoped she would be braver when she faced death, relieved to cross from this world to the next, but she was frightened. It was too early. She had so much to do. So much. She looked down at her hands, gnarled as they were, the knuckles swollen and oftentimes painful; as a young woman, her fingers had been supple and strong.

She should accept her own death, trust in the fates that had plotted her destiny, and yet she could not. As a raven called in the darkness, she took a step closer to the pond and stared into the deep water. So still. So dark. Only a hint of moonlight added a tiny sheen to the pond's surface.

Don't look!

But she took another step forward and stared into the silent waters.

Her own reflection gazed up at her and there was fear in her eyes. Knowledge. Worse yet, she was not alone, and though there was no breath of wind, the water seemed to stir, to swirl as behind her image arose a shimmering red dragon and atop his back was Arawn, god of the underworld, a hideous smile slicing his face.

Her old heart clutched painfully. She spun to face the beast, but of course no one was behind her; the red dragon and his master of death were invisible.

She quivered, her every sense heightened, her eyes searching the darkness as she sent up another tremulous prayer, this one to Morgan le Fay, not for her safety but for death to he who would try to kill her. "Please," she whispered, "goddess of death, come from Glamorgan, hear my plea, cast a curse upon the evil one!"

But it was too late. Already the lots of fate had been cast. Her vision could not be changed.

Be not afraid, she told herself. *Death comes to us all.* And yet wrapping her cloak more tightly around her body, she felt despair as cold as all of winter.

There was no cheating death. When it came, she'd always told herself, she would surrender peacefully, go eagerly through the portal to the other side. But now, facing death's certainty, she wanted to run, to hide, to remain here in this earthly life.

Old joints aching, she started for her room. Inside, she would light candles, burn herbs and bark, tie strings for safety, and, lastly, arm herself with a weapon. Though Arawn himself could not be slain, whoever he sent as his messenger would, no doubt, be mortal. And evil. She sensed it, felt it in the still, frigid air.

Bustling up the path through the garden, she thought of the bone-handled knife her mother had left her, the one with a blade sharp enough to slice an eel from the tip of his head to his wriggling tail with one quick cut. Even so, she would hone the blade tonight, make certain it was sharp.

A cloud slid over the moon.

Isa's arms prickled with bumps.

The night grew dark as obsidian.

Isa felt a tremor. Either within her or from without, she knew not, but there was a shifting.

Arawn!

She raced faster, her old feet slipping on the flat stones. She was near the chapel now, and then it was but a sprint through the chapel garden to the doorway. Only a few more steps! *Run, Isa. Make these old legs move faster!*

Her lungs burned as she dragged cold air into them, but she was close now. Through the garden gate to the path leading toward the great hall. Surely the guard would see her . . . but there was no guard at the doorway, no sentry.

Something was amiss! 'Twas too early for the changing of the guard and Sir Cowan would never abandon his post.

To one side, she saw a figure approach and she sighed a breath of relief. The guard had just stepped away from the door, probably to stretch his legs.

"Oh, Sir Cowan, you gave me a fright," she said, gulping in deep breaths of air.

Too late, as the clouds shifted again and a bit of moonlight filtered through, did she realize that the man was not Sir Cowan. He was but a farmer, wearing the garb of a peasant . . . or was he? Nay . . .

He was on her in an instant!

Before she could scream, he leapt, one gloved hand pressed hard over her mouth, his other arm fast around her waist.

She had not escaped.

Arawn had come for her in the guise of someone she knew.

Fear drove deep into her soul.

She struggled, flailing and kicking, but was no match for his strength. Steely muscles dragged her backward again through the gate as she clawed and squirmed to no avail.

Once in the shadows of the chapel, his sweat and foul breath a stench as vile as Pwyll's piss, he drove her to the ground.

Bam! Her chin smashed against the rocks and for a blinding instant a flash of light exploded behind her eyes.

Morrigu, help me. She thought of trying to scream, to move, to somehow slither away from this beast. She tried to bite his hand, but all she got for her trouble was the taste of dry old leather. His body weight held her down. Breathing hard, he shifted, no doubt to find his weapon.

He rolled something in front of her face and she saw the glint of metal, a ring. Her heart sank. Carrick of Wybren's ring. This monster must be the very same vile beast who had butchered Sir Vernon. She struggled harder, all her muscles working together, her arthritis forgotten, her body soaked in sweat with the effort, her mind screaming to fight him off. Valiantly she attempted to buck him off her back, but it was no use. He was strong. And determined.

Great Mother, give me strength.

From the corner of her eye, she saw a flash of steel.

His knife.

'Twould be over soon.

The knife plunged downward.

There was no escape.

No denying death.

Tonight, she knew, Arawn would take his due.

CHAPTER TWENTY-TWO

Carrick?

Why did the name still bother him? Still cause his stomach to curdle a bit? He hid behind the gong farmer's smelly cart and waited for just the right moment. Every nerve ending stretched tight, every muscle ready to spring, he crouched deep in the shadows.

Everyone here at Calon, from the sheriff to the kitchen maids, assumed he was the murderous bastard. People who had met Carrick long before the accident, aye, before the fire, recognized him as the murderous bastard. Morwenna believed him to be Carrick of Wybren, and he'd been wearing a ring with the castle's crest upon it.

Even he himself had accepted the name of Carrick as his own.

But it didn't feel right. It chafed and itched and caused him to cringe each time he heard it, as if he, as much as anyone else, despised the man he was supposed to be.

Mayhap it's because you nearly died. Once faced with your own mortality, Carrick, *you changed your ways.*

He nearly snorted at the absurdity of the thought but caught himself as he heard footsteps in the garrison, the sound of soldiers ready to change positions.

Perhaps your personality changed while in the sleep near death. Perhaps you were purged of all your sins.

His lips twisted wryly at that thought. One thing he was certain of — he'd not been a religious man before the attack, nor had he been especially just and good. No saint was he, but though he'd sinned, he found it impossible to believe himself capable of murdering his family.

Whatever the case, he was determined to uncover the truth and he was certain that truth lay in the fortress that was Wybren. He'd be damned if he was going to carry the name around with him if it wasn't his.

But Morwenna was in love with Carrick, and she felt so right last night. As if you'd loved her all your life.

Well, soon he'd find out. 'Twas nearly time to leave Calon for Wybren.

Gray light rose in the east, sending feeble shafts to pierce the fog as it crept through the bailey, wrapping around the huts and walls, settling over the ponds and sluices, rising in thin fingers toward the heavens.

To him it was a gift, a gossamer cloak that would help him slip through the gates.

Within the mist he heard the changing of the guard and saw the soldiers, like shadows, moving about, taking the time to speak to each other.

With a grinding of ancient gears the portcullis was slowly raised, the gates creaking open. The huntsmen, already astride their mounts, disappeared into the fog.

Now was the time.

Knife in hand, cowl hiding his features, he slid silently through the shadows, slipped into the open stable door, and found a solitary boy raking out the stalls. Whistling to himself, his rake scraping while the horses in the surrounding stalls snorted, the lad was busy with his work, unaware anyone else was inside.

His fingers tightened over the knife's hilt. 'Twould be a simple matter to vault over the rail, plunge his knife into the youth's neck, and kill him swiftly.

But it seemed such a waste. Quickly he glanced around and spied several ropes coiled and hanging upon the wall. He grabbed one; then, with the scent of horse dung and piss filling his nostrils, he put one hand on the top rail, sprang into the stall, and grabbed the boy from behind in one swift instant.

A horse whinnied nervously.

The stableboy tried to scream and kick before he felt the blade at his throat. "Be quiet and you'll survive!" he hissed as several horses in nearby boxes stomped and snorted, tossing their heads. "But scream or make one move against me, and I swear I'll slit your throat."

The boy complied. Crumpled in his arms. Wet himself.

Using the rope, he bound the boy's wrists and ankles and then ripped off a sleeve of his tunic and used it for a gag. Once the stableboy was properly trussed, he hauled him to a far corner of the stable, behind bags filled with grain. He tied his feet and hands to a post.

"Do not move until I'm gone," he warned, though it would be nearly impossible for the boy to work himself free or kick or hit anything to attract attention. He would be found only when someone came looking for a missing stableboy.

Once the boy was no hindrance, he searched through the horses tethered in the building and found a barrel-chested bay with sturdy legs and a wild eye. Not only did the animal appear strong and swift, but the steed would also blend into the forest much better than the gray or white animals he noticed. Ears straining to hear anything out of the ordinary — a footstep or cough — announcing another worker's arrival, he located a bridle and saddle that would suffice.

There was not a peep from the dark corner where the lad was tied.

Good.

He heard over the rustle of straw in the stables the sound of a dog's bark and the movement of sentries as they walked along the walls of the castle, but otherwise the early morn was quiet.

Within minutes he'd saddled and bridled the bay and, before dawn had completely broken, led the horse outside.

As expected, the guard was still in the process of changing and the gate to the keep was opened wide. A few farmers' carts pulled by mules and oxen and laden with goods were already slowly rolling into the bailey. Three more hunters rode out of the bailey, raising their arms to the sentry as they passed under the yawning portcullis.

Now was the time.

He climbed onto the horse's back and trotted the beast toward the gate. No one seemed to notice.

Yet.

He rode tall, as if he had every right to come and go as he pleased, and as he reached the gate, the two sentries were talking as one replaced the other. They both swept him a quick glance and he raised an arm, just as he'd seen the men in the hunting party do.

The guards barely paid him any notice and he rode through. Across the draw-bridge and down a muddy road he walked the horse, but all his senses were height-ened, his muscles tense. When he was at a fork in the road, he kicked his steed and felt the big horse's muscles bunch and then surge as the beast sprang forward.

Upon its back, Carrick leaned forward, guiding his mount out of instinct, feeling the cold winter sweep by in a rush of wind that shoved his cowl from his head. Through the mist the big horse ran, and in the distance, through the shifting fog, rose the forest.

He knew the way to Wybren, had heard his caretakers whisper of a shortcut across the river at Raven's Crossing.

He felt himself smile despite the cold.

Soon after nightfall, he'd reach Wybren.

And when he did, he was certain all the demons in hell would break loose.

The bastard!

The lying, cheating, murdering son of a flea-riddled cur had left her again!

So enraged she could barely speak, Morwenna surveyed the bed, the *empty* bed, where only she lay. Carrick, that miserable piece of snake dung, was gone. *Gone!*

"Christ Jesus," she swore, the grogginess she'd felt upon opening her eyes rapidly chased away by stone-cold fury.

She slammed a fist into her pillow. "Damn, damn, damn, and double damn!" she growled, anger and shame washing through her. How could she have been so stupid? So trusting? So ridiculously naive — *again?* Both fists curled and pounded the mattress. If she ever saw him again, ever got her hands on him, she'd strangle the life out of him!

She sat in the bed and thought about the night before. The lust. The passion. The pure, sublime eroticism. Her anger slowly dissipated in the dark room. Tears burned at the back of her eyes and she pulled a pillow to her chest.

Oh, God, what had she done?

This was her fault. *Hers.*

He was gone. Like a whisper on the wind. Like before.

She tossed her pillow aside and shot from the bed as if she could deny what had happened. Shoving her tangled hair from her eyes, she refused to think of the passion she'd shared with the bloody cur and closed her mind to the erotic images still conjured by the scent of sex that lingered on the bedsheets.

By the gods, what kind of fool was she? she asked herself morosely. Then her blood boiled again as she recalled how easily she'd been seduced with the crook of his dark eyebrow, the twitch of one side of his mouth, the flash of fire in his blue, blue eyes.

Bloody piece of swine dung!

"Fie and fiddlesticks," she muttered, her mind racing in circles.

How had he escaped?

And where had he gone?

Throwing on her clothes, she ignored the sharp needle of pain that pierced her heart, that jab of knowledge that he'd callously and determinedly plotted against her . . . . luring her in with sweet, sensual kisses and a touch of pure magic only to deceive her yet again.

But you were the one who came to him. He could not have done this without your oh-so-willing help, she reminded herself.

"Bother and bloody broomsticks!" She swept her angry gaze into every corner, under the bed, and into an alcove and yet knew with heart-stopping certainty that he was gone.

He'd left her.

Just like before.

"Damn your soul straight to hell, Carrick," she growled through clenched teeth, kicking at a pillow that had dropped to the floor. Feathers flew as the pillow hit the wall before falling into the rushes. What a fool she'd been! What an idiot! She had no more brains than Dwynn! Maybe less!

Full of recriminations, she swiftly went through the motions of searching the room once more, peering under the bed, looking into the alcove, even glancing at the cold embers of the fire and up the damned chimney though all the while she knew full well that he was far away.

Halfway to . . . where?

Where would he go?

A headache thudded behind her eyes as she concentrated. Where the bloody hell would he try to find shelter? Sanctuary?

Who would take him in?

Through the window came the sound of a cock crowing. She looked up and saw daylight. She realized then that the room wasn't dark despite the lack of fire or the burned-out candles in the sconces. She froze, trying to listen over the fury of her own heartbeat, and she heard the distinctive sounds of the servants already at work, their voices and footsteps. She also heard the sounds of men and women shouting out morning greetings, along with the grunts of pigs and clucks of chickens. The smoky scent of cook fires and sizzling meat and the sweet aroma of baking bread reached her nostrils. Her stomach growled but she felt no hunger.

With the realization that the morning was well under way came a new mortification. She couldn't just slip through the darkened hallways to her own room and hope no one noticed, not when all the servants and freemen had arisen for the day. No doubt half the castle staff — those who lit fires, cleaned rushes, replaced candles, and brought up fresh linens, along with the soldier who guarded the door to this very chamber and anyone he'd gossiped with during the night — already knew that she'd spent the night in Carrick's chamber.

When she walked through the door, she would have to face them — and their curious stares or smug smiles or knowing glances.

And soon they would all know that after he'd bedded her and she was lulled to sleep, he'd slipped away from the keep. Heat crawled up the back of her neck.

'Twas one thing to have people rumor about one; quite another to step into the hallway from a lover's chamber when the servants were already awake and at their duties.

A new wave of embarrassment flooded over her, but she found no way to avoid it. Better to face everyone head-on. Stiffening her spine, she squared her shoulders. Then tossing her hair away from her face, she lifted her chin and yanked open the door.

Sir James was at his post, one shoulder propped against the smooth stones of the corridor, his eyes definitely closed, his mouth slightly agape, his breathing regular. The rushlights in the corridor had burned down to nothing, as had the candles in their sconces. None had yet been replaced. For the moment, it seemed, no one save the sentry knew of her nightly visit to Carrick.

She let out her breath as the sounds of

voices drifted up the staircase. It would be only a matter of minutes before the servants would start working on this floor.

"Sir James!" Morwenna said, touching the guard upon the shoulder of his tunic.

He started. "Wha — ? Oh!" Blinking rapidly and pulling himself to attention, he focused on her. "M'lady," he said in a rush, his eyes filled with regret as he realized he'd been caught napping. "Oh, 'tis sorry I am. I . . . er . . . I must've dropped off."

"Was that before or after Carrick escaped?"

"What?" Sir James's Adam's apple bobbed wildly. "Escaped?" The sentry's gaze centered on Morwenna and she felt her cheeks burn with embarrassment. "But I thought you were with . . ."

"Yes, yes, I know. I *was* inside, but I fell asleep and somehow Carrick managed to leave without rousing me. Or you."

"He did not pass me," Sir James said firmly, but his own cheeks reddened, and she realized the man had no idea how long he'd dozed in the corridor. "He must be yet inside." On a mission, Sir James hurried into the chamber where Carrick had resided for nearly a fortnight. As hers had before, the sentry's gaze swept every corner and nook and cranny within the room. He studied the floor, the walls, and even the ceiling, as if he expected Carrick to appear.

He found nothing, of course.

Not even when he searched under the bed and inside the alcove where linens were kept.

"Call the captain of the guard," she ordered once Sir James saw the chamber was truly empty. "Have Sir Alexander double the sentries at the gates and then have his men begin scouring every inch of this keep. Every inch! Then ask Sir Alexander to meet me in the great hall."

She crossed the hallway quickly, slipped into her chamber, and slammed the door shut behind her.

"Fool, fool, fool!" she railed as she walked to the basin left on a stand near the window. What had she been thinking? *What?* Why was she so weak whenever Carrick of Wybren was concerned?

Angrily she splashed the cool water upon her face and rinsed her mouth. Mort, who had been lying upon the wrinkled bed-clothes, pushed himself to a standing position. As she cursed herself, the dog stretched and yawned, showing off black lips and yellowed teeth and not concerned in the least about Carrick's whereabouts.

"This is a crisis, you know," she scolded, and he wagged his tail. "Oh, for the simple life of a dog." Again he wiggled his back end, but this time gave up a quick, sharp bark. "Okay, okay. Good morning to you, too," Morwenna muttered. "Though, trust me, it's anything but good."

Eager to be petted, he continued to whine until she finally crossed the room and plopped down beside him. "Miss me?" she asked, taking the time to scratch his grizzled chin and ears. He washed her face with his tongue and she almost laughed. Almost. Patting the bristly fur on his head, she said, "I guess I should have stayed here last night." Sighing loudly, she pushed herself upright, found her shoes, and then reached for her wool mantle hung upon a hook near the door. "It would have been a much wiser thing to do."

The dog wagged his tail wildly and hopped off the bed to wait at the door while she tossed the russet-colored mantle over her head. The minute she unlatched the door, the dog shot through, bounding down the hallway just as Fyrnne and Gladdys, toting large baskets of fresh laundry, candles, and herbs for the rushes, appeared at the top of the stairs. "Good morning, m'lady," they said in unison.

"Good morning," Morwenna responded and realized that so far they knew nothing of the night before. So far. Soon the gossip would blaze throughout the keep.

Finger-combing her hair, she flew down the stairs. She expected Sir Alexander to be waiting for her in the great hall. She'd already braced herself for the rebuke she was certain to see in his dark eyes. How many times had he insisted that her "guest" be treated like a captive? How often had he suggested that Carrick be kept under lock and key and that she not visit him alone?

Oh, 'twas more than an embarrassment to have to tell the captain of the guard about Carrick slipping away; 'twas downright humiliating. On more than one occasion she'd sensed that Sir Alexander was in love with her. Though he'd tried to hide his feelings, bury them deep, she'd both witnessed the way he looked at her when he thought her gaze was directed elsewhere and felt the heat of his eyes upon her back when she was turned away.

She'd attempted to ignore the warning signs, hadn't wanted to acknowledge his attraction to her, and yet there it was, forever between them, making her more and more uncomfortable each day since Carrick, battered and bleeding, had been dragged into the keep.

But today in the great hall, she saw no sign of Sir Alexander.

Instead she found his second-in-command, Sir Lylle, standing in front of the fire with Sir James.

Lylle was a tall, thick-bodied soldier with thinning brown hair, a scraggly beard, and a voice that usually boomed when he spoke.

However, this morning Lylle's voice was soft, a whisper that couldn't be heard over the shouts of the cook, the shuffle of feet, the crackle of the fire, and the general hubbub of the castle getting ready for the day.

Preparations were being made for the morning meal. Trestle tables had already been pulled from their stacks against the walls and carried to the middle of the room. Benches had been hastily arranged around the plank tables while the scents of sizzling meat, baking bread, and cinnamon and ginger wafted through the room. Servants moved quickly from the kitchens to the great hall and back again while Mort explored beneath the tables, his nose pressed into the rushes as he searched for leftover scraps that hadn't been swept away or discovered by the other dogs.

She glanced at the stack of firewood that lay untouched near the fire. Though the castle dogs were in their places near the grate, and the flames were crackling and popping as they consumed the dry wood, the fire was unattended. Dwynn, who usually seemed nearly omnipresent, was, for the moment at least, missing. Probably carrying in another load of wood. Or listening at someone's keyhole.

Lylle, warming the backs of his legs, had the decency to redden as he caught sight of her. He whispered something to Sir James, and Morwenna stiffened. It didn't take a sage to understand that he and James had been discussing her part in Carrick's escape.

Get used to it. This is just the beginning.

"Where's Sir Alexander?" she asked.

"There was a disturbance last night, m'lady," Sir Lylle explained. He'd taken off his gloves and held them both beneath one arm as he rubbed his hands together. "A farmer's wife claimed that her husband was attacked by a group of men in the middle of the night. They didn't get good looks at the attackers but assume they are the same band of thugs who have haunted the woods near Raven's Crossing. Sir Alexander, along with the sheriff, left before dawn to speak to the man who was ambushed. They've yet to return."

Nothing was going right this morning, she thought crossly. "I assume Sir James told you that Carrick of Wybren is missing."

"Aye." Lylle nodded. "I've already dispatched five groups of three soldiers to search the keep. They are starting with the gates, sally port, towers, and wall walks — the perimeter of the castle — and then slowly working their way inward toward the center of the keep."

"Good."

"I've also sent another search party into the town, just in case he somehow slipped outside."

His plan seemed sound. "Let me know if you find anything."

"At once, m'lady," he said.

Morwenna felt sick inside. Carrick had left last night. Somehow, because she'd been with him, he'd taken the opportunity to make good his escape.

But why last night? Why on a night when she was in the room? Would it not have been easier to sneak away when he was alone and all he had to do was slip past the guard?

And the farmer who was attacked . . . Was it coincidence that the assault had happened on the night Carrick slipped away?

Or had Carrick done the deed?

Could the band of thugs who had been harassing travelers be the same group who had attacked Carrick and left him for dead?

The questions swirled round and round in her head, and though she tried, she came up with nary an answer.

Frowning, she made her way outside, where a steely sky threatened rain and a brisk wind chased away a few lingering wisps of fog. She needed to talk to someone, to bare her soul, and yet she cringed when she imagined what Isa would say to her. The old woman would speak in riddles and omens and curses when Morwenna needed answers.

Morwenna grimaced, flipping up the hood of her mantle. Nor could she confide in Bryanna. Her sister would try to find some romance or heart-wrenching drama in her seduction and Carrick's escape. And though she could not confess her sins to Father Daniel, she could pray in the solace of the chapel.

And what if you find the priest as you

did before, naked, prostrate, and flailing himself?

Then she'd leave. Find a private place to talk to God, hope for some divine intervention for the first time in her life. Mayhap through prayer and God's help she could force Carrick of Wybren out of her life forever.

The first drops of rain began to fall and she held her cowl closer over her face. Her pattens squished in the mud as she wove her way along a narrow path leading to the chapel.

Foolish, foolish woman. Will you never learn?

A flash of lightning sizzled in the sky. Somewhere a child cried and a horse neighed in fright.

Fires glowed in the candlemaker's hut, and the farrier was at his forge, his hammer ringing as he pounded out red-hot horseshoes. Boys were opening the sluice dams to the ponds, fishermen retrieving the eel traps. One young girl, the potter's daughter, gathered eggs while her younger sister spread seed to the ever-ravenous noisy chickens, ducks, and ill-tempered geese. A peacock screeched and preened, his bright tail feathers plumed, as nearby peahens scratched at the dirt along the cattle sheds.

A clap of thunder echoed over the hills and the little girls cast worried looks at the sky. "Come, Mave," the older one said, grabbing her sister's hand. "We'll do this later, once the storm passes." Together, carrying their baskets, they scampered toward the kitchen.

Morwenna watched them go and felt the cold drizzle of the rain. It seemed a long time since she had been so young. She dismissed the thought and walked rapidly toward the chapel. The rain was spitting madly now. She had almost reached the door when she spotted Isa sitting in the garden, her back propped against a tree.

"What are you doing?" Morwenna called to the old woman. But she knew. The sorceress had probably stayed up all night, drawing runes and whispering prayers to Morrigu and Rhiannon and Morgan le Fay and the like.

She'd be furious all her work was for naught and that not only had Morwenna given herself to Carrick, but then the rogue, true to his character, had abandoned her.

"Isa, come in. 'Tis freezing and you will be soaked to the bone." Morwenna approached the old woman, but Isa didn't respond. "Isa?" she asked, and the first whisper of dread raced up her spine. "What're you doing?"

It was then she saw the blood.

Deep red stains covered the old woman's neck.

"No, oh, God, no!" she cried, rushing forward, horror burrowing deep inside. "Help! Guards!" she screamed, praying that it wasn't too late, that Isa was yet alive, that . . . that . . . Morwenna's knees gave way as she reached her old nursemaid.

"Isa!" she cried, grabbing Isa's shoulders, shaking her, hoping for some signs of life in those blank eyes. "Isa, please. Say something. Oh, please, please wake up!" She was screaming, demanding, praying, and yet knew it was already too late. "Help! For God's sake, someone help us!" she yelled, cradling the unmoving body. "No, no, no! Isa!" She clung to the woman who had helped raise her, holding her, rocking her, willing life into the cold flesh.

Footsteps rushed forward, splashing through the puddles. Men shouted as Morwenna desperately searched for some sign of life, a hint of breath, a faint pulse, a tiny heartbeat, but it was too late. Isa's skin had already grown icy.

Tears fell from Morwenna's eyes.

"Lady!" someone cried, as if through a long cavern. "Lady Morwenna! Please. Let go! You've got to let go! Mayhap we can help her."

It was Sir James's voice and Morwenna finally turned her face upward toward the sound. Through the drops of rain, she saw the worry in the lines in his face, the deep regret in his eyes.

Still holding the old woman, cradling her head and rocking her as the rain peppered the ground and soaked through her clothes, Morwenna heard the sound of approaching soldiers and peasants as they hurried forward, shouting and talking among themselves.

"Call for the physician."

"And the priest!"

"God in heaven, what's going on?"

As they closed in, their faces twisted with dismay and their eyes grew round with horror.

The mason's wife, carrying her toddler, sheltered her son's eyes as he shivered from the cold. A crippled man who had once been a tanner made the sign of the cross over his thin chest.

"Please, Lady." Sir James bent down. Rain ran down his nose as he offered help. " 'Tis in God's hands now. Let me carry her inside, where it's warm."

Still Morwenna could not let go. She bit her lip and tried to quiet the rage that welled in her blood.

I will find who did this to you, Isa, she silently pledged, her throat raw with unbroken sobs, her fingers trembling as she gently closed the old woman's eyes. *Whoever did this will pay and pay dearly. I will hunt him down if it takes the rest of my life!*

This I vow.

She slowly released the woman who had been with her all her life, and as she did, she noticed for the first time that there was something clutched in Isa's fisted hand. With care, she pried open the dead woman's fingers, and there, glittering wickedly in the gray light, was Carrick of Wybren's ring.

A woman gasped. Dully Morwenna glanced upward. The woman's horror-struck eyes were transfixed on Isa. Automatically Morwenna followed her gaze.

Isa's throat had been slashed in a jagged W.

CHAPTER TWENTY-THREE

"Nay! Not Isa!" Bryanna face was a mask of pure horror. She sat on a stool in her chamber as Fyrnne worked at braiding her unruly hair.

" 'Tis true, Bry. I found her myself. By the chapel."

"Someone killed her?" Bryanna brushed Fyrnne away and crossed the room. Tears filled her eyes and her lower lip quivered. "Why?"

"I know not."

Blinking rapidly, Bryanna drew in a long, shuddering breath. "This has something to do with Carrick of Wybren, doesn't it?"

"Probably." Morwenna motioned Bryanna to sit down on the stool again and then asked Fyrnne to leave them alone. Once Bryanna was seated, she told everything she knew about Carrick's escape, Isa's death, and the ring that was discovered clutched in her fist.

"Carrick killed her," Bryanna said, her jaw thrusting in anger as tears fell from her eyes. "That spawn of a maggot sliced her throat and probably Sir Vernon's as well."

"We don't know that." Why was she defending him?

"Who else could have done it?"

"I — I don't know. But when Sir Vernon was killed, Carrick wasn't able to move."

"We think he wasn't able to move. It may have all been an act."

"You saw him, Bryanna. He was beaten black and blue, could barely speak."

"He was conscious enough to whisper a woman's name, was he not? Didn't he repeat the name Alena over and over again?"

Morwenna felt as if a thousand knives made tiny cuts all over her heart. "But he did not know what he was saying; he was still unaware."

"So you think."

"And when Vernon was killed, Carrick was guarded, unconscious, and lying in a room with only one way out."

"Just as he was last night! But he got past you, didn't he?"

Morwenna sighed. "Yes."

"And somehow slipped past Sir James as well."

"But —"

"After which he eluded every bloody sentry in the damned keep!" Bryanna made a broad, sweeping gesture with her arm, a motion that was meant to include everyone residing within the solid walls of Castle Calon. "How do you explain that?"

"I can't." Morwenna shook her head. The questions that had been plaguing her for hours still had no answers. Carrick's escape was a mystery. She walked to the fire and warmed her hands, but deep in her soul she was cold as ice. It was as if every stone that had been used to construct Calon's walls had been placed solidly upon her shoulders.

"Let me see her."

Morwenna's head snapped up. "I don't think you should —"

"Let me see her," Bryanna insisted, her eyes shimmering with tears. "Now."

"But the physician has yet to examine her."

"I don't care." There was a new fire in Bryanna's glare, a determination that wouldn't be denied. Not as tall as Morwenna, she angled her head upward and met her older's sister's gaze. "You wouldn't forbid me one last moment with Isa, would you?"

"Nay, but I don't think this is the right time."

"Where is she?"

Morwenna hesitated and then decided

there was no dissuading her. "She's in the physician's quarters."

"I thought you said she hadn't been examined."

"She hasn't. I'm waiting for Nygyll to return. He was called into town. The smith's son started shaking and convulsing in the early hours of the morning. Nygyll should be back soon."

Bryanna raked her fingers through her hair, tearing out the half-finished braid as Morwenna led her through the keep. The castle was abuzz with the news of Carrick of Wybren's escape and Isa's murder. Everyone was edgy and gossip was rampant. The gates had been locked and now the guards were occupied searching for Carrick, a quest that Morwenna believed was not only useless, but a distraction from their more vital mission to find and arrest Isa's murderer.

Outside, the day was brisk and cool, a few shafts of sunlight penetrating the clouds. Workers were at their tasks, the carpenter's hammer rang, and fires blazed under the vats of ale being stirred by the alewives. The weaver's loom clacked, and knots of women and children gossiped and whispered as they washed clothes, gathered scraps of food for the poor, or plucked feathers from chickens, geese, and ducks.

Morwenna heard snippets of the gossip as she passed. Two boys in wool caps sniggered as they walked the dogs. The tanner spoke in low tones to one of the huntsmen, but upon spying Morwenna, he quickly closed his mouth and his ears reddened.

'Tis going to be a long day.

With Bryanna at her side, she rounded a corner near the candlemaker's hut and saw two women sitting on three-legged stools near a fire. They didn't look up from their tasks, didn't realize that Morwenna had stopped short near the seamstresses' hut.

"A shame about Isa," Leah, the beekeeper's toothless wife, said, her meaty hands rotating a plucked bird over the flames as she singed off the pin hairs.

The smaller woman, Dylis, widow of a slain soldier, plucked a goose skillfully, her hands quick as they sorted through the feathers, piling them by size and weight into separate bags. " 'Tis almost as if God punished 'er for praying to the great goddess," Dylis said, and as if to make certain she wasn't in the same state of fallen grace as Isa, Dylis quickly made the sign of the cross over her scrawny chest.

"I wonder what it has to do with Carrick of Wybren," Leah pondered. "Isa is said to have found his ring. That it was clasped so tightly in her hand that the W was impressed upon the skin of her palm."

"And 'er throat was cut the same way, I 'ear!"

Leah's voice lowered conspiratorially. "You know, Carrick was practically a prisoner, and he vanished into thin air, as if he were a bloody ghost." She snapped her fingers. "Just like that!"

Dylis raised a knowing eyebrow as a blast of wind swept through the bailey, catching on the straps of her hat and blowing them around her face. "Is that so?" Quickly she tied the strings beneath her bony chin.

"Aye. And the way I heard it, the lady, she'd been with him all night long." Leah nudged her friend with a hefty elbow.

Morwenna winced. She knew she should announce herself but couldn't stop listening. Sometimes one learned more from the servants' conversations than from actual interrogation. She felt Bryanna bristle at her side and placed one hand on the younger woman's arm, staying her.

As they watched Leah dipped the singed goose into a large tub of cold water.

Dylis sniffed loudly. "If ye ask me, she's still in love with 'im. I 'eard she was with

Carrick afore the fire and 'e left 'er without a second thought."

"For Alena, Lord Ryden of Heath's sister." Leah's small eyes sparkled. "And a randy one she was, let me tell you. Almost as if she were a man. Had herself several lovers, including a commoner." She giggled at that little tidbit of gossip.

"She were married to one of the brothers of Wybren, weren't she?"

"Aye, but not Carrick. I can't remember which one. . . . Wait a minute and I'll call it up. Let's see, there was Owen and Byron and . . . one more, I'm thinking."

"Yes. Theron 'is name was," the smaller woman said, nodding as she stuffed into sacks smaller feathers that would be used for bedding, the larger feathers set aside for arrows and writing quills. She was tightening the laces of a full bag when she happened to look up and lock gazes with Morwenna. Instantly she snapped her gossiping jaws shut.

"Aye, that's it. Theron," the toothless one said as if tasting the name. Despite the cold, sweat trickled from beneath her cap. "The cuckold." Laughing so hard she snorted, Leah placed the singed, dipped goose into a basket and caught a warning glance from her friend. Finally she glanced up and, to her credit, turned a dozen shades of crimson. "Oh, m'lady," she said, pretending she hadn't been spreading rumors. "I did not see you."

"Obviously," Bryanna said, seething.

"Well, good mornin' to you, to both of you." Leah was busy wiping her hands on her apron.

"And to you, Leah." Morwenna's jaw grew tight. She thought of reprimanding the woman for her talk and then decided to hold her tongue. But Bryanna had no qualms about speaking her mind.

"Mayhap it would be best if you two paid more attention to your work and less to talking about the lady who rules this keep!" she warned. Anger radiating from her, Bryanna turned and marched stiffly toward the physician's quarters.

" 'Tis sorry I am," Leah said quickly. "If I said anything to offend you, m'lady, please . . . forgive me." Studying the muddy, feather-strewn ground at her feet, she looked absolutely miserable and completely contrite. If it was an act, it was a good one.

"Just be careful in the future," Morwenna warned. She'd learned nothing more than that people liked to talk and embellish stories, glad ill-fate had occurred to someone other than themselves.

As she hurried on to the physician's residence, Morwenna told herself to remain calm, to keep her anger under rein, but she had the feeling that time was wasting. Whoever had killed Isa was getting away, and Carrick, too, was escaping farther into the distance.

As soon as she had a chance to speak to the sheriff and captain of the guard she would leave, head up a search party herself, and ignore the arguments from both men that were certain to come her way. This was her castle; she was the leader. Two innocent people had been slain under her very nose; another, perhaps guilty of murder himself, had slipped through her fingers. 'Twas her duty to aid in the apprehension of both criminals.

Or just one man. Though unlikely, as you pointed out to Bryanna, 'tis not impossible that Carrick was somehow behind Isa's and Sir Vernon's deaths.

Following Bryanna, she continued toward the physician's residence, a suite of two rooms that abutted the wall near the south tower. She caught up with her sister on the path only steps from Nygyll's home, where a guard had been posted. Without any arguments, he allowed Morwenna and Bryanna entrance.

Inside, the rooms were dark, smelling of dried herbs that hung from the ceiling. The candles had burned out and the only illumination came from a single window. 'Twas enough.

Morwenna's stomach slammed against her spine as she viewed Isa again. Stretched upon a heavy table that had been covered with a long sheet lay Isa, her cloak blood soaked, her skin pale as a November moon, her throat a jagged, open gap.

A cry escaped Bryanna's throat as she spied her old nursemaid. "No, no . . . oh, God, no!" she whimpered before letting lose a keening wail that scraped the sides of Morwenna's soul. "Oh, Isa . . . nay, nay, nay," Bryanna whispered hoarsely, her eyes filling with fresh tears. She grabbed one of the dead woman's hands in her own and fell to her knees. "Who did this to you?" she demanded, as if the dead woman could not only hear her but answer as well. Shaking her head, Bryanna echoed her sister's words as she whispered, "I swear you will be avenged. Your death is not in vain. I shall not rest, Isa, not one second, until this vile murderer is caught and punished, his eviscerated carcass hanging for all to see!" She was sobbing and choking on her own tears, her hands massaging the old woman's unmoving fingers. "I promise Mother Morrigu and all the gods and goddesses you trusted that justice will prevail."

Morwenna's insides twisted. She, too, felt Bryanna's grief and despair for a woman who had tended to her, guided her, taught her, a woman who had been an integral part of her and her siblings' lives for as long as Morwenna could remember. She glanced down at the shell of the woman she'd known and fought her own bitter tears.

"I — I would like to be alone with her," Bryanna whispered, staring up at her sister with red-rimmed eyes.

"Of course." Morwenna nodded. They both had much to consider, much to do. "I'll be in the great hall." Wrapping her cloak more tightly around her, she walked outside and knew her life had changed forever.

He pushed the horse hard. Sweat and lather covered the bay's dark hide. They would have to rest, once he was assured that he was alone. By now, he was certain, he'd been discovered missing, and he closed his mind to the thought of Morwenna's expression when she realized that he'd duped her. Glancing over his shoulder, he saw no one following, and yet he'd been plagued by the sensation that someone was close behind ever since he left Calon.

'Tis nothing! Just his own fear . . . and yet . . .

His fingers tightened around the reins and he glowered at the dark, menacing sky. The steed galloped onward, and at each fork in the road, the rider instinctively turned toward Wybren, where the answers to his identity lay. Somewhere in the thick stone walls he would find the truth, no matter how dire his past was.

And if you are Carrick?

A murderer?

"So be it," he said to the wind and nudged his horse ever faster with his heels. He leaned forward, feeling the slap of his mount's mane against his face as he guided the animal unerringly toward Wybren.

He rode through a forest of dry, brittle oak trees that rattled in the wind until he found the river and a place where there was no bridge, just a narrowing of the river's chasm. Upon the shoreline, mashed deep into the mud, were hoofprints, proof that this was the spot known as Raven's Crossing. This was where the daring, upon horseback, chose to reach the opposite bank.

The bay balked at the edge of the water.

"Come on," the rider urged as his mount sidestepped and minced, tossing his great head, his dark eyes showing white. "'Twill be all right," he soothed, though he knew not how deep or swift was the current. "Easy . . ." Slowly the horse entered the river, plunging his legs into a torrent of icy water that swirled and frothed.

Deeper and deeper they went, the water rising to the beast's chest, the rider's boots submerging. Gritting his teeth against the cold, he let out the reins, let the horse find his own way. He sensed the moment the animal began to swim, the eerie feeling of floating as the horse strained against the power of the current.

Nostrils above the surface, the bay swam forward, struggling against the surging water and all the while being pushed steadily downstream. Carrick's breeches were wet, the hem of his mantle floating around him, the saddle nearly submerged. "That's it," he said, as he felt the jar of a hoof striking the bottom. "Come on, boy!"

In an instant the horse lunged forward, water cascading on either side as the bay strained, trying to gallop, his hooves sliding as Carrick held fast to the saddle pommel lest he be swept away.

With one mighty leap, the animal climbed upward, out of the frigid depths, fifty feet downriver from the crossing. He stopped to shake himself of the extra water and then walked eagerly forward to the trampled edge of the bank and the road leading upward through the forested hills.

To Wybren.

In a splinter of memory, the rider saw this road as it had been in spring, which year he did not know. His brothers had been with him, their faces but blurs. They had been riding together . . . but there was more than family comradery in the group as they traveled along this road; there was something in the air between them, something dark and sinister.

Shivering, the cold from the river seeping into his blood, causing his hands to shake as he held the reins, he tried to concentrate, to call up the memory.

Think, damn you!

But the glimmers that taunted and teased him swiftly fled.

Frustrated, he rode farther, passing few other travelers on the road. A minstrel troupe, an oxcart laden with stone, a farmer's wagon driven by a boy, and two lone horsemen were all that he met.

The day wore on, clouds scuttling across

the sky, the sun never managing to pierce the ever-moving veil. His teeth chattered and his fingers felt frozen over the reins, yet he scarcely noticed as he rode closer to Wybren. He saw an ancient, abandoned cathedral and a near-rotted bridge that seemed familiar and then passed a farm where pigs rooted for acorns beneath spindly oak trees.

Flashes of memory flirted with him, starting to form, only to dissipate before he could latch onto any clear image. Yet he sensed he was getting closer, felt that it was only a matter of time before he would recognize something and all that had been lost to him would be recalled.

He passed two boys riding in the opposite direction. They were racing along the road, yelling at each other, oblivious to the frigid weather, impending storm, or anyone else. Laughing, baiting each other, they thundered past, mud flinging from the hooves of their horses.

As they swept by, a vision formed behind his eyes. *He* was one of those hellions, riding without regard to anything except his own need to race headlong into the open sky. His laughter carried on the wind as the four of them . . . that was right, *four brothers,* raced their horses through spring green fields, carelessly disregarding anyone but themselves.

"I'll get you!" one shouted. A challenge. He saw himself leaning far over his black horse's shoulders, burying his face in the steed's mane, feeling the stiff hairs slap his cheeks and tears gather in his eyes at the rush of wind. He was ahead and he wasn't going to allow any of his brothers to win!

From the corner of his eye, he saw the nose of one of his brothers' horses, the animal breathing hard, legs driving into the soft loam, so close he felt the steed's warm breath.

"Go!" he yelled to his stallion, releasing the reins a little. He wouldn't lose. Not again! "Go, go, go!" His horse sprang forward, but he couldn't shake the other steed, and as the forest rose before them, he heard his brother's laughter, an evil sound that crawled up his spine. Then there was a movement, a flash of a quick glove as the bastard leaned closer and slapped the black's buttocks with a short whip.

His horse squealed. Flinched and bucked. He lurched forward. Lost his grip. Scrabbled for the reins that slapped at the ground and his mount's forelegs. Fear shot through his blood. He was going to fall and be trampled.

He heard shouts.

His other two brothers!

The ones lagging behind on their slower horses. Surely they would avoid a collision somehow, guide their steeds out of way. His mount shied, stumbling and veering crazily to the right. Straight into the path of the two trailing racers.

Jesus, God, no!

Grasping the pommel in a death grip, he tried to push his body back into the saddle, to throw his weight onto the charging horse's back, but gravity pulled hard and the saddle started to slip.

"Damn it, stop!" he yelled impotently. "Stop!"

The ground rushed up at him in a blur of lush grass being mashed by flying hooves. His arms ached, his back arched as the saddle slid lower and lower, stirrups beating against the horse's sides.

He could hold on no longer!

And then . . . and then . . .

Nothing!

The memory was suddenly lost to him. As quickly as it had surfaced it retreated. Like a snake striking only to recoil. He was left with nothing more than the empty black void of his past once again.

He blinked hard as the first drops of rain fell from the sky, cold beads against his already frozen skin. The four boys in his memory — surely they were he and his brothers? And he would remember more. He was certain of it. The dam holding back the truth was cracking and soon it would all come back in a rush.

Renewed, he pushed his horse forward, urging the flagging beast along the muddy road. He knew he was getting closer to Wybren, felt a difference in the air. Memories tickled his brain, touching and receding. He spied a near-overgrown road leading through a thicket. He also remembered spotting a stag in the underbrush there while out hunting. With his brothers . . .

He took a breath, easing his tortured brain, picking slowly through the wreckage of his shattered recall.

But they hadn't been searching for deer or game, he remembered. It had been early fall, leaves beginning to drop from the trees, the air crisp, the harvest reaped. . . . He again had been out riding, but this time he was alone and a golden moon had hung low in the sky.

He'd ridden wildly, anger firing his blood, the lust for vengeance seething darkly in his soul. Hatred had spurred him onward, the desire to kill and kill quickly thundering in his brain.

He'd been hell-bent to rid this world of an enemy.

Now, as he pulled on the reins, stopping the bay short, he tried to recall whom he'd been chasing, whom he'd wanted to slay. But his enemy's face was a blur, a distorted image.

Who would have caused him such fury? Goose bumps traveled up the backs of his arms as he realized it was someone close, someone he had trusted.

The memory bit at him. Just on the edge of recollection.

Who was it who had betrayed him?

Every muscle in his body tensed and a headache pounded behind his eyes. Who?

"Bloody hell," he growled. As the rain began to sheet, another memory assailed him. No longer blurry, the image of his enemy formed: a tall, strong man with a black beard, a calculating grin, and eyes as blue as his own.

His heart pounded and his fingers twisted the reins as he pictured his cousin, the man who had always thought he'd been somehow cheated out of his lot in life, a man, he knew now, who would do anything to further his own ambition.

Graydynn!

Lord of Wybren.

A black rage stormed through his blood-stream.

Bile climbed up his throat, the bad, bitter taste of betrayal spreading into his mouth.

He leaned to one side and spat into the undergrowth.

'Twas time to face the enemy.

CHAPTER TWENTY-FOUR

Morwenna had no appetite as she sat at the raised table and surveyed the great hall, where soldiers and peasants were eating. When meals were served, there was usually a buzz of conversation, outbursts of laughter, and a sense of joviality, but not today. Everyone was subdued. Quiet as they ate from shared trenchers. Even the castle dogs seemed to notice the change in the air and their begging seemed less frantic, their eyes and ears straying toward the doors, as if they, too, expected to hear something, *anything* about the missing captive.

Morwenna barely touched her salmon pie or coddled eggs, and the gravy that covered her food soaked into the bread of her trencher. Nor did she have any interest in the bites of roasted eel and onions that were usually her favorite.

She wasn't the only one whose appetite was missing. Bryanna had sat without saying a word throughout the meal. She hadn't tried so much as one bite, not even tasting the almond pudding decorated with honeyed dates, the cook's pride and joy. She'd sat white-faced and morose, and the instant the last dish had been served, she was on her feet, quick to leave the table. She had offered no excuses as she hurried though the great hall and upstairs to her private chamber.

Morwenna picked at the pudding but anything she ate seemed to curdle in her stomach. Her thoughts were both with Isa and the last terrified moments of her life, and with Carrick and how he'd somehow slid out of the bed she'd shared with him and slipped past the guard at the door. Had he bided his time, waiting until he was certain Sir James was dozing? Or had he just been fortunate enough to push the door open at the right moment so that no one in the keep, not the sentry at the bedroom door, nor anyone awake, nor the guard at the main door, would have seen him?

Was security in the keep so loose that anyone, including Carrick and Isa's murderer, could come and go at will? Or were they all working together — a band of traitors and cutthroats who were not only undermining but rebelling against her authority? Hadn't she felt it often enough? That unseen eyes were watching her? That there was a malevolent presence within the keep? Had not Isa herself warned her of just that kind of treason — omens of death and destruction?

And Isa was the one who had ultimately paid.

Had the old woman been right?

Was this keep cursed?

Was it possible that everyone she trusted was a traitor?

Morwenna's stomach tightened and she looked up quickly, her eyes scanning the large room and everyone within it. Was it her imagination or did the tanner avoid her gaze? And the atilliator, did she not see rebellion in his glare whenever she spoke with him? She'd thought it because she was a woman. . . . And where the devil was Alexander, the captain of the guard, the man supposed to keep the castle safe? He'd been gone all morning supposedly on a mission of justice, but could she really trust him? Had she not heard the people who were supposed to pledge themselves to her gossiping about her, talking behind her back, sniggering that she'd been left by her lover again?

She couldn't stand sitting at the table another second. Leaving her barely touched meal to congeal, she wiped her hands on a napkin and crumpled it into the boat-shaped nef sitting on the table. Before the cupbearer could pour more wine into her mazer, she pushed past him and headed upstairs. To think. To figure out what to do.

She couldn't wait for everyone else in the keep to come up with ideas and plans; she, as the ruler, would decide what course of action to take. She started for her own room and then paused and walked into Tadd's chamber, the room she'd shared with Carrick.

Her face reddened when she noticed the bed, now freshly made. No candles or rushlights burned in the room; no fire had been built in the grate. She walked around the bed, remembering entering the room the night before, seeing him lying there, touching him, feeling the heat of his lips, surrendering to the magic of his touch.

She'd thought she could fall in love with him again.

And she'd been wrong.

Sighing, she left the chamber. She spent the next hour in the solar, standing at a window, gazing down at the bailey and wondering how Carrick had escaped so easily. Did he have conspirators? Others who aided in his flight? Did one of them stumble upon Isa and kill her, leaving the ring of Wybren as a sick souvenir?

Why, why, why?

And how, damn it, how?

"Great Mother, forgive me," Bryanna murmured, grief tearing through her soul. She closed her eyes to block out the image of Isa lying on the physician's table, her skin cold and ghostly white, her throat crusted in her own blood, but the impression remained as if burned into her brain.

As she knelt beside the woman who'd raised her, the wet nurse from whom she'd suckled when her own mother's milk had dried, she touched Isa's stiff fingers and felt something, not life but the remains of it, as if Isa's soul still lingered.

"Do not leave me," Bryanna whispered as her tears ran onto the dead woman's fingers.

I will be with you always.

More startled than frightened, Bryanna's gaze flew to the dead woman's lips. Isa had spoken! Yet words had not been uttered.

Heart thudding, Bryanna asked timidly, "But how?"

She heard Isa's voice as if from within herself: *In your memory, child, and in those things that I've taught you. Not in embroidery, nor hemming, nor spinning, but in my teachings of the old ways, of the spirit world, of the heart.*

"I believe not in such things."

Ah, Bryanna, 'tis there you're mistaken. . . . You of all of Lenore's children know of the great treasures of the earth. You who drank from my breast have the knowledge of truth. You alone have the sight.

Bryanna could scarcely breathe. "The sight? Nay, nay, I see only what is in front of my eyes."

Only because you were looking but not seeing, hearing but not listening, touching but not feeling. From this moment forward your life will change, daughter, and you will know things others do not. Always seek the truth, Bryanna.

"You are wrong about me!"

Am I?

"Yes!"

Then why do you hear my voice?

Bryanna dropped the lifeless hand. " 'Tis a trick," she cried. "Only a voice in my head. I — I am going mad." Scrambling to her feet, she started to make the sign of the cross over her breast as she had a thousand times before, but her hand stopped in midair and she gazed down upon the one they had called a sorceress.

388

She listened hard over the pounding of her heart against her ribs, and though Isa was no longer speaking, she heard the rustle of the wind outside, the pepper of rain upon the roof, and something else . . . something that trapped the breath in her ears. 'Twas the whisper of something dark and malevolent.

She glanced down at Isa's corpse. "Who killed you?" she asked, and though she quivered inside, she linked her fingers with those of the dead woman. "Who, Isa?"

That is your quest, Bryanna. To flush him out and make him pay.

"I will," she swore, bending low to kiss Isa's forehead, and she knew just where to start. Carrick of Wybren had disappeared on the night Isa had been killed.

She would start with him.

Leaving Isa's body, she stepped outside, where the day was as gray as twilight and rainstorms rolled in one after the other. 'Twas gloomy and dark, perfect for her task. She walked quickly through the kitchens to a back staircase, and the scents of smoke and rendering fat followed her to the third floor. She passed by her room and eyed the doorway to her brother's chamber, the room where Carrick had lain, supposedly ailing for so long.

Once inside she surveyed the chamber with its high ceiling, large fireplace, and raised bed. Closing her eyes, she concentrated, hoping for some sign, a hint of the sight Isa had sworn was hers.

Concentrate, she told herself when nothing came.

She knelt as Isa would have, placed her hands on the stones beneath the rushes as if she could divine something about Carrick from this chamber made of mortar, stone, daub, and wattle . . . yet nothing came to her. Heart pounding, she approached the bed and sat on the edge. As she did she imagined Carrick and Morwenna together last night, two long-lost lovers reuniting. There was a magical, romantic quality to it.

Except Isa died and Carrick disappeared.

Running her hand over the bedclothes, she thought perhaps a vision would strike her. But all she saw was the room as it was, cleaned and fresh, the maids having erased all evidence of the coupling.

She waited and nothing happened.

"You're wrong, Isa," she growled. "I have no sight. I see nothing here. Nothing!" Flinging herself back onto the pillows, she gazed upward to the ceiling, her eyes searching for answers in the sturdy timbers.

As she did she noticed cracks in the mortar high overhead. The same kind of even slits between the stones that she'd observed in her own room. She'd always assumed that when the castle had been built, the slits had been allowed to help air move through the chambers, to keep them from becoming stale, but it was odd, she thought, for they did not vent to the outside. This was an inner wall.

She walked to her own room and eyed the narrow crevices, then went to the solar and Morwenna's room. All the chambers had the same strange pattern cut into the wall just below the ceiling.

But so what? 'Twas not a revelation. She wasn't reading in bloody letters the name of Isa's killer. She had no visions of Carrick sneaking through the bailey or slicing Isa's throat. At that thought she cringed.

She remembered Isa was forever lighting candles and tying them with string and sprinkling herbs upon them, and then gazing at the flame. Well, so be it. She'd heard the old woman's prayers often enough.

Quickly she hurried to Isa's room, where she filled a sack with candles and stones and dried herbs and colored string. She spent the next half hour setting up a tiny altar in Tadd's chamber.

She didn't bother wondering what would happen if anyone found her — they'd either think her distressed and mad with grief, or dismiss her as a silly goose, just as they always had. So behind the closed door of her brother's room, she lit candles, rushlights, and the fire. Once flames were crackling in the hearth and emitting a glow around the room, she sent up prayers to the Great Mother, sprinkled pinches of herbs into the tiny flames of the candles upon the altar, and waited for a sign that did not come.

Do not be discouraged, she told herself and tried again and again to hear the words of the spirits, to envision some kind of signal from Isa, to start her quest.

And yet she failed.

An hour passed and all she got for her prayers was an aching back and sore knees from kneeling before the fire.

"A bloody mistake," she growled.

Disgusted with her feeble attempt at sorcery, Bryanna doused the flames of the tapers at her altar and walked to the corner of the room to extinguish the candles in the wall sconce.

And then she noticed a scratch on the

floor — no, several scratches, even scrapes that arced from the wall, as if someone had repeatedly dragged something from one wall to the next. Except that the scratches ended several inches from one wall, but on the other, they seemed to go to the wall . . . even through it. Using a candle for light, she knelt and examined the floor more closely. Was it her imagination or was there the slightest draft beneath this section of wall?

Heart in her throat, she picked up a piece of straw from the floor and began pushing it against the wall where it joined the floor. The straw bounced back at her for a while until she came to the place where the floor was scraped. At that point and for nearly a foot farther, the straw slid beneath the stones, as if there was another chamber on the other side of the wall.

Her heart was racing as fast as a hummingbird's wings. Biting her lip, she rocked back on her heels and observed the wall. Could it be? Was this the vision? Or was she making something out of nothing?

She saw no doorway, no perfectly cut stones . . . and her fingers found no slice visible to her eye . . . but somehow . . .

Bryanna pried at the rocks, tried to force her fingers into the minuscule opening beneath the wall, but she found no latch, no secret key. All she got for her efforts were broken nails and bloody finger pads.

It has to be here, she thought, though the first doubts crept into her mind. Carefully she began to run her hands along the wall as high as she could reach and all the way to the floor. She started at the corner and worked her way to the far side of the room.

Nothing.

Back to the corner.

Inching her way down the wall again, concentrating on the rough texture of the stones, she closed her eyes, listening, feeling, centering her thoughts on her task, closing out all other thoughts, noises, smells. . . . Slowly she felt each stone, and after fifteen minutes she found it, a small latch hidden in one of the stones near the corner.

Finally!

Her breath nearly stopped.

What now?

Eagerly she worked the tiny piece of metal, pressing, pushing, pulling . . . to no avail. Nothing happened. "Oh, for the love of Saint Jude," she whispered and then remembered Isa's advice. "Mother Morrigu, help me," she said. "Guide me and please aid me in finding the monster who took Isa's life." Then she took a deep breath, pushed hard on the little finger of metal, and heard a soft, distinct click.

Heart leaping, she pushed against a stone near the scrapes on the floor and ever so slowly a portal opened, a jagged door as no rocks had been cut to create an even entryway.

So this is how the bastard escaped!

Bryanna put two candles in her pocket. Then, taking one of the lit tapers from the sconce, she stepped into the dark, musty corridor, determined she would learn how Carrick of Wybren had gotten away with Isa's murder.

CHAPTER TWENTY-FIVE

Morwenna was still pondering the questions, coming up with no answers, staring out the solar window and feeling utterly useless. She rubbed her arms and glanced upward, feeling again as if unseen eyes were silently observing her every move.

A soft rap at the door announced the steward. "So where is everyone?" she asked as Alfrydd brought in his damned ledgers. "And do not talk to me of taxes today, please." Unpaid taxes were the least of her worries. "I have too many more important matters to consider."

Alfrydd, forever weary, was decidedly more glum than usual. And argumentative.

"But, m'lady, we have things to discuss and I think it would be best to do so, even though we are grieving, before Sir Ryden arrives."

Ryden!

She'd forgotten that he would soon be at the gates of Calon, anticipating to be welcomed into the keep. He would expect a feast and . . . oh, no . . . "God in heaven," she whispered. Before the last spate of trage-dies had occurred, she'd planned to tell Ryden that she couldn't marry him, that a union of their two baronies was out of the question. She'd hoped that he would under-stand; surely he would want a bride who was attracted to him. "I can't think of Ryden now," she said, ignoring the look of reproof in Alfrydd's eyes. She walked to the window again and gazed outside to the bailey, where soldiers were still searching the grounds. "Where the devil is Alexander?"

"It's my understanding that Sir Alex-ander and the sheriff left at dawn to search for the band of cutthroats and thieves that have been operating in the forest not far from Raven's Crossing. Another man, a farmer, I think, was robbed last night," he said, bolstering what she'd already heard hours before.

"What of the physician?"

"Nygyll is in town tending to a woman who is having trouble laboring. She's car-rying twins, I'm told, and the midwife who would be in attendance has another woman who is birthing."

"And Isa can't help," Morwenna said with a catch in her voice.

"Aye. The poor babes chose a poor night to try to come into the world."

He set his ledgers onto the table and reluctantly Morwenna left her spot by the window.

"Why has Father Daniel not returned?" she asked. "Does anyone know where he is?"

"Also in town," Alfrydd assured her. "Helping the chaplain hear confession and then giving alms to the poor."

"He's been gone for hours."

One side of Alfrydd's skeletal mouth lifted in a sad, world-weary smile. "There are so many sinners," he said, opening his book. "Always."

"I suppose. . . ." Morwenna briefly considered Alfrydd, wondering if he, too, was against her. He seemed such a kind and patient man, one who had never raised his voice, nor mentioned the fact that she was female, but sometimes those who seemed most innocent were the most deadly. Unless one had knowledge and looked closely, it was nearly impossible to tell a poisonous spider from one without venom.

She tapped a finger on the open ledgers. "When we're done here, send me the scribe. I want to write a letter to Lord Ryden. And one to my brother."

"As you wish," he said, and when he glanced up at her, questions in his eyes, she only shook her head and refused to confide in him.

" 'Tis a private matter." Already a plan was forming in her mind, a course of action that she would share with no one, for there was no one she could trust. Except for her sister, and to confide in Bryanna was to endanger her.

She spent the next hour trying to listen to Alfrydd's concerns about thievery within the keep; he seemed convinced that someone was pilfering everything from herbs, sugar, and rice to honey, dates, and even wine. He showed her where the clerk's inventory didn't agree with what he'd calculated had been purchased and used.

He was starting in on the delinquent taxes again when she cut him off.

"Another day," she said. "This one is for mourning."

"Of course." He managed a patient, if strained, smile and immediately called for the scribe. After Alfrydd left, she had the scribe write two quick letters, one telling Lord Ryden that she could not possibly marry him, a letter she intended to leave with instructions that should Ryden arrive when she was gone, he should be given the letter. The second one was to her brother, telling him that Isa had been killed and she would like him to send help in the form of soldiers she could trust. She would give the letter for Kelan to Sir Fletcher, one of the men who had ridden with her from Penbrooke, a man who had spent years with her brother. He was one of the few here who, she was certain, would lay down his life for her.

Once the scribe had left, she hurried to her own room. Her plans forming in her mind, she threaded a belt through the back of a leather purse and strapped it around her waist before donning a warm wool mantle with a hood trimmed in black fur. No longer could she sit around and wait. It had been hours since she'd found Isa, longer still since Carrick had left. If she stayed another minute in the keep, she'd lose her mind. Yanking on her boots and with a plan of action propelling her, she dashed down the stairs, surprised that she didn't trip over Dwynn. He, too, was missing, no longer sitting listening at keyholes.

She wasted no time in seeking out Sir Lylle. She was walking so rapidly she was nearly running, her breath fogging in the cold air. In her hurry she passed groups of peasants and servants gathered in the inner bailey. She nodded to their greetings but didn't bother listening to their gossip. Let them wag their tongues and spread their rumors; she would no longer let whatever they were talking about concern her.

Following a heavily trodden path to the gatehouse, she splashed through puddles and sank into mud that nearly covered the toes of her boots.

Ignoring a guard's question about her business, she barely scraped her boots before flying into the gatehouse. Up the stairs she pounded to burst through the door to the captain of the guard's room.

As expected she found Sir Lylle seated at Sir Alexander's desk and looking for all the world as if he enjoyed his new command, as if he was already dreaming about someday replacing the current captain of the guard.

At her entrance he stiffened and stood abruptly. "M'lady, what brings you to —"

"Have the soldiers found anything that might tell them who killed Isa?" she demanded.

"Nay." He shook his head and frowned, his long face lengthening as the corners of his mouth drew downward. "Only impressions upon the mud, runes near the eel pond where they think Isa may have been praying."

Morwenna's heart caved at the thought of poor Isa chanting and praying to the Great Mother, tossing herbs into the wind and scratching out runes for protection, for *Morwenna's* protection, even as she was no doubt seeing her own death. Morwenna wrapped her arms around her waist, her fingers curling into fists, her nails cutting into her palms as she mutely renewed her oath to find Isa's killer.

"The sentries last night heard her chanting out near the eel pond but thought nothing of it." The soldier's eyes beseeched hers. "It was her custom, m'lady. No amount of talking to her would make her stop."

"I know. I sanctioned her actions," Morwenna admitted, another jab of guilt jarring her. She'd allowed the old woman to practice her own form of religion despite everyone from the priest to the physician scoffing at Isa's pagan ways. Father Daniel thought her work to be heresy; Nygyll considered her "hen scratching" and "baying at the moon" as religious nonsense. Even Sir Alexander had tried to dissuade Isa from her practice, but no one could convince her otherwise and Morwenna had seen no harm in letting her pray as she always had.

And it had cost Isa her life.

"Have you found no one who saw anything?" Morwenna asked, refusing to dwell on her mistake. 'Twas time for restitution. "The guards, did they not see anyone near Isa? Not hear her cry out? Not sense something amiss?"

"Nay, Lady, I told you — nothing."

"What of the baker who may have been up early? Or the priest? Does not Father Daniel sometimes wake long before dawn?" As he shook his head, she felt a deep sense of despair wrap around her heart. She itched to do something, *any-*thing to help. "What of the monk in the south tower? Brother Thomas? Has anyone questioned him?"

"He rarely leaves his room."

"So we think," she said, "but who really knows what he does, especially at night?"

"Surely you don't think he killed Isa." Sir Lylle stared at her as if she'd gone mad.

"No, no! But I think he might have seen or heard something! Did no dog bark suddenly last night? A horse neigh nervously? Dwynn . . . did he not see anyone? He is forever lurking about! Or . . . or . . . or what about a new mother up with her young babe? Does not the master mason's wife have a colicky babe? She may have been awake and could have heard something amiss, a noise or smell that was out of the ordinary." She was suddenly angry again, her blood racing through her veins, her own impotence infuriating her. "And where the devil is everyone? Why are they all gone this day? The priest, the physician, the captain of the guard, the sheriff — all gone. Even Dwynn who is forever underfoot seems, despite all our guards, to have vanished!"

A new horrid thought came to her. "Oh, God," she whispered, having trouble finding her voice. "You . . . you do not think that something has happened to them, that they all have suffered the same terrible fate as poor Isa?"

"Nay, Lady, you're making too much of this."

"Am I? I think not. Isa was slain last night, her throat slit in a W from ear to ear, and Carrick escaped. Now most of the people I trust are missing. Something evil is happening here, Sir Lylle; something vile and evil and hungry." She swallowed hard, noticing that she finally had the soldier's attention. She leaned over the desk and jabbed a finger at the worn wooden planks. "Someone in this keep knows something about the events of last night, Sir Lylle. We just have to find out who. Now, I suggest we should start with Brother Thomas, the sentries, the mason's wife, and the baker. Who else is known to rise early — the hunters? The steward . . . aye, Alfrydd is always awake. It seems the man never rests." She was thinking hard now, pacing in front of the desk and tapping her chin with a forefinger. "And who goes late to bed — the jailor, perhaps?" Her eyes narrowed as she turned and faced Sir Lylle. "Let us question them all again."

His lips paled and his nostrils flared a bit for he was a proud man and obviously didn't like his authority questioned. Nonetheless he nodded curtly. "As you wish." He rounded the table just as the sound of hurried footsteps thundered up the stairs.

"Sir Lylle," a voice shouted, and seconds later Sir Hywell pushed open the door. With him, being pulled by his arm, was a sullen lad whom Morwenna recognized as Kyrth the stableboy. The boy's eyes were downcast and hay was stuck to his clothes and cap. "Kyrth, here, knows what happened last night," Hywell announced triumphantly and then upon seeing Morwenna gave a quick nod. "M'lady."

"What is it you saw?" Morwenna asked, and the boy, swiping his woolen hat from his head, leaving his hair standing on end, barely looked up.

"I was attacked."

"Who attacked you?" she asked quickly.

He shook his head. "I know not. 'Twas dark and I was mucking out the stable, didn't see him, but he had a knife to me neck, right here" — he touched a spot near his Adam's apple with one grimy finger — "and . . . and he swore he'd cut my throat if I so much as said a word."

"Tell me everything," Morwenna said.

Haltingly Kyrth explained how he'd been bound and gagged and left in the stables. He'd been unable to move or cry out and hadn't been discovered for hours. Whoever had trussed him up and left him had also stolen a horse, a big bay stallion named Rex.

" 'Tis sorry, I am," he was saying as another set of footsteps lumbered up the stairs. The stable master appeared in the doorway and upon spying Kyrth swore under his breath.

" 'Tis your fault we lost a fine steed," he accused, pointing a gnarly finger at the boy. "Christ Jesus, what were ye thinkin', or do ye?" Red-faced and tight-lipped, he barely glanced at Morwenna. "I never could trust ye," he spat, his thick eyebrows slamming together. "How could this have happened? By the Christ, Rex is a fine steed and now he's been stolen!" He turned his worried eyes to Morwenna, and some of the wind seemed knocked out of his sails, his anger, now that he'd spewed at the boy, spent. " 'Tis sorry, I am, m'lady." He plucked his cap from his head as if finally remembering his manners. "This . . . this disgrace should never have happened." He shook his big head slowly from side to side. "First the man escapes. Then Isa, poor woman, is slain . . . and now this."

Morwenna's eyes narrowed at the man's speech. The sadness in his eyes was contrived. John had never trusted Isa, had often made fun of her ways, and here he was acting as if he mourned a woman he'd muttered was a "heretic, a damned witch," over a cup of ale. He was just trying to save his position by blaming the boy and pretending to care about a woman he despised.

"We'll find the horse," Sir Lylle assured her, his long jaw hardening. "Along with the rider."

"Good," she said, though she didn't believe him for a minute. It seemed everyone in the castle was inept and incompetent.

She'd already decided that it was best not to trust others with her own mission.

Though she didn't voice her mistake, she realized it was she who had refused to listen to Isa's warnings. She'd allowed the self-proclaimed sorceress to do what she wanted — and that leniency may have cost Isa her life. Morwenna also knew she was the one person within the keep who had given Carrick his chance to escape, she who had insisted he not be jailed, or bound, or returned to Wybren under lock and key.

So it would be her task to locate him.

"Assuming Carrick stole the horse," she said, and everyone in the room nodded slightly, "where do you think he's gone?"

Kyrth shrugged. John didn't venture an answer, and Sir Hywell snorted, "Who knows where the likes of him would be goin'?"

Sir Lylle thought a minute, a smug, nearly patronizing smile pinned to his lips. "Carrick is getting as far from here and Wybren as possible," he said. "He took the strongest steed, one with great stamina. I would guess he would travel toward the sea, mayhap to a town where he could secure passage on a vessel leaving Wales." His eyes thinned as he thought, his grin widened, and at that moment, Morwenna realized Sir Lylle was an idiot of the highest order. Though she knew Carrick to be a liar, a womanizer, and a cheat, deep in her heart she didn't believe him to be a murderer. In the time she'd been with him, nothing had changed her opinion.

She thought that what he would want more than anything was to clear his name. And the only way he could do that was to return to Wybren. The opposite of what Sir Lylle thought.

And precisely where Morwenna planned to follow.

The castle loomed, a behemoth of a keep with rounded turrets, massive walls, and a wide moat that surrounded the hillock on which it stood. Red-and-gold standards snapped in the breeze, and as twilight was fast approaching, torches had been lit.

Wybren.

From atop his spent horse, he stared at the keep.

Zing! Like an arrow, a memory sizzled through his mind. He was in bed with a woman with flaxen hair. She glanced up at him and smiled, as if she had secrets he would never uncover, and then pulled his head to hers.

Alena.

He'd loved her once . . . or thought he had.

Zing!

Another memory, a sharp-edged picture of one of his brothers . . . which one he knew not . . . whipping a horse as it balked at jumping a rail. The frightened animal reared, blood at the corners of its mouth from the bit, lather forming on its dark coat.

As more splintered memories cut through his mind, he had no doubt that this was his home.

He remembered the apple tree in the orchard from which he'd fallen as a child, recalled a small shaggy-haired pony that had tossed him to the ground before he learned to ride, called up images of swordplay with weapons made of sticks before he was allowed to use a real blade of steel.

Zing!

A fleeting picture of his father — a big bear of a man — smelling of ale and sex as he stumbled up the stairs, heading to the door of the chamber he shared with his wife.

As for his mother, his memories of her were still dim. It seemed she was weak, her eyes always sad, her touch lifeless.

His father and mother had lived here in a cold state of marriage where they were formal to each other and treated their children distantly, through the service of wet nurses, nursemaids, teachers, and anyone who would keep them occupied. There had been grand balls and dark secrets and a childhood littered with fantasy and fun and despair.

Aye, this was the place he grew up. More fragments of memories rose to the surface of his consciousness: apple fights and catching frogs and having his ears boxed for stealing the priest's chalice upon a dare . . .

Guilt twisted his insides as he stared up at the watchtowers. How had he survived? Why, with all the memories that assailed him, could he not remember who he was, or the horrendous night when most of the people he remembered in bits and pieces had died, caught in a fire from which there was no escape?

Because you were a part of it.

If you didn't set the fire, then you aided someone who had and he double-crossed you. Elsewise, you would not have escaped. Only one person survived the blaze, one person who rode into the night wearing the ring of Wybren. One person who has been blamed for this tragedy.

You.

Carrick of Wybren.

His throat closed in on itself. It seemed certain. He had to be Carrick . . . and if so, he was a part of what had happened.

His eyes narrowed as rain began to fall.

One person knew the truth.

The answer to everything lay with Graydynn, Lord of Wybren.

"I'm coming, you miserable son of a dog," he muttered through clenched teeth. He kneed his mount toward the main gate. "Be forewarned."

The Redeemer slid noiselessly through the inner bailey of Wybren.

His home.

Where he belonged.

Fires from the huts of the potter and tanner and smith warmed the night, casting the glow of inviting patches of light. From the great hall he heard the sound of voices, even merriment, as soon the evening meal was to be served.

Rain misted from a near-dark sky, but the cold of winter didn't settle in his bones. It was staved off by the thrill that pulsed through his blood, the anticipation of finally realizing his dream. 'Twas so close at hand.

He glanced upward, to the second story and the lord's quarters. The keep had been rebuilt stronger and loftier than before, but if he closed his eyes and drew in a long breath, he could recall every detail of that night, the night he'd heard God's voice. Even now he could still smell the scent of burning oil. He remembered the crackle of the flames as they'd moved hungrily under the doors to the rooms of those sleeping unaware.

Even now he felt a thrill just imagining the fire creeping through the rushes, surrounding the beds, igniting the drapes hanging from the canopies, crawling relentlessly through the linens to the slumbering sinners. That they had died in their own little hells was fitting. . . . More than fitting . . . 'twas sweet, sweet justice.

And redemption.

He smiled to himself, satisfied at a job well done . . . well, almost done.

Soon all that he had planned would be realized.

The mistake he'd made earlier, inadvertently not killing everyone he'd intended to in the blaze, would be rectified.

This night.

And all he had worked for would be his.

Including Morwenna of Calon.

Frustrated, he felt the same tremor of lust run through his body, the heat of desire. He tamped it down with an effort.

He would wait.

Finish what he'd started first.

Suffer a little more torture by not being able to touch her . . . yet. But soon, mayhap on the morrow, she would be his. He rubbed his hands upon his breeches, drying them, creating heat on his thighs.

Tomorrow.

His work would be complete.

And God would be pleased.

CHAPTER TWENTY-SIX

"Halt! Who goes there?" The sentry's voice boomed through the night, ricocheting off Wybren's thick walls.

For a heartbeat, he froze upon his steed. But he'd already formed the lie, and it was easy enough to say, "My name is Odell. I come from Castle Calon with a message from Lady Morwenna for Lord Graydynn." He spoke in a raspy tone, as much from his injuries as to alter his voice lest this guard remember him, for now he was certain he had lived here, grown up here as a son of Dafydd.

He'd hidden the small knife inside his sleeve and appeared unarmed. He wanted to say more, to start talking to convince the man, but held his tongue. If need be, he could pull his knife quickly and force the man to let him pass, but he didn't want to cause any trouble, didn't want anyone to see a commotion. No, he wanted to float into the keep as quietly as a soft breeze.

The guard held his torchlight aloft though a curtain of rain kept the flame low

and helped disguise him. "Odell?" he repeated as if the name sounded strange.

"Aye. I came with m'lady from
Penbrooke, where I worked in the service
of Lord Kelan."

"Ye seem familiar."

"You were at Penbrooke?"

"Nay, never." The guard shook his head.

"Then maybe we shared a cup of ale in
Abergwynn or at the Cock and Bull near
Twyll?"

"Nay, I think not but —"

Two horsemen approached from behind,
and the sentry's attention shifted for a
second. The newcomers were loud and demanded to be allowed inside. "Hey, what's
the holdup here? C'mon, mate, we need a
fire and a woman and a cup of ale to warm
our bones! Belfar, is that you?"

The guardsman, standing in the illumination from his dying torch, scowled and
muttered something unintelligible. He cast
one last glance at the solitary rider. "You
can pass," he said. "Sir Henry will escort
you to the lord." He motioned toward the
gatehouse. "Henry, you there, take this
rider from Calon to see the baron."

A man darted from the gatehouse.

Upon his worn steed, the rider's heart
was beating hard, and he hoped that the

new man wouldn't recognize him. Sooner or later someone would. He'd grown up here among these people, and surely they had heard that Carrick had been found near Calon, so he was pressing his luck if he met too many people. Fortunately most of the guards were mercenaries, men whose allegiance was paid for in gold and who often found a higher bidder for their services, many of whom were new to Wybren.

With one of Graydynn's soldiers walking briskly beside him and carrying a small lantern, he rode through the gates and into the lower bailey.

In the dim, flickering light, as rain poured from the heavens, a barrage of memories hammered in his brain. He knew instinctively where the flock of sheep were penned. Though he couldn't remember the name of the one who sheared the animals, he saw him in his mind's eye, a spry little man with a balding head and a big belly. . . . Richard, aye, that had been his name, and he had a son, a red-haired lad with a gap between his teeth and who was deadly with a slingshot.

The rider also recognized the farrier's hut, where, this night, he caught a glimpse of the brawny man silhouetted in front of the fires of his forge. . . . Timothy was his name, and his wife, Mary, was a big woman with large breasts, who had flirted mercilessly with all the boys in the keep.

He swallowed hard as memory after memory assailed him and yet he attempted to keep his mind on his duty, to act as if he had not woken every day to the sounds and smells that were Wybren. He and the guard stopped at the stables, where a young lad, a page whom he didn't recognize, took the reins of his horse. "I'll see that the stableboy, 'e takes care of 'im. Feeds 'im, waters 'im, and brushes 'im," the boy promised.

As the page led the big stallion to the overhang of the stable, another recollection came to mind, one of York, the stable master, a robust, bowlegged man who was always up at dawn, checking the animals and the stores of feed, calling each horse by name.

York's daughter was Rebecca, a girl with doe eyes, an innocent smile, and an infectious laugh. Rebecca had been the first girl he'd ever kissed, just inside the stable door.

"Jesus," he whispered.

So why couldn't he remember the fire?

If he was Carrick, why didn't he recall setting flame to straw, or running from the keep to ride away while the castle burned. . . . Why, why, why?

Tonight, he would find out.

Gritting his teeth because he wanted to flee to the great hall, he let the other man guide him. Fortunately, the guard took a path that was familiar to him. He knew just where to make his move, where to pounce. Though he appeared to be paying the guard no attention, when the path jogged and they were in a tight spot between the miller's quarters and the windmill, out of view of everyone, he let his knife slide into his palm, his fingers curling over the hilt. The guard was half a step in front of him.

In one swift motion, he leapt, held the knife to the guard's throat, and with the man sputtering, eyes wide, forced the surprised sentry against the wall. "Drop your weapon," he ordered through clenched teeth.

The guard struggled. The lantern went flying, the candle's flame fizzling out, the metal clanking against the wall.

"Fine." He kneed the man in the groin and, as he doubled over, took his weapon. His knife was at the man's throat again.

"Do not kill me," the sentry whimpered, holding on to his groin and looking as if he would throw up or piss all over the stones and mud of the path.

" 'Tis your choice," he said quickly. He couldn't afford for the man to soil his uniform. "Trust me. If you obey, I'll let you live. If not, I swear, I'll run you through with your own sword."

"Nay, I —"

He placed the tip of the man's sword to his chest. "As I said, your choice!" Eyes upon his captive, one hand steady on the sword, he removed his belt and quickly put it over the man's mouth as a gag. Once assured the sentry could not call out, he shoved him into the base of the windmill and stripped him of his clothes. The air was thick with dust and the smell of crushed grain, the room black as pitch.

Working quickly, he sliced off the sleeves of his own soldier's tunic and used them to bind the sentry's wrists and ankles, and then ripped off the hem of the tunic and used it to tie the naked sentry to a post near the center of the building. No doubt the man would be able to struggle free of his bonds or someone would find him, but with any luck, hours would pass before he was freed.

In the dark he finished stripping and then dressed in the uniform of Wybren. He made a few mistakes, wasting precious time by pulling the tunic over his head backwards before twisting it around, and he struggled with the laces of his breeches. The clothes fit poorly, the tunic tight over his shoulder, the breeches snug over his thighs. And they smelled of the guard. But they would have to do.

He slid the knife into his sleeve again and carried the stolen sword. He was ready.

Stealthily he slipped into the night and, with the rain as his shield, crept along the familiar paths that wound across the large middle bailey. He found his way to the back of the great hall, eased through a kitchen door, and then noiselessly climbed the servants' stairway to the second floor. To the lord's quarters.

To Graydynn.

Teeth clenched, hand tight upon his weapon, he moved into the upper hallway, different from what he remembered, yet the same. Rushlights burned in new sconces and the hallway seemed wider, its whitewashed walls clean and new.

His heart thudded. *So this is where it had happened. This is where they died.* His blood pulsed hard through his veins and different emotions tore at him. He'd loved her. And hated her. Trusted her. And been betrayed.

He remembered a woman. "Alena."

Pausing at a spot where he knew the doorway to his private chamber had been, he touched the wall. A sense of déjà vu overcame him and he saw her inside the room, whispering to him in words he didn't understand. She curled a finger toward him, inviting him inside, and though he knew he was making a mistake crossing the threshold, he couldn't resist, had never been able to resist her.

His chest tightened until he could scarcely breathe. He'd never been able to breathe when he thought of her and how she'd died and now, because he'd survived, he felt a wedge of guilt cut deep into his heart. He'd loved her. But maybe he hadn't loved her as much as he could have.

Alena! He momentarily closed his eyes and saw her: gold hair that fell to her waist, impish eyes, perfect breasts, and a nipped-in waist. "Come to me," she'd whispered, and though he'd known he shouldn't trust her again, he'd walked willingly into the room. . . .

"So it's true!" A voice cut through his vision and he whirled, weapon drawn. Too late, he realized he wasn't alone. Someone else was creeping in the hallway.

There, but a few paces from him, was his cousin.

Graydynn of Wybren smiled, his white teeth slashing beneath his beard. "So it's true," he said with a shake of his head. "Carrick is, indeed, alive."

"I hate to bother you, m'lady. I know you've got much on your mind," Sarah, the sheriff's wife, said anxiously. "But 'tis unlike my husband to not return." She stood in front of Morwenna in the great hall, wringing her hands nervously.

"He's the sheriff, Sarah," Morwenna said. "Surely he's been gone for longer than this before." Morwenna motioned to the chair beside her and the big woman dropped down. She sat on the very edge of the seat as if she wanted to bolt at any second.

"Aye, but he's always told me . . . how long he thought he'd be gone. 'Sarah, I'll be gone three days, and if 'tis longer, I'll send a messenger to let you know so you don't worry,' he'd say. Or 'I'll be back by nightfall; mind that you keep the porridge warm.' But in all our years of marriage, never did he say, 'I'll be gone but a few hours' and then be away far into the night. Aye, I've waited up for him a time or two, when something prevented him from returning as planned, but always only a few hours."

"This time is different," Morwenna said.

"Aye." She nodded sharply several times. "He told me he was off to talk to a farmer with Sir Alexander, and this was before dawn, mind ye." She bit at her lower lip, realized what she was doing, and stopped suddenly. "He said he'd miss the first meal, to be sure, but be back by midday."

"And now it's nightfall."

"Aye, I'm sure he would have sent word if he could . . . knowing how I worry and all." She clasped her hands in front of her. "I fear something's happened to him, m'lady," she said in a voice that was little more than a squeak. "And with all that's gone on around here . . . with what's happened to poor, poor Isa and, oh, Sir Vernon." She clapped a hand over her bosom, swallowed hard, and looked away. " 'Tis a worry, m'lady. 'Tis a worry and then some."

Morwenna wanted to dismiss the woman's fears, to console her, to advise her that everything was as it should be, but it would have been a lie. "We must wait through the night, Sarah," she said, "but I've already decided that with the new day, I'll send out a search party."

"Must you wait?" Wide eyes blinked. "By then it could be too late."

Inwardly Morwenna agreed. She, too, was concerned that something dreadful had happened. "I fear there is nothing we will find in the storm, at least not before morning's light." She offered a smile and patted the woman's hand. "Have faith," she suggested when her own was in tatters. "Mayhap he'll return soon. I know that he and Sir Alexander are both intelligent, strong men, unlikely to be duped, and each is handy with a sword."

"Aye, but sometimes a sword is not enough," Sarah said as she stood. She took her leave. For a long moment Morwenna sat in silent agreement. She drummed her fingers on the arm of her chair and tried to console herself with the thought that she had not sat idle. Mort, rousing from his spot on the other side of the fire, came to her side, and she scratched his ears.

Earlier this day she'd asked Sir Lylle to dispatch messengers into the town to locate the physician and the priest. So far, the two men hadn't returned. Nor had the messengers. "How odd," she said, and felt a niggle of fear, a sense that treason was afoot. Why else was it that everyone who had left Calon today had then disappeared, as if they'd fallen off the face of the earth?

Her eyes narrowed on the fire.

In all the years she'd hoped and worked toward running her own barony, she'd never considered how difficult it might be. She'd been tested, aye, when she first arrived at Calon and, as a woman, had expected it would take time for her subjects to accept her. She'd hoped that by ruling with a level head, firm hand, and warm heart, the people would come to trust and respect her. But it hadn't happened as she'd planned, and she'd often felt the tension in the air between those who did accept her as the lady of the keep and those who would never trust an unmarried woman to make their decisions for them.

Until Carrick had been brought through the castle gates, she'd worked diligently toward the single end of being the best ruler she could be, but the sight of her old lover, beaten and nearly dead, had proved her undoing. Everything she'd worked toward, all her hopes had not only been challenged but dashed, and it was she who by sleeping with him had sealed her own fate: She would never be trusted in her own keep.

So what are you going to do about it, Morwenna? Sit here and feel sorry for yourself? Call yourself a thousand kinds of idiot? Or are you going to do something to prove your worth? Are you a leader, or just a pampered woman with a dream of being a lady?

"Fie and fiddlesticks!" she grumbled under her breath, and the dog beside her whined. "You're all right," she said to him, though she felt ice in her blood at the thought of treason within the keep. Was that it? Was someone plotting to take over Calon?

She glanced around the room. A few servants were stacking the tables against the walls after the evening meal as a cat slunk through the shadows. The castle dogs barely lifted their heads at this intruder. Even Mort didn't seem to notice the black feline. Was she like the dogs, filled with a false sense of safety?

Who at Calon could she trust?

That question was a ghost stepping through her mind.

The people you trusted are gone. Her jaw slid to one side and she wondered if she'd somehow become the center of a plot. Had she not felt that she was being spied upon? Had she not overheard snippets of conversation questioning her abilities, primarily because she hadn't been born a man? Had she not sensed the tension, noticed the tight, disapproving smiles, the mistrust in several sets of eyes? Some of her enemies were obvious: the alchemist, the tanner, and two or three of the huntsmen had done their best to avoid her. Whenever they did have to deal with her, they were curt and rushed. And the potter was a crafty man. She did not believe she could ever trust him because he seemed to speak from two sides of the same mouth. The miller's wife was a cold woman who always fancied other women had their eyes on her toothless, leering husband. And then there was the priest and physician — she'd never known where she stood with either of them. Now both were missing, despite the messengers. Aye, something was amiss.

And it had started with finding Carrick outside the keep. He was the key. Since bringing him inside there had been two murders and now people were missing. According to Sir Lylle everyone in the keep had been questioned and questioned again.

Not everyone, she thought. For some reason Sir Lylle had balked at speaking with Brother Thomas, which was a mistake. Not his first.

Again she reasoned she could rely only upon herself. As she'd promised Sarah, she would ride at dawn and try to locate Sir Alexander and the sheriff. But she would not sit around until then. Tonight she would approach the south tower and speak to the old monk herself. According to Fyrnne, Brother Thomas had lived in Calon as long as anyone, and there was a chance that from his position high above the bailey, he had witnessed something out of the ordinary the night before.

She only hoped he hadn't taken a vow of silence!

"Just get on the damned horse!" The voice was loud. Imperious. Used to giving commands.

Alexander wanted to fight. To take his sword and run the thug through, but it was too late for that. Blindfolded, he climbed upon the steed — his horse, he thought, for the saddle felt familiar and the animal's gait was the same steady walk he was used to. That at least was something — to be upon his own steed.

But not enough, he feared, his hands bound, his jaw aching with a blinding pain.

He and the sheriff, thinking they were going to the aid of a farmer who'd been the victim of a vicious attack, had instead been played for fools. They'd come to the farmer's house at dawn and pounded loudly on the door.

When no one had answered, they'd

broken down the door and found the farmer in the center of the room, chickens, pigs, and goats running free around him on the packed dirt floor. The fire was no longer burning, but they'd seen that the man was beaten to a pulp, his hands and ankles bound and tied together, a rope strung through his blood-crusted mouth.

The farmer had yelled as they entered, his eyes widening in horror. Too late Alexander had realized he and Payne had walked into a trap. They'd been attacked from behind. Been hit hard enough upon their heads to send both he and Payne to their knees. Chickens had squawked and scattered; a goat bleated and ran over his legs in terror. A blackness had pulled at his brain, though he'd managed somehow not to lose consciousness.

He'd tried to stand and whirl, to lash out with his sword, but the men — and there had been many of them — had quickly knocked him down again, his face hitting the hard, packed earth. Before he could react, they'd covered his head with a rough sack and stripped him of his weapon. Roaring, he'd managed to fling himself to his feet and swing around, kicking hard and wounding one of his would-be captors. He'd heard the man howl in pain before someone hissed, "Bloody stinking bastard!"

Bam!

A bootheel had cracked hard against his jaw.

Blinding pain had burst though his head. His teeth had rattled and his legs had finally given out. He'd gone down like a mortally wounded stag, falling to his knees again. Before he could breathe his hands were jerked roughly together and his wrists bound with leather straps that slashed deep into his flesh. A gag had been forced over the bag and pulled tight about his head.

"There ya go, mate, trussed up like a damned Christmas goose!" the same foul-breathed man had said before cackling at his own pathetic joke.

Such mortification.

Now, hands tied behind his back, his mouth aching as he sat astride the horse, he strained his ears. The men were talking, but he could not identify any of the voices. He wasn't even certain that Payne had been brought along with this party of thugs, but Alexander thought he must still be in the ragtag party. He fervently hoped they were together, that somehow they could overcome their attackers.

And how will you do that, captain of the damned guard?

His big shoulders slumped. By the saints, he'd failed.

Not only himself and the keep, but Lady Morwenna, the woman who depended upon him, the woman he loved.

Aye, he was a sorry specimen for captain of the guard of Calon Keep. The days of wishing that he were of a noble station, that he could dare ask the lady to be his wife, had been as easily stripped from him as his own sword. In truth, that particular dream seemed a lifetime ago, as if it had happened to another man.

Don't give up!

Fight, damn it!

You owe it to her!

To yourself!

You may yet find a way to get out of this.

You have to!

Despite the pain, Alexander tried to concentrate, to keep his wits about him. Where were these cutthroats taking him and why? He knew not in which direction they were riding, but he smelled the scent of wet bark and leaves over the smell of rain. Straining to hear, he listened hard and a few of the words whispered between the men came to his ears. Some were unintelligible, but others were clear. "Calon" and "Carrick" and "vengeance" all were mentioned.

What did they mean?

Dear God, what was their plan?

Had this band of thugs lured them out into the night only to return them to Calon to be ransomed? Nay, that seemed unlikely. 'Twas too risky and had nothing to do with Carrick or revenge. The wheels in his mind turned and he tried to climb inside the thoughts of the men who had ambushed him.

Did the criminals plan to kill both the sheriff and himself? Perhaps for sport or to make a point to others who tried to stop their thievery? What better way to flaunt their authority and prove how clever and invincible they were than to slay the captain of an army and the sheriff?

But it seemed far-fetched.

He listened to the steady plop of the horses' hooves in the mud and felt the sting of rain upon his face. Suddenly, without provocation, the truth hit him.

Like a punch in the gut.

He and the sheriff weren't going to be taken to the castle for an exchange of prisoners or money. Nor were they going to be murdered outright, at least not yet.

Nay.

He knew in his heart they were being taken back to Calon for one purpose only.

To be used as bait.

CHAPTER TWENTY-SEVEN

Morwenna half ran up the stairs, her dog following at her heels. The walls of the great hall had seemed to shrink and she couldn't sit still another second.

She hadn't lied when she'd told Sarah that she was forming a party to leave at dawn. She planned to take five of the best men she could find within the ranks of the soldiers. She only hoped that the missing men would arrive by morning. Maybe they'd have Carrick, that cur, with them. Oh, she'd love to face him again! Tell him what she thought.

And what is that, Morwenna?

What do you think of him?

Do you imagine that if he were here, standing in front of you right here and now, you would not fall victim to his charms again?

"Damn it all." She wouldn't think of Carrick, mangy rat that he was, not now. At the moment she had to concentrate on finding the captain of the guard and the sheriff. What she'd said to Sarah was true:

stronger or smarter men did not exist in Calon. If Sir Alexander and Payne had met with ill fate, she doubted she and the lesser men she would ride with could triumph.

But she'd try.

And then she'd ride to Wybren, not only to tell Graydynn what she'd done, how she'd lost the man he'd been searching for, but also to see if, as she suspected, Carrick had ridden to the very keep where he was considered a wanted man, a criminal accused of treachery and murder.

But first she would seek out Brother Thomas.

At the top of the stairs she paused before walking to her sister's door. Biting her lip, she knocked softly on the heavy door and waited. "Bryanna?" she called, but there wasn't a sound coming from inside the room. "Are you all right?"

Still her sister didn't answer. Bryanna had been holed up in her chamber for most of the day, ever since viewing Isa's body, and Morwenna had let her sister be.

Now she placed a hand on the door handle, but before she entered she changed her mind. Bryanna just needed time alone to accept Isa's death. Morwenna would give her that time. She understood Bryanna needed to face the hole in her life

Isa's passing had created. Later Morwenna would tell her sister of her plans to lead a search party. She only hoped Bryanna would not insist upon coming along.

In her own chamber, Morwenna tossed on a squirrel-lined cape and slid her shoes into her wooden pattens, as her boots were drying by the fire. Grabbing a lantern from a shelf, she carried it with her as she clomped down the stairs, Mort still at her heels. Once on the ground floor she headed out the main door, where a guard, Peter, tried to suggest she wait for an escort. "You should have someone with you, m'lady," he said, his gray eyes filled with worry. "Think of Isa last night."

"I'll be fine," she assured him. She didn't mention that she had a dagger in the leather purse cinched by a strap to her waist, nor the tiny knife in her shoe.

Outside, a storm raged. Thick dark clouds blocked the moon. Rain peppered the ground and washed down in little gullies, cutting into the pathways of the keep. Mort, beside her, stepped outside, blinked and shivered, and then promptly turned around. Tail between his legs, he bolted toward the fire in the great hall.

"A fine watchdog you are if a little bit of rain scares you," Morwenna muttered as she made her way along the rock-strewn trails, her lantern seemingly feeble and small.

Nerves stretched thin, Morwenna picked her way past huts where firelight shone from the windows. She passed by the sheriff's quarters and saw Sarah by the fire, sadly mending a pair of breeches.

Quickly sketching the sign of the cross over her chest, Morwenna sent up a prayer for Alexander and Payne's safe return. Crossing the grass beneath an orchard, she thought about the others who were missing also and belatedly mentioned Nygyll, Father Daniel, and Dwynn in her prayers as well.

The south tower, stretching skyward at the corner of the wall walk, was the tallest in the keep. A watch turret rose even higher from the tower's battlements, seeming to pierce the sky.

By the time Morwenna reached the tower doorway, the flame on her candle had died and she had to relight it from a sconce inside the tower.

Leftover rain dripping from her cape, she began climbing ever upward, the spiraling staircase seeming without end. Her own shadow fell against the thick walls, and aside from the scrape of rodents' claws and the pounding of the rain, she heard nothing.

When was the last time she'd seen Brother Thomas? Had he come down to eat for the Christmas Revels? She didn't think so, and remembering the Revels reminded her that the deadly fire at Wybren had been set a year earlier on Christmas Eve.

The people who had later died that night had been celebrating, probably singing and dancing and passing the wassail bowl. Mayhap they'd been entertained by a passing troupe of mummers while warming themselves at a great yule log . . . only to end up dead, hopefully dying from breathing smoke before the ravenous flames were upon them.

Shuddering at her thoughts, she continued ever upward and reminded herself that Carrick had escaped the blaze at Wybren . . . just as he had found his way out of his room at Calon. . . .

Refusing to dwell on the bastard, she climbed faster, passing several vacant hermits' cells on her way up before finally stopping at the cell located at the highest point, just before one final flight of stairs narrowed to the watch turret.

'Twas time. Inhaling a breath of fortitude, she rapped upon the door to Brother Thomas's cell.

She waited but heard no response.

"Brother Thomas?" she called, knocking more loudly. She'd spoken to the man only once, in the first week she'd arrived, climbing this very staircase to make certain she met everyone within the keep. What she knew of him she'd learned from others — Alfrydd, Alexander, and Fyrnne — who had known him for years. "Brother Thomas, it's Lady Morwenna. May I come in?"

Again there was no answer.

Refusing to give up, she tested the door and found it unlocked. "Brother Thomas?" she called one more time and then pushed the creaking door open.

Inside, the monk knelt, head bent in prayer, his fingers sliding skillfully over the beads of a rosary. A single candle sat in a holder on a three-legged stool, its tiny flame casting the compact room with a dim, flickering light. Aside from the cot, stool, and pail, there were no furnishings. The only adornment upon the walls was a wooden cross nailed over the bed and two small hooks that held nothing. She waited in the doorway, and when he'd finished his prayers, he turned to her and nodded his head.

"M'lady," he said, pulling himself to a

standing position. Once a tall man, he appeared to have shriveled and become stooped, his skin sinking into his bones. With a monk's tonsure, snowy beard, nose hooked like an eagle's beak, and eyes as black as night, he wore a brown robe tied with a rope and looked a hundred years old if a day. "What can I do for you?" he asked in a voice that cracked like dry straw.

"I'm trying to find out what happened to my nursemaid, Isa," Morwenna said. "She was killed last night. Slain by an unknown assassin. I thought mayhap you had heard something or saw something that might help me locate whoever did this. I know — I mean, Sir Alexander has mentioned that sometimes you climb up to the turret for fresh air in the middle of the night."

" 'Tis true." He nodded, his wrinkled face a mask of patience. "And, aye, I was outside last night searching for the stars, hoping for a glimpse of moon." He sighed sadly. "I heard her pagan prayers whispering on the wind." He hung the rosary on a hook over his bed, and she noticed his white, nearly translucent skin stretching taut over the bones and cords of his hands. "Sometimes I think God handles heresy in His own way."

"You think God killed her?" she said, horrified.

"Nay . . . you misunderstand me. . . ." He held up a hand.

"I hope so, Brother Thomas, because someone actually slit Isa's throat last night, sliced it in the shape of a W, dropped Carrick of Wybren's ring into her hand, and then disappeared. Whoever it was, he left her to bleed to death, like some kind of sacrificial lamb." Anger began to thrum through her bloodstream again. "I want that person found and brought to justice."

"Your justice," he said.

"And God's. Whoever killed her committed a mortal sin." She took a step toward the stooped man. "Now, please, Brother Thomas, tell me what you saw last night."

He shook his head. "I saw little. 'Twas dark, you know. I heard her chanting and I looked toward the sound. My hearing's not what it used to be, but I think she was near the ponds. Then she stopped, not abruptly, not as if someone attacked her, but as if she was finished with her talk. It was late. I was tired. And I didn't want to hear any more of her blasphemy if she started up again, so I walked down the staircase and into my room."

"And that's all? You saw or heard no one else?"

"I told you all I know."

Her shoulders slumped in disappointment and she mentally chided herself. What had she expected? That this man had actually witnessed the deed and then never said a word?

"A man escaped last night," she told him.

"Carrick of Wybren," he said. Morwenna's head snapped up and he added, "I hear the guards talking. They are right above me, you know. Their conversation often drifts through my window. And the boys who bring up my food and water, they, too, gossip. They seem to think he vanished into thin air, like that." He snapped his fingers and managed a kind smile. "I'm sorry, m'lady, but I did not see Carrick leave, nor did I witness the death of your nursemaid."

She waited, sensing he was about to say more. When he didn't, she prodded him. "But you hesitate, Brother Thomas. As if you know something."

His eyebrows quirked upward and he studied the floor for a second.

"You do!" she charged, her weariness suddenly gone. "What is it, Brother Thomas?" When he paused, she wanted to step forward and shake whatever it was from his tongue. "Please, you must tell me.

For the safety of everyone in the keep."

"I've lived here long," he said, obviously wrestling with his decision to speak. "In fact, I've lived here longer than most. Perhaps the longest. I was here as a lad, long before I found my calling."

"Yes," she prodded when he hesitated.

"My grandfather was the mason who constructed this keep." His lips folded over his teeth for a second, and he rolled his eyes to the ceiling as if searching for a sign from above before speaking.

It was difficult to wait, not in Morwenna's nature at all. But she sensed the monk was choosing his words with care. She needed to be patient.

"My grandfather designed this castle for Lord Spencer," Brother Thomas continued at length. "Lord Spencer required a . . . unique set of hallways within hallways within the great hall."

"Hallways within hallways?"

"Aye. Secret passageways and rooms that only the lord knew about. Originally the lord said they were to be used in case of an attack, as a place to hide from the enemy, or even a way in which the lord could escape, get away unnoticed, but it was a lie. When all was said and done, my grandfather realized most of the hallways were used as viewing areas, places where the lord could spy unseen upon his guests or his wife."

"What? Spy unseen?"

"Yes, from the hidden chambers."

"But where are they?"

"I know not. I . . . I only know what I heard growing up in my family. I've never seen them for myself, never tried, nor, do I think, did my father or any of his brothers."

"But someone knows," she whispered, the hairs at the back of her neck rising as she remembered how often she'd felt unseen eyes upon her, how she'd thought someone was observing her in her chamber as she'd slept or dressed or bathed. Anger surged through her.

"For years, all of my lifetime, no one that I know of has used the hallways, and even the rumors of them have died. Anyone who talked of it always thought it was a joke or . . . or a legend . . . one that was fabricated to begin with and enhanced as the years went on." He stepped to the wall and leaned his back against it. "But now, I fear, those hallways have been discovered and used." His eyes found hers. "It explains so much."

"Yes," she said, trying to imagine who

had the knowledge of the secret rooms.

"After Sir Vernon was killed, I wondered. Through gossip I learned no one could understand how the killer got away so quickly and completely. I didn't say anything because I thought the killer might just be clever. But then Isa . . . ."

And Carrick.

"Then we must find the hallways," she said, already thinking ahead, her blood pumping at the thought of discovering the killer's lair, his escape route, his identity!

Brother Thomas sighed and made a sign of the cross over his chest. "My grandfather's fear was that his architectural masterpiece would be used for evil and so, it seems, it has."

"You must help me find them, the rooms, the hallways, the . . . what? Secret doors?"

"As I said, Lady, I know not where they are or how to access them, just that they exist."

Was it possible? The idea seemed outrageous, yet . . . Her skin crawled at the thought of someone lurking in the shadows, ever watching, coming and going at will.

Carrick?

Is that how he escaped?

445

Did he know of Calon's secrets?

Could he have left his room and killed both Vernon and Isa?

Her stomach wrenched, but she wouldn't believe it. Nay, nay, nay! There was someone else. There had to be.

"Come with me," she said to the old monk.

"Nay, I must stay here."

"Not tonight, Brother Thomas."

"I have a duty to God. A promise to keep."

Her fingers circled his wrist. "And you will not break it, but tonight, Brother Thomas, you will come with me and we will find these lost secret tunnels and rooms or whatever. I have a feeling it's God's will." His eyes rounded at her blasphemy, but she ignored it. She was done with following a strict code of conduct — it had never fit her anyway. She was always breaking the rules, so tonight would not be that much different.

Her lantern swinging, she tugged on the old man's arms and helped him down the stairs. "Heathens and heretics," she whispered under her breath.

"What say you?"

"Nothing, Brother Thomas," she said. "Come along."

446

"M'lady, really, I have no idea where to start looking."

She wasn't deterred. "I do," she said and thought of the chamber where just last night she'd given herself so eagerly to Carrick of Wybren.

"I didn't kill them," he said as he stood in the hallway outside the lord's quarters at Wybren. He glared at his cousin and the handful of men behind him — huge bodyguards with their swords glinting wickedly in the dim light from the candles mounted upon the walls. "I didn't kill them," he repeated, stepping forward, "but you did."

"I?" Graydynn, weapon drawn, shook his head and laughed. "Oh, no, Carrick, you'll not pin your crimes on me!"

"Who is the one person who has profited from all their deaths?" he demanded. "Certainly not me." He walked closer, suddenly unafraid of Graydynn's blade. Graydynn's eyes met his, and a perplexed look crossed his features as he scrutinized his face. " 'Twas not I nor anyone else who set the blaze, but you. Now you are Lord of Wybren, Graydynn, but before the fire, what were you?"

"This is madness!" But there was distraction in his proclamation.

"I think not." His gaze drilled into that of the baron. Did he see something flicker in Graydynn's eyes, a bit of guilt? Was there just a fleck of spittle at the corner of his mouth? Did one of his eyelids twitch slightly?

"Do not try to turn the tables on me. Use none of your tricks, Carrick." Graydynn stumbled over the name, and his eyes narrowed a fraction as he studied his cousin. "They won't work here. You, in fact, are not just a trespasser, but also a murderer and a traitor." His words seemed to bolster him, to restore his own sense of power. "Did you not think I expected you? If not this night, then one soon thereafter? I knew of the attack against you, heard through my spies that the idiot Lady of Calon gave you refuge and helped heal you! But I knew once you were strong and able you would return here." A thin smile played upon lips buried within the nest of his beard. "Why do you think you were allowed through the gates so easily?" he asked. "Hmmm? Why was only one simpleton of a guard allowed to escort you to the great hall? Did you really think I would just sit and wait for you to burst in, sword drawn, making the outrageous claims I knew you would? Didn't you know that I expected you to outfox that one sentry? Where is he? In the potter's hut?" He snapped his fingers and cocked his head to one side. "No, my guess is that I'll find him in the mill."

So, it had been a trap. Graydynn had set him up! Jaw tight, he poised for the fight bound to come. He looked for a chance, just one moment's hesitation, to best Graydynn.

As if he could read his enemy's thoughts, Graydynn grinned and a sparkle of invention came to his eye.

"And don't expect anyone here to believe that you and I were . . . what? In league together? I see the lie forming in your eyes, Carrick." He waved a hand near his head as if the idea had just occurred to him, but there was more to his words, an underlying warning, and yet more than that, too: Graydynn was worried. He went on, but it seemed as if it was for the benefit of the guards, as if Graydynn was playing a part. "I suppose you were going to say that I was the one who came up with the plot to kill your family and you were but the henchman, willing to do whatever I asked."

That caught his attention. "What are you saying?" he demanded.

"No one here will ever believe you, Carrick!"

But there was something there. Something in Graydynn's words that he had not considered. "You are saying you and Carrick plotted the fire together —"

"I said that ploy would not work!" Graydynn declared loudly. He swept his free arm toward the guards standing ready behind him. "We all know of your lies."

Something was wrong here, something he was missing. Something very important. "You are blaming Carrick for your own deeds," he said slowly.

From below came the sound of shouts and footsteps. "Lord Graydynn," a deep voice called up the staircase. "Lord Graydynn! We've caught him! We've caught the spy!"

"Now what?" Graydynn glowered and pointed an accusing finger at his cousin. "Seize him and bring him downstairs!"

Now was his chance! In motion as the thought crossed his mind, he spun and broke into a run, his sword swinging in a wide arc in front of him. The guards sidestepped his blade and then thundered after him. "Halt!" a guard cried.

"Go to bloody hell!"

He was tackled from behind, a body slamming into his before he reached the doorway. He and his attacker fell together.

His sword flew from his hand. He tried to lunge forward, but the guard atop him put a knee into his back and his spine popped. Fighting with every inch of strength, he nearly broke free, but another guard threw his weight upon both of the struggling men.

Smack!

His face smashed against the floor.

He tasted blood.

Within seconds his hands were lashed by thick rawhide cords, his arms forced against his body. A gag was thrust into his mouth and roughly tied. Hauled to his feet, he was nudged forward, down the steep winding staircase and into the great hall.

Blood ran into his eye from a gash on his head as he gazed at the room before him. A fire crackled in the grate and torchlights glowed, reflecting in the gold threads of the ornate tapestries draping the white-washed walls. Huge wheels hung suspended on chains from the ceiling and upon the wheels, interlaced with antlers, burned hundreds of candles, causing the room to glimmer and sparkle.

As before.

His heart clutched.

As he looked at the raised dais.

He'd sat there. With his mother, father, and siblings.

His heart thudding, the shutters to his mind suddenly flew open.

In a jolt, the curtain lifted.

His life snapped back into his memory. He saw himself at the great table, his sister on one side of him, his wife on the other.

His breath swept in through the gag as every piece of his life fell into place.

In the span of a single heartbeat, he finally understood who he was.

CHAPTER TWENTY-EIGHT

"M'lady!"

Morwenna and Brother Thomas had just reached the few steps leading to the main door of the great hall. She turned quickly and found Sir Hywell running toward her.

"Please, wait," he said.

"What is it?" She tried not to snap, but she was tired and anxious to get at the task of finding the hidden doors and secret hallways within the keep — if indeed there were such things. On her way from the south tower she'd wondered more than once if the old monk was not quite in his right mind, if he could have created the idea of "hallways within hallways" in all those years of solitude. Still, it was something to do, to search for.

"There is a party of men outside the main gate and they want to speak to you."

"Now?" she asked, glancing up at the dark sky. Though the rain had abated, the wind was cold as Satan's breath, the night pitch dark, and the promise of more rain or sleet heavy in the rumbling clouds overhead.

"Aye, they have come with prisoners."

"Prisoners? Who are these men?"

"I know not, but Sir Lylle has detained the two who have shown themselves. They claim there are more waiting in the woods with their prisoners."

"What do I want with their prisoners?" she snapped and then stopped herself. "They have found Carrick? Or the killer?"

Sir Hywell shook his head. "Nay, m'lady, they claim they have Sir Alexander and the sheriff."

"What!"

"That's what they're saying."

"As captives?" she demanded. "But why would anyone imprison the captain of the guard and Sir Payne?"

"I know not," he admitted, and even in the darkness Morwenna read the confusion on his features.

"I'll be right there." She turned to the monk. "Brother Thomas, please, wait for me inside. You can warm yourself by the fire and I'll be back. We can then start our search."

"Mayhap I should return to my room."

"Nay! Please . . . just give me a few minutes. I won't be long," she promised. "Sir Cowan," she called to the guard at the door, "would you please see that Brother

454

Thomas has a mazer of wine and ask the cook for some jellied eggs, or cheese, or a bit of smoked eel."

"Please, do not go to any trouble." But there was a glimmer in the monk's eyes and she swore she heard his old stomach rumble.

" 'Tis none," she assured him quickly. She was in a hurry and she did not want to have to retrieve him yet again from the tower. "Come along." She shepherded the man up the steps, delivering him to the door. "Sir Cowan will take care of you." Over the monk's bent shoulder, she met Sir Cowan's eyes and silently insisted that he take charge of the man. "As I said, I'll be back directly."

Then she was off, following Hywell along the dark paths, feeling the night close in on her. Her pattens collected mud and the wind cut through her cloak as she made her way in the darkness and wondered who had the nerve, the outright audacity, to take Sir Alexander and Sir Payne captive.

You know who, Morwenna.

It can be no one else but Carrick.

"God's teeth, I swear I'll kill him with my own hands," she said through clenched teeth.

"Pardon, m'lady?" Hywell said.

She shook her head and lied, " 'Tis nothing."

Firelight glowed from the windows of the gatehouse and most of the garrison was awake. Those who had dozed had been roused and the few who had been up playing dice and chess had abandoned their games. Some of the men had collected in a large chamber of the gatehouse; others were posted strategically on the wall walks.

Sir Hywell escorted her to the captain of the guard's chamber, where a guard stood at the door. Inside, Sir Lylle and five knights surrounded two men she'd never seen before. The taller of the two had a brand upon his cheek, was missing a front tooth, and wore an air of indifference that bespoke a soullessness that Morwenna noted immediately. The mark on his cheek told her he'd already been branded a criminal, and his eyes were lizardlike and cold. The second man was three inches shorter and years younger, not more than a boy. His skin was unblemished, his hair a mop of red-brown strands. He held a cap in his hands and worried the brim, nervous as a mouse in a roomful of cats.

"These men insisted on seeing you, Lady

Morwenna," Sir Lylle said, and Morwenna met the taller man's eyes. "They surrendered their weapons."

Morwenna didn't wait for introductions. "I understand you have two of my men, that you're holding them hostage." She advanced toward Lizard Eyes. "You are to release them both immediately."

"That's why we're here," he said. "To bargain for their release."

"Bargain? Why would I bargain? Tell me, where are they?"

The branded man's smile stretched to show off the gap between his teeth. "With Carrick of Wybren."

She knew it! That lying underbelly of a snake! So angry she was almost shaking, she curled the fingers of one hand tight and said, "Then why is he not 'bargaining' with me? What kind of coward is he, and how is it you work for him? Why did he send you?"

"To ensure that he's not falsely accused and arrested."

"*Falsely* accused? He's kidnapped two men and is worried about *false* charges?" She shook her head and slowly uncoiled her fist. "I'll not deal with either of you. If Carrick wants to bargain for his life or his freedom, then he should do it himself."

She leveled her gaze at the taller man, and from the corner of her eye she saw the shorter one squirm. "You know, I should toss both of you into the dungeon, or better yet, the oubliette. We have one here at Calon." The younger one was sweating now, biting at his lip. "And then I should just forget about you."

"If any harm comes to us, then your men are as good as dead," Lizard Eyes said.

"Then go. Tell Carrick that he'll have to deal with me himself, and if any harm comes to Sir Alexander or the sheriff, I'll see that he's hunted down like the lying dog he is." She glanced at Sir Lylle. "Do not return their weapons to them, but escort them out of the keep." She turned her attention back to the taller man. "I expect to see Sir Alexander, Sir Payne, and any other free man in your . . . 'custody' by dawn. With or without Carrick."

The branded man's eyes narrowed even farther and his lips twitched beneath his scraggly beard. "I imagine you'll see him and see him soon, m'lady," he mocked. Abruptly he turned on his heel, nodded toward his cohort, and, as the men around her parted, left the gatehouse.

Two soldiers saw that the men were walked out of the keep. Only when she heard the gates creak closed and the portcullis grind down did Morwenna breathe again.

"I don't like this," Sir Lylle said as the men went back to their posts. He clasped his hands behind his back and paced in front of the desk. "It feels wrong. As if it's some kind of trap."

"I don't like it, either. I assume we have men following those two."

"Aye, but the thugs will know it, too, will assume we've sent men after them. They will probably lead my men on a merry chase but I doubt they'll lead us to Carrick or the captives."

"Then we'll just have to find them," Morwenna said. "Whichever way the men go, even if they split up, we must track them all. And our men are not only to be looking for Alexander and Payne, but the physician and Father Daniel and whoever else is missing as well — including the two men we sent to search the town earlier."

He nodded.

"It would seem that Carrick's camp would be close if he was waiting for word of my decision from his men."

"He may not even have made camp," Lylle pointed out.

She agreed, her heart heavy when she

thought of Alexander who, though he'd never voiced his feelings, had loved her silently. Then there was Payne and the distress of his loving wife.

"Mention this to no one; make your men swear to silence except to you and me. There is no reason to worry anyone in the keep until we know more."

Again he nodded and she sighed loudly, a headache starting to pound behind her eyes. She started for the door. "Let me know the second you hear anything." Pausing, she placed a hand on the doorframe and looked over her shoulder at the man who so feebly filled the captain of the guard's shoes. Not only a smaller man than Sir Alexander, Sir Lylle was so much weaker. "Find them, Sir Lylle," she ordered. "And report back to me immediately."

"I'm not Carrick."

His voice echoed through the great hall at Wybren as he managed to spit off his loosened gag.

The soldiers holding him and those who had gathered in the cavernous room turned, eyeing him suspiciously.

Imperious as ever, Graydynn laughed without an ounce of mirth in his voice. "Of course you're —"

"Nay, Graydynn, I'm not and you know it," he charged, his fury white-hot. "You recognized me." With a quick hitch of his shoulders, he threw off the guards' arms. "I'm Theron. Dafydd's son. Carrick's brother, aye, and I look like him, but I'm *not* Carrick."

"Theron died in the fire," Graydynn said, but his voice held less conviction as he studied the marks on Theron's face, searching below what remained of his bruises and scratches, looking beneath his beard.

"I wasn't in Wybren that night," Theron insisted, memories of his past solidifying in his head. He stepped closer to Graydynn. "I left this keep when I discovered my wife in bed with another man, her lover, and no, the bastard wasn't Carrick, either." His lips barely moved as he spoke and everyone in the great hall became silent. " 'Twas someone she'd known from Heath Castle, a man her brother Ryden had sent to watch over her." Theron's lips twisted at the irony of this, his wife's ultimate betrayal. "I didn't even know his name, but he was the one who died in the fire with my wife. He's the one everyone assumed was me."

"You're lying!"

"Am I, Graydynn? Look at me. Look closely. All of us brothers, the sons of Myrnna and Dafydd — Byron, Carrick, Owen, and, yes, even I — looked so much alike we could fool those who didn't know us well. Only Alyce, our sister, took after our mother; the rest of us were the image of our father. But you, Graydynn, you should realize the truth when it stares you in the face."

"This is impossible," Graydynn hissed over the murmurs of his men and the pop and crackle of the fire burning hot in the grate.

"Is it? Then how do I know that you stole wine from my father by bribing the cellarer?" he demanded, edging yet closer, smelling the scent of fear mixed with Graydynn's sweat. "Because I did it with you. I was there. I think Wynn is still here, is he not? He can verify this."

"Theron could have told you about the wine, Carrick," Graydynn insisted. The tip of his tongue nervously licked his lips.

"Would I have told Carrick about the other secret you and I shared?"

"I know not what you're saying." But Graydynn's nostrils flared a bit and there were doubts surfacing in his eyes.

"Sure you do, Graydynn. You remember."

Theron's jaw was stone. "I caught you stealing Carrick's knife, the one with the jeweled handle, remember? 'Twas summer . . . six years past and Carrick swore that if he ever found out who did it, he would cut off the culprit's balls and stuff them down his throat!"

Graydynn visibly paled.

"I see you do recall that event. I assume you still have the knife."

"You are Theron," one of the soldiers said, stepping closer, his gaze scraping over the captive's face. "I see it now."

"And I remember you, Sir Benjamin," Theron said to the thick-bodied man with a heavy red beard.

"Aye, and I know you, too," another, smaller man, concurred. "I was in the service of your father for twenty years."

"As was I."

Other voices chimed in, agreeing. A laundress wiping her hands on her apron smiled through a sheen of tears. "Thank the Lord that you're safe, Sir Theron. Thank the Lord!"

One man with thinning brown hair and eyes with crow's-feet spreading from them stepped forward and stared at Theron long and hard. "You saved my life, or at least kept me from prison," he said solemnly. "A

463

man had accused me of stealing from the lord and you stepped forward in my defense. A week later the true thief was found."

"You're Liam," Theron said, nodding. "Your wife, Katherine — nay, Katie, you call her — had twin sons a year ago."

"Nearly two years past it is now," the man said, a grin crawling across his face.

"By the saints, I thought you were dead!" another soldier yelled.

"My liege," yet another called and fell to one knee. Several others followed, swearing their allegiance to the son of Dafydd, the rightful lord.

"Up! Up! All of you!" Graydynn commanded furiously, swinging his arms toward the ceiling as if willing his subjects to their collective feet. His sword was still in his hands and it cut a wide arc as he pointed toward the heavens. "This is . . . this is preposterous! This man is Carrick! A traitor! A murderer!"

"You lie!" Benjamin said and in one quick movement relieved Graydynn of his sword.

Theron narrowed his gaze on his cousin. "Have them cut me loose," he ordered, but before the Lord of Wybren could respond, Benjamin, using Graydynn's sword, sliced the bonds and cut the gag from his neck.

Liam rose from his knee. " 'Tis sorry I am for my part in your capture, m'lord. I should have recognized you."

"He's not the lord here!" Rage and fear twisted Graydynn's face. "Do not release him! Do *not!* We know not why he's here."

"He's here because he belongs here!" one man shouted, and others yelled in agreement and held their weapons high.

"I came for the truth. I came to face you." Theron's voice was low as he tried and failed to control his own simmering fury. "And I came to avenge my family." So angry he quivered inside, it was all he could do not to wring the bastard's neck. "You killed everyone."

"Nay."

"You thought I was in the room with Alena, and you thought you murdered every last one of us, so that you could claim this barony as your own, as the rightful heir, the firstborn of my father's brother. Only Carrick survived, and after he escaped, or did the dirty work for the two of you, you blamed the fire on him."

"No, Theron . . ." Graydynn paled, hearing his own voice betray him and call him by name. "I . . . I had nothing to do with your family's death."

"Liar!" Theron shouted. "I know not how it worked between you and Carrick. Perhaps you two were partners. 'Tis no secret that Carrick despised our father, but what I don't understand is why he would trust a snake like you."

"I swear to you, I had nothing to do with the fire!"

"Prove it."

"I don't have to. I'm the lord here!"

"But you shouldn't be. Not when one of Baron Dafydd's sons is alive," Benjamin pointed out, and suddenly a dozen sets of angry eyes were trained on Graydynn. The room went deathly quiet. Only the pop and hiss of the fire remained.

Sweat beaded upon Graydynn's brow. "Listen," he said and squared his shoulders, stiffened his spine. "You men — each and every one of you — have sworn your allegiance to *me*, have promised to lay down your lives for king and country. I am your lord, so take this man to the dungeon and lock him away or you'll each be charged with treason."

"We swore allegiance to the rightful heir of Wybren," one man said, his lips tight.

"The king has recognized me as such."

"But the king don't know what you did."

"I did nothing!" Panic strangled

Graydynn's words before he could compose himself. Anger took rein of his emotions. Fury radiated from him and a red vein throbbed at his temple. "If you do as I say, I'll forget this bit of rebellion. If not, you will all be jailed. So understand me and understand me well. Take the prisoner away. Place him behind bars. I'll decide what to do with him in the morn."

"Wait!" A high-pitched voice cut through the room, and a soldier wrestling a smaller, wiry man entered from a side hallway. With another man's help the soldier managed to subdue the captive.

Theron's heart jolted as he recognized the man he'd seen lurking by the door to his room, the one he guessed from the gossip he'd overheard was Dwynn, the half-wit.

"I'm sorry, m'lord," the soldier, red-faced and breathing hard, apologized to Graydynn, since he'd missed what had just happened. "After I called up to you to tell you about the spy, he bolted, and then got out a back door and halfway to the stables. We" — he gestured to the other sentry — "had to capture him again." He cast his captive an angry glare. "Earlier I found him hiding near the well. I think he followed the other one here." He pointed at

Theron. He stopped then, his expression growing nearly comical in its confusion as he noticed Theron was neither bound nor held. "What's going on here?"

Graydynn's eyes narrowed on Theron. "So you brought allies with you?"

"Nay."

"I come from Calon!" Dwynn said, nodding his head frantically.

"He seems to disagree," Graydynn pointed out.

"He may have followed me, but I knew nothing of it."

"I come alone. There — there is trouble in the keep!" Dwynn said, his gaze meeting Theron's for a second before dropping to the floor again. "She needs help."

"Who?" Theron demanded, but he knew. Morwenna's image cut through Theron's mind. His blood turned to ice. "What kind of trouble?" he asked, his heart thudding at the thought that she might be hurt, or worse.

"She —"

"The lady? Morwenna?"

Dwynn nodded. "She's in danger."

"How?"

"The brother," Dwynn said, but still he wouldn't meet Theron's gaze. He bit his lip and acted as if he was giving up a great secret and was afraid he would be punished for it.

"Carrick," Theron guessed tightly. "Carrick has returned?"

But Dwynn turned mute suddenly and wouldn't say another word.

"Tell me!" Theron demanded, grabbing the smaller man by the shoulders. "Damn it, Dwynn!"

"The brother!"

It was useless. Frantic, Theron turned his attention to Benjamin. "I need five men and fresh horses. To ride to Calon."

Ten soldiers stepped forward.

"Good." He was thinking fast, already making plans, and he noticed Graydynn searching the faces of the men who hadn't volunteered. He said to his cousin, "I'll take care of my brother, Graydynn, worry not. But in the meantime I think your idea of the dungeon is a good one. I suggest you spend the night there and consider what you've done."

"I did nothing," Graydynn protested. "You can't . . ." His gaze swept the room, his words dying in his throat as he counted all the men who seemed more than willing to carry out Theron's wishes.

"No?" Theron's smile was cold as ice. "Then, *Lord* Graydynn, you have no fear of retribution or of being punished, do you?" He slid a glance at Sir Benjamin and added, "Lock him away."

CHAPTER TWENTY-NINE

The Redeemer fingered his knife.

He was ready.

Anxious.

His nerves stretched to the breaking point.

From his hiding spot behind the curtain in the balcony, he'd observed as Carrick was captured and dragged into the great hall, only to learn that the cur was really *Theron.*

The Redeemer's insides curdled at that thought. He'd always assumed that Theron had died in the fire, and it made him feel unworthy to know that not only Carrick but now also Theron had escaped the blaze meant to wipe out the entire house of Wybren.

But now he did know the truth and that knowledge gave him power. Insight.

Worse yet, though, had been witnessing Dwynn, that idiot, as he'd been hauled into the great hall and inanely blathered things he should have kept to himself. To think that all the Redeemer's carefully laid plans could be undone by that pathetic half-wit was irritating beyond reason. Dwynn, too, would have to pay the ultimate price.

Now Theron and his group of soldiers were on their way to Calon. Another irritation. One he would have to deal with. But first, Graydynn.

He'd managed to sneak from the balcony and down several flights to the dungeons — a horrible, dank place where only pestilence and despair could breed. The cells were, for the most part, uninhabited aside from the rodents, insects, and snakes that crept and slithered through the rusted bars of the jail. Water dripped somewhere, and the scents of mold, urine, dirt, and rotting straw mingled into an odor that burned one's nostrils.

But he wouldn't have to stay long. As soon as Graydynn was behind bars, he'd sneak up to the unsuspecting guard, drive his blade between the man's ribs to his heart, and then unlock the door. Graydynn would assume he was being freed. Only when Graydynn attempted to step out of the cell would he understand. For then he would feel the blade at his throat and within seconds he would be slain, a perfect W carved into his lying throat.

From his hiding spot, the Redeemer felt a tremor of excitement race through him;

the warm buzz of anticipation made his pulse beat hard. He ran the pad of his thumb over the razor-sharp edge of his blade and waited, listening.

Within minutes the sounds of boots tromping down the stairs reached his ears. Along with the heavy footsteps, he also heard Graydynn ranting, proclaiming his innocence, offering bribes of money, women, or anything the guard so desired.

Oh, it was good to hear him barter for his life. To plead with the guard. To make promises that he couldn't possibly keep. To know the fear and frustration of losing everything he'd thought he'd earned.

Chains rattled, a rusted key turned in the lock, and in the dim illumination of two rushlights, the Redeemer witnessed Graydynn's final mortification as he was cast into the stinking, dingy jail.

Graydynn whimpered and then shouted out obscenities.

He never knew that he should be sending up prayers for his soul.

To the Redeemer's amazement, the guard locked the cell door and then left, hanging the ring of keys on a hook set into the wall near the staircase.

"You're not leaving me down here! You can't!"

The guard turned, looked Graydynn square in the face, and then spat on the floor. A second later his heavy tread thudded as he climbed up the stairs.

"Bloody hell! You can't leave me down here!" Graydynn, frantic, held on to the bars and shook them wildly. "I command you to set me free!" he ordered. "Sir Michael! Come back down here! Sir Michael!" Graydynn drew in a long breath and kicked at the floor, sending something, a piece of bone or a dirt clod or a rock, sailing into the wall, where it hit with a hard thud. "Damn it all to hell!" Graydynn raged.

The Redeemer almost smiled. He heard a door above close and then no other sound but the prisoner's rantings. Stepping away from the shadows, he moved into the weak light.

So caught up in his fury was he, Graydynn didn't see his approach until he was nearly at the cell.

"Who are you?" he asked, startled, eyeing him in the darkness.

"I'm here to help."

"Well, you can bloody well start by unlocking the damned door." With both hands, Graydynn shoved his hair from his eyes. "I can't believe this! Locked down here like a common criminal! Can you hurry it up a bit?"

The Redeemer nodded and walked to the staircase to retrieve the keys. As he did, he slid his knife from its sheath with his other hand.

Graydynn didn't notice.

All he saw was the key ring and freedom.

The Redeemer considered toying with him, taking his time, even teasing the would-be lord of the keep, but he thought better of it, for he needed to return to Calon and the hours to dawn were waning.

He inserted first one key into the lock and turned.

Nothing happened.

"Christ Jesus, must you be so slow?" Graydynn growled.

Another key.

Still no opening click.

"Give me the key ring, you idiot!" Graydynn said and snatched the heavy circle from his hand. One after another he tried the keys, and when at last the lock clicked open and he pushed open the door, the Redeemer was waiting.

Graydynn stepped past him. The Redeemer grabbed hold of the man's hair, pulling back his head and carving a quick, neat W across his throat before Graydynn opened his mouth to scream.

"I'm sorry, m'lady," Brother Thomas said as they searched the solar one last time. "Mayhap when it's light out we'll find something, but I fear we'll discover nothing tonight — mayhap not at all."

Morwenna wasn't about to give up, but she could tell that the old man was already overly tired. The dark smudges beneath his eyes were more pronounced and he was slowing down. Worse yet, they'd been searching for hours and had discovered nothing.

"You've done all you can, Brother Thomas," she said, her eyes noticing the first light of dawn creeping over the eastern hills. 'Twas morn again, the roosters already giving up their raucous cry, the sentry in the watchtower blowing his hunting horn, signifying the changing of the guard. "Have Cook give you some porridge, blood pudding, or finch pie before you go back to your room."

"Mayhap," he said softly, his old eyes glinting at the mention of food.

As he started to turn toward the door, Morwenna touched him lightly on the arm. "You need not spend all your time up there. I would find you a warm place with a fire and a mattress for your cot."

"Nay, child," he said with a faint smile, "but thank you. Now, get some rest."

Rest! 'Twas the last thing she could do. Already the castle was stirring and she had much to do.

She saw the old monk to the kitchen, where one of the pages promised to walk him back to the tower after feeding him some of Cook's mutton stew. Morwenna then returned to her room, splashed water over her face, and renewed her determination to find the secret rooms.

They could be just the idle thoughts of a half-addled old man, she reminded herself. Toweling her face, she shook her head. She still believed him. In the hours she'd spent with the monk, he'd been clearheaded and had barely repeated himself. He insisted that his grandfather had created a hidden series of passageways.

There was one room they had not yet checked, but now, with the morning light, it was time to search it as well. Besides, she wanted to speak to her sister. Mort, who had been sleeping curled on the bed, lifted his head when she passed, and then thumped his tail as she petted his head. He promptly returned to snoozing, having tagged after her most of the night.

"I don't blame you," she admitted,

eyeing the bed and thinking it would be heaven to sleep for a few hours. Just not yet. She'd made promises that she herself would ride at dawn to search for Alexander and Payne; she would have to tell Sarah of the meeting last night with two of Carrick's men.

Carrick!

The betrayer.

Why had he wanted to bargain for her men's release? Was it for money? But no ransom had been demanded from the two lying dogs he'd sent inside. Mayhap she should have thrown them in the dungeon, but she'd been afraid Carrick would slit Alexander's and Payne's throats.

Her heart nose-dived.

Mayhap they are already dead. If the thugs return, demand proof that the men are alive.

She wouldn't think that way, wouldn't believe it. Not yet. Nor would she think that something dire had happened to the other people missing in the keep, though if the physician, priest, and Dwynn didn't appear today, she would search the town herself.

She rapped upon Bryanna's door and waited.

No answer.

"Bryanna?" she called, knocking more loudly, as sometimes the girl slept like the dead. "Bryanna, I need to speak with you." Again she waited, then pounded again. When there was no sound of her sister's footsteps, Morwenna shoved open the door. "Bother and broomsticks, Bryanna, wake up. I know you're grieving about poor Isa, but —"

Inside the room was cold. Empty. The bed without a wrinkle.

Morwenna's heart pounded crazily. Her sister had to be in here, *had* to! But she searched. The room was smaller than her own with but a tiny alcove by the fireplace, where shelves had been built. Her sister wasn't under her bed. Nay, she wasn't in the room. But she had to be!

Morwenna rushed to the window. It was high, but could be reached if one pulled one's self up, and it was large enough for someone of Bryanna's size to escape through it. The ledge was wide and solid but the drop was steep, three stories down. Morwenna peered outside to the misting dawn and the bailey far below. No ropes dangled from the ledge. Even if a person was foolish enough to jump to the soft, muddy ground, she would risk serious and almost certain injury, if not death. No,

Bryanna had not leapt out the window.

Morwenna gazed around the room helplessly. Bryanna had to have left by way of the door. Had her sister sneaked away, unable to deal with the tragedies and pain that had occurred in the keep? But where would she run? To Penbrooke?

Had she been kidnapped?

Morwenna's stomach clenched. The hairs on the backs of her arms lifted. Had Bryanna, sweet sister, suffered the same fate as Isa and Vernon? Had the monster taken her and sliced her young throat?

"Oh, God," Morwenna whispered, her knees threatening to give out. She looked up at the ceiling. Had the same killer who had struck before been watching?

She flew toward the door, but as she was about to run into the hallway she nearly collided with a man entering Bryanna's room. She would have screamed, would have yelled for the guards, but her throat failed her as she stared into the eyes of her old lover.

Her hand flew to her mouth and she felt as if she'd been tossed back to another time, another place.

Carrick of Wybren was before her. There was no doubt in her mind. Nowhere was there a scar or bruise upon his face, no evidence of a nose that had been broken, just the same blue eyes she remembered from three years past.

"Don't say a word," he ordered. He shut the door behind him with a distinct thud. Morwenna's heart thundered painfully. Her mind scattered.

"But . . . you're not the man . . . we found. You . . . you've suffered not a beating?"

"Shh . . ." he said, and though he held a sword in front of him, she felt no fear of him.

"Who was he?" she whispered, her world spinning when she thought of the wounded, scarred man, how she'd lain with him, trusted him, believed him to be the very man standing before her — the very strong, unbruised warrior she'd known before. "Who was he?"

"My brother."

"They all died in the fire," she protested, but the resemblance between the two men was unmistakable.

"Not Theron."

Morwenna struggled to take it all in. "Theron? Alena's husband?" she said, remembering the woman's name on the wounded man's lips, the name he called in his delirium. She felt as if she might collapse. *Theron.* Did he know? Had he lied to her? Pretended to be Carrick?

What had he said? In an instant she recalled his confession:

"I know not if I've ever taken a man's life . . . and there are pieces of memory . . . a rage that flows through my blood, but I swear on all that is holy, I did not slay my family. Nor do I believe I would ever have left you. With or without a child."

She swallowed hard as shock gave way to rage. "Where is he? Theron . . . where is he?"

"I know not. I thought he was here with you."

"You beat him, left him for dead!"

"No!" Carrick's eyes glinted. "I made a mistake. He'd been in the service of the king, far away, using a name that was not his own, and I found out that he'd returned and was riding to Wybren. Already everyone thought I'd killed my family, and Theron, too, believed so. I knew that he would cause a new interest in the fire and that I'd be hunted again, as I was just afterwards."

"You set the fire."

"I did not!" he swore, his eyes flashing, his lips curling in disgust that she would think such a thing. "I told my men to stop him, and they . . . they took it too far. By

481

the time I arrived, he was nearly dead."

"And you left him?"

He nodded, his chin sliding to one side.

"That's as good as murdering him."

He drew in a long breath. "I've done much in my life I'm not proud of, Morwenna. As for Theron, I heard the hunters, knew they would find him. He had no chance with me, living in the forest, but if he was brought here, to the keep, he had a chance, albeit a sorry one, to survive. I took off my ring and forced it onto his finger, knowing that you . . . you would try to help him."

"And if he died, everyone would assume he was you and that you'd gotten what you deserved, that you had been punished for murdering your family. You would allow that to happen? And then what? Did you not think people would still recognize you?"

"I hoped that Theron would survive."

"To be tried as a killer? To take the blame for your crimes?"

"I did not kill my family!" he swore again. "I did not know that when Theron awoke, if he awoke, he would not have his memory!"

"So that was just convenient. How did you know that he could not remember?

Oh!" She inhaled sharply. "You have spies in my keep." She recalled all the times she'd heard people whispering, seen looks exchanged, felt unseen eyes upon her — and all the time it was Carrick!

"There are men who would take a coin for information," he admitted, and she thought first of the potter — a crafty, nosy man whom she didn't trust. Yet he was only one of several.

"So your spies have been walking through the secret hallways of this keep?" she challenged.

"*Secret* hallways?"

"Do not pretend that you don't know about the hidden chambers, the secret portals, the corridors within corridors that run throughout Calon." She was guessing, but he did not know that.

"What are you talking about?"

"The means by which your spies slunk through this keep!"

For once Carrick appeared tongue-tied.

"You deny knowing about them?"

"I deny that they exist," he said, baffled. "I've had spies here for nearly a year and never have I heard of these . . . passages you speak of."

She stared at him and didn't know what to believe. He seemed genuinely lost, but she knew he was a consummate actor. Had he not pretended to love her? Had she not believed him that summer that seemed so long ago?

Her head spun with all the lies he was weaving. Untruth after untruth fell off his tongue as easily as spittle. She could never trust him again. Never! She knew how callous and heartless he could be. "You left me," she charged, "when I was with child."

His eyes flickered and he paled a bit, but he didn't deny it, and her heart broke into a thousand pieces all over again.

Still she plunged on, her fury firing her blood, her disdain palpable. "You left me pregnant, and then you returned to Alena, your brother's wife — *Theron's* wife — who died in the fire."

Carrick did not deny it.

"And now you expect me to believe that even though you had your men set upon Theron and beat him to an inch of his life —"

"That was a mistake!"

"— and even though you have taken some of my men prisoner as a means to bargain with me, apparently — for what is still not clear — you want me to believe your intentions are honorable. That is the point, is it not? That you are not the murdering bastard everyone thinks you are?"

He struggled for an answer. She lifted a brow and waited.

"Yes."

"And you want me to believe you would not further hurt Theron?"

"Yes."

"You expect too much! You are the lowest of the low, Carrick of Wybren," she charged. "For all I know, you've not only killed your family, but one of my sentries and the midwife who was my nursemaid."

"I swear to you, Morwenna, I did not."

"Swear to me on what? The life of our child who never was born? The graves of your sister, parents, and brothers? The freedom of the men you have held prisoner so that you could sneak into my keep?"

A muscle worked in his jaw, but he held his head with a pride that was undeserved.

"Understand this, Carrick, that I trust you not. I believe you not. I would be better off bargaining with Lucifer and all the demons in hell than to help you." She advanced upon him, her jaw set, her eyes trained on his seductive and oh so traitorous blue gaze. "What the hell have you done with my sister?" she demanded.

"Your sister? I know not."

"Liar!" she nearly screamed, her fists

clenching. "Tell me where you took her and pray God for your mortal soul if you've harmed her in any way!" Morwenna stopped only when the toes of her shoes touched the tip of his boots. She had to crane her neck to glare up at him, but she did so, skewering him with a look of pure loathing. Inside she was quaking, her stomach in knots, and her words came out in a hiss between gnashed teeth. "If Bryanna is hurt or . . . or worse, you pathetic piece of filth, I will see that you are strung up by your heels and sliced end to end so that your innards spill out before you are even dead!"

His gaze didn't falter.

"I swear, Carrick, you miserable son of a dog, I'll kill you myself!" She flung herself at him, pummeled his chest with her fists, and felt his arms surround her. As she fought and clawed he had the audacity, the damned nerve, not to so much as strike her or defend himself. He merely held her close as she spat and swung and swore, damning him to hell, reviling him to the heavens. Fear and anger caused her to flail wildly, furiously, broken sobs coming out of her mouth, until the rage had quieted and she was spent, sweating, gasping in his arms.

She looked up at his handsome face and saw not the man she'd loved but a liar, a cheat, a traitor. When her heart pounded it was not with love, nor lust, nor temptation, but only with fear for those she did love and the frustration of not being able to save them.

Doubts assailed her. Had all her hopes, her dreams, her plans to be the Lady of Calon, ruler of this barony, caused all the pain, deceit, and death in these thick, solid walls?

Finally she realized she was still in his arms, her breasts held tight against the wall of his chest, his square jaw pressed to her forehead, the scent of him invading her nostrils.

Revulsion tore through her. "Let go of me!"

"If that's what you want."

"I do!"

He cocked a dubious black eyebrow and she wanted to beat the bloody piss out of him.

"What the hell are you doing here?" she demanded as he released her and she stumbled backward before catching herself.

"I've been waiting for you," he said in that same deep voice she remembered. "Here in this room. I just stepped out when you took the monk downstairs."

"How do you know what I've been doing, and where the bloody hell is my sister?"

"I know what you've been doing because I've been watching, waiting for the chance to get you alone. Most of the time I hid out here because no one bothered to come inside. As for your sister, I know not where she is. When I arrived, her door was shut, the fire out, the bed made."

"When did you sneak in here?"

"When you all were distracted by my men." She thought of the two men who had come to the keep's gatehouse. " 'Twas a simple matter," Carrick went on. "I knew you would send men after them, just as you sent men looking for Carrick, so I instructed Will and Hack to split up and lead your soldiers in opposite directions, away from the camp. While they were discussing all the plans with you and the guards were distracted, I slipped through the gates and into the keep."

"So easily?" she asked bitterly.

He nodded, looked at the floor, and then again into her eyes. "Your security, *m'lady,* is . . . less than you might want."

In this, she believed him. People had been murdered or gone missing, and no one — not one of her soldiers, spies, scouts, or huntsmen — could find any clues to the identity of the killer or knew how to find those still unaccounted for.

She blew out her breath. "You have my men?"

"Aye. Hidden away."

"All of them? The physician and priest and . . . and another man who is considered a half-wit?"

"Nay, only the sheriff and captain of the guard."

"But the others are missing."

"Not at my hand," he said, frowning. "You are certain they didn't leave of their own accord?"

"I do not know," she admitted. "But it seems strange that they are all gone, all left the night Isa was murdered and Car— Theron escaped."

"You thought my brother was me," he said. "I knew everyone else did, but I thought that you . . . you might have known the difference."

She flushed and bit her lip. "I thought you were dead," she said, her voice a whisper. "And then this man appears, wearing your ring. I had to believe . . . nay, I *wanted* to believe that you'd survived."

Carrick nodded as if this were so, which

enraged Morwenna anew.

"You lured my men from me so that you could use them to bargain," she said tightly. "Tell me, what bargain do you wish to make?"

"I need your help," he said, and she was instantly wary.

"*You* need *my* help?" She nearly laughed at the absurdity of the situation. Shaking her head at the folly of it all, she said, " 'Tis ridiculous. You've never needed anyone's help in all of your miserable years!"

"Until now. I want your help in proving that I did not set the fire that killed my family. To that end, we will have to convince Theron of that."

"The man you had beaten nearly to death? That might not be easy."

"And we must find the real killer. Or killers."

"It's been more than a year since the fire. Everyone at Wybren has tried to do just that."

"Have they?" He shook his head. "Not the current lord. Graydynn is satisfied with things the way they are." He rubbed his chin. "Listen, Morwenna, I know you have no reason to trust me and, aye, every reason to hate me, to consider me your worst enemy, but if you help me in my quest, I will help you in yours.

"For your assistance, I will release your men," he went on, "and help you find your sister and anyone else who is missing. I will put all my resources into uncovering who killed the guard and the old woman and . . . above all else, Morwenna," he said solemnly, "I will help you locate my brother." His blue eyes held hers. "That is the best I can offer, but it's sincere. You have my word."

"I do not trust you or your word."

"My word is as good as any of the people who live in this keep, half of which would love to see you fail or be replaced just because you're a woman."

In this, Morwenna could not argue.

He removed his sword and tossed it onto the bed and then reached into his boot and pulled out a wicked little knife. It, too, landed on Bryanna's mattress.

"So what will it be, Morwenna?" he asked. "Will you let me help you, or would you rather be on your own?"

She walked to the bed and retrieved his weapons. Looking him squarely in the eye, she yelled, "Guards! Sir James and Sir Cowan, I need you here immediately!"

Footsteps pounded up the stairs.

Carrick snorted. "This is your answer?"

"As God is my witness, Carrick, I will never trust you," she said, her lips barely moving, "but I will let you have your freedom. You'll work with my most trusted soldiers. They will be armed. You will not."

"Lady Morwenna?" Sir Cowan called.

"Here, in Bryanna's chamber!" She gazed at her old lover. "Make no mistake, Carrick, I will never, as long as I draw a breath, trust you again, but I will give you one last chance to prove yourself. And if you dare cross me, lie to me, or endanger the lives of those I love, I swear I will spend the rest of my life making yours a living hell!"

CHAPTER THIRTY

"Tell me again, what is the trouble at Calon?" Theron demanded as they paused at a creek for the horses to drink. The animals needed a rest, having been driven hard from Wybren. Ten men from Wybren rode with Theron, including Benjamin, and Liam, the best of the lot, and Dwynn, the odd one. The men had dismounted and were either chewing on dried beef the cook at Wybren had given them, or relieving themselves in a copse of oak trees.

Theron knew not what he faced at Calon. The idiot had turned silent, only muttering about "trouble" and "brother" and "God."

"Did you see Carrick?" he asked for the twentieth time, but Dwynn just shook his head.

"Brother."

Theron sighed. "My brother. I know."

Or was it something else?

"Do you mean a monk?" He remembered the disguises he'd found in the secret room, and one of them had been the robe

493

and cowl of a monk. "The 'brother' you're speaking of, does he live at Calon?"

A spark showed in the half-wit's eyes, but it quickly faded.

Theron scowled. Maybe he misunderstood the man. For all Theron knew Carrick was dead, though he was sure he had escaped the fire. Theron remembered that the man in his chamber with Alena had not been his brother.

So where was Carrick now?

The men were returning, the horses somewhat refreshed. Calon was still nearly two hours away, so Theron climbed onto the back of huge red steed and said, "Let's ride."

"To Calon," Liam said, his eyes bright.

"To Calon," Theron agreed, and he only hoped that whatever the trouble was, Morwenna was safe. "God be with her," he whispered and then dug his heels into his big horse's flanks. The steed shot forward, the other horses thundering behind.

Lord Ryden's spy sat on the opposite edge of the campfire and picked at his teeth with the point of his knife. Two rabbits and a pheasant were roasting on the spit, fat sizzling into the coals, smoke rising to the heavens. The other men, ever vigilant for the outlaws, were tending the horses or pacing the perimeter of the camp.

Ryden, sipping ale from a jug, was propped against the trunk of a tree, his legs sore from riding for hours. He'd hoped to arrive at Calon before nightfall.

"I'm tellin' ya, m'lord, it's Carrick's gang," Quinn insisted. The spy was a rat-faced little man. His features were set in the center of his face — a long nose and ridged brow out of proportion to his small eyes and mouth, where yellowed teeth crowded together. He pointed his dirty knife toward the western hills. "Hidin' out down by the old rock quarry." Waggling his blade toward the encampment, he nodded to himself, pleased with what he'd discovered. "And they've got captives."

"Morwenna?" Ryden heard himself ask a little too quickly. The spy's eyes lightened a bit as he flicked a piece of old meat from his teeth.

"Don't think so."

"But you're saying that Carrick of Wybren is alive? Just not the man who was dragged, near death, into Calon Keep."

"That's right."

Ryden tried to quell the fury that boiled through his blood as he thought of his intended's lover, his sister's murderer.

The spy grinned a bit and then cut off another chunk of charred rabbit from the carcass on the spit.

"I thought Carrick was half dead. Lying in the keep."

Quinn gnawed on the burned meat and shook his head. "Seems that Carrick is the leader of this band. He wasn't hurt at all in any attack." Quinn's chin was tucked as he chewed. He looked up at Ryden from the tops of his eyes. "Nay. 'Twas his brother."

"Brother? They were all killed in the fire."

"So everyone thinks. But one managed to escape."

"One as well as Carrick?"

The rat-faced man nodded. "Theron, his name was."

Ryden nearly choked on a swallow of ale. "Alena's husband survived?" he whispered, disbelieving. "While *she* was killed?" In his mind's eye he imagined the fire, the flames, the burning bed . . . "But she was with Theron."

The spy wisely didn't say the unspoken thought hanging between them.

"Nay, this is a lie! Two bodies were found."

"And is there not a man missing? One you sent to Wybren? One who knew your sister?"

Ryden's throat closed in upon itself. He shut his eyes. Alena. Beautiful, headstrong Alena. Would she have taken another lover to her bed, one other than Carrick? The man he sent, aye, had been a stableboy at Heath as a lad and had helped Alena learn to ride. He thought that spy he'd sent to watch Alena had disappeared with his hefty fee. Apparently that was not the case.

His jaw clenched so hard it ached. If he could believe what Quinn was suggesting, then the man who was in his own employ had gone to Wybren and set upon seducing the woman he was supposed to watch over.

Ryden's muscles tightened. A bad taste rose up his mouth. He realized that Quinn, on the other side of the fire, was staring at him, trying to read his reaction.

When Quinn saw he had Ryden's attention again, he said around a mouthful of rabbit, "So you see, m'lord, the rumors about Carrick being alive are true."

"Who told you this?" Ryden asked.

"One of the Carrick's thugs himself, a man who goes by the name of Hack. Odd-looking fellow. Got a brand on his cheek and eyes that hardly blink." Quinn chewed and cleaned his teeth with his tongue. "Anyway, Hack, he was well into his cups one night at the alehouse, and he bragged to me about being part of Carrick's gang."

"Why to you?"

"Cuz I was buying the ale," Quinn said smugly. "I learned a lot that night."

Ryden wanted to shake the information from him but contented himself with tossing a wet, mossy branch of oak onto the fire. The flames hissed, smoke churning upward.

Afraid the lord had lost interest in his tale, Quinn added, "So this Hack and two other men, they beat the brother senseless, nearly killing the man, and Carrick found out and threatened them all with their lives. Turned out he didn't want him killed, just warned not to raise trouble about the fire at Wybren. Carrick, he got all upset. Furious at the men. Said they weren't supposed to kill him, just warn him. Anyway, they left him for dead."

"And Morwenna's hunters found him." Ryden rocked back on his heels and felt a little better knowing that the man Morwenna had tended to these last weeks hadn't been her old lover after all. Mayhap all his worries about her changing her mind about their impending marriage were for naught.

He considered what would happen if he

chose the right course of action.

Wouldn't he appear the hero, her champion, if he brought Carrick and his band to justice? He smiled at the thought and motioned for one of the men to bring a second jug as he drained the first. Not only would he rid the barony of a wicked band of thieves and cutthroats, but he'd also bring Carrick of Wybren to justice for the murder of his family *and* free Carrick's hostages!

Satisfaction filled him as he considered his future as the Baron of Calon as well as Heath, Wynndym, and Bentwood — the last two keeps compliments of his prior wives. Ah, yes, his power would stretch far and wide. . . . He sipped from his cup and congratulated himself on his foresight. Before he'd left Heath, he'd sent three spies ahead of him to search for the band of robbers who were reputed to inhabit the forests near Calon. Ryden had decided to flush them out before he and his party were attacked. His plan, it seemed, had worked perfectly.

"Have another swallow of ale," he said to the spy. "Once it's dark, you'll take me to Carrick's camp, where we'll surprise the bastard and free his prisoners." His smile deepened at the thought of turning the tables on the traitor once and for all.

Carrick's capture at Ryden's hand would be sweet, sweet justice.

Finally Alena would be avenged.

And Morwenna would become his bride.

She clutched the knife to her chest.

Alone in the dark, she waited.

For him.

The murderer who took Isa's life.

He would be back, Bryanna thought, as she sat on a pile of clothes that he'd left. Disguises. To hide his identity and to allow him to walk through the keep unnoticed.

She'd spent hours exploring these passageways, and her heart had pounded in fear that she would unexpectedly come across the monster, that he would slice her as he had the others. But she'd kept on her mission, making it a quest to explore as many of the dark corridors and chambers as she could, carrying one torchlight after another as they burned down. There had been several torchlights in place along these narrow passageways, waiting to be lit. She'd risked collecting others by stepping into the hallway near her chamber, or by the kitchens, wherever she found a door and listening until she heard no sound from the other side. Twice, she'd nearly been spotted by guards searching the keep, but each time she'd managed to slip into the hidden corridors once again without being seen.

She'd learned a lot about this unknown labyrinth.

Mazelike, the corridors sprouted off each other, some ending in chambers with no other exit, others leading outside. In the hours she'd been in the semidark, she'd found wider areas where the monster could watch through the slits in the wall, stare down into private chambers, observe without being seen.

Goose bumps crawled up her arms at the thought of him lurking in the dark, waiting, watching, perhaps smiling, or licking his lips or touching himself.

But it would end soon.

He would return; she was certain of it.

And when he did, she would be ready.

She reached to her neck, where hung the leather strap with its smooth stone. She did not feel a second's guilt about sneaking back to the physician's hut and taking Isa's necklace from her. Nor did she feel bad about creeping into Isa's chamber and taking all her treasures: herbs, candles, string, stones, dice, a book of runes, and this, her tiny dagger with its wicked, curved blade. Bryanna had stuffed the lot of it into an apron that had been hanging upon Isa's wall, and then she'd carried everything back here, to this chamber, where she was certain he would return.

"Worry not, Isa," she whispered. "I will end his miserable life."

Be careful, child. He is like the wind, unseen but ever-present. Do not let down your guard.

Ever.

"So there is supposed to be a second set of hallways, and you think Theron used them in his escape," Carrick said as they once again searched through the solar and chambers that were her quarters.

"Aye. I know not how else he could have gotten past the guard."

Carrick slid her a glance that said he knew more, but he didn't voice what was on his mind. "Let's go through the room he was in again, inch by inch."

"I've been through it three, nay, four times!"

"But it's the only place from which we know for certain someone disappeared. You cannot even be sure that Bryanna was in her room when she went missing."

Bryanna!

Dear Lord, where was she? Why had she not returned?

Upon agreeing to a pact with Carrick, Morwenna had taken Sir Lylle into her confidence. The knight had been aghast at her alliance, but she had insisted that he accept her decision. Only Sir Cowan, Sir James, and the temporary captain of the guard knew that Carrick was in the keep, and while he and Morwenna had searched the upper story, other soldiers had been sent to the lower rooms of the keep as well as the buildings, shops, and huts inside the inner and outer baileys. Another small group had been sent into town, and the castle itself seemed empty, only a few servants going about their tasks.

Once again they entered Tadd's chamber and for a moment, Morwenna wished her brother were visiting. Tadd was a pain in the backside, aye, always looking to lift a skirt or drink a pint, but he was true of heart and . . . Oh, fie and fiddlesticks, what was she thinking? Tadd would only get in the way. He would point out time and time again her failings, so it was best that her brother not visit anytime soon. Not until she had restored some order and found their sister.

Spurred by her thoughts of saving

Bryanna, Morwenna walked to the center of the room and stared at the four walls.

Carrick was measuring the floor by his strides. "We know that if there is a passageway, it does not run along the main hall, for there is not enough room. The walls into which the doorways are set are not wide enough."

"Aye."

"And the wall to the outside of the keep is unlikely as well — see the width of the windowsill — which leaves the wall between this chamber and the next, to the left of the fireplace, elsewise whoever was building it would run into the corridor." Morwenna nodded and Carrick continued. "The only place for a secret door in this room is there, near the grate, running toward that wall, or on that long wall without window or door or fireplace."

"Or the floor," she said, and he nodded, smiling a bit.

"Or the ceiling, but there seems to be no way to reach the ceiling, no ladder nor stones that are pushed out a bit to allow for climbing."

She eyed the floor as he studied the ceiling. "Have you noticed that these chambers, up here on this level, are different in that they are not covered in whitewash?" Carrick asked. "The stones are allowed to be their natural color; the mortar, too, is gray."

She nodded. "I thought it odd when I first arrived but decided it was the style of the lord who constructed the keep."

"Perhaps it was done this way to hide the secret doorways, to make certain that no one would come in and fix the wattle and daub or limewash the walls." His eyes narrowed as he examined the stone and mortar that reached to the ceiling.

Morwenna kicked the rushes out of the way, studying the mortar, even scooting the bed to one side. "Nothing," she muttered. Shadows had deepened as their fruitless quest had continued. Now Carrick lit the fire with an ember from the hall rushlights as she did the same with all the candles in the room.

" 'Tis impossible," she muttered.

"Only if you think it so. If you believe that there is a doorway to this room, then we shall find it."

She silently prayed he was right but was about to give up when she saw the scratches, long marks upon the floor near one corner. Her interest quickened. "What's this?"

Carrick was beside her in an instant. He

bent to one knee, touched the stones. Feeling along the crack between the wall and floor, he grinned. "You found it, Morwenna!" he said. "There's an opening here." He ran his fingers over the crack. "Now we have to find a lever, or a latch, or a keyhole, or something . . ."

And then she saw it . . . an unlikely niche in a rock. She reached inside, felt a piece of metal, and held her breath. "I think I found it," she whispered and pushed hard against the latch.

Slowly the doorway appeared.

Before she could step through, a soldier's voice boomed down the hallway. "Lady Morwenna!" he cried.

"Bother!" she muttered. Hurriedly she handed Carrick one of the rushlights. "Go!"

"You don't want them —" He hitched his chin toward the door where the sound of boots pounded.

"Not yet. Now go. Hurry!"

Carrick ducked through the newly found portal and Morwenna ran to the door.

Sir Lylle reached her just as she shut the door to Tadd's bedroom behind her. "What is it?"

"Lord Ryden has arrived," he said, a bit breathless as he approached. "And he's not alone. He and his soldiers have captured Carrick of Wybren's band of criminals." His smile was wide. "Now you will no longer have to deal with him, m'lady," he said proudly.

Morwenna's heart dropped. Carrick was already deep in the hidden passageways of the keep. "Good. You stand guard here and I'll go greet the baron. Don't let anyone in or out. Including yourself."

He seemed puzzled, but she said, " 'Tis a test, Sir Lylle," and she didn't explain, knowing that he thought it was probably a test of his loyalty, to see if he truly was worthy of the position he had filled while Sir Alexander was gone. "Is anyone else with them?"

"Just the cutthroats and the sheriff and the captain of the guard," he said, and she wondered at the whereabouts of the others. Theron? Dear God, was he still in the dark passageways she had yet to explore? And Bryanna? Had she followed after him? Where the devil was Nygyll? And Dwynn? And Father Daniel?

The longer they were missing, the more worrisome it was. "Please take me to Lord Ryden and send a messenger to the sheriff's wife that he has returned. Bring her to the great hall. Then return here, to your post."

"But Carrick could escape."

"Place sentries at each end of the hallway, at the top of each staircase," she ordered. She was already marching rapidly toward the main stairs, bracing herself for the confrontation with the man she had vowed to marry.

"Death and dog's breath," she said, tossing her hair over her shoulders.

She had nearly reached the bottom step, had already heard the sound of male voices coming from the great hall and recognized Lord Ryden's laugh, when another horn sounded outside and Sir Hywell threw open the door.

Now what? Morwenna thought in frustration.

A blast of winter air blew inside, causing the rushlights to flame brighter. "A party has arrived from Wybren," he announced. *Graydynn. No!*

Morwenna ground her teeth. Stiffening her shoulders, she strode into the hall just as Theron, wearing a tattered and muddy uniform, entered from the other side. Her heart leapt and her breath seemed stolen from her lungs. She stared into his blue, blue eyes, shocked by her overwhelming sense of joy.

"Morwenna," he said as other men

joined him. "I'm not —"

"I know!" Without a second thought she threw herself into his arms. "Thank God you're alive . . . Theron."

She held fast to him, felt the comfort of his arms surround her, and only when she heard a cough did she realize that Sir Ryden of Heath, the man she'd agreed to marry, was standing only a few feet way, his gaze blistering, his face red with suppressed fury. His nostrils quivered and he managed to somehow look down his nose at them both, as if the spectacle Morwenna had created disgusted him.

"Ryden," Theron said as Morwenna stepped out of his arms.

"Theron." Ryden stared at the younger man with eyes that could bore through granite. "Mayhap you can tell me how you escaped the tragedy of Wybren," he said, moving slowly forward, his words as measured as his steps, "while everyone else, including your wife, my sister, perished?"

"I had left Wybren before the fire broke out."

"Left your wife to fend for herself?"

"She was with someone else."

"And you could not fight for her honor?"

Theron's lips barely moved. "I see you do not question her fidelity. Alena had little honor, Ryden, and we both know it. 'Twas her choice to be with the man you sent to spy on her." He glanced at Morwenna. "We cannot discuss this now," he said, "for on our ride here, we found Father Daniel."

"Finally! Where was he?" she asked, irritated for a second that the priest had abandoned the keep. Her anger quickly dissipated when she noticed the solemn set of Theron's jaw, the sadness in his gaze.

"He, too, was murdered, Morwenna, his throat slit in the same manner as the others."

"Oh, God," she whispered, feeling the blood rush from her head. "Not another one." She thought back to the day she'd seen him through the doorway to his private chambers, the cruel whip in his hand, the scars and blood upon his back. A tormented soul.

"Take me to him," she said.

"Not yet," Ryden ordered imperiously. "We have but arrived."

"Now." Morwenna met his gaze, a challenge in hers. Ryden looked thunderous, but she didn't care. Castle Calon was not his, and if she had her way, it never would be.

With Theron leading the way, she swept from the room.

CHAPTER THIRTY-ONE

The Redeemer slipped unnoticed through the inner bailey. He had ridden from Wybren like a messenger from hell, driving his horse mercilessly to shorten the time it took to return to Calon.

As he'd expected, chaos had erupted with the discovery of the priest's body. He smiled as he remembered their last meeting. Father Daniel had been exhausted, spending all day first giving alms and then sitting with a dying man as the old merchant had coughed and hacked his way into the kingdom of heaven.

No amount of bloodletting nor prayers had saved him, and when finally the priest, after consoling the family, had been ready to return to the keep, night had fallen. He'd been walking alone in the streets and had been surprised to hear a familiar voice.

"I thought you'd already returned," he said as they continued toward the keep through the rain.

"I decided to wait for you. We can walk together."

The priest had nodded, and once they were outside of town, each caught up in his own private thoughts, the Redeemer slid his knife into his palm. His blood had been warm with the need of another kill, his nerves on edge at the thought that he might be caught.

He'd said, "I think there's someone ahead. I see something."

"Where?" the priest had asked, squinting into the darkness.

And then he'd struck. Plunging his dagger deep, up beneath the breastbone to slice into the heart.

"Wha— oh, merciful Father!" Daniel had cried in shock. The Redeemer pulled out his weapon, and as the priest fell to his knees in the mud, he had grabbed hold of his head.

As Father Daniel prayed for forgiveness from God, the Redeemer had stared into the eyes of his victim. Quickly, cleanly, he had slit his throat, carving a deep W for Wybren into the man's skin. It was all part of the plan, a way to brand all the pretenders to the barony as well as those who distrusted him. Though that dull-witted Vernon and the heretic of a midwife had been only stumbling blocks in the way of his ultimate goal, the Redeemer had enjoyed dispatching each of them from this earth. The same was true of Father Daniel. The priest was forever prying, watching, eyeing him suspiciously.

Well, no more, he thought.

A fitting end for so tormented a soul. No more flailing the skin off his back. No more lust for the lady of the keep! No more hours of atonement.

Father Daniel had met the Redeemer.

Now hours had passed and he heard all the noise in the great hall, people rushing in and out, more than he would expect. . . . He wondered as he hurried along the path from the well if more was happening than he knew. Surely the priest's murder would cause a stir, but there was something other than just the panic and horror he'd expected — more shouts, harsh words, raised voices. . . . His insides curdled as he realized Theron had beaten him back here. Theron and Dwynn, that traitorous moron.

To think that Dwynn would be the one to warn them — after all the Redeemer had done to protect him and care for him. Now he envisioned the dull-witted one as dead.

But you can't kill him.

Did you not vow to care for him? To see that he was protected?

And how has he repaid you?

By treachery and deception. By throwing in his lot with the sons of Wybren. The Redeemer owed him nothing. As for the woman to whom he'd sworn to protect Dwynn, surely she would not have asked had she known the little half-wit was a lying double-crosser. The fool deserved no better fate than the priest.

Furious, the Redeemer rounded the corner of the beekeeper's hut. He then cut through the garden and entered a side door by the kitchen that led behind the huge hearth, where the fire was now banked for the night.

Hardly daring to breathe, he sneaked into a hallway and down the servants' stairs to a short tunnel that opened to the jail cells, where, during Morwenna's rule, no prisoners were kept. The dungeon was quiet aside from the footsteps and voices filtering from above.

From the empty jailor's area, he slipped through a doorway and crawled into the oubliette deep in the bowels of the keep. The stench of the tiny cell was still foul though he could remember no one ever being shoved into this hole — at least not in the time he'd been here, nearly twenty years. At the far end of the cell, he applied pressure to the hidden latch and shoved hard on the stones. And while the rest of the castle cried, whimpered, and wondered at the priest's fate — or celebrated that Theron of Wybren was alive — the Redeemer slid into the dark, cobwebby maze that had become his home.

"This man is bloody Theron? Not Carrick?" Alexander's dark eyes glowered suspiciously as he stared at the man who had lain in Tadd's chamber recovering from wounds, the man he'd thought was Carrick. Morwenna, Alexander, Theron, and Payne were walking to the gatehouse to see the slain priest for themselves. They'd left the others, including a loudly protesting Lord Ryden and the sheriff's tearful but relieved wife, in the main house with instructions to the staff to keep them warm and fed and contained. "But Theron died in the fire," Alexander said as they passed the well. Two boys were hauling buckets of water to the great hall, sloshing water as they hurried in the opposite direction.

"Obviously I survived," Theron said through tight lips.

The two prisoners had assured Morwenna that they were not unduly abused by Carrick's outlaws, but it was clear to her this statement was given to convince her of their ability to take over their duties as before rather than a tale of truth.

Theron pointed out, "You should have known I wasn't my brother if Carrick was the leader of the damned group who captured you."

"He was never there," Alexander protested.

"That's true," Payne agreed. "We never saw the leader. Where is he again?"

"Under guard at the keep." Morwenna slid Theron a glance. "In the room you occupied. The capture of Sir Alexander and Payne was only a ruse so that our guards would be distracted and Carrick could get inside."

"You've spoken with him at length," Theron said.

"Aye."

" 'Tis not enough to have him guarded in that room," Alexander spat angrily. "If this one" — he hooked a furious thumb in Theron's direction — "was able to escape, then bloody Carrick can as well!"

"I don't think so," she said, but her mind went down a dark path. Her last impression of Carrick was of him slipping through the hidden doorway, pulling it closed behind him. Who knew what he was really planning? She'd agreed for the moment to help him, just as he would help her, but now she doubted his intention, and her stomach twisted at the thought that she'd not only given him his freedom, but mayhap also sent him straight to Bryanna. Where else could she be but in the passageways?

He won't hurt her. He wouldn't. He didn't harm these men, did he?

She hazarded a glance in Sir Alexander's direction and saw the swelling and discoloration upon his face. Payne, too, showed signs of a severe beating. Carrick may not have struck them himself, but he had instigated their wounds. Their capture had been his plan.

She looked up at the man she loved . . . and was surprised at the emotion she felt. It had so easily come to her, that she loved Theron of Wybren. Her heart broke to look at him. To think she'd once believed fervently that she'd loved Carrick.

Another snake. Was not Carrick behind everything? Aye, he claims not to have set the fires, nor killed Isa and Vernon . . . but how do you know he did not? Lies, lies, lies! Mayhap he did not do the actual murders but only ordered them. . . . Think of the one called Hack with his emotionless lizard eyes and brand upon his cheek. Do you not think him capable of the vilest of deeds? Yet his allegiance was sworn to Carrick. . . .

She tried to shove the horrid thoughts aside and take solace in the fact that Carrick had given her his word.

The word of a liar. And worse. If not a murderer, at least a thief and a man who thinks nothing of having his brother attacked and beaten senseless! Oh, he didn't want him dead, he said, but that was afterward. He knew what his thugs and henchmen were capable of.

She went cold inside. Slid her fingers through Theron's.

Carrick could do no harm in the secret hallways.

Are you daft? From there he can do the worst of his deeds. Slip in and out of rooms as if invisible.

She felt sick inside.

What if he comes across Bryanna?

Morwenna's stomach clenched.

Remember, even if Carrick seems innocent, he's now trapped, and even a caged animal will strike its master if threatened.

They reached the gatehouse, where every rushlight was lit and a fire roared in the hearth. Yet Morwenna felt cold as death, and she rubbed her arms as she viewed the priest.

Father Daniel's corpse was lying upon one of the tables that had been draped in sheeting. Blood stained his cassock from a wound in his abdomen as well as the horrid jagged cut across the front of his neck. His skin was white, as if all the blood had truly drained from his body, his eyes staring blankly at the ceiling until Payne reached out and closed them gently.

"If only Nygyll were here," she said, but as the words passed her mouth, she felt a shiver slide down her spine. "Where is he?"

The sheriff was examining Father Daniel's wounds. "Has he been gone long?"

"Since the night Isa was killed, you two, Dwynn, Father Daniel, and Nygyll have all been missing. Bryanna's missing, too."

"Bryanna?" Alexander's head snapped up. "What happened?"

Morwenna let out her breath. She glanced at Theron. "She may have found the hidden door. The one you used."

"What hidden door?" Alexander said, his gaze centered on Theron.

"The one I think the murderer used. It links to hidden hallways and chambers, even leads outside. I think that's how he came and went."

"And Carrick's in the room where there's an entrance to these hallways?" Alexander roared.

"Yes," Morwenna admitted.

Theron grabbed Morwenna by her arm. His fingers clenched tight, his jaw chiseled in stone. "Don't tell me he knows about the damned door."

"Yes," she said again, feeling a fool. How could she have trusted Carrick again? How? "He went inside just before you arrived."

"Bloody hell!" Alexander glanced at Theron. "You know the entrances to the passageways?"

"Some of them."

"Then let's go!" The captain of the guard glared at Morwenna. "I only hope we're not too late."

He sensed it.

Another presence.

Someone else in his domain.

The Redeemer listened hard, heard the barest of whispers. A female voice. Chanting.

His insides twisted. Who dared enter his domain? He instantly promised himself that he would slay whoever it was . . . and then he recognized her voice. The breathless prayers were not the deep seductive tones of Morwenna, but those of the sister.

He remembered watching her in her chamber: her curling hair that shone a deep brown red in the fire glow, the smaller but high breasts with their rose-colored nipples, the thatch of hair at the juncture of her legs, again with that same erotic, reddish hue.

His member twitched at the thought of her sleeping restlessly, naked on the bedcovers, obviously in need of a cock to be thrust inside her. His cock.

At the memory, his member twitched and he licked his lips as he thought of what he would do to her.

Eventually she would die.

She was not the chosen one.

But now, with so much of his quest accomplished, certainly he could allow himself a bit of pleasure?

'Tis a sin. She is not the one.

But she was a virgin. No man had been near her and, oh, to feel her tightness around him, to experience the shattering of her maidenhead, to hear her gasp in delight and horror as he thrust into her again and again, pushing, delving, claiming her . . . !

He closed his eyes, realized that his breath was coming out in hard gasps, that his manhood was already rock hard and his heart was hammering wildly, pumping blood through his veins so fast that he couldn't think.

Stop! Do not lose your vision. This one, she would be but a dalliance. . . .

And yet he knew he wouldn't be able to stop.

It had been so long.

First the young one. The virgin. He would claim her and then kill her, and then . . . then Morwenna.

The chanting stopped, as if she sensed he was near.

But it mattered not.

He knew where she was.

The sounds had come from the chamber where he'd stashed his disguises. An evil smile pulling on his lips, he stepped unerringly toward her.

Morwenna and Theron entered the secret hallway through the doorway in Tadd's room while Alexander placed his men in the other areas that Theron had mentioned, including the portal in the gardens and another hidden entrance in the solar. Even Lord Ryden, though he was clearly irked, had his men join in the search. And Dwynn, who kept nattering on about "the brother," had insisted upon helping as well. They were all under Alexander's command.

Morwenna couldn't move quickly enough through these unknown passageways. She believed somewhere Bryanna was waiting. Somewhere she was in danger.

Somewhere she might already be dead or dying, the lifeblood flowing out of her in these dark, lifeless corridors.

Using a torchlight, Theron led her into and through the incredible maze. He had insisted she not call out, not warn Bryanna or Carrick or anyone else who might be creeping through the labyrinth of their whereabouts, and Morwenna had agreed to his plan, though her heart was tearing inside. *Bryanna, oh, sister, where are you? Where?* With each step her dread mounted, and she found herself straining to listen for any noise — a muffled footstep, a quiet sob, the sound of frightened breathing — but all she heard was the rapid, uneven beating of her own heart.

Morwenna couldn't help but imagine the worst. What would they find in these dark hallways and secret chambers? More bloody, mutilated bodies? Bryanna's? *Oh, God, please, no. Please keep her safe!*

Theron showed her the viewing area with the slits looking down into her chamber, the solar, Bryanna's room, and, of course, Tadd's room, where she and

Theron had made love.

She wondered if the hideous creature who inhabited these dank corridors had watched as Theron and she had joined, their lovemaking wild and exhilarating and oh so private. Her stomach turned at the thought, but she couldn't let her mind stray. Above all else she had to find her sister.

She'd already come to believe that Carrick, true to his opportunistic nature, had used looking for Bryanna as a ploy to make good his escape. Well, so be it. As long as her sister was safe, Morwenna cared not what he did with the rest of his miserable life. That he'd played Morwenna for a fool yet again was of little consequence. All that mattered now was Bryanna.

She heard footsteps.

Morrigu, Great Mother, be with me this night.

A soft but distinct tread.

Isa, if you can hear me, I am your messenger of death. I will avenge you.

And through the doorway to this hidden chamber Bryanna saw a light flickering, smelled the scent of tapers burning.

He was close.

Morgan le Fay, give me strength. Help me defeat this villain and rid this world of him.

She thought of all the innocents he had slain, all the havoc he had wreaked, all the pain caused by his hand. She breathed in silently, imagining Isa's face, hearing her voice, feeling her strength through the amulets, charms, and unlit candles she'd spread around her. She'd drawn runes in the dust, listening . . . waiting. . . .

He was near.

Her nerves tingled. She bit down on her lip.

A shadow appeared in the hallway.

Her heart nearly stopped. Her gaze never left the small opening to this airless chamber.

Please, please, give me strength.

He showed himself — a dark figure looming in front of her.

As he lifted his light to peer into the darkness, she sprang, Isa's knife in her hand. "Die, bastard!" she yelled, plunging the blade deep. "And if there is a hell, go forth and never return!"

Theron froze as Bryanna's voice echoed through the hallways.

"This way!" he urged, guiding

Morwenna down a short flight of steps.

"Bryanna!" she yelled, no longer able to hold her tongue. "Bryanna!" Blindly she raced after Theron through the tight hallways. Fear pushed her onward; dread pounded in her heart. Surely her sister was safe! *God in heaven, do not let her die. Please, please, do not let her die!*

Theron rushed into a small chamber and stopped short, his rushlight flooding the room with an eerie gold light. There on the floor was Bryanna, surrounded by piles of clothes, runes scratched into the dust, pebbles, candles, and odds and ends of things Morwenna recognized as Isa's scattered throughout the chamber. The fallen body of Carrick, blood running from his side, lay at her feet.

"He's not yet dead!" Bryanna said, and in her hand she held a dagger with a curved blade. Blood was smeared upon it as well as on Bryanna's hands. Her eyes were round with horror and something else, a bit of triumph. "I did it," she whispered, standing and dropping the knife. Pale and unsteady, she looked about to swoon. "I avenged Isa."

From the floor, Carrick groaned. He rolled an eye upward and saw Morwenna with Theron. His lips moved slightly, pulling up at one corner. "Brother," he whispered.

"That you can still call me that after what you've done," Theron growled.

Carrick closed his eyes. "I . . . I . . . did not . . ."

"Liar!" Theron said. "I trusted you with my life, and what did you do? Steal my wife? Kill our sister and brothers! Leave Morwenna pregnant! Christ Jesus, you deserve to die here alone or worse!"

Carrick didn't respond, and Morwenna stared down at the man who had been her lover. How had she trusted him? Why? Had she still felt a bit of love for him? . . . Nay, she thought, and she touched Theron on the shoulder. This was the man she loved. Never had she cared for Carrick as she did for this man, this good man.

"We cannot leave him here," she said.

Theron let out an angry breath.

"We cannot," she repeated.

"He killed Isa and Sir Vernon!" Bryanna said.

"He told you this?" Theron asked.

"I did not . . ." Carrick's words drifted off and Theron bent down to his brother.

"Whether you did or not, that is between you and God." Handing Morwenna his torchlight, he said, "Take this and hold it aloft. I will carry him."

She did as she was bidden. "Come, Bryanna," she said, but her sister didn't move.

"Wait," Bryanna whispered, and the hairs on the back of Morwenna's neck lifted. "We are not alone."

"I know, Bryanna. There are others searching the hallways. Sir Alexander and Sir Lylle and the sheriff and . . . Come on."

Bryanna didn't move and Morwenna realized that her sister was beyond grief, beyond rationality. The fact that she had actually stabbed someone was so unlike her. "Please, Bryanna," she said softly. "Show me how to get out of here."

" 'Tis too late," her sister said, her eyes widening in horror. "He is here."

"Who?" Theron asked, steadying Carrick's unconscious body, which was slung over his shoulder.

From the corner of her eye, Morwenna saw movement. Turning, she cast the light high. In its wavering light, looming in the doorway, sword in hand, was Nygyll the physician, wearing the bloodied garb of a farmer. His eyes were bright and feverish in the light, his gaze trained on Theron. "Pretender," he whispered and lunged, his sword swinging wildly in an arc that would surely decapitate Theron.

"No!" Morwenna flung herself at the physician.

Theron ducked, dropping Carrick onto the floor.

"Die, Arawn!" Bryanna ordered and shoved the rushlight into the physician's face.

He screamed in pain and dropped his deadly weapon. Morwenna reached for it, but Theron grabbed the hilt and with both hands buried the sword deep into the physician's flesh. Eyes round, he howled and fell to his knees, the blade protruding from his back.

"Curse you!" Nygyll said. "Curse you and all the sons of Dafydd of Wybren!"

There was another scream and the rush of feet. Dwynn, careening through the passageways, shrieked as he saw Nygyll. "Nay! Not the brother! Not the brother!"

The physician spit blood. "You should have died at birth," he said. "You are not my brother, *not* my twin. . . . You . . . have only . . . been . . . my burden. . . . My . . . my curse." He fell forward then, his head hitting the floor with an ear-splitting crack.

Dwynn, his body racked with horrible sobs, tears raining from his eyes, fell onto the slain man's body just as lights appeared in the outer hallway and men rushed forward.

Alexander slid to a stop in the door of the chamber and held his torch high. "Holy Mother of God," he whispered. "What happened?"

Morwenna felt as if all the strength had seeped from her body. She slumped against the wall until Theron wrapped a strong arm around her shoulders.

"It's over," she said, looking at the carnage around her. "It's finally over."

EPILOGUE

Castle Calon
February 20, 1289

"I don't want you to go."

"I know," Bryanna said from atop the spirited white jennet Morwenna had given her. "But I must." She stared down at Morwenna and Theron, who were standing in the yard near the stables. The air was crisp, still holding on to winter, but Bryanna knew it was time.

Isa had come to her last night in a dream.

You must make your own way now, child. You have your own life to lead. Your own private quest.

She knew not where the dream would lead, but she'd packed up all of Isa's private belongings as well as a few clothes and a leather sack of dried food from the cook.

" 'Tis not safe for a woman to travel alone," her sister insisted.

Theron nodded his agreement. "You can stay with us here or at Wybren."

"Aye, and when we move to Wybren, you could be the Lady of Calon. I've already spoken to our brother of it."

"Someday. Mayhap," Bryanna said. For now she needed to leave this place where so many had died. She stared up at the keep and thought of Dwynn, the pitiful twin brother of Nygyll, both of whom had been fathered by Dafydd of Wybren and born to another man's wife. There had been rumors of the birth, of course, but it had been assumed that one twin had died, the birthing cord wrapped around his frail neck. In truth, he'd survived and his younger brother, Nygyll, had helped raise the half-wit. But somewhere along his road, he'd succumbed to a rage at being treated as an insignificant bastard by his father, Dafydd — a rage so deep it had become obsession and insanity.

Ryden, having both read the note Morwenna had written him and been witness to her challenge of his authority, had reluctantly ridden back to Heath. He had not missed the powerful love shared by Theron and Morwenna, either. He had bade them a curt farewell and went, no doubt in search of another bride, perhaps with a larger dowry.

Dwynn had stayed on at Calon, but

Carrick, though wounded, had been able to leave on his own power, disappearing in the middle of the night yet again, leaving no note nor word. He'd been gone nearly a week and Theron had refused to chase after him.

He was no longer cursed as being the killer of his family and burning Wybren, but he was still responsible for the thievery and attacks made by his men, including nearly killing Theron.

Now Bryanna felt a moment's guilt, for Carrick was not whole. The wound he'd suffered at her hand had cut deep into the muscles of his shoulder and upper arm, perhaps damaging tendons or nerves. He seemed to accept it as some sort of perverse punishment for his crimes; she knew it only as her biggest mistake.

"Please reconsider," Morwenna said, her hand upon Alabaster's bridle.

"I can't." She offered Morwenna a final smile and then pulled on the reins, and Morwenna let go of the leather straps. "I have much to do."

"I fear for you!" Morwenna whispered, and Theron hugged her close.

"Fear not!" Bryanna saw a ray of sunlight piercing the clouds and took it as a sign from the goddess. Though her own future was murky and unclear to her, she was certain Theron and Morwenna would marry and be happy, having many, many children with black hair and blue eyes.

On impulse, she blew her sister a kiss and then, before she changed her mind, she guided her horse through the gates and under the yawning portcullis of Calon.

A cool breeze greeted her and lifted her hair.

The trees sighed.

The gods and goddesses were watching.

And somewhere Isa was hiding in the clouds, guiding her on her newfound and secret quest.

Bryanna leaned forward. She sensed that her life was changing. Without knowing what was in store for her, she dug her knees into her horse's sleek sides. The jennet responded, her legs stretching, then bunching. Bryanna let out the reins and felt the rush of air as it tangled her hair and caused tears to streak from her eyes. "Run, Alabaster!" she encouraged, leaving Calon far behind. "Run like the wind!"

Dear Reader,

I hope you enjoyed *Temptress*.

I had a great time writing the novel, let me tell you. I love turning back the centuries to another time, another place, another perspective. This time was special for me because I was able to blend my love of sharp-edged suspense with romance and backdrop the story with the intrigue and mystique of medieval Wales.

Ever since I'd finished writing *Impostress*, where the character of Morwenna was introduced, I just knew she had to have her own story. She was just such a likable, take-charge kind of woman, one who knew her own mind but had one fatal flaw: her love for Carrick of Wybren, who also was mentioned in *Impostress*. I knew Carrick had to show up in *Temptress* so that Morwenna could face her past: her dreams, her mistakes, and her disappointments. And of course, I had to have a villain whose chilling obsession with Morwenna was second only to his thirst for blood and revenge. So the Redeemer crept onto the pages and the suspense really took off.

At least for me. While writing the book, I was lost in this darkly romantic world I'd created. Though I hadn't planned it, I again fell in love with several new characters, especially Bryanna, Morwenna's younger, self-involved sister, who, during the course of *Temptress* not only grew up but discovered that she'd been endowed with a special gift: the ability to see into the future. She wasn't sure she wanted this keen sense of what we'd now call ESP, but we left her about to face the rest of her life as well as the curse of her special "gift." Wouldn't it be great if Bryanna were to show up in a future book? And just possibly run into Carrick again? Let me know what you think by writing to me through my Web site. Tell me if you agree.

To celebrate the publication of *Temptress*, I've created some special pages on my Web site, www.lisajackson.com, and www.thedarkfortress.com, which is a site dedicated to *Temptress* and my other medieval novels. While you're there poking around, why not enter a contest, take a poll, or e-mail me to tell me what you think of my historical novels. And please e-mail me to let me know how you liked the blend of romance, suspense, and historical fiction in *Temptress*.

Keep reading!

Lisa Jackson

ABOUT THE AUTHOR

LISA JACKSON lives with her family, two cats, and an eighty-pound dog in the Pacific Northwest. She can be reached by e-mail at www.lisajackson.com.

The employees of Thorndike Press hope you have enjoyed this Large Print book. All our Thorndike and Wheeler Large Print titles are designed for easy reading, and all our books are made to last. Other Thorndike Press Large Print books are available at your library, through selected bookstores, or directly from us.

For information about titles, please call:

(800) 223-1244

or visit our Web site at:

www.gale.com/thorndike
www.gale.com/wheeler

To share your comments, please write:

Publisher
Thorndike Press
295 Kennedy Memorial Drive
Waterville, ME   04901

Withdrawn from
Carmel Clay Public Library

CARMEL CLAY PUBLIC LIBRARY
55 4th Avenue SE
Carmel, IN 46032
(317) 844-3361
Renewal Line: (317) 814-3936
www.carmel.lib.in.us